Haven of Swans

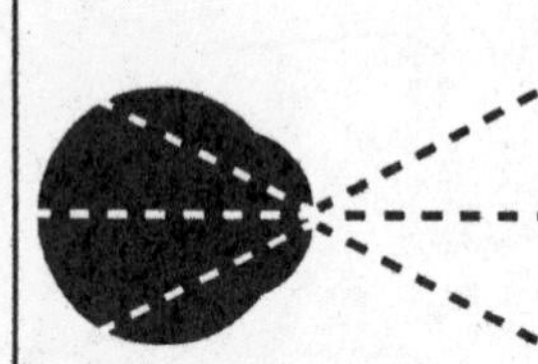

This Large Print Book carries the Seal of Approval of N.A.V.H.

HAVEN OF SWANS

COLLEEN COBLE

THORNDIKE PRESS
A part of Gale, Cengage Learning

Farmington Hills, Mich • San Francisco • New York • Waterville, Maine
Meriden, Conn • Mason, Ohio • Chicago

GALE
CENGAGE Learning

Thorndike Press, a part of Gale, Cengage Learning.

Thorndike Press® Large Print Christian Fiction.
The text of this Large Print edition is unabridged.
Other aspects of the book may vary from the original edition.
Set in 16 pt. Plantin.

LIBRARY OF CONGRESS CIP DATA ON FILE.
CATALOGUING IN PUBLICATION FOR THIS BOOK
IS AVAILABLE FROM THE LIBRARY OF CONGRESS

ISBN-13: 978-1-4104-9961-5 (hardcover)
ISBN-10: 1-4104-9961-8 (hardcover)

Published in 2017 by arrangement with Thomas Nelson, Inc., a division of HarperCollins Christian Publishing, Inc.

Printed in Mexico
1 2 3 4 5 6 7 21 20 19 18 17

To my parents, George and Peggy Rhoads.

Your faith in me has never wavered.

Prologue

Night crept over the hills, smothering the landscape in a cocoon of darkness that would hide him in a few minutes. He'd abandoned his real name for one more fitting of his strength and intellect. Gideon was what he called himself when clouds hid the moon and the shadows gathered. Gideon, the Destroyer of Evil.

Before the moonlight could fade completely, he flipped down the sun visor and stared into the face of his wife, Miranda — a photo of her as she had once been.

As she would be again.

The blare of a horn startled him, and he slapped the visor back into place as a gray SUV careened past where his car sat on the narrow shoulder. The vehicle splashed water from a mud puddle over his car. He bit back an expletive, knowing such words ill befit a man of his intellect. He twisted the key and heard the car engine purr to life. Easing onto the road, he hunched over the wheel and stared into the fog. The turnoff to the lake was just ahead. No car lights illuminated the road ahead or behind. He turned the vehicle onto the muddy track and rolled down the window to let in the fresh scent of the water. The lane was meant for tractors, and visitors rarely trespassed. The owners would never even know he'd been here.

The lake reflected the golden orb of the moon. He parked and turned off the car. The cacophony of crickets and tree frogs paused, then started up again as he stepped into the mud and went around to the trunk. The lid sprang open at his touch, and he looked down into the woman's face. As with the others, preludes to the grand finale, he'd stripped her of beauty. This one would never lash a man with her tongue again.

Securing the gray wool blanket around the body, he hauled it out and dumped it on the ground. He tucked a partial peanut butter sandwich under the sinner's blouse. He took hold of the end of the blanket and pulled the bundle down to the water.

Reaching the small pier, he paused and listened, then stepped onto the rickety boards. The body slid easily across the worn wood. Once he reached the end of the dock, he dropped the end of the blanket and settled onto the weather-scoured boards to wait. He pulled his GPS from his pocket and noted the coordinates. Close enough. He didn't plan to go far from shore.

A hint of pine mingled on the night air with the scent of water. The chilly night began to creep into his bones. Loons called, and he straightened and stood to stamp his feet.

Then the angels came.

Gideon held his breath as they glided into the shaft of moonlight. Silent and beautiful, they moved as one along the placid surface of the water. He counted one, two, ten. The largest one's wings spanned at least eight feet.

He shoved the body into the bottom of a small boat, where it lay amid the flotsam of tackle boxes, tarps, and fishing poles. Gideon hurried to the shore, where he gathered rocks in a bucket. Carrying his burden, he went back to the boat and set the bucket into the boat as well. The boat tipped when he stepped in, but he was quick on his feet and moved to the center, where he settled onto the seat.

Years of use had worn the oars smooth, and they fit into his palms as if they'd been carved for his hands. His muscles flexed, and he dipped the oars into the water. The boat moved smoothly through the ripples. They barely noticed his approach. Their voices raised the hair on his arms and back.

About five feet from them, he laid the oars back against the sides of the boat, then crouched beside the body. Opening the blanket, he piled rocks from the bucket inside, then tied the ends with the rope he'd brought.

They moved around him. One bent her neck and looked at him. Something about the way she held her head made him catch his breath. She glided nearer. They would wait with him, patient, long-suffering, until he secured the ultimate prize. Then one rose into the air. The others soared heavenward as well, and he was left alone with a single feather wafting toward him on the shifting fog. He caught it in his hand and brought it to his face. He brushed it over his lips like a kiss. A benediction.

His gaze lit on the body. Frowning, he put the feather in his pocket. He balled his fists, then stooped and heaved the bundle over the side. The water rippled, then closed over the space. He turned around and began to row back to shore.

The house was quiet when he got home. He peeked in on his daughter, Odette. Seventeen years old with a soul as old as

Moses, she slept with one hand on her cheek. So innocent the sight made his heart swell in his chest.

What would happen to her if he were caught?

His lip curled. They weren't smart enough to find him. Besides, he was surrounded by a mantle of protection. He was invincible as long as his angels stayed with him. Pressing a kiss on his daughter's hair, he went down the hall to his office and entered, shutting the door. The computer screen lit as soon as he lifted the laptop's lid. He launched the browser and went to the geocaching site.

After he put in the GPS coordinates, he typed:

ABOMINATIONS WILL FIND YOU.

1

She didn't know how far she'd driven — all she knew was that it wasn't far enough. The lights on the dash moved in her vision, growing and receding as she gripped the steering wheel and struggled to hang on to consciousness. Nothing but the moon illuminated this lonely stretch of highway. The clock read 8:03.

Panic beat in her chest like a bird trying to escape her rib cage. She had to get away, had to find a place to hide. Her hand touched her ribs and came away with sticky wetness. How much blood had she lost? Her fingers probed the spot again, and she discovered a six-inch gash. Had she been in a car accident?

Her gaze wandered to the rearview mirror, and she moved it so she could see the child in the car seat in the back. Confusion clouded her mind. She struggled to put a name to the little girl who looked to be about two. Her child? Her gaze took in the worn backpack beside the sleeping child, but nothing looked familiar.

A green sign flashed past as the car weaved. Rock Harbor, ten miles. She had no idea where this town was located, not even what state. Maybe she was just tired. Too frightened to think, to plan. Her head ached abominably, and her vision continued to waver.

Headlights haloed with distorted rings of color sprang into view behind her, and the panic surged into her throat again. She pressed her foot to the accelerator.

He couldn't find her.

The car responded to the acceleration at first. Her tires zoomed along the road, their hum sounding loud inside the car. The other vehicle receded in her rearview mirror. But her elation faded when the wheel shuddered in her hands. The engine coughed.

"No, no," she moaned. "Not now." He would catch her. She struggled for a name to put with the danger, but it wouldn't come. If her head would just quit aching, she could think.

The car convulsed again, then began to slow. The warning lights on the dash blinked, then held steady, glaring their threat into the night. She fought the wheel as the power steering failed with the engine. The sore muscles in her arms screamed.

She managed to steer the car onto the shoulder of the road. Glancing behind her, she saw the lights were no longer following her. But that didn't mean he wasn't back there somewhere. Every moment that ticked by brought him closer.

Cranking the key, she tried to start the engine. "Come on, come on," she whispered. "Oh God, please help me!" The engine turned over slowly but didn't catch. She tried again, and it coughed to shuddering life. It wouldn't run long the way it missed. She had to get the car out of sight, throw him off her trail.

A small path opened between thick, ice-frosted brush. Though it wasn't a real lane, she pulled onto it and caught the glimmer of moon on water. A plan sprang to life, but she found it hard to think through all the ramifications. She put her hand on her pounding temple, and her fingers brushed a bump on her scalp, a lump so big and tender that her misery increased.

Her stomach convulsed with nausea. She stopped the car, opened the door, leaned out, and threw up. She couldn't remember ever hurting so much. She could still feel the knife slicing through her flesh.

A knife. Where had that thought come from? Surely she hadn't been stabbed. Had she? She groaned and laid her forehead against the steering wheel. Someone had tried to kill her. Somehow she knew this.

The car engine still sputtered. He would find her, kill her, finish the job he'd started. She got out and inhaled the cold night air tinged with moisture. The fresh, clean scent penetrated her mental fog and gave her hope. Staggering and dizzy, she managed to get the toddler out, car seat and all, and set the seat with the sleeping child on the ground. The child's parka lay inside the car by the backpack. She tucked it around the little girl.

Her vision blackened, and she thumped down beside the child and put her head between her knees. Once her sight cleared, she crawled to the car door again and hauled herself to her feet. She took out the backpack, then sat on the edge of the seat with her feet on the ground. Unzipping it, she checked the contents: a small purse, changes of clothing for the child.

She dropped the backpack beside the child, then staggered back to the driver's door and got in. She pulled the transmission lever into drive, then guided the car toward the lake. The water showed under a light coating of ice, so the car should plunge right through.

The speedometer showed 25 miles per hour. She shoved open the door and sprang from the car. Her shoulder slammed into the ice-slicked knoll. The impact knocked the air out of her.

She lay facedown in mud while the pain thundered in her head and her side. The agony pushed out all other thoughts. The blood running down her side and pooling under her felt warm.

With a groan, she welcomed the darkness that blotted out her pain and terror.

Her dreams were punctuated with screams and the sound of crying. Gradually she became aware that the cries were real. She moaned, then sat up and pushed her hair out of her face. The level of pounding in her head had eased off, maybe enough to think. She lurched to her feet.

The car.

Glancing around, she saw the vehicle was gone. How long had she been unconscious? Staggering, she started toward the toddler. "It's okay, baby," she crooned, her voice hoarse and sore as if she'd been screaming. Maybe some of the screams in her dreams had been her own.

The little girl held up her arms. "Mama,"

she sobbed.

Lifting the toddler into her arms, she cradled the child's head against her shoulder. "It's okay, sweetie," she whispered into the child's soft blonde hair. Had a child's hair ever smelled so sweet? It felt strange and familiar all at the same time.

"Mama." The little girl nestled close and popped her thumb in her mouth.

A wave of maternal love rose in her chest. This was her daughter, even if she didn't know the little girl's name. "What's your name, sweetheart? How old are you?"

The little girl took her thumb out of her mouth. "Two," she said. She held up chubby fingers. "Two."

"You're two," she agreed. "But what's your name?" The little girl didn't answer. The wind kicked up, and she realized she needed to put the child's coat on her. The toddler cooperated by sticking her arms into the sleeves.

Now that she was shivering, she dimly remembered seeing her own coat on the seat. How stupid not to grab it.

The backpack she'd pulled from the car before she disposed of the vehicle lay at her feet. Her purse was in there. Surely she had a driver's license. Still holding the child, she knelt beside the backpack. She rooted out the purse she'd seen and unzipped it. One by one, she examined the contents by the bright light of the moon.

There was no identification in the purse. It actually seemed to be the child's play purse. She found cherry ChapStick, a broken green crayon, a tiny doll, and a bib. Where was her own purse? She should have checked the floor and the glove box before sending the car into the lake.

She touched the ring finger on her left hand. A ring had worn a groove there, but her finger was bare. Was she divorced? Was it her husband she was fleeing from?

Struggling to think, she pulled a bulky shape from the dark shadows of her mind and shuddered. He couldn't find her now. Surely she'd come far enough. She touched the goose egg on her head. It had started to bleed.

"Mama has to put you down a minute," she told the little girl. The child didn't complain when she set her on the frosted grass.

She started to shoulder the backpack, then felt something swing along her chest. Her fingers touched a necklace. Fumbling with the latch, she managed to get the necklace off and held it up to the moonlight. Small ballet slippers swung on a delicate chain.

She turned it over and noticed something engraved on the back, but it was too dark to make out the word.

Clutching the necklace in her palm, she shouldered the backpack, then lifted the child into her arms. Holding the toddler on her right hip with her right arm steadying her, she picked up the car seat and went through the trees back to the road.

She set her feet on the deserted road and began to walk in the direction she'd been traveling. An owl hooted from a tree overhead, and other night sounds rustled in the brush. Were there bears here? Wolves? She tried to quicken her pace, but she was weak and unsteady.

Her breath fogged the air, but carrying the little girl warmed her. One bare foot in front of the other. Where were her shoes? There were no lights in the distance to beckon her, but desire to protect the child drove her. Her ears rang, and it was all she could do to hang on to her senses.

She glanced behind and froze. Headlights loomed. They weren't there the last time she looked. The vehicle was nearly on top of her. She tried to step back into the shelter of the trees, but the vehicle rolled to a stop and a woman's voice called out.

"Are you okay? Do you need a ride?"

Her knees nearly buckled. It wasn't a man. The woman sounded worried. And friendly.

The woman exited the car and gasped as she rounded the hood. "You've got a child. What are you doing walking out here alone? And barefoot?" She took the car seat and set it by the Jeep. "You don't have a coat."

The welcome dome light spilled onto the pavement. A small boy peered from the backseat. Red hair like the woman. Maybe seven years old or so. A dog, a mutt mixture that looked part German shepherd, stuck its head out the window and barked.

A family. Tears welled in her eyes. Thank God. "I'd be grateful for a ride," she said.

"I'm Bree Matthews." Bree's gaze went to the lump on the woman's head. "You're bleeding. I'd better get you to the hospital."

"It's not that bad. I just need to find a hotel or something." She gulped. "I . . . I don't have any money though," she stammered. "I lost my purse."

"You don't have to be afraid. I won't let anyone hurt you," Bree said. "What's your name?" She opened the rear hatch, reached in, and pulled out a blanket.

Would Bree think she was crazy? She had to risk it, since her head hurt too badly to make up something. "I . . . I don't know. I can't remember. My head hurts so much."

Her stomach rebelled, but she managed to swallow the bile that burned her throat. She set the little girl down, took the blanket Bree held out, and draped it around herself.

"We need to get you to the doctor." Bree opened the passenger door. "Here, sit down."

Panic burned more intensely in her chest. "No hospital." She took her daughter's hand and began to walk away, then stumbled and went down on one knee.

Bree knelt beside her and put an arm around her, helping her rise. "It's okay. I've got a friend who's a doctor. He'll come to my home."

The young woman wasn't very big, maybe five-three, but she possessed a reassuring sense of strength. "Where am I?"

"Just outside Rock Harbor. The west side of Michigan's Upper Peninsula." Bree reached under the blanket, took one strap of the backpack, and began to ease it off her shoulders. "We'll sort this out in the morning. You and your little girl are about to drop. I've got room at my house. Let me help you."

Tears sprang from her eyes. "Thank you," she whispered. Maybe she could find a safe harbor there for a few days. If she could just sleep, maybe her memory would come back.

2

The lighthouse beacon flashed from the cliff that overlooked Lake Superior. Bree hoped the sight gave the young woman beside her as much comfort as it always gave her. "This is home," she told the woman.

About five-four, the woman was as icy and beautiful as a Swedish princess, but terror and uncertainty haunted her blue eyes. Someone had abused her for sure. In the soft wash of light from the dash, Bree saw that her long blonde hair was filthy with blood, dirt, and twigs.

"We have to call you something," Bree said. She flipped on the dome light and glanced into the backseat. "What's your name, sweetie?"

The little girl looked at her mother in the passenger seat, then back to Bree. "Terri. Terri two." She held up two fingers.

Bree smiled. "You're adorable, Terri. What's Mommy's name?"

Terri looked up at the woman. "Mama."

Bree stifled a sigh. Of course the little girl would only know her as Mother. "Maybe when you get some rest, you can remember your name," she said to the woman.

The blonde opened her hand, and something glinted in her palm. She held it to the light and squinted at the necklace. "I think my name is Elena," she said, holding out the necklace.

The name was engraved on the back of one of the golden ballet slippers. "You look like an Elena," Bree said.

Elena put the necklace back on while she peered through the window. "You live in a lighthouse?"

"My first husband and I bought it. When he died, I made a commitment to restore it. My second husband, Kade, hung the Fresnel lens, and we activated the light again." Bree glanced at the woman's hands as her long, slim fingers worried the space where a ring had left an indentation on her left ring finger. She'd bet Elena was running from an abusive husband. Poor thing. "That's my son, Davy, back there. And our dog, Samson."

Elena smiled at the little boy. "Hi," she said, pressing her fingers against her temple. "Won't your husband be upset when you come dragging in some vagabonds?"

"Kade's great. He'll want to help. Are you sure there isn't someone I can call for you?"

Elena's lips twisted, and she held up her hands. "Please, no. No questions tonight. I just need to sleep."

"I've got a bed all ready," Bree said soothingly.

Samson whined. He pushed his nose against Elena's hand, where she'd laid it on her armrest. She flinched, then relaxed and stroked the dog's head. "You've got a nice dog," she said.

"Samson is a search-and-rescue dog, one of the best in the country. But more than that, he's part of our family."

"Two." Terri said, holding up her fingers. "Terri two."

Bree laughed. "I take it she just had a birthday."

"I . . . I . . . think so," Elena stammered.

She didn't know her own daughter's birthday? Bree glanced at her. The woman belonged in the hospital, and Bree was tempted to take her there in spite of her protests.

Elena's gaze went past the lighthouse to the buoy across the water. The buoy foghorn blared out, and the light flickered on and off. "It's peaceful here."

"You're safe," Bree assured her. She got out and opened the Jeep's back door for Samson, Terri, and her son. She led the way past the dogwood dusted with a trace of snow. They'd often had more snow in late March, but the weather seemed to be indicating an early spring.

Kade had turned on the porch light for them, and the welcoming beams spilled into the yard. She pushed open the door. "Kade, we have a guest," she called.

He was probably at the kitchen table working on his swan relocation plan. His boss at the park service wanted a flock of mute swans moved before they harmed the population of the native trumpeter swans. She led Elena down the hall, past pictures of their wedding day three years ago and other photos that showed Davy from infancy through his current second-grade school picture.

They walked through the living room to the kitchen. Still dressed in his brown park-service uniform, Kade sat bent over a swath of paperwork that nearly covered the table. His dark hair fell across his broad forehead and stuck up at the back where he'd evidently swiped at it with his hand.

"Hi, honey," she said. "Come say hello to our guest."

His blue eyes held a faraway look, but they sharpened when his gaze went past her to Elena. He frowned, and Bree knew he'd seen the goose egg on the woman's face. "She's okay," she said.

Kade's gaze sank lower. "No, I don't think she is."

Bree turned and saw where his eyes were fixed. Elena had let loose of her grip on the blanket, and it gaped to reveal that her shirt from the right rib area down was saturated with blood. A fixed, glazed stare made her think Elena might pass out.

"Here, sit down." Bree lowered her onto the sofa.

"I'll get blood on your couch," Elena muttered.

"It's leather. It will clean. Kade, get me some hot water and soap. And some clean rags. Call Dr. Matilla."

"Let me see," Bree said. Without waiting for an answer, she lifted the woman's top and winced when she saw the slash. Long and nasty, but probably not life-threatening. "You'll need this stitched."

"I think I'm going to pass out," Elena whispered.

"Here, lie down." Bree raised Elena's bare feet onto the sofa, and she laid her head back. Bree kept pressure on the back of her head. "Better?"

"Yes." The words were faint but clear.

Kade came in carrying a pan of water and some clean rags. "The doctor is on his way."

"Lie still." Bree began to dab the blood from Elena's abdomen. The woman winced when the cloth passed over the raw edges of the cut. The water soon turned as red as the cloth. "I need some fresh water," she told Kade.

He nodded and took the pan.

"Mama?" Terri said, her mouth puckering.

Bree had forgotten the little girl. "Mommy will be okay. The doctor will fix her." She looked at her son, who stood watching the situation with a somber expression. "Davy, take Terri to your room and show her some of your toys."

"Okay, Mom." He took the little girl's hand in a protective stance. "Do you like LEGOs? I've got lots of them."

What a little man. Bree's smile dimmed. He'd asked for a little brother or sister for months. It wasn't as though she and Kade hadn't been trying, but her womb remained stubbornly empty.

The doorbell rang, and Kade sprang to answer it. Bree heard the doctor's deep voice. He lived just down the street and was always willing to help out in an emergency.

Kade ushered him into the living room. "Looks like a knife cut," he told the doctor.

Dr. Matilla went straight to the sofa and began to examine Elena. "She's going to need some stitches." He touched the lump on her head. "You might have a concussion. Double vision? Memory problems, nausea?"

"All the above," she murmured.

"We need to get you to the hospital."

"No!" The woman rose on her elbows. "I can't go to the hospital. I have no money. Can't you just put butterflies on the cut?"

The doctor sighed. "Yeah, but you'd be better off in the hospital where a nurse could monitor your symptoms."

"There's no real treatment for concussion. I can rest better here."

"That's true." The doctor stared at her. "Do you have medical training?"

"I don't know." Elena closed her eyes.

"She was a little confused earlier," Bree murmured. "The only reason she knows her name is because it's on her necklace."

"Is that true? You don't know who you are?" the doctor asked.

"I'm sure I'll be fine in the morning."

"What do you remember?" the doctor asked, drawing supplies out of his bag.

Elena bit her lip and shot a pleading

glance toward Bree, who ignored it. The doctor needed to know the full story. "She doesn't remember anything. Not her name, where she lives, what she's running from, who did this. Nothing."

"Could be emotional amnesia, or retrograde amnesia from the injury. Someone worked her over pretty bad, and it could be either the blow itself or the emotional trauma of it. You may be fine in the morning," the doctor told Elena.

Tears slid from under her lids, and Elena rubbed her forehead. "My head hurts."

"I'll give you something for that," the doctor said. "Now let's get that wound closed."

Bree and Kade stepped into the kitchen while the doctor stitched her up. Bree could see the questions in Kade's eyes, so she told him how she'd found Elena stumbling along the side of the road.

He shook his head. "Only you, Bree." His tone held admiration.

"You would have stopped too. Anyone would have."

The doctor called them from the living room, and they stepped back through the doorway. Elena's eyes looked a little clearer.

"Get some rest," the doctor advised. "I have office hours tomorrow. Stop by and see me when you get up."

"I'll see she does." Bree ushered him to the door and thanked him. When she returned to the living room, Elena was sitting up, but she was as pale as Bree's sheer curtains. "I've got two spare rooms, but I imagine Terri will feel more secure if she stays with you," Bree said. "Let me show you." She carried the backpack up the steps and down the hall to the guest suite at the end. "There's a bathroom here if you'd like to shower."

"I . . . I don't have any clothes," Elena said. "I've got things for Terri though."

"My underwear might fit you, but there's no way my jeans would fit. You're so tiny." Bree tried to think if she knew of any woman as slim as Elena but couldn't think of any. Her best friend, Naomi, was a little heavier than Bree. "I've got a nightgown you can wear. You'll swim in it, but that's okay. What are you, about a 2?"

"I don't know." Elena's gaze darted past Bree to the dark spare room.

"It's okay, no one's here," Bree said, flipping on the light. The soft overhead light illuminated the queen bed covered with a peach-flowered quilt. White ruffled curtains gave the room a homey feel she hoped would reassure the woman.

"It's lovely," Elena said, stepping through

the doorway. “I can’t thank you enough.” Her lids drooped, and her body sagged.

Terri peeked into the room after them, and Elena called her daughter and began to undress her for bed.

“You’re exhausted. Let me get the nightgown.” Bree set the backpack on the floor and went to the master suite. She found the smallest nightgown she had in the big dresser just inside the door and grabbed a pair of her panties as well. At least Elena could have clean underwear, even if they were a little big. Tomorrow they’d go find her something to wear.

When she went back down the hall, she peeked in on Davy and found Kade slipping their son’s pajamas over his head. “Thanks,” she mouthed, then went on to the spare room. Elena had Terri in her pajamas.

“She’s too sleepy for a bath, and I . . . I think she’s clean.” The woman’s voice quivered.

“That’s a good idea. You should just fall into bed yourself. Don’t worry about getting the sheets dirty. We can change them tomorrow.”

Elena nodded. The little girl was asleep when her mother slipped her between the sheets.

A head injury, a knife wound. Bree had to wonder if whoever had hurt Elena might come looking for her. She leaned against the door frame. "Should I call the sheriff? Are you in danger tonight?"

"No! No police."

"Why? I don't understand."

Elena rubbed her forehead. "I don't know, but I just know I can't talk about it."

Bree walked to the bedroom window. "I won't do anything you don't want. But we need to keep you safe."

"I think I'm safe here." Elena's voice trembled.

Her fear was beginning to transfer itself to Bree, and she glanced out over Rock Harbor, peaceful and serene with the village lights twinkling.

Elena slipped into bed next to Terri. "Thank you so much for your help, Bree. I'll try not to be a bother."

Bree crossed the room and turned off the light. "You're no bother at all. Get some rest."

She was going to have to be patient. Her heart welled at the other woman's predicament. Whatever it was, it was very bad.

3

The smell of stale coffee, sweat, and despair seeped through the Michigan State Police District 3 headquarters like an invisible stain. Captain Nikos Andreakos — Nick to his friends — propped his boots on his desk and stared at a glossy eight-by-ten crime scene photo from yesterday's sniper attack. His stomach gave a sour rumble from too much caffeine and too little food, and his brain felt about as alert as a turnip at this unreasonably early hour for a Saturday. As the lead in a special violent crimes unit, he saw these types of photos too often to sleep well at night. He hadn't slept at all in the last twenty-four hours.

What would possess a man who had just lost his job to go on a shooting spree? The perp had positioned himself on an overpass and taken potshots at passing vehicles. Three people died in a fiery car crash before he dropped his gun and hightailed it out of the area. It was Nick's job to track him down. He sighed, dug in his pocket, and pulled out a pack of Rolaids. He thumbed one loose without looking and popped it into his mouth.

The door to his office burst open, and his father stepped into the room. Colonel Cyril Andreakos stood at Nick's height of six feet. Their broad shoulders fit the same size shirts, but Cyril's waist had spread out to about thirty-eight inches. People who saw pictures of Cyril at Nick's age thought they were looking at Nick.

"We've got a bad one, Nick."

Nick thumped his feet back on the floor. "Worse than snipers?" He grabbed a pen and paper.

"Couple of geocachers found a floater at Wilson's Pond about an hour ago. Nasty. The perp took her tongue and her face. And here's something weird — there was a partial peanut butter sandwich tucked inside the corpse's clothes, next to her skin."

Nick's fatigue fell away as it always did at the prospect of a new case. "Geocachers? What's that about?"

"Geocaching. Players use a GPS unit to find stuff other people have hidden. People plant what they call caches, then log the thing onto the site for other people to find."

"Kind of a treasure hunt?"

His father nodded. "Exactly. Thousands are doing it all across the country. Even more thousands in other countries. This body was found at what the geocachers call a *benchmark,* in this case a historical marker. The GPS coordinates of the benchmark were listed on the geocaching site. When the geocachers got to the marker, they found a white bucket with a logbook and a note inside a plastic bag. The note told them to check the lake. So the perp was clearly having fun with the sport. It wasn't a fluke."

Nick jotted down some notes. "It doesn't come across like a crime of passion. Too much planning involved. I don't like the sound of this."

"You and me both. Maybe this is a serial killer coming to call in our area. It feels ritualistic. Fraser is looking for similar cases elsewhere in the U.S. Look at the stuff posted at the site." He handed Nick a paper.

Nick scanned it. "The first part is what the cache is called?"

His dad nodded. " 'Abominations will find you.' "

Nick read on to the clues. " 'Then Musa cast down his staff and lo! it swallowed up the lies they told.' " He looked up. "Do we know where it's from?"

"The Koran."

"And he took her tongue." Nick grimaced. "What leads do we have from the post?"

"The geeks are on it. Give 'em an hour."

"Any ID on the vic?"

Cyril shook his head. "Not yet. The on-site coroner said she's got the build of a dancer." His eyes locked with Nick's for an extra second.

Nick rubbed his temples.

"If it pans out, maybe you could ask Eve —"

Nick gave a short, bitter laugh. "Eve is steamed that I didn't show last night. She hasn't returned my messages."

His father's mouth turned down. "I'm sorry, Son. I know it hurts. You thought about asking Evie for one more try?"

"No." Nick narrowed his eyes to warn his father to back off.

"She loves you, and you love her. Work it out."

"Drop it, Dad."

"Your mother won't drop it. Expect her to bring it up on Sunday."

"Sunday?"

Cyril sighed. "Her birthday. I won't tell her you forgot. She's been cooking all week."

Nick nodded, suppressing a wince. If there

was one thing his Greek family loved, it was a chance to have a big family dinner. His mother's birthday was something none of them was allowed to miss, though he'd sure like to sidestep her interrogation.

Eve's face flashed into his mind, but he refocused on the computer screen and pulled his keyboard toward him.

"Did anyone check out the abomination angle?" he asked his dad.

"What abomination angle?"

"The listing." Nick pointed. " 'Abominations will find you.' "

"What kind of angle?"

"Who uses the word anymore? It's old-fashioned, kind of literary, religious. Might be a clue."

Cyril shrugged.

"I'll check it out," Nick said. Intent on the computer screen, he barely noticed his dad close the door behind him. He typed the word *abomination* into the search box and watched the results appear. The first result took him to Wikipedia. All sorts of references were listed, so he clicked the first entry, the biblical references. Considering the passage came from the Koran, he figured the perp intended some kind of religious significance.

He scanned down the list of possibilities.

Shepherds were an abomination to Egyptians. That didn't seem obviously relevant. There was an end-times reference that might be a possibility. Maybe the guy thought he was a prophet.

He stopped at a reference to Proverbs 6:16. The verse encompassed a whole list of things that were an abomination to God. He read them, then read them again. The woman's tongue was missing. "A lying tongue," he said.

Realizing he was talking to himself, he hit the print button. It was too soon to jump to conclusions, but he could keep the list for reference. His phone rang. He picked up.

"Andreakos."

"We got a name on the geocaching site post, Captain. Guy goes by Gideon."

State forest fronted the complex on the north, making it easy to forget that the city was only an hour away. Gideon rolled the van through the gate under a sign that read "Mount Sinai," then parked in front of the meetinghouse. The enclave of twenty or so cabins and tents cluttered the clearing around it.

The white-board structure had once been a Methodist church and still turned blind stained-glass windows toward the road. Gideon nodded to several members as he strode up the steps. Inside, the wooden planks of the church resounded under his heels. He walked tall, knowing those in attendance whispered about him in a respectful tone.

The church held about forty people. Moses Bechtol, the group leader, rubbed his hands together as he approached the podium. The place quieted. "We're honored to have our special guest today. Just as Gideon judged the children of Israel and led them into the right worship of God, so our man Gideon has much spiritual wisdom for us today." He clapped, and the rest of the group joined in.

Gideon walked to the podium. "Archimedes said, 'Give me a lever long enough and a fulcrum strong enough, and single-handedly I will move the world.' We have that lever and fulcrum."

"Preach it, brother," one of the young men on the front row murmured.

The audience nodded, ready to accept his message. They were worthy vessels. Bechtol had prepared them well. "Most of you are here because you are seeking something more from life than having the best toys, the most expensive TV, the newest phone. Some of you come from painful, even shameful pasts. You think you deserve nothing because of what you've done." He paused to watch some of them avert their eyes and cast their gazes to the floor.

"Our experiences are the womb — or matrix, if you will — to give birth to all we might become. Pain engenders power. The power to change your life is within you." He tapped his forehead. "It resides here. You can take your past and use it to shape your future. Let it empower you to change yourself, and then the world."

"How do we do that?" a young woman called. Her direct blue eyes challenged him.

He hesitated, aware that only those who were ready for his message would really accept it. Maybe 5 percent of this motley group. The rest would need more time. More pain. "Relish the trials you've been given. See what they have taught you. Embrace what they have made you become. Feed your strengths and ignore your weaknesses." Satisfied when she dropped her gaze, he went on with his lecture.

When he ended the speech, he invited any of them who sought more out of life to join him in the group he called Job's Children. Bechtol nodded his approval. Excitement hummed around the room as the young people discussed his new group. Gideon watched with a satisfied smile. Some might ask why he bothered to show others the way when he himself had so much important work to do, but he knew what it was like to wander on his own, searching for truth. There was much satisfaction in speeding others on their journey.

When the room emptied, he joined Bechtol for a stroll through the compound. They passed a lake that reflected the few shafts of sunlight piercing the tree cover.

The chilly wind began to creep into his bones as he followed Bechtol along the path. Gideon started for a small cabin on the other side of the armory, and Bechtol redirected him.

"This way," Bechtol said, his dark eyes shifting away from Gideon's gaze.

"Why?" Gideon asked, stopping in the middle of the path. He pulled his arm out of Bechtol's grip and started for the cabin again.

Bechtol hurried after him. "I have a . . . um . . . a guest."

As Gideon neared, he could hear a woman sobbing. He stopped outside the door. "Tell me."

"She's going to be my wife when she's properly broken." Bechtol made no apologies for what he'd done.

"You kidnapped her?"

"Yes."

"You already have two wives," Gideon pointed out, though he and Bechtol were merely colleagues, and neither claimed the right to pass judgment on the other man's actions.

"I desired another one."

A face appeared at the window. Straight black hair, sloe-eyed face, olive skin. Gideon covered his surprise by swiping his hair out of his eyes, then decided to say nothing.

The scent of something sweet drifted into the room. Elena hadn't thought she would sleep a wink, but her exhaustion and the bed's comfort sucked her into oblivion. Terri still slept beside her. Her blonde curls lay across the pillow, and her cherubic cheeks were flushed with color.

Sunshine streamed past the curtains. She didn't want to move, didn't want to try to think. Her fingers touched the knot on her head, and she winced. Even the light touch of her fingers caused pain. She was afraid to look at it.

Her name was Elena . . . Elena what? Surely she could remember the full name this morning. No pictures rose to the surface of the fog that shrouded her memories. Nothing about the home she lived in, the yard, her parents, siblings. Her gaze touched the sleeping child. No memories of Terri's birth came. No snippets of past events like a first tooth or the day she crawled or walked. Nothing.

Just an empty blankness. And fear. Terror leaped out of the shadows of her mind, and she bolted upright. Throwing back the bedding, she swung her legs out of bed and stumbled to her feet. She had to get away. Stepping to the window, she looked out on a town worthy of Currier and Ives. An idyllic small town with Victorian storefronts, the blue of a lake on one side, and green forest on the other.

Her fear began to swirl away as she drank in the peaceful scene. Surely she was safe here. While she had no real idea of where she was, the place seemed remote. Later she would ask Bree to show her the location on a map. The car was gone, sunken in the lake. No one knew where she was.

Elena turned away from the perfect view and found Terri's backpack. No phone with information. But even if she'd found it, she would have been afraid to call anyone. What could she say?

Hello, this is Elena. Who are you, and how do you know me? What's my last name? Where do I live?

She sighed and glanced around for her clothes. Gathering them up, she went to the bathroom. It was charming, with a claw-foot tub encircled by a shower curtain that hung from the ceiling. She turned on the water and let it warm. Once she was showered and dressed, she'd figure out what to do.

A movement to her left caught her eye, and she flinched. A woman she'd never seen stared back at her. She realized it was her own image in the mirror. Long blonde hair, haunted blue eyes, a bruise that covered nearly her entire forehead, and a lump the size of a boulder on her temple. Scrawny too. Her breastbone stuck out of her skin, but her arms and legs were muscular.

She stepped closer and peered in the mirror. Running her fingers over the planes and angles of her face, she willed herself to remember. Anything, even a single memory would have reassured her. But there was nothing.

She dropped her hand and went to the tub. Stepping into the flow of water, she flinched when the hot water touched the raw cuts on her head and face. The water at her feet turned pink from the blood in her hair. She had a feeling she was lucky to be alive.

Someone had tried to kill her. She didn't know how she knew, but she recognized the seriousness of the attack.

She scrubbed herself all over, watching the red and brown swirl together down the drain. When she washed her feet, she noticed they were calloused and ugly. The nails were devoid of polish. She was obviously no princess. Her fingers touched the necklace around her neck.

Ballet slippers. Could that be why her feet were in such rough shape? Maybe she was a dancer. Standing in the shower, she flexed onto the balls of her feet. It felt good to stretch, to use the strong muscles in her legs. Maybe it was a clue.

Fifteen minutes later, she went in search of the heavenly smell wafting up the steps. Maybe food would help revive her memory. Terri was still sleeping, so she followed the sound of voices.

Kade's voice was loudest. "Did you find out anything about our guest?"

"Not really," Bree answered. "She's really scared though, Kade. I wonder if her husband abused her."

Elena couldn't even remember what her husband looked like. Her fingers curled around the doorjamb. Her right hand crept to the ring finger of her left again. She knew she'd been married but had only this circumstantial evidence, not any memory of a man, to prove it.

She straightened her shoulders and stepped into the kitchen. These good people needed some kind of pleasantry from her. "Something smells good."

Bree spun from where she stood cooking at the stove. "Good morning." She stared. "Your bruise is bigger."

Kade stood from his seat at the table and pulled out a chair. "Have a seat. Bree is learning to make *pannukakku.* This attempt is pretty good. I don't think it will poison you."

Elena felt a smile curving her lips. Her tension began to melt away in the presence of these two. "Does she commonly poison people?"

Bree made a face. "I'm not the best cook in the country. But Kade here has gained fifteen pounds since we married, so he shouldn't be complaining." She fixed him with a stern stare that changed to a giggle when he crossed his eyes and stuck out his tongue.

"I'm starving. What is *pannukakku*?" She'd never heard the word.

Bree turned back to the stove. "A Finnish pancake. Kind of a custardy one with a fruit sauce. Boysenberry in this case."

"Sounds yummy. Maybe I should wake Terri." Before sitting at the table, Elena went to the windowsill. "Your African violet needs help." She deadheaded the wilted blossoms and gave the plant a drink of water before caressing the leaves. What a lovely, velvety texture. She sniffed the aroma of soil. Such a fresh, new scent. And how had she known what the plant needed?

Lost in thought, she went to the table.

"I don't have a green thumb." Bree scooped up some pancake. "This warms up well. You can let her sleep if you want." She put a plate of food down in front of Elena.

Elena spooned a bit of the concoction into her mouth. The sweetness felt like a shot of adrenaline. "Oh, this is great." She began to wolf it down.

"Good." Bree sat down in the chair next to her. "Is there anything I can do to help you today? Someone I can call?"

"No, no one," she mumbled. She wasn't prepared for questions. She took another bite, but the pancake lost its savor. Bree would want to dig until she found out who Elena was. The thought of discovering who had done this made her shudder. Whatever it was, the pain was too great to face now.

"You still don't remember anything, do

you?" Bree asked in a gentle voice.

Elena grasped for a memory, anything. A dim hint of music floated in her mind. She could see a dance floor, hear the pounding of ballet slippers. Someone called out a name. Elena Cox.

Her fingers clutched the golden ballet slippers at her neck. "I . . . I remembered," she gasped. "My name is Elena Cox." Her gaze fell to the floor. A worn pair of ballet slippers superimposed themselves over her bare feet. A high laugh tried to escape her throat. She was remembering.

"Oh, good." Bree's voice rose on the end with a hint of relief in it. "We want to help you," Bree said, exchanging a glance with Kade. "And don't worry, Kade and I discussed it. You're welcome to stay until you get on your feet."

"I don't have any money. Maybe I could find a job in a convenience store or something." Ballet hardly seemed something marketable.

"There's a little shop in town, Finnish Imports. The owner happens to be my first husband's mother. She's looking for sales help. The pay isn't much, but it would be enough to get by for now."

"She's Finnish?"

Bree nodded. "Many of the residents of

Rock Harbor are of Finnish descent. Or Cornish who came over to work the copper mines of the Keweenaw. I think you'll like it here."

"What do you do?" Elena asked.

"I train search-and-rescue dogs. I also have an animal shelter. Do you like animals?"

"I . . . I think so." Her eyes filled, and she looked down. "Your job must be very interesting."

"I like it."

"You've been very kind," Elena said. "When could I talk to the owner of the store? What's her name?"

"Anu Nicholls. We'll go over after Terri gets up. You'll love Anu. She's always been there for me, even after Rob died."

"Mama?" Terri stood in the doorway, rubbing her eyes.

"Hi, sweetheart." Elena held out her arms, and Terri ran to climb onto her mother's lap. The little girl's hair was sticky with something and stuck up on end, but the aroma of little girl was even more appealing than that of the Finnish pancake. Elena pulled it into her lungs, dragging it in deep like an oxygen-starved diver. "We need to give you a bath. Are you hungry?"

Terri nodded. Her mother offered a

spoonful of *pannukakku,* and the little girl's eyes widened.

"Good?" Elena asked her daughter.

Terri nodded and opened her mouth like a little bird for more. The child soon finished a whole pancake.

She wiggled down to the floor. "Music," she said, pointing to the radio on the counter.

Bree smiled and flipped it on. The melody filled the room, and Terri began to dance.

Elena watched her daughter twirl and pirouette around the room. She was incredibly graceful for a little girl. Elena couldn't drag her eyes from her daughter. Each limb so exquisitely made, so perfect. Her limbs twitched with the desire to dance with Terri, but knowing the Matthewses would be watching kept her in her chair. Elena's love of dance was her first clue to knowing herself.

"Looks like she's had dance lessons," Bree said.

Elena just nodded. It was obvious Terri had been taught, but Elena had no memory of the lessons. "Let's get you bathed and dressed, Terri." She scooped her daughter up. "I'll be right back," she told Bree.

By the time she bathed Terri and dressed her in denim pants and a pink shirt that read "Daddy's Girl," her assurance lagged. She didn't want to leave the safety of this lighthouse home and face anyone in town. Maybe this wasn't such a good idea. A job where she didn't meet people might be better. What if *he* came here and just walked into the shop?

She glanced sideways at Terri. The little girl hadn't mentioned her father. Was that a telling omission? If only Elena could name the threat. It was hard not knowing who was a danger.

Terri patted her mother's cheeks. "Mama sad?"

"Mama is fine." She kissed Terri's cheek. "Maybe we can find a park and go swing later."

"Swing!" Terri agreed. "Daddy go?"

So much for Terri not asking for her father. How should Elena respond? She not only didn't know the answer; she didn't know all the questions. "Daddy isn't here. We're visiting friends."

Terri frowned but didn't say anything more. She held on to Elena's hand as they went down the steps to meet Bree by the door.

"Anu is expecting us," Bree said. She held the door open. "Kade went on to work."

Elena stepped out into brilliant sunshine

and the fresh scent of water. The sound of waves hitting the shore lent a peaceful calm to the day. It was like standing at the beginning of a new world, a place she'd never dreamed existed. This place cast a spell of deep peace over her heart. If only she could stay here.

Maybe she could. It might be safe.

She rolled down her window as they drove the few blocks into downtown. Bree pointed out the landmarks, and Elena drank in the beauty of the small village. The smell of the big lake made her think of new life, and she prayed this was a chance for her and Terri to start over.

Whatever was behind her was something she didn't want to face.

"Rock Harbor is surrounded on three sides by old-growth forest. The west side of town runs along a bluff above Lake Superior. We live there. Rock Harbor's downtown area is nestled at the base of Quincy Hill." Bree smiled. "If you can call three blocks *downtown.* Most of town's major businesses are lined up on Houghton Street, which is intersected by Jack Pine Lane and Pepin Street."

Elena nodded. "It's like stepping back in time."

"That it is." Bree parked outside the store.

"Here we are. Don't be nervous."

Elena followed Bree's petite figure to the shop. A charming Victorian storefront done in the Painted Ladies style in several shades of blue with red accents made her smile. The front window held displays of wool sweaters in muted tans and browns. The bell jingled on the door as they went inside.

A slim, middle-aged woman looked up. Her stylishly short blonde hair lay in a cut that accentuated her chiseled features. She smiled at Terri. "I have some toys in the back room, little one. Would you like to see?" She held out her arms for Terri.

To Elena's surprise, the little girl went right to Anu. Terri patted Anu's face. "Hungry," she said.

Anu smiled. "She is used to being around her grandmother?"

Elena held out her hand to avoid answering a question she had no answer for. "I'm Elena Cox." She barely stumbled over the name. It was growing more and more familiar, like a pair of comfortable shoes that had been rediscovered in the back of the closet.

Anu grasped her hand in a firm grip. "I'm Anu. Bree has told me of your situation. Do you have any sales experience, Elena? Not that it should matter. I shall hire you for this little darling's sake alone." She smiled at Terri, who was staring at her with fascination.

"I . . . I don't think so," Elena stammered. Her bright hope began to flag. This was a mistake.

Anu waved her hand. "No matter. All I really require is someone to smile and be friendly. You will just need to learn the merchandise. I shall show you. Can you start tomorrow? Or are you unwell?" Her focus went to the knot on Elena's head.

"I'm fine. Tomorrow is fine. Is there a day care around?"

"My friend Naomi said she'd keep Terri," Bree said. "Since her little one's been born, she hasn't yet returned to the Kitchigami Search and Rescue. The kids'll get along just fine. I'll take you over to meet her when we leave here." Bree took Terri from Anu to show her the toys.

Everything had happened so fast, Elena could barely take it in. "I don't know what to say," she said in a choked voice.

Anu patted her cheek. "Say yes, *kulta.*"

"Yes," Elena whispered past numb lips. She would stay here as long as she could. She hesitated when Anu asked for her Social Security number but then made up one. It would probably be weeks before Anu turned in any money to the government. And Elena didn't think it was the government that represented the danger.

4

Nick pulled his Dodge Durango to the curb and glanced at his watch. One o'clock on the button, just like he'd told her a week ago. He couldn't figure out why she hadn't returned his calls. She must be really ticked.

The house looked the same as always. A French country two-story, it had been Eve's dream home. And Nick had been only too happy to give her whatever she wanted. The grass was still dormant and brown, waiting for spring.

The house was silent as he approached.

He braced himself for her fury and risked it only because he wanted to see Keri. Monday the divorce papers would go to the judge, and it would be over for good. He still didn't understand how they'd ever come to this place.

He'd done all he could to save his marriage, but it had been like clawing at sand on a hillside only to hurtle to the bottom anyway.

No one came to the door, so he pounded on it. "Eve!" The house seemed empty, but she'd promised he could have Keri for the weekend, and if there was one thing Eve held sacred, it was her word. Maybe he'd crossed the line this time, made her mad enough to run off. The drapes were open on the picture window, so he stepped into the flower bed, his boots stomping into the petunias Eve had planted. Ignoring the stink of crushed flowers, he cupped his hands around his eyes and peered inside.

A chair lay upended. His gaze traveled the room. Another chair had a rip in it, and a bloody handprint marked the wall behind it. Disbelieving what his eyes had just seen, he clawed out his cell phone and called it in.

"I'm going in," he told the dispatcher. "Get someone here now." He clicked it off in the middle of her protest.

The key to the house still dangled amid the other keys on his keychain. Fumbling, he got it out and jammed it into the lock. He twisted it the wrong way first, then finally got it to unlock. His gun in his hand, he stepped into the foyer. The coppery scent of blood hit his senses.

"Please, God, don't let them be dead," he whispered. He stepped over a shattered vase into the living room. "Keri?"

His throat thickened, and he felt a certainty that he would find her and Keri lying somewhere in the house in a pool of blood. He heard the dim scream of sirens approaching the house. The house felt closed up, alien. He searched the living room, blanching at the amount of blood on the floor and wall, then went to the kitchen. A peanut butter sandwich lay on the floor with one bite out of it.

There was a sandwich on the body at the lake.

Nick doubled over. "Oh God, oh God," he cried. "Please, God, no." He crumpled to his knees on the floor.

The door banged open, and he heard his father's voice calling him. "In here," he mumbled past numb lips.

His father stood in the doorway. "Nick? I heard the call on my way home."

Nick looked up as his father's gaze lit on the peanut butter sandwich. "That geocacher guy has been here, Dad. He took them," he whispered. Cyril's big hand came down on his son's shoulder and tightened in a grip that should have been painful, but Nick was past physical pain.

"They're missing?"

Nick's partner, Fraser Warren, came into the kitchen behind Cyril as Nick nodded. "There's blood in the living room. A lot of it."

"Don't jump to conclusions, Nick."

"Maybe she had an accident," Fraser said.

"Too much blood. What if it's her? What if the body is Eve? Oh God! Where's Keri?"

"This might have nothing to do with the other murder," Cyril said. "I'll call in the team right now. We'll find something. Have you checked upstairs?"

"No." He looked wildly toward the steps. What an idiot.

"I did," Fraser said. "No one there. But the car's gone. Any idea where it could be?"

Nick sprang to the garage door. Sure enough, the garage was empty. "Maybe she got away," he said.

"Maybe," Cyril said, but his voice lacked confidence.

"I'll go talk to the neighbors," Fraser said. He gripped Nick's shoulder. "Hang in there, buddy. Call your pastor. Have your church pray. We'll find them." But his gaze dropped away when Nick stared into his face.

Nick's cell phone rang. The number wasn't familiar, but Nick answered it.

"Eve?" he barked.

An eerie laugh sounded in his ear, almost like Daffy Duck in the old cartoon. "Figured it out yet, Nick? Have you checked the geocaching site? I left a clue just for you."

"Gideon?"

There was a click, then silence. Nick couldn't think, couldn't face what the taunting voice meant. Summoning reserves he didn't know he had, he forced the emotion down to a dark place to be examined later.

He ended the call and turned to Fraser. "That was him. He says he left us a clue on the geocaching site. Where do I find it?" Fraser told him the URL. Nick veered down the hall and into the office.

"I'll get the laptop," his dad called after him.

Fraser followed and grabbed Nick as he started to type. "Nick, don't touch anything. There might be prints."

Nick dropped his hands and stared at the keyboard. "Get me some gloves. I have to see what he left."

Fraser glanced around the office. "There's a wireless router. Wait for your dad to bring the laptop."

Nick stood and followed his partner out of the office. His dad met him in the living room with the laptop in his hand. Nick grabbed it, opened it up, then navigated to the site. "How do I find a cache?"

Fraser pointed out the first link. "Now type in the zip code of your house."

Nick typed it in and nearly groaned. "Over three thousand caches," he said.

"It will probably be one of the most recent," his dad said.

Each cache had a different title, like GERM'S PURGATORY and DÉJÀ VU. How would he find Gideon's clue in all these? He started at the top. Five caches down he stopped. "This reads 'Sins of the Past.' Sounds ominous." He clicked the link. The page held a set of coordinates, a tiny map, and gibberish he didn't understand.

Scrolling down the page, he found more. " 'For pride is the beginning of sin, and he that hath it shall pour out abomination: and therefore the Lord brought upon them strange calamities, and overthrew them utterly,' " he read.

Cyril put his big hand on Nick's shoulder and glanced at Fraser. "What were the coordinates for the woman in the pond?"

Fraser pulled a small notepad out of his pocket and flipped it open. He rattled off some coordinates.

Nick and Cyril exhaled in unison. "Not the same as these," Nick told Fraser. "Go check the coordinates on the GPS unit in the car." His partner nodded and vanished out the door.

"I don't quite recognize that text," Cyril said. "It sounds like something out of the Bible, but it's not familiar."

Nick nodded and opened another browser window, where he typed in the first part of the saying. It brought up another site. "Hmm, it's from the Apocrypha. Sirach 10:13. I'm not familiar with it."

While Fraser was gone, Nick decided to return to the geocaching site and check the entry for the first woman they'd found. Under the logged visits, he found a new message from Gideon. "Dad, look here!" He turned the screen around so his father could read it.

Cyril leaned over the computer. " 'Abomination upon abomination. You have left her body unclaimed and unburied. Check out the Blue Gate Bar.' "

Nick moved the computer screen back to face him. "He doesn't seem to like the fact that we haven't identified her."

"I'll send someone to the bar. It's down by the water," Cyril said.

The investigators arrived and talked in low tones while they took blood samples and gathered evidence. Nick had never imagined this familiar scene would be played out in his own home. *Eve's home,* he corrected himself. She'd kicked him out months ago.

Fraser came in and stuck his thumb in the air. "The coordinates are for here."

Cyril scratched his head. "Okay, stay with me here a minute. The killer is using religious verses, but not from any one text. The first was the Koran. This is the Apocrypha. He calls himself Gideon. Could mean nothing, but that's one of the big-shot judges from the Old Testament. Think it's a missionary killer?"

"They usually target prostitutes or homeless people," Nick said. "Why Eve?"

"That's what we have to find out. We need to start digging into Eve's past, and this other woman's as soon as we get her identified. Sorry, Nick."

Nick nodded without meeting his father's gaze. No one said anything else. He knew they were all thinking that Eve's body would be the next one to be found — minus a body part.

Body parts. "I might have something else," he said slowly. "Let me get Eve's Bible and show you." He went to the bedroom and found her Bible on the nightstand. He flipped to Proverbs and carried it back to the living room. "I saw this on a Google search this morning."

"What?" His dad peered over his shoulder. Nick read aloud.

"These six things the LORD hates,
Yes, seven are an abomination to Him:
A proud look,
A lying tongue,
Hands that shed innocent blood,
A heart that devises wicked plans,
Feet that are swift in running to evil,
A false witness who speaks lies,
And one who sows discord among
brethren."

"You think the floater was the lying tongue?" Fraser asked.

"Maybe." Nick wasn't ready to assume anything. He prayed he was wrong about all of it. "If we find the woman's identity, let's try to keep it out of the media as long as possible. Maybe he'll get more agitated the longer she goes unclaimed. He seems to care about that for some reason."

Elena got the deposit ready, turned out all the lights, and headed for the door. Anu had left her in charge tonight, so she double-checked to make sure she hadn't overlooked anything. Had she really been in Rock

Harbor for two months? It seemed like only a few days, yet it had been forever as well. She felt as though she'd lived here all her life.

Terri would be looking for her. Bree's best friend, Naomi, had invited them to dinner tonight, which would be a nice change of pace. Bree and Kade were coming too. Elena really needed to look for another place to live and quit mooching off the Matthewses, but Bree had insisted that she and Terri stay for now. What she made at the shop wasn't much.

Elena wanted to relax, to settle into Rock Harbor, but everything could come tumbling down in a moment. Anu could hear back from the government about that fake Social Security number anytime, or the man who had hurt her could come walking in the door.

Not that she would recognize him.

With the door locked behind her, she stepped out into the sunshine. Had she ever realized spring was so glorious? With her lids closed, she lifted her face to the light. A dozen fragrances burst on her senses: flowers, sunshine, cut grass. A smorgasbord of scents. Though she guessed she was in her early thirties, this was the first spring she could remember.

So many people had welcomed her to Rock Harbor, made her feel a part of the community. Slowly, she was beginning to let down her guard, to think she might be safe here.

To make a fresh start.

The sidewalks bustled. A gay-rights group had come to town for the weekend, and the participants had waved banners and made plenty of noise. A magazine was doing a spread on the event, but Elena made sure to stay out of their way. She didn't want her picture to get out to the media. The wrong person might see it.

She crossed the street and dropped the deposit off at the bank, then retraced her steps in the direction of Naomi's home, where she was to meet Bree. Two women with their arms around each other careened into her. "Sorry," she said, even though it was their fault.

"Hey, where's a good place to eat?" the dark-haired woman asked.

Elena smiled and nodded toward the café. "Have you tried the food at the Suomi? It's pretty terrific."

The redhead returned her smile with a warmth that put Elena's guard down. "What would you suggest?"

"You have to try a pasty. Get a beef one.

They're the best in the UP."

"We'll do that." The redhead's smile widened, and her gaze shifted past Elena's shoulder.

Elena turned in time to see a flash go off. Someone had snapped a picture. He was leaning against a van emblazoned with the name of a Detroit newspaper. "Oh, please, you have to erase that picture." She ran toward the photographer, a young man with broad shoulders and shoulder-length hair. He lifted the camera above her head when she grabbed at it. "Please, you can't use that."

"Chill, lady. You can barely see your face. I was just getting the town." He went to his van and got in.

She ran after him and tried to wrench open his door, but he stared straight ahead, dropped the gearshift into drive, and pulled away. Only by snatching back her hand did she escape being pulled along with him.

Maybe she was overreacting. Her past might not even be in Detroit. Even if it was, whoever was looking for her might have given up by now. She could only hope. She caged her fear again, squared her shoulders, and started toward Naomi's. She was making a new life. No one would find her here.

She stared in fascination at purple phlox

spilling down a slope. Were the colors up here brighter and more vivid, or was she simply seeing everything for what felt like the first time? Flowers bloomed along the sidewalks, and wildflowers dotted the countryside on her route to Naomi's.

She was so blessed to have this place, to experience this life.

The children played in the front yard and didn't notice when she entered the gate. Naomi O'Reilly pulled weeds in the flower bed by the walk. Her baby, Matthew, played with a top on the sidewalk.

"Hey, girl," Elena said. "I'm a little early. Need some help?" She put down her purse, squatted beside her friend, and began to tug weeds loose from the soil. The rich scent smelled like home.

"Thanks." Naomi swiped at a stray lock of brown hair that hung over one eye. At thirty-three, she was about Elena's height. Pretty rather than beautiful, her real beauty was in her sprightly attitude. Nothing ever got her down for long.

Her search dog, Charley, bounded to greet Elena. She rubbed him and kissed his muzzle. "Hey, buddy." He was a beautiful golden retriever with large, expressive eyes and a sweet soul.

Naomi gave her a sly smile. "I have a present for you."

"For me?"

Naomi stood and dusted her hands. "Wait here and keep an eye on Matt. He keeps trying to eat the dirt." She disappeared inside the screen door.

Elena waved at Terri, who was swinging, then knelt next to the baby. "Hey, little guy." She opened his tiny fist and dumped the dirt out of his palm. His lips had traces of dirt at the corners when he smiled up at her.

"Close your eyes," Naomi called from the other side of the screen door.

Elena stood and shut her eyes. "Okay," she called. She heard the screen door squeak, and then a small ball of warm fur was deposited in her arms.

Her eyes flew open, and she looked down at the most beautiful face she'd ever seen — well, other than Terri's. A pure white kitten with blue eyes.

"The neighbor cat had babies," Naomi said, beaming like a proud grandmother. "Isn't she darling?"

"Oh, she's beautiful." Elena didn't think she'd ever been the squealing sort, but a sound very much like one came from her lips. The kitten's tiny pink tongue came out and licked her cheek. Sharp milk teeth nibbled her chin, and Elena laughed.

A vehicle rumbled behind her, and she turned to see Bree and Kade pulling up in Kade's truck. Bree waved and leaped from the vehicle as soon as it stopped. "You were supposed to wait until I got here," she scolded, her teasing gaze going to the kitten.

"I couldn't stand it," Naomi said. "I just gave it to her."

"What are you going to name her?" Bree plucked the kitten out of Elena's arms and held her up in the air. "Oh, you are just adorable."

The kitten mewed and struggled. Bree held it against her chest and laughed when it nibbled the neck of her blouse. Samson whined at her legs, and she held the kitty down for him to sniff. His curly tail wagged frantically, and he licked the little white head.

Elena held out her arms. "Hey, she's mine. I want her back." Bree dropped the kitten back into Elena's arms, and she nuzzled the little fur ball. "What do you think I should call her?"

Both women stared at the kitten as if contemplating a great mystery. "Gracie," Bree said. "I think she looks like a Gracie."

"I like it." Elena kissed the fuzzy head. "I

could use a little grace in my life."

Bree touched her arm. "I had some time to look around on the Internet today. I found an article about you helping some underprivileged kids take dance lessons."

"Really?" Elena asked.

"I checked for a Facebook profile and hit every social media site."

"Any idea where we lived?"

Bree's nod was vigorous. "In a Detroit suburb. I'll show you the link when we get home. I bookmarked it."

Not that it would help. How much could there be about an obscure dance teacher named Elena Cox? Bree hadn't even been able to find a phone number. And maybe that was for the best. Elena could settle here, put the evil in her life behind, and start fresh with Terri.

5

"Anything?" Nick asked his partner. His family had been missing for two months. The constant ups and downs between hope and despair had begun to even out into depression, much as he tried to hang on to the thin strand of possibilities.

"Nothing new." Fraser had been checking regularly with police districts up and down Lake Huron. "I don't get it. This guy likes attention. He notifies us on a site used by thousands of people. If her body was somewhere, wouldn't he tell us like he did with the first vic? Why is he holding off?"

"I wish I knew. You can bet he has a plan."

Nick's cell phone rang. He grabbed it, then groaned when he saw his mother's name on the screen. She'd called every day since Eve and Keri disappeared.

"Nothing new, Mom," he said when he answered the phone.

"Did you sleep last night? I made some

kreatopita. Stop by and pick it up."

Food was the last thing he wanted, not even his favorite meat pie. He'd been living on coffee and Rolaids. A tone indicated he had another call. "Gotta go, Mom. I'll call you later."

"Nicky —" she started.

He cut off her voice and answered the other call. "Talk to me."

His dad's voice was grave. "We've got another body, Nick. At a geocaching site. Partial peanut butter sandwich too." He gave Nick the location.

Nick swallowed. "Eve?"

"Can't tell. Animals got to the body, and all we have left are scattered bones. We'll have to work on identification."

"On my way." Nick hung up and grabbed his jacket. "There's another one. We gotta go," he told Fraser.

They drove out to the location north of the city and parked behind a row of police cars. The spring air held a chill, but it wasn't the weather that made Nick shudder. Yellow police tape marked off the woods. Forensic detectives had sifted every cubic foot of soil as the bones were slowly retrieved from the area.

Eve might be in this grave. And Keri. He wasn't sure he was ready to face the reality, even if it meant closure. He slipped booties on his shoes and stepped over the tape, then approached the men who were intent on their work.

"Any idea who it is?"

One of the men glanced up and shook his head. "No identification yet. Clothes are missing. The grave was so shallow that animals got to it. I think the woman was moved here from somewhere else."

"Who found it?" Nick asked.

The guy nodded to two men who stood talking with an officer out by the road. "A couple of geocachers."

Same MO. Nick thanked the man and went over to join the men. He flashed his identification. "You found the body?"

The younger man had his arms clasped around himself. "When can we go home? We've been here five hours. My daughter is going to be worried." The guy looked like some kind of professional. His hunting jacket looked new, and his hair was a sleek cap. Skinny and in his late thirties, he stared Nick down with the assurance of a man used to commanding other people.

The other man looked about ten years older. Graying hair curled up around the edge of a plaid hunting cap that matched his vest. His beefy arms were crossed over his chest, and he was frowning. "We've told you all we know."

"Go over it one more time for me," Nick said.

The older man's face reddened and seemed to swell. "Look, we had nothing to do with this. We were just out geocaching. We found the body at the coordinates listed in the computer bank."

"How did you find it? Was it partially uncovered?"

The older man spoke first, earning an annoyed glare from the other guy. "We didn't see a canister or anything, so we looked a little closer. Most things aren't buried, but we couldn't find anything obvious, and Judd saw a freshly dug spot." The man jabbed a thumb in Judd's direction. "I had a small shovel, so we dug down a few inches." He swallowed hard. "We stopped when we saw a bone. That's when we noticed other bones scattered around above ground. They looked too big to be an animal's. I already called the police."

Nick nodded. "Thanks." He glanced at the other policeman. "You done with these guys?" The man nodded. The men thanked them and headed toward their truck, a beat-up green Ford.

Fraser walked over to join him after talking to Cyril. "Think they had anything to do with this?"

"I doubt it. Any clues on the Web site?" He knew his partner would have checked already.

"Yeah." He handed Nick a sheet of yellow lined paper.

Nick glanced down and read the clue silently. *For pride is the beginning of sin, and he that hath it shall pour out abomination: and therefore the Lord brought upon them strange calamities, and overthrew them utterly.*

Pain exploded deep inside. "The same verse left at the house," he whispered. He sagged against a tree. Nick should have been prepared for this.

"We don't know that yet, Nick. It will take awhile to get DNA back."

He knew. Nick looked back toward the collected bones. "I've got someone who can help us identify her faster." He dug out his phone . . .

Green Glade Community was the glorified name for the facility Gideon always thought of as Den of the Zombies. Many of the residents walked around with blank expressions and fixed smiles. Some were violent, and he could imagine them stalking the residents of the nearby town.

Birds chattered at him from an aviary in the sitting room as he passed. Brightly colored wings flashed by in his peripheral vision, and he paused to watch them a moment.

"Do you like birds?" A woman in her late twenties with hollow eyes paused long enough to question his scrutiny. "I like to look at them. They don't even realize there's a whole world outside. They don't have to face it."

"You don't have to stay here, you know."

Her gaze darted to his face. "It hurts out there."

"Pain is good for us. Without it, we would never do anything with our lives." He indicated the peaceful surroundings with a sweeping hand. "What is there in here? Food, a bed, no pain. But no life either. No growth. Pain is better than pleasure."

"It's safe here." She didn't wait for an answer but wandered off, her slippers making scuffing sounds along the tile.

Gideon shook his head and continued down the hall. Stupid sheep without a shepherd. Miranda was lucky to have him, to be spared from the same fate.

He pushed open her door and stepped into the room filled with flowers. His monthly Visa bill reflected the cost of these weekly arrivals of carnations. Pink ones, her favorite.

"Hello, Miranda," he said.

She kept her face averted like she always did. Not that it mattered, since he couldn't bear to look at her destroyed beauty. Though she hadn't spoken a word in ten years, her body language screamed of despair.

The doctors called it a catatonic state. He knew she'd just given up. Her pain had lasted long enough. It was time for her to rediscover life. He would give her a reason to live, and she would turn her blue eyes on him and really *see* him again. She would know all he'd done for her, all he would give up for her.

She would finally love him again.

"You'll have a new face soon, Miranda. I promise," he whispered, adjusting the pink lace shawl around her shoulders. "I'll be able to see you as you really are."

He'd tried harvesting a few faces after the one he wanted had escaped, but none of them had worked out quite right. Only one face would be perfect, and he would find her again soon.

"How long before you have a bust to show the media?" Nick rubbed his burning eyes and watched Oliver Harding press clay onto the cast of the skull they'd found five days earlier. The forensic sculptor was one of the best in the country. Police departments as far away as California had flown Oliver in to help identify remains.

The man could have been a shoo-in for a most realistic Santa Claus if he were about fifty pounds heavier. Nick guessed Oliver's age as forty or so, though he'd grayed early. His rosy cheeks and ready smile had children ready to climb into his lap and ask for a bike for Christmas.

He'd driven down from Cheboygan as soon as Nick called him. The two had worked on several difficult cases over the past few years and had become friends as well as colleagues. Oliver was a fishing nut, and he'd talked Nick into going out a time or two. Nick had never picked up the passion for sitting in a boat and watching a bobber.

Oliver's other passion was bringing closure to hurting families, and Nick always called him when he was in a tight spot.

The sculptor looked up and blinked his reddened eyes. Bits of clay clung to his neatly trimmed white beard, and his smile had dropped. Glancing at his watch, Nick realized the man had been at it for twelve solid hours so far today, after five days of the same grueling schedule. If the need wasn't so great, Nick would have been ashamed of his insistence.

Oliver walked around to the other side of the face he was sculpting. "Nick, you know you can't rush this. There is a time for everything under heaven. It normally takes a couple of weeks."

"I don't have a couple of weeks," Nick said.

"I'm going as fast as I can. I should have something to look at by late tonight or early in the morning." He glanced at Nick. "You should have called me when the first faceless woman turned up. I could have gotten her back to her family sooner."

"I thought you only worked with bones."

"Not always." Oliver bent back over the table.

"Anything I can do to help?"

"No, my friend." He glanced at Nick. "Anything on dental records?"

Nick shook his head. "There was a fire at Eve's dental office a month ago. All the records were lost. The backup hadn't been done in a while either so they couldn't recover anything. No matches to anyone else yet."

"Seems rather convenient."

"I thought so too. I bet Gideon torched

the place. You're our only hope."

"I'll do what I can. You look exhausted. Take a nap."

Nick wished he could sleep. His eyes burned, and his throat felt sore and scratchy. He turned away and went to look out the window. The rain had come for three solid days, and the landscape looked as dreary as he felt.

Eve's birthday was today. In past years he would bring home flowers — carnations were her favorite — and DeBrand truffles that he ordered online. He'd turned down an invitation from his parents for dinner, but he suddenly didn't want to be alone. Maybe he'd go after all.

Nick turned his gaze back to the worktable. The bust looked eerily like his wife. He squeezed his eyes shut. Maybe it was a trick of the light. Opening them again, he stepped closer. Eve's face sharpened into better focus.

"It's her," he said hoarsely. The strength ran out of his legs. He stumbled back and fell into the chair.

"Don't jump to conclusions," Oliver said. "The painting still needs to be done. We don't have the results back from the lab on when she died either. As backed up as they are, that may not come for weeks. What are you seeing?"

Nick couldn't take his eyes off the bust. "The bone structure, the way the eyes are set."

Oliver winced. "Just remember, it's hard to tell at this stage."

He nodded, unable to trust his voice to speak. Keri. Where was she? Would Gideon have killed a child? It would be outside his MO. Nick could only pray she was alive.

He stared at the bust again. "When will you be done with the painting?"

"No later than tomorrow morning. I'll work all night on it if I have to."

"Call me when you're finished. Maybe I'm seeing things." Now the face looked like a shapeless blob. He reminded himself that the clue left on the geocaching site was the same one left at Eve's house. He already knew the outcome — he just didn't want to face it.

"Maybe. You've been under a lot of stress. Your dad can take a look when it's done."

"I've got to get out of here." Nick bolted to his feet and left the room. Driving to his parents' house, he kept blinking moisture out of his eyes. He parked on the street and swiped the back of his hand over his cheeks. He'd had maybe four hours of sleep a night ever since Eve and Keri had vanished. Now he understood that knowing their fate wouldn't bring him rest. He might not truly rest again until he brought Eve's murderer to justice.

Feeling older than his thirty-five years, he threw open the car door and dragged himself up the walk. Even the aroma of *mousalia* wafting out the screen door failed to lift the lead from his feet.

His parents had lived in this Victorian-era neighborhood in Bay City all his life. The three-story home held memories of kids running in and out, lots of good food and laughter, and almond biscuits in front of the TV while the family watched *Family Ties.*

Some hard memories lived on, too, like the night his father had been shot by a robber fleeing a convenience store when Cyril was a city policeman.

Nick walked inside the house. "I'm here," he called.

His mother came from the kitchen, wiping flour on her apron. "Nicky, you said you weren't coming." Her smile changed to a frown that deepened when she glanced at his face. "You've probably lost fifteen pounds. Are you sleeping?"

"Not much," he admitted. He dropped a kiss on her upturned cheek. "Everyone else here?" He wanted to tell her about Oliver's sculpture, but he couldn't talk about it. Not yet.

"Layna is making the salad. The boys are watching baseball with your father. Go on in. Dinner will be ready in a few minutes."

"I'll say hi to Sis first. Besides, I hear those black olives calling me."

The kitchen had always been his favorite place growing up, and not just because he liked to eat. The white cabinets always held surprises like *loukoumades,* Greek-style donuts his mother made weekly for his father. Fresh cookies always filled the cookie jar. But mostly it was the room where his mother was likely to be found, dispensing advice and love to her family.

His sister, Layna, looked up briefly when he entered. "I thought maybe you weren't going to make it." Two years his senior, she'd been divorced five years ago and had two boys who adored their uncle Nick. The divorce had twisted her mouth and hardened her eyes, which saw the bad in everything.

Nick loved her, but it was hard to spend much time around her. "I wouldn't miss playing video games with the boys."

She finally smiled then, an expression that transformed her into the girl he used to know, the one who borrowed his clothes during the grunge trend and who cheered at his football games.

She tapped her fist on his shoulder. "You're a great uncle. It's a good thing when their father cares so little." She slapped his arm. "You haven't been around much either lately."

"Sorry, Sis." He made no excuses.

"Any new info?"

He fished a black olive out of the jar and avoided looking in her direction. Once Oliver finished painting the actual bust, he'd let someone else make sure he wasn't putting Eve's features onto it.

Layna pressed on with the questions. "You don't have to be so driven about it. You're divorced."

"Sure, bring that up." He made a face. "It doesn't change a thing."

"You need to move on with your life, Nick. Once you find them, I mean. Don't make the mistake I did of clinging to the past."

"You're still holding on to it," he pointed out. "It's still all you talk about. Have you dated anyone in the last five years?"

"Men are pigs," she said. Her gaze met his, and she shrugged. "Present company excluded."

"Tom had an affair. I didn't."

"Oh, but you did," his mother said from behind him. "An affair with your job." She moved past Nick and went to lift the *mousalia* out of the oven. The scent of lamb and *tahinial* sauce enveloped the kitchen.

His mom had made insinuations like this before, and he'd ignored them. But not this time. "What is it with women that you don't get how important a job is? It's how you eat and buy pretty clothes and purses. And shoes. Don't forget the shoes. Eve had enough shoes to fill three closets. How did she think she got to buy those tiny bits of leather? They didn't just fall into her lap."

He knew he was being too harsh when he saw tears flood his mother's eyes. Hurting her didn't bring Eve back. He buried the apology on his tongue with another olive.

"Eve wanted you, not the shoes, Nicky. They were just something to fill a void." She shook her finger at him. "And don't talk about her in the past tense. You'll find her."

The truth waited to be spoken, but he swallowed it. He'd failed his wife all around. Now it was probably too late. "I'm going to go play with the boys."

His mother's face softened. "I'm sorry I'm so hard on you, Son. I just want you to be happy. When you find Eve, you make it up to her."

Nick heard his father's booming voice from the entry, then his dad's bulk filled the doorway. One look at Cyril's face and Nick knew.

His father had seen the bust. He knew it was Eve too.

6

Bree fed the last dog and turned out the lights at the animal shelter. Her muscles ached but not unpleasantly. Today's training session in the woods had gone well. Samson continued to show that his ability surpassed that of most other dogs.

She snapped her fingers, and her dog ran after her. His nails clicked on the concrete floor, and he was at her side by the time she opened the door. "Let's go home, boy."

He woofed deep in his throat and ran to the Jeep, which sat under a poplar tree. Birds had deposited a few gifts on the windshield, and Bree made a face. She'd have to wash it this weekend.

Her cell phone rang, and she pulled it from her belt. "Kitchigami Search-and-Rescue."

"Bree, it . . . it's Ruby." The aide's voice was tentative. It also held a note of fear that kicked Bree's adrenaline into high gear.

Bree clenched the phone in her hand. "Is something wrong, Ruby?"

"I . . . I'm afraid so. Your father isn't in his room. I checked everywhere. I think he's gotten out."

For Rock Harbor Nursing Home to admit he was gone meant they'd truly looked everywhere. Bree tried not to panic. "I'll be right there." She had Samson. He would find her father.

She flung open the back door of the SUV. The dog jumped in and lay down on the seat. Bree ran around to the driver's side and slid under the wheel. The back wheels fishtailed when she stomped on the accelerator, but she maintained control of the Jeep and wheeled it around toward town.

The North Woods was no place for a frail old man with Alzheimer's to wander. Black bears roamed the woods. And while the DNR denied it, she'd seen a cougar with her own eyes last summer. She glanced at her watch. She could call her sister, who was on temporary assignment in England, but there was no need to worry her. Not yet.

After parking the Jeep, she hopped out and opened the door for Samson. She reached in and grabbed her ready-kit. Samson's ears perked when he saw her lift out the backpack that held his vest. His tail began to wag.

He followed her up the walk. Ruby rushed to her and apologized, but Bree brushed the apology aside and walked straight to her father's room. Samson wouldn't need a special article. She'd take him to the room and let him sniff the bed. Her dog bounded ahead of her. They'd been here many times, and he knew the way.

When she entered the room, Samson was nosing around the floor. Opening her kit, she pulled out his vest and slipped it on him. He immediately went alert. She snapped his leash onto his collar and led him to the bed. He sniffed the sheets.

"Search, Samson. Find Grandpa."

He leaped for the door and led her down the hall. Residents called to them as they roamed through the sitting area, but she just waved and didn't stop. Samson raced toward the sliding glass door that led into the fenced backyard. If her father had gone out there, he should still be around. There was no exit except by coming back through this area.

His nose in the air, Samson crisscrossed the open area, searching for an air scent.

A man ran toward her with his arms out. "Stop, wait, what are you doing?"

A newbie evidently. Bree motioned for him to follow as she trailed after the dog. "Samson is a search dog."

"He doesn't have his nose to the ground."

"He tracks by air scent. Every human scent is different. The skin gives off about forty thousand dead skin cells called *rafts* every minute. The rafts carry bacteria that release a vapor that makes up the unique scent we all carry. He has my dad's scent, and he'll find him. You can count on it."

The man stopped and stared, but Bree rushed on. Samson raced back toward the door, back through the sitting area, and out the front door. Her father had walked right past the receptionist? Bree had wondered about their security, and this was proof it wasn't very good.

Once back outside, Samson made a beeline for the trees across the street. Bree unclipped his leash. Samson plunged into the wooded area, and Bree darted after him. The cool, dim forest blotted out the sun. She had to find her dad before sundown. The temp would lower, and he wouldn't be dressed for it. And the mosquitoes would eat him alive.

Samson's ears were pointed, and his tail swished like windshield wipers on high, sure signs that he had a hot trail. Maybe Dad was just a little distance ahead. The dog put on an extra spurt of speed, leaping over a brook and bounding across a fallen tree. He disappeared over the hillside. Moments later, she heard him begin to bark.

Samson had found him. She kicked up her own speed, but in her haste she slipped on a mossy rock and landed in the swiftly flowing water. It wasn't deep, but she was soaked to the waist by the time she regained her feet and hurried in the direction of Samson's barking.

She reached the top of the hill and looked down. A small pond lay at the bottom. So did her dog and her father. The old man sat on a log and stared out over the water. He seemed not to notice the dog licking at him. Two swans glided along the lake's surface. She noted their bright orange bills. Mutes. Kade would want to know.

She approached slowly so she wouldn't startle her father. "Dad?" she said softly when she reached him. Even when her hand touched his shoulder, he didn't move. He was lost inside his mind today.

She blinked against the moisture in her eyes. All she could do was call off the search and take him back. Nothing was going to change here.

■ ■ ■ ■

Nick suspected that Gideon belonged to a geocaching community. But which one? He'd attended several local meetings where the groups talked about which GPS unit was best and explained how to plan the best adventures. Their passion for the hunt hummed in the air.

The geocaching community was vast, global. Nick's poking into it was about as ineffectual as a puppy nipping at the heels of a giant. If he stumbled onto Gideon like this, it would be a fluke. Still, the puzzle drove him day and night. He hoped that concentrating on figuring it out would help him get through what he had to do today. Searching through Eve's things for clues to her disappearance would bring back more memories than he wanted to deal with.

The sun glinted through the windows of his SUV. He sat looking at the house where he used to live. The grass was beginning to green up, and he could see soft shoots emerging. His own life felt as dormant as the rosebushes.

The job wouldn't get done by sitting here.

With a supreme effort he pushed open his door and got out. When he reached the house, he heard the engine of a car and turned around. His mother waved to him and got out of her Lumina.

"What are you doing here?" he asked when she reached him.

"You don't think I'd let you do this alone, do you, Nicky?" Her dark eyes held empathy.

"I can do it, Mom."

"We're hurting, too, your Dad and me. Let me help you." She looked past him to his key still in the deadbolt. "Are you going to open it, or do I have to?"

His grin felt genuine for the first time in two months. "Thanks, Mom." The pain of stepping inside and seeing Keri's little patent-leather shoes in the entryway wasn't quite as bad with his mom along. He could do this.

He let his mother take Keri's room while he went to the master bedroom. No way could he stomach looking at those little-girl clothes. Eve's presence still occupied the master bedroom. Her fragrance clung to the bedding; her laughter echoed from the bathroom. He expected to see her come dancing into the room on her toes, doing one of those pirouette things.

Gritting his teeth, he opened the closet door and began to lift out the racks of Eve's clothes so he could go through the pockets for clues. *Don't think about it — just do it.* His gaze snagged on her pink nightgown. The garment was soft as gossamer, and he remembered the last time he'd seen her in it. The anger in her eyes had overshadowed the tearstains on her face.

He'd been the cause of both emotions.

He lifted the garment in his hands and buried his face in it. The gown still bore her scent, sweet and seductive. Thrusting it away, he dropped it to the floor. Those memories were unbearable.

"I'm glad you hired someone to clean the bloodstains," his mother said from the doorway. Her gaze swept the pile of Eve's clothing he had laid on the bed.

At least she hadn't seen him with his nose buried in the nightgown. "Yeah," he said. "I didn't want to look at them again either."

"How are you handling this, Nick?" Rhea took a tentative step into the room.

"How do you think, Mom? Some sicko has murdered my wife and daughter —" His voice broke, and the weakness spurred his anger. "I'm going to find him, and he will pay," he muttered past clenched teeth.

"You don't know that for sure. The bust looks like her, but we still don't have the DNA back or anything."

"I have to face facts, Mom. So do you. I'm going to find who did this." He clenched his fists.

"Revenge? You know better than that."

"Justice — I have to have justice." He expected platitudes about how God would bring Gideon to justice, but she said nothing, just turned away. The sadness in her face defused his anger. He lifted a hand toward her, then dropped it back to his side. "I'm sorry."

"So am I, Nicky. So am I." She walked away.

Man, he was a jerk, taking his pain out on his mother when she only wanted to help. He started to go after her, but the phone rang on the bedside table. Eve had been gone over two months. No one should be calling this number.

The phone vibrated against his palm like a rattler when he lifted it. He punched the talk button. "Nick Andreakos," he said.

He heard only silence at first. Then a high-pitched laugh hit his ear, the Daffy Duck inflection from his nightmares.

"It's a fine joke, don't you think, Nick?" The caricature of a voice chortled. "Did you like the way she looked in her pink nightgown? She wouldn't look that lovely now. Not at all. But you already know that."

Nick leaped to the window. As he peered through the glass, he saw a van pull away. The signage read “Mount Sinai.”

“Hello? Hello?” he said into the phone. But there was only silence.

7

Samson lay sprawled on the rug. Gracie, her back arched, prowled around on top of him, pausing occasionally to knead him. He opened one eye to see what she was doing, then flopped his head back down and went back to sleep.

"Leave him alone." Elena scooped up the kitten and sat down on the sofa with her. Terri sat on the floor, building a house with LEGOs. It was almost five. Bree and Kade would be home anytime.

She heard the front door open, then Bree's voice called her name. "I'm in here," Elena said. Bree's face was white and strained when she entered the living room, and a worried frown replaced her customary smile. "You look upset. What's wrong?"

"My dad wasn't well today. He didn't know who I was." Bree settled on the sofa beside Elena.

Her father had escaped the nursing home

just last week, Elena knew. She wished she could confide to Bree that she didn't even remember if her father was alive or dead, but she didn't dare. Not only would it be insensitive; it would also tip off Bree that Elena remembered less than she pretended to. If she kept up the facade long enough, maybe she could slip into this new life and the old would be gone forever. Rock Harbor had cast a healing net over her, and she didn't want to slip from under it.

Her past was bound to catch up to her though.

"I'm sorry," Elena said finally. "It has to be hard."

"It's not going to get any better." Bree dug into a bowl of pistachios on the coffee table and offered some to Elena, who shook her head and made a face. "Um, your clothes don't match."

"They don't?" Elena glanced down. "I guess I was thinking about something else when I got dressed."

"Any new memories today?"

Elena's smile faded. "No."

It was a familiar question. For a while the dance memories had come fast, but they led to no real insight. Bree wanted to contact some dance studios, but Elena didn't want to run the risk that her attacker might be connected to her profession. Every discreet path they'd followed had led nowhere.

"Let's make some more calls tonight," Bree said.

Elena nodded. The women had been methodically calling every Cox in the Detroit area and asking if they knew Elena. So far, out of fifty-two calls, no one had heard of her.

Through the glass, they watched Kade park his truck. The passenger door flew open. Davy tumbled out. Moments later the sound of his small feet thundered across the entry floor, followed by the heavy tread of Kade's boots.

Davy burst into the living room. "Hey, Mom, I got to help Dad feed the peregrine falcons. One falcon ate three mice!"

"Ew," his mother said. "You're a ghoul."

"Birds have to eat too," Kade said, dropping a kiss on her red curls when he reached her. "What's for dinner?"

"Whatever you want to cook tonight. I'm beat."

"I'll cook," Elena said quickly. "I picked up stuff for spaghetti." She put Gracie on the floor, and the kitten immediately went back to pester Samson.

"I knew we kept you around for a good

reason." Kade sat on the sofa on the other side of his wife. "Nice house, Terri."

The toddler frowned and knocked over the house. "Daddy help." She looked at her mother. "Where Daddy?"

Elena struggled for some excuse, but nothing came to mind. "Oh, look, Terri. Samson is cuddling Gracie." The kitten nestled between Samson's front paws. They were both asleep.

The distraction worked. Terri crawled over to the dog and laid her head on his flank. "Terri sleep."

Elena knew the questions weren't going to stop. And she had no answers. Every time she thought about the man who had fathered Terri, she ran up against a blank wall and stark terror.

Kade yawned. "I found a place to relocate the mute swans," he told the women.

"That's wonderful news," Bree said. "I really thought they'd make you shoot them."

"I'd hoped it wouldn't come to that. I'm going to move them in a couple of days. I'll have to sedate them or they'll peck my eyes out. And then I'll have to destroy the eggs in the nests. I can put oil on them so they won't hatch."

The phone rang, and Bree answered it. Listening for a moment, she handed it to

Elena. "It's Anu for you."

Her boss had never called her before. Elena told herself it was nothing, that maybe Anu wanted her to work some extra hours. Anu normally let her off at four. She took the phone Bree held out. "Hi, Anu."

"Elena, I must have written down your Social Security number wrong. I got a letter today saying it was incorrect. Could you give it to me again?"

Elena's fingers tightened on the phone. She'd known this day would come sooner or later. "I thought I had it memorized, but I must have slipped up. Let me get ahold of the Social Security department and double-check it. Of course I don't have my card any longer."

"That would be fine, *kulta.* I must respond to this letter within thirty days though, so you must handle this as soon as possible."

"I will." She ended the call and handed the phone back to Bree, who gave her a curious glance. "Everything okay?" Bree asked.

"Fine. My Social Security number is wrong. I need to get it straightened out."

"You made it up, didn't you?"

Elena nodded. "I couldn't remember it at the time."

"Do you now?"

She shook her head. "But if I go to the Social Security department and give them my name, they can look it up, can't they?"

"Yes, but will they give it to you without any identification? We'll have to check that out." Bree's gaze stayed on her face. "Elena, is there anything you'd like to talk about? I have a feeling there's still something you're ashamed to reveal to us. We're your friends. You can tell us anything."

Elena looked down at her feet. "No, there's nothing." She waited to see if Bree would press the issue, but her friend let it ride. The silence stretched out until Kade got up and left the room.

Bree touched Elena's arm. "Are you sure? Kade's gone now, so if you just didn't want him to hear, we can talk now."

"There's no reason to talk about the past. The present is all that matters." Elena dared to raise her gaze to meet Bree's.

"Oh, honey, that's so not true. The past affects everything we do, all that we are. Believe me, I know. You're going to have to face it sooner or later." Her eyes went to the scar at Elena's temple. "I still want to know who hurt you. Don't you want to know too? We could go to the police, get them to discreetly ask some questions."

"I've told you before — I can't risk tipping off the man who attacked me. I've got Terri to protect. He didn't hurt her last time, but he might if he finds us again."

"The police would protect you."

Elena nodded at the familiar argument. They would try hard, but what if they failed? She clasped her hands together and stood up. "I'd better go fix supper."

Nick looked up everything he could on Mount Sinai and discovered a survivalist community that went by the name. It had offshoots like Liberty's Children and the newly formed Job's Children. What he learned about them only intensified his hunch that Gideon might have a connection with them.

Some of the derivatives weren't as radical as the Mount Sinai group. The parent organization was suspected of an assassination attempt on the governor last year. They had unknown quantities of stockpiled arms, and there were consistent rumors that the group was affiliated with white-supremacist efforts and even the occult. Not a group to mess around with. Several murders had been laid to their account, though nothing had been proven.

The only way to prove anything would be to get inside the organization. Doing *some-*

thing would be better than sitting around staring at four walls. He needed a diversion to make him forget that his wife was dead and his daughter still missing.

Nick packed his Durango with camping gear, a rifle, and canned food. Dressed in camouflage gear, he drove to the camp, about 130 miles from Bay City. Fully expecting to have to convince the group that he was sincere, he was surprised to find that no one challenged him when he passed into the confines of the enclave. The lane had more muddy potholes than gravel, and he bottomed out several times before he reached the heart of the camp.

There were more cabins than he expected and fewer tents. It almost looked like a small frontier town. Men dressed in camouflage hunting clothes and boots meandered across the road and into the woods. Nick saw one man with a dead fox slung over his shoulder.

It wasn't hunting season.

Nick parked his SUV in the lot by the church and got out. With a smile that felt as tight as his new boots, he nodded to two women who walked along the side of the road. They carried buckets of water in their hands.

"Good morning. I was wondering where I might find Moses Bechtol?" His research indicated that the man with the biblical name was the leader of the organization.

The women looked at each other. "Maybe you'd better wait at the office," one said finally. She pointed toward the church building. "He'll be back sooner or later." The women avoided Nick's gaze and moved away from him.

From the women's reactions, he had to wonder what this Bechtol guy was up to. When the women were out of sight, Nick moved between the buildings. Everyone seemed to be out. The cabins were deserted.

He reached the outermost cabin and turned to go back to the church when he heard a woman cry out. The cry seemed to come from the woods. Entering the trees, he saw another cabin hunkered under a huge oak. He glanced around to make sure he wasn't seen, then approached the building.

The cabin door rattled, and he darted behind the trunk of the big tree. A man stepped through the battered door. Burly and sporting a blond beard, he attached a padlock to the cabin door, then stalked off. Nick waited until the man disappeared through the trees, then, careful to make no sound, moved to the cabin.

The door was solid wood, though old and

nicked, and the shiny padlock was sturdy. He moved around the cabin, searching for a window. The back of the cabin had one tiny window. The glass had been busted out, but bars covered it. He cupped his palms around his eyes and peered into the dark interior.

A woman sat on a small cot, her head in her hands.

"Hey," Nick whispered. "You okay?"

Her head came up, and her tearstained face swiveled toward him. Terror marked the twist of her mouth.

He smiled to reassure her. "My name is Captain Andreakos, with the Michigan State Police. I can help you."

The woman looked familiar, but he couldn't place where he'd seen her. About thirty, she had long black hair and Asian features. Slim and attractive too.

She stood and cast a fearful glance toward the door before sidling to the window. "Moses will be back. Get me out of here."

So the big man was the group's leader. "I need a bolt cutter for the padlock. I'll have to go get help."

She gripped the bars. "No, don't leave me here. He's kept me prisoner for three weeks!"

Then it clicked. Nick had seen her face

on a missing-persons poster. "You're Iris Chen?"

"Yes!" She rattled the bars again. "Please get me out of here."

"Don't worry. Let me get some help. Is anyone else held prisoner here?" He couldn't help but hope he'd find Keri. "Any children?"

"No one, just me. Please get me out."

"I'm going to go for help now."

"Hurry!" She hesitated. "Don't hurt anyone though."

He nodded, though hurting these scumbags seemed justifiable. Pulling out his phone, he checked the bars. No signal. The tree cover was too heavy. "I have to get out of the forest. I'll be back." He patted her hand and moved off through some thick spruce trees in the direction of his Dodge, keeping off the paths.

Needles crushed under his boots and released the scent of pine. He finally emerged from the trees and stepped onto the dirt parking lot. A group of six men saw him and headed his way. Led by a burly man Nick recognized from pictures as Bechtol, the men squared their shoulders and clenched their fists, apparently intending to confront him.

His SUV was only a few feet away. He

made a break for it, and the men began to run. They surrounded his vehicle even as he managed to get the doors locked. Flashing his badge was unlikely to do any good. His best option was to get out of here, get some help, and stage a rescue.

Bechtol pounded on his window. He turned and gestured to another man, who approached with a tire iron.

Nick started the engine and pressed the accelerator. They'd either get out of the way or get run over. The two men standing in front of his vehicle leaped aside a fraction of a second before the bumper could hit them. A thump sounded behind him, and the back window shattered. A tire iron lay in the back amid tiny crystals of glass.

A man was only about two feet behind, his hands reaching out to grab the back of the SUV. Nick accelerated, and the vehicle leaped away from the man's outstretched hand. Nick zoomed out of the compound. When he reached the highway, he thumbed a Rolaids into his mouth, got out his cell phone, and called his father.

"We got trouble, Dad." Nick launched into an explanation of what he'd found.

"Let me try to get ahold of some help close by," Cyril said. "I'll call you back."

Nick closed his phone and looked back at

the lane into the compound. He decided to try to circle back and lay low. If the group moved Iris now, he might never find her.

The only weapon he had was a pistol. He'd be hard-pressed to withstand the firepower the group was likely to muster. Rolling forward in his vehicle again, he searched for a spot that would hide his SUV. There — a tiny opening in the forest that grew thick along the road. He jerked the wheel and drove the vehicle into the tiny space. Branches whipped around the cab and screeched along the metal. He doubted his shiny paint would emerge unscathed.

The branches closed behind him. It was all he could do to force open his door and exit the vehicle with his gun. Pressing forward through the brush, he stumbled clear of it into a copse of spruce. A cut on his arm bled, and he wiped the smear of blood away with his thumb, then struck out in the direction of the camp.

Stopping for a moment to get his bearings, he listened for voices but heard only the wind and birdsong overhead. The cabin was back this way. He'd always had an innate sense of direction, and he plunged through the cool shadows toward the compound.

His phone was set on vibrate, and it shuddered in its case on his waist when he stepped into a meadow with clear skies. Nick pulled out his phone. "Andreakos," he said softly.

"Nick, I got some help from Alpena. They're at the entrance to the compound now," his father said. "Where are you?"

"On the south side. Tell them to wait for my signal. I'm going in now." He closed his phone and jogged on. When he got close enough to see cabins, the place was hopping. People ran from the buildings to pack up vehicles.

The compound was bugging out.

Iris's face peered desperately from the window of a van. He had to do something right now. He darted into the road and out of the trees. Pulling out his phone as he ran, he called his father. "Send them now," he said and ended the call.

They still hadn't seen him. Pulling his gun from its holster, he slipped off the safety and approached the van where Iris was imprisoned. There was no one else in the vehicle that he could see. She hadn't seen him either.

He was dressed like the others, so he didn't stand out. Maybe he'd be able to get to the van and get her out unnoticed. He had to try at least.

The big man he'd seen earlier headed toward the van. Car keys dangled from Bechtol's right hand. His head turned, and his gaze locked with Nick's.

"Get him!" he shouted, waving his arm toward Nick.

Nick dove behind a boulder as gunfire erupted around him. Revved engines sounded over his shoulder, and he saw the police vehicles come tearing into the compound. Peering over the boulder, he saw Bechtol fumbling to unlock the van door. He was going to escape with Iris.

The gunfire intensified as the Alpena police returned the bullets from the men crouched behind vehicles, rocks, and trees.

Nick narrowed his focus, blocking out the sounds of shouts and car engines. He rested his gun on the boulder and took aim at the van tires. He sighted down the barrel, and his finger hovered on the trigger.

Bechtol looked up. He fumbled for his own gun and swung it up to face Nick. The steady black barrel of the pistol pointed right at Nick's chest.

Nick adjusted his sighting, aiming the crosshatches on Bechtol's trigger hand. His finger tightened on the trigger, and he squeezed. Bechtol moved. The bullet Nick had meant to strike the man's wrist hurtled toward his chest. Nick saw Bechtol jerk when the bullet hit, then the man's big hand pressed against his chest, and he slowly crumpled into the dust.

The crackling gunfire began to sputter out. People turned to look at their leader and the other men lying in the dirt. Women and children began to wail. Without Bechtol to guide them, they bolted and scattered. Men grabbed up children and tugged women toward cars, trucks, and SUVs. But the Alpena police moved in, heading off the inhabitants before they could flee.

Nick walked to where Bechtol lay and kicked the pistol away from the man's fingers. He picked up the fallen keys, then jogged around to the passenger side and unlocked the door.

Iris's hands were handcuffed behind her back. "I asked you not to hurt anyone," she shouted. Her eyes blazed with anger.

"He was going to shoot me!"

Tears hung on her lashes. "I hate killing anything, even animals." She looked at the weeping children. "There are fatherless children here because of you."

"Hey, I just saved your bacon. The least you could do is say thanks."

She gave him another angry glare and stumbled from the van. "Unlock these cuffs," she demanded.

Nick handed Iris off to an Alpena officer. He moved around to the dead man again and rummaged through his pockets for Bechtol's ID. His fingers touched paper, and he drew it out. A picture. He stared down into the face of his wife.

8

With June's arrival, the wildflowers burst out in profusion. Anemones and marsh marigolds blanketed the roadsides. Elena spent as much time out of doors as she could. She felt reborn along with nature.

Bree had been right about the Social Security office. They'd refused to give Elena her number without some kind of identification, so now she was unemployed.

She tried not to think about it as she jogged along the dirt road through the forest, pushing Terri in one of Bree's old jogging strollers. The morning was a perfect blend of temperature and sunshine. Bree had no trouble keeping up with her, and Samson ran ahead of the two women, then circled back to check on them every few minutes.

"You're quiet. You're worried about losing your job, aren't you?" Bree asked, not even short of breath.

"How am I going to support Terri?" Elena tried to keep her voice even and quiet so she didn't frighten Terri.

"Elena, you have no choice now. You have to find out more. If you can get your ID, you can have a normal life."

Everything in Elena recoiled at the thought of signaling her location to the man who attacked her, but she had to be able to work. Her memory wasn't coming back by itself. She'd remembered only her name and the ballet. Everything else still swam in an impenetrable black fog.

Bree and Kade couldn't support her forever.

"I don't have much choice."

Their feet hit the path in rhythmic unison, raising puffs of dust.

"When we get back, we'll go to the sheriff's office. Mason and Hilary are in Finland with Zoe, but we can talk to Deputy Montgomery about it," Bree said.

Elena nodded, struggling to keep her expression from betraying her dread. But it was time, and she knew it. She couldn't hide from her past forever.

Elena heard the rumble of vehicles behind them and turned to look. A caravan of cars, trucks, and SUVs drove slowly past. Some of them had words written on the windows.

SAVE THE SWANS. SWANS ARE SACRED. MUTE NO LONGER.

Bree groaned. “Kade was afraid there would be protests today.”

“Is he having trouble with the relocation?” Elena watched until the last vehicle turned onto a lane leading to Reed Lake.

“I think the park service was expecting this and had plenty of rangers ready.”

“Why are they so mad? Kade is just moving the swans, not hurting them.”

“These folks think the mutes have just as much right to the habitat as the trumpeters, even though they aren’t native to this area. But there are just as many people who think they’re dirty and want them killed.” Bree stopped running to pull out her phone. “Montgomery might need to know about it though.”

Elena listened to Bree explain the situation to the deputy. Some of the people in the vehicles were shouting and waving. Elena shifted and looked down at her daughter. Terri needed to be out of this. It might get ugly.

Bree ended the call. “Montgomery is coming out. Let’s get going.”

“I think I should go back,” Elena said. “I don’t want Terri in any danger.”

“The ranger station is between here and

the lake. You can stay there while I go on to join Kade."

Before Elena could answer, a truck zoomed down the road. An engine backfired, then roared louder. The truck barreled toward them, and she could see a man hunched over the wheel. He wore a baseball cap low on his forehead, and she couldn't make out any details of his features.

The women stepped off the road, and Bree called Samson to her. She entwined her fingers into his collar as the truck approached. "Sit," she commanded. The dog settled onto his haunches.

With a cloud of dust in its wake, the truck came abreast of them. The man directed a dark glance their way, then his eyes widened. Truck brakes squealed, and the back end of the pickup fishtailed. When the truck came to a stop, the man jumped out and ran toward them.

"What the heck?" Bree whispered. "Let's get out of here."

She didn't have to tell Elena twice. The women bolted for the trees. Elena rolled the stroller over the rough ground as fast as she dared.

Samson planted himself between the man and the women and snarled in a way that would stop a charging bear. It worked on the man too. Elena dared a backward glance and saw the dog herding the man away from them.

"It's me, Will!" the man yelled after them. "Come back, I won't hurt you!"

Will? The name meant nothing to her. She and Bree plunged on into the woods and out of danger.

The depression that had surrounded Nick since Bechtol's death a week ago refused to lift. He'd killed Gideon. Nothing was going to bring Eve back. And now he'd never find Keri.

Nick had about worn out the faded picture of his wife that he'd found in Bechtol's pocket.

A new case came across his desk, a serial rapist, which normally would have engrossed him in work, but he couldn't focus on the details of the case. His mother had called repeatedly with supper invitations, but he turned down all of them. The only thing he needed was some space to mourn his family.

At least he'd stopped the monster, shot him dead. Nick should have found satisfaction in that, but vengeance was a cold bedfellow. He'd talked to everyone who knew Bechtol but had turned up no real clue to which geocaching group the man belonged to.

He thrust his chair back from his desk and stood. This morning he'd checked the list of caches in the area and discovered an event at the park this morning at ten. It was a quarter till ten now. He'd just mosey down there and see who showed up. Snatching up a picture of Bechtol, he headed out of the building.

He might as well walk. The day was sunny and warm. Joggers passed him in spandex shorts, and he waved at an acquaintance, then crossed the street when she acted like she was heading his way. The last thing he wanted was another condolence.

Several fathers threw softballs with their children, and Nick had to avert his eyes when a toddler shouted, "Daddy!" and ran to her father. He passed his hand over his stinging lids and walked past quickly.

He found the geocaching group at the flagpole. They were impossible to miss with their GPS units in their hands and the packs they carried on their backs or on their belts. Dressed in jeans and hiking boots, two women and three men stood talking, energized. A cloth bag swung from one woman's hand. One man consulted a compass.

Nick's gaze lingered on a familiar face.

"Zack, what are you doing in town?" Until he moved to the UP a year ago to expand his lumberyard business, Zack lived down the street from Nick and Eve.

He was a German Baptist dressed in black pants, a white shirt, and a flat-rimmed black hat. Nick guessed him to be about forty-five. Zack's red beard seemed to expand as he greeted Nick with a surprised smile. "Nick, my friend, how pleasant to see you." He squeezed Nick's hand in a firm grip. "My manager retired, and I'm down for a few weeks to hire another," Zack said. "How about you? What are you doing here?"

"I thought I'd come learn about this sport. It sounds fun."

"Ah, yes. I'm quite fond of geocaching and thought I might hook up with old friends today. Let me introduce you." Nick intended to pick Zack's brain when the others weren't around. Maybe he'd seen or heard something in his previous excursions with the group. "This group is the Bay City Searchers," Zack said. "I was part of their group before I moved north."

He rattled off the names of the other members so fast, Nick knew he'd never remember them. "Nick Andreakos," he said, shaking their hands. "Where are we going today?"

A fair-haired man about forty smiled. "I've downloaded three caches out near the bay. It will be fun to have a geomuggle with us."

"Geomuggle?" Nick asked, trying to place where he'd seen the man.

"A newbie," Zack said, smiling a little. "You can ride with me, Nick," he offered.

"Thanks." Nick followed him to his van, a shiny black Chrysler Town & Country. "Who was the fair-headed guy again?"

"That's Judd Haskell."

Then it clicked. "He found a body out geocaching, didn't he?"

"So he told me yesterday. Were you on that case?"

"Yep." Nick didn't want to get into it. If Zack didn't know about Eve, Nick didn't want to tell him now. "So how does this work?" He climbed into the van and discovered it was much dirtier inside than out. Gum and candy wrappers littered the floor. Big books that looked like research works sat in stacks on the back bucket seats.

Zack glanced around. "I apologize for the mess. The class I'm taking for my master's requires a lot of study. I'm learning a new language." He drove out of the lot and headed toward Saginaw Bay. "As Judd said, he downloaded some caches that we thought might be interesting. They're in the same general area, so we don't have to spend too much time driving. What we're going to do first is follow a MapBlast map to the general area."

"So we're not using the GPS yet?"

"Not yet." Zack turned onto the access road to the bay. Glancing at his instructions, he cranked the wheel and drove along the waterway to the parking lot.

"So what's the draw to this sport anyway?"

Zack grinned. "It's a treasure hunt, my friend. The search for the unknown, a way to feel like an explorer. People who hide the items find it a way to share their own interests with others."

"I guess that does sound fun."

Zack parked. He opened his door and got out.

Nick hopped out too. "Now what?" he asked as the other vehicles parked and the searchers came to join them.

"Now our enjoyment begins." Zack fiddled with his GPS unit. "It's this way," he said, heading off to a stand of trees.

Nick could see the draw of the sport. There was an air of excitement in seeking out the "treasure" and wondering who'd spot it first. He joined in as they tromped around the small stand of white birch.

"What are we looking for?"

"We're uncertain of what it is we seek," Zack said. "Look for hiding places. The cache is close."

Nick spied a flash of red in the fork of a tree. "Is this it?" He reached up and grasped a red metal canister.

"You've found it!" Zack said, consulting his GPS unit. "Over here, friends."

The rest of the group gathered around to watch Nick unscrew the lid and draw out the contents: a signed score of *Swan Lake,* two tickets to a showing of the ballet in New York City, and a DVD of the same ballet.

"Ooh," the women said in unison. "We can take something if we leave something."

"I'm game for a trip to New York if you are," the younger woman said.

"They're ours," the redhead agreed. "Did you bring anything to put in it?"

"Yeah." The brunette pulled out a DVD of *Pride and Prejudice.*

"Are we supposed to take that?" Nick asked.

"It's allowed," Zack said. "You need to sign the guidebook. We're FTF."

"FTF?"

"First to find." Zack said. "Sign your name and write a small paragraph about how you found it."

"Can't I just sign my name?" Nick hated reports.

"That will suffice." Zack chuckled. "I'll jot down a tad about our experience. I'll sign our names as well." He waited until Nick handed him the logbook, then began to write.

Nick looked around while Zack finished up. He could see glimpses of blue through the trees and the white from boat sails. The scent from the bay began to lift his depression. It was good to get outside and try to move on with his life.

Zack gave him the canister to put back in the tree. "The next cache is new also. They both just came up this morning. This way." He set off away from the water to a deeper part of the treed area.

Flies came to greet them as they pressed deeper into the woods. Nick walked through mayapples and moss. They climbed a wooden stile that was more rotted than good. On the other side, Zack held up his hand and pointed.

"It should be right over there."

The women dashed for the clearing. A large tree lay across the opening and hid the downward-sloping side of the meadow from view. The redhead reached the tree and stopped.

Nick saw her hands go to her eyes. She began to shriek. Alarms rang in his head as he ran toward her. It was probably a snake or something. Then he saw where she was looking.

A blonde woman lay snuggled up against the fallen oak. Her hands lay on her chest, but they were severed from her body. A peanut butter sandwich was clutched in one hand.

She had no face.

A wise man must always be willing to alter his course of action as God demanded. Abraham Joshua Heschel said wisdom was the ability to look at all things from the point of view of God.

Gideon began to click on sites, glancing at them and shaking his head, then going to the next one. They proved his belief that the human race was corrupt and evil to the core. He had a ripe field.

He checked his favorite news site and frowned when he found a snippet that said his dear Sophie hadn't yet been identified. It wasn't acceptable. Did he have to do everything? Such incompetence.

He moved on. One blog entry caught his attention. The person bragged about going on vacation with a homosexual lover. The picture of the two women, fingers entwined, made his stomach clench. Still, the world had a way of dealing gays their fair share of pain without his assistance. They weren't his mission.

He started to go on, but then the woman in the photo's background caught his interest. She stood half hidden by the sweep of bare branches overhanging a bench.

The hair was hers. And the arrogant chin. If only he hadn't lost his picture. He'd dropped it somewhere at the Mount Sinai camp. Gideon's gaze scanned the text of the blog. Rock Harbor. He'd never heard of it. Near the Keweenaw. That was a place he did know. The UP was a place of deep spirituality for him, and his group was there.

How ironic that she'd found sanctuary there. He smiled, clicked off the site, and went to find his daughter.

Odette was in the kitchen. She dried her hands and smiled when she saw him. "Hey, Pop, you're home early."

Her beauty made his heart ache. So like Miranda had been once. Blonde hair, blue eyes, pink cheeks. The boys hadn't been too much of a problem yet, but lately she'd been pressing him to buy more fashionable clothes than the shapeless dresses he made her wear.

He kissed her cheek. "Yes, my dear. I thought I'd spend the evening with you. I have a trip coming up, and I'll be gone a few weeks."

"Oh?"

"A job out of state."

She sighed. "There seem to be a lot of those lately. Do I have to stay with Gram? I'm seventeen, Pop."

"Too young to stay alone. I'm going to study a bit," he told her. "Want to keep me company?"

She nodded, and they went down the hallway into the study. Gideon took down a copy of the Yajurveda.

"You've sure got a lot of books," Odette said, pulling an Italian edition of Dante's *Divine Comedy* off a shelf. "I think you've got every old book there is. Why do you read so many of these outdated things?" She flipped through some pages, then closed the book, an annoyed pout on her face. "They're all in other languages too."

"Most people are content to cling to one belief. Stupid sheep. Truth is everywhere. Don't ever forget, Odette, that finding truth requires digging, determined study, and an open mind. And you need languages. You learn the truth by reading it in the original. That's why I've always demanded you take a couple of languages, and why I'm always learning a new one."

"I hate Spanish."

She had never questioned him before. "Why so many questions, my dear?"

Her gaze went to the floor. "We never talk. You're always gone."

"Are you sure you're not just trying to get out of having to stay with your grandmother?"

He knew he'd guessed her motive when a blush graced her cheeks. "Sit," he said. "It's time you broadened your education. Do a good job and I might let you stay with your friend Betsy this time — if her parents approve."

"Really?" Her voice had a glad ring.

He flipped to Kandi I, a passage about the new and full moon sacrifices. The Vedic proverb, "Sacrifice is the navel of the world" was his mantra. Tonight was a new moon.

His gaze fastened on the fourth stanza, verse G. *Thou art the oblation-holder that wavers not.*

"You look shocked," his daughter said. "What are you reading? Is that what you want me to study?"

"The Kandi," he said. "New truth is always shocking."

"What's it say?"

"We're not to waver when we know the right course," he said, knowing she wouldn't understand the profundity of his words.

The game was just about to get intriguing.

"So really all we've got is your name?" Deputy Doug Montgomery scribbled in his small notepad, then put it back in his pocket. He was a tall, raw-boned man, and Elena found him to be more a bumbling dimwit than a competent officer of the law.

Seated on Bree's sofa, Elena sipped her tea and tried to calm her shaking hands. This felt all wrong. "I seem to have lived in the Detroit area from the little we've gleaned from the Internet. And I taught ballet."

"I'll make some inquiries." Montgomery fixed her and Bree with a stare that tried for stern. "You should have come to me sooner."

"I know." She kept her voice meek in the hope of turning his displeasure. "I was afraid. I'm still afraid. Someone attacked me, almost killed me. I can almost see his face in my dreams."

"I can understand that. I'll make sure a deputy keeps an eye on things."

"Thanks, Doug," Kade said. He walked the deputy to the front door.

"Are you feeling okay about this?" Bree

asked when the front door banged. She put her tea on the coffee table and brought her feet onto the sofa beside Elena.

Elena shook her head. "I'm not confident he'll be discreet." The sunset had ended, plunging the room into darkness, and Elena leaned over to switch on a light. Distant thumps echoed through the ceiling above her head, and she could hear the children giggling. At least Terri had no notion there was anything wrong.

"Doug isn't the smoothest operator around, but he's good at what he does. Let's help speed up the process, make some more calls," Bree suggested. She grabbed up the phone and pulled out the list of the Coxes in Detroit.

Elena took the pages Bree held out but then laid them on the sofa between them. "It feels pretty hopeless, Bree. I don't think I can face another 'Sorry, I can't help you.' Maybe Montgomery will turn up something."

Bree studied Elena's face for a long time before she nodded. "We need some fun. Let's go geocaching after church on Sunday. I can dig up some locations that won't take all day to get to."

Elena had heard Bree talking about the sport for weeks, but there'd been no time to actually do it. "How'd you get into that anyway? I would think it's too much like search-and-rescue work to be fun for you."

"I think that's why it *does* appeal," Bree said. "It's the other side of what I do. I love being out in nature and looking for something frivolous instead of serious. I get such a kick out of finding crazy things out there. Like the set of California Raisins that started singing when I opened the lid."

"How'd you get started?"

"One of the clubs had an event up here two years ago. Kade was asked to coordinate sites for the caches, and I got roped into helping. After one weekend, I was hooked."

Elena giggled at the rapture on Bree's face. "You're so weird."

"But you love me anyway."

"Yeah, I do." Elena touched Bree's knee. "I don't know what I would have done without you and Kade, Bree. Where I might be. Maybe six feet under." She shook her head. "I wish I could remember more."

"If all of your memory doesn't come back, you've got the important things," Bree said. "Yourself and your daughter. I think all of us have wished we could start over a time or two. There's something very appealing about a fresh slate."

"I've been thinking about that. I've got no

baggage right now." She smiled. "That's a good thing, right?"

"Right." Bree returned her smile.

"I'll never be able to thank you enough for the past months."

"It's what friends do." Bree patted the top of Elena's hand as the phone rang on the stand. Bree reached over and grabbed it. She glanced at the screen. "It's Doug." With a click, the phone was on and at her ear. "Hey, Doug, what's up?" She listened for a few moments. "I see," she said, glancing at Elena. "You're sure?" Nodding, she listened a few more moments, then clicked off the phone and put it back on its cradle.

"He hasn't found out something already, has he?" Elena didn't like the stricken expression on her friend's face. Or the way Bree was avoiding her gaze.

Bree sighed. "Yeah, he did. It came right up when he ran it. The only Elena Cox in the Detroit area is a teacher who died two years ago. That's the one we read about on the Internet. It's not you."

Not her? She absorbed the news in silence a minute. The little tidbits of information they'd collected were all wrong too. She hadn't expected quite this clean a slate.

"Then where did I live? Where's my family?"

"Doug is checking to see what other Elena Coxes are in Michigan, but it may be days before he figures it out."

She didn't even know her own name. Maybe it was a good thing. Maybe her attacker wouldn't ever know it either.

9

The stocking Gideon wore over his face the night he'd entered Eve's house should have kept his identity safe. But his first day in Rock Harbor, he tensed, then relaxed when Eve's gaze touched his face and moved on.

He could take his time, observe her behavior in anonymity. It was nearly three weeks before the next full moon. He could choose his moves carefully, perfect his approach. Finish what he'd started with the others before ending at the beginning.

He headed to the coffee shop and passed two men in park service uniforms, talking in front of the sheriff's office. He slowed when he heard what they were talking about.

The bigger man stretched. "Well, you ready to go shoot some more swans? I'd hoped we could get them all the other day, but that darned protest slowed us down. We've only got another ten or so to handle."

Gideon barely choked back his gasp.

Shoot swans? What kind of maniacs would do such a thing? His hands curled into fists at his side.

"I sure hate to do it, Kade. I hope none of them drown when we knock them out."

So they were just going to tranquilize them. But why? Gideon pretended to examine a shop window.

"Me too," the one called Kade said. "But it's got to be done. I hope moving them works. If they come back to the trumpeters' lakes and ponds, we'll have to kill them. I've got my tranquilizer rifle in my truck. Did you bring yours?"

"Yeah, I brought it."

Kade went to his vehicle, parked along on a side street, and took out a gun. Then he slid into a truck with the other man, and they drove off. Gideon clenched and unclenched his fists. There had to be some way to make the man pay. Glancing around, he saw no one on the side street.

A shovel lay in the back of Kade's truck. Gideon gave another quick glance around, then pulled a glove out of his lightweight jacket. He slipped it on and lifted the shovel out of the truck. With long strides he went to his vehicle around the corner and got in. He tossed the shovel in the back.

Perhaps he could kill two birds with one

stone here. That was an unfortunate but fitting metaphor, all things considered. He contemplated a plan that would make this Kade pay for his abuse of the natural order *and* let Eve know for sure her sanctuary had been invaded. The site of his first kill lay only an hour and a half from here. No one had ever discovered the grave.

He dug around under his seat and pulled out a CD. When the music of Tchaikovsky filled his ears, he sighed and leaned back to let the swelling instrumental sounds minister to him. With the song blaring out of the speakers, he made his way to Highway 45. The music made him drive faster, and it was only an hour later that he spied the national forest road he needed.

He hadn't been here in five years, but he remembered the night he'd first answered his calling. Parking in the trees, he put on his gloves and grabbed the shovel and a plastic bag. A fifteen-minute hike brought him to the site, still undisturbed and peaceful.

Half an hour later, sweating and dirty, he carried his burden back to his vehicle and put it in the back. Now to find a worthy place.

Gideon ended his productive day at his

sanctuary. He wasn't sure anyone knew it was here. To reach it, he drove a barely recognizable path that was mostly covered with grass. Huge jack pine trees, stands of birch, and giant oak trees hovered in a protective canopy over the two-room cabin. And his angels guarded the place as well. It was as secure as any place in heaven or on earth.

The first day, five years ago, when Gideon forced open the door and stepped into the cobwebbed cabin that smelled of mildew and rat droppings, he'd known. Known it was his place. The heart of his plans, the soul of his new life.

Now, carrying a sack of groceries, he stepped to the porch and dug out the padlock key. It fit neatly into the shiny new lock and opened without a sound. Stepping to the single wall of cabinets, he set the sack on the counter and began to put away the food. He alphabetized the soups, stacked the boxed foods neatly so he could read the tops, then folded the paper sack and placed it under the sink.

Only when the kitchen was in perfect order did he allow himself to enjoy the main reason he loved it so. He made a peanut butter sandwich, pushed open the back door, and stepped out on the porch. A small, beautiful pond backed up to the cabin. The water reflected the spill of moonshine. Loons cried out. The tremolo they made had been described as insane laughter, but the deep, rich tones reminded him of a moaning aeolian harp.

His angels were here somewhere. He stepped down off the porch and strolled to the water's edge. He'd known the minute he saw the pond that the swans he loved would hover over these waters like gods. Deep-throated cries came to him now. Sonorous like trumpets and just as thrilling.

They glided into the moonlight. Their beauty swamped his senses. Ethereal and glowing with white light, they came nearer. "My angels," he crooned, throwing the bits of the peanut butter sandwich in his hand to them.

The darkness of the island in the middle of the water drew his gaze. He'd go there later tonight to make sure everything was ready for her.

After church, Elena accepted Bree's offer to take her geocaching. They stopped to pick up Naomi, then went out to the woods.

"We won't stay out long," Naomi said. "Donovan is taking me out for dinner tonight."

"Are you sure Anu is okay with keeping Terri and Davy?" Elena asked.

"She's in her element," Bree assured her. "We'll only be gone a couple of hours. She'll let them bake cookies or something."

Bree parked the Jeep along a bank of blooming columbine. Humming, she opened the back door and let Samson and Charley scamper out. The dogs nosed through the wildflowers and moss.

"This is going to be so fun," Bree said. She unzipped her backpack and pulled out a GPS unit, then shouldered the pack. "Let's go."

Once in the woods, the clouds of biting, stinging insects descended to feast on every bit of uncovered flesh. The incessant buzzing alone was enough to drive a person mad. Only an idiot would endure this for the sake of "fun," Elena decided, but she kept her opinion to herself when she saw the eager way Bree and Naomi plunged through the thickets.

So what did she enjoy most in life? The natural beauty of this place pleased her. Did she prefer art galleries and museums? Spas and manicures? Whatever she had been in the past, she could change now if she wanted, while she didn't remember.

But it wasn't this.

Elena's nylon head net trapped her warm breath and added to her discomfort. "How much farther?" she called to Bree and Naomi as they started up a hillside.

Bree brushed her short red curls out of her eyes and consulted the GPS. She wore no netting, relying instead on insect repellant. "Not far. It should be just over the hill." She pulled a handful of pistachios from her pocket and offered some to Elena.

Elena shook her head and turned to survey the hill Bree had indicated. Charley romped in last autumn's leaves on the hillside while Samson rolled on his back in the vegetation.

"I'd like to find something fun today," Naomi said. "Bree has been hooked since she found a rare Elvis album in the original sleeve."

Bree's smile flashed. "There are snippets of culture just lying around. You'll be hooked too."

Elena paused and looked toward the sky. The trees seemed to crowd in on her, and she found it hard to inhale enough oxygen. The peace of the forest should have soothed her, but her gaze kept darting from bush to shrub. Her ears strained for evidence of a hostile presence. What was wrong with her?

"We should bury something ourselves,"

Bree said.

Elena tried to enter into the spirit of the hunt. "What do you have in mind?"

"Maybe something about search-and-rescue and dog training?"

Naomi punched her lightly on the arm. "We're the only ones who care about that. Other people probably think we're nuts. Hey, what am I saying? I think we're crazy sometimes." She swatted at the flies buzzing around her head.

"A lot of people are fascinated with what the dogs can do," Elena said. "I had no idea until I met you. We could put in some pictures of your most memorable finds — like the day Samson found a body under the water. Well, that might be gruesome. How about when Charley found that little girl who had been missing for two days?"

"You've been paying attention to our stories," Naomi said, her smile breaking out.

"A little." Elena smiled back. She caught a glimpse of blue through the trees. She started toward it. "Hey, water. Is it a pond or a lake?"

"It's a pond," Bree said. "Real pretty. We could take a break and eat our snack."

Elena moved through the trees to the pond. Once she was in sunlight, she'd feel better. She fought through a thicket and stepped into the clearing. Her next breath took in the sweetest air. If only she could stay here and not have to go back into the woods.

"Oh, look, swans," Naomi said from behind her. "They're so beautiful."

At the sight of the beautiful birds, Elena's knees went weak. She could almost hear ethereal music, but it must be in her head. She closed her eyes and listened to the melody. She began to move with her eyes closed. Behind her lids she could see a stage, and beautiful women dressed in white twirling across it.

She became aware that her arms were out from her body and she was dancing on her toes. Opening her eyes, she blinked and came out of her trance, if that's what it was.

"You looked beautiful. What was that you were humming?" Bree asked.

Elena hadn't realized she was humming, but she could still hear the music echoing in her head. " 'Dance of the Little Swans,' " she said. Until she uttered the words, she hadn't realized she knew them.

"From *Swan Lake*?" Bree asked.

"Yes."

"Did you dance in it sometime?" Naomi asked. "You were dancing like a real ballerina. Did you dance professionally?"

Did this mean her memory was coming back? It was the first clear memory Elena had had in weeks. She began to smile. "Maybe. I remember lights and a stage."

The wind shifted, and Samson lifted his nose in the air. Charley's tail drooped, and both dogs began to howl. In perfect synchronization, they raced up the hill away from the pond and disappeared over the crest. Their howls continued to punctuate the air.

Bree went pale and looked at Naomi. Both women wore expressions of dread. "What's wrong?" Elena asked. Her fingers tightened on her walking stick.

"Maybe it's a dead deer," Naomi whispered.

Bree shook her head. "We know better. We'd better go take a look." She and Naomi plunged after the dogs.

"What's going on?" Elena shouted after them. She wasn't sure she wanted to know. Reluctant to be left alone, she followed the women and looked ahead to the dogs. They dug at the ground and continued to whine and howl.

Naomi swallowed hard, and her gaze locked with Bree's. "Should I call it in?"

"Let's check for sure." Bree stood a few feet from where the dogs cowered with their tails tucked between their legs. She glanced at her GPS. "I have a really bad feeling about this."

Elena gulped, and her gaze went to the dogs and to the bundle they had uncovered. Samson was defecating. Charley retched and coughed. "I don't understand," she whispered.

Bree squeezed her hand. "I'm sorry you had to see this. The dogs have found a dead body. Human."

"Are you sure?" Elena couldn't bring herself to look.

"Positive. The dogs are giving an unmistakable death-scent reaction. The grave looks to be shallow. Samson, Charley, come," Bree commanded. The dogs turned and moved to her. Both still had their tails tucked.

The two women approached what appeared to be a pile of rags peeking out from the dirt. Elena hung back, telling herself there was no reason for the terror that darkened the edges of her vision.

Naomi stooped and peered at the shallow grave. "Don't get too close. We don't want to contaminate the evidence," Bree warned.

Elena swallowed the sour taste in her mouth and stopped about five feet from the bundle. A tuft of blue clothing that looked like silk poked from the grave. The detailing clearly signaled female. She caught a glimpse of white bone. The victim had been buried awhile.

"Elena, could you call it in?" Naomi tossed her phone to Elena.

The women blocked her view of the grave. Elena's hands shook. She stepped back to the pond and called 911. Her trembling intensified, and it was all she could do to choke out their coordinates to the dispatcher. She managed to mumble the details to the man on the other end of the line, then she returned to Naomi.

Samson pushed his nose against Elena's hand and whined. She rubbed his ears. "I'm okay, boy," she whispered.

Bree touched her shoulder. "Are you really?"

"No, but I'll deal."

"If you want to go back, we'll wait here for the deputies."

Elena straightened. "I'll wait with you." Her gaze went back to the body. "Has Samson found many dead bodies?" Clasping her arms around herself, she took another step back.

Bree's lips flattened. "Some. He'll be upset for a few days. When we get back, we'll play with the dogs. That will help." She pointed toward the grave. "What's weird is there's a peanut butter sandwich on the remains. It looks fresh."

"How odd," Elena whispered. She felt the blood drain from her face.

Bree studied Elena's face. "What's wrong, Elena?"

Elena shivered even though the air was oppressively warm. She rubbed her arms. "Something about peanut butter." Was it her imagination, or did she hear someone move in the thicket? She peered into the dark shadows but saw nothing.

"Oh, Elena," Bree whispered. She moved toward her and put her arms around Elena's shoulders. "This poor woman has been dead for several years. It can't have anything to do with you."

"You're right. Of course you're right." Elena clamped her lips shut, but they trembled anyway. She could feel Bree's stare, could sense Naomi's speculation and concern. Lodgepole pine reached for glimpses of blue sky. She'd found solace in these quiet hills and valleys where moose and black bear still roamed. The peace of this place had been shattered. Elena knew it as clearly as if she'd heard the foghorn of Bree's lighthouse home.

He'd found her.

10

"Iris Chen is squawking about the people who died last week." Cyril tossed a manila file onto Nick's desk. "She doesn't seem ready to let it go."

The picture of Eve was in Nick's hand. He didn't want to relinquish it long enough to look at the file his dad had brought in. "I killed the wrong guy, Dad." He'd been immersed in the Gideon case.

"You only did what you had to do."

"I know." Nick rubbed his aching head, then thumbed loose a Rolaids and popped it into his mouth. "I was sure Bechtol was Gideon. Now we have no leads."

"What about the geocaching group?"

"I pumped Zack for information, but he only goes with this small group and hasn't gone to any bigger events. One interesting thing — the guy who found Eve's remains was in Zack's group."

His dad paused. "You think he could have

anything to do with it?"

"Zack says he's harmless." He turned the picture over and looked at it again.

Cyril saw the picture in Nick's hand. "You've got to let it go, Son. There are no clues in that picture."

"I like looking at it." Nick put it down on the desk, but his gaze strayed back. "It was taken the night Eve danced in *Swan Lake.* He had to be there. The stage is in the background, and she's wearing her white costume."

"Maybe it was a media picture," his dad suggested.

Nick shook his head. "It's just a Polaroid. A news photographer would have used a better camera. This might have even been the night we met. I'd never seen anyone more beautiful." He could still see her in his mind, his heart. So light, so fragile.

"Don't, Nick."

"I wanted to kill him, you know." Nick stared into his father's face. "I wasn't aiming to, but I was happy when that bullet struck home, when he crumpled. He deserved to die. Iris told us he intended to force her to become his third wife. He was scum." He slumped back in his chair. "But he's innocent of hurting Eve and Keri. I don't understand why he had the picture though." He picked up the folder. "Tell me about Iris."

His dad pulled up a chair. "She's claiming there was no need to use deadly force to free her. I have no doubt you'll be exonerated, but you'd better expect some heat for now."

"I can handle heat. What I can't handle is not knowing what's happened to Keri. Finding Eve's body was hard, but at least there was closure, you know? I keep waiting for the other shoe to drop."

"Maybe it won't. Maybe Keri is alive and happy somewhere."

"She adored Eve. She wouldn't be happy without her."

"She's young. Children forget."

Nick didn't want to hear it. So long as he and Keri kept Eve in their memories, she wasn't truly gone.

Cyril stood. "Your sister is in the waiting room."

"What's she want?"

His father shrugged. "She wouldn't tell me. I fended her off until I had a chance to talk to you, but she's not going anywhere until you see her."

"Send her in. I might as well get it over with."

His dad nodded and left the office. There

was no telling what Layna wanted. She could have stopped by to see how he was holding up, or she could have come to cry on his shoulder. Either way, she was a trial. He wished she'd go back to the way she used to be when they were growing up. The bitterness she held like a shield got tiresome.

At least she was smiling when she came into the office. "Hey, brother of mine."

He stood and went around his desk to hug her. Her strong perfume made him sneeze. "Hi, Sis." Stepping back, he pulled the chair away from the desk. "Have a seat."

Dressed in black jeans with a red jacket over a black lace thing that Eve used to call a camisole, Layna looked cool and elegant. Her hair was swept up in some kind of knot on her head.

Nick went around the desk and dropped into his chair. "What's up?"

"Does something have to be up for me to stop by and visit my favorite brother?"

"I'm your only brother." He tried not to look at his watch. There was a ton of work on his desk.

Her smile widened. "I wanted to invite you to dinner tonight."

"That's it? You could have called for that." She looked down, and he knew there was more to her intent than a simple dinner invitation. "What?" he asked.

"Um, I invited Jessica over too."

Nick leaned back and blew out his breath. "Why do you do things like this?" he asked, careful to keep his voice down.

Her chin jutted out. "It's time you move on, Nick. Jessica has never gotten over you. If Eve hadn't moved in on you . . ." She bit her lip when he glared. "I think you could care about Jess again."

"Layna, I'm not interested. All I want to do right now is find Keri."

"She's not even —"

"Not even what?" He stood. "Look, let's not fight about this. I'd be happy to come to dinner sometime, but not when you're trying to fix me up. I still love my wife."

"Your ex-wife," she pointed out, getting to her feet. "Nicky, she was never good enough for you. And she proved it with that affair with that dancer . . . Will, or whatever his name was."

"It wasn't an *affair*!"

"You caught them at dinner," she pointed out.

"She was just lonely, eating with a friend. Nothing happened." He saw the pity in his sister's eyes and tried to hold on to his temper.

"Nothing you'll admit to yourself."

Maybe she was right — he didn't want to believe more than he saw. Eve had sworn there was nothing more than friendship between them, and Nick let it drop. And tried to get home more for dinner. His new pledge to be there for her had lasted all of four days.

Birds chirped overhead, a much too cheerful sound for the drama playing out in the middle of the woods. Elena tried to tell herself it wasn't so, couldn't be true. There was no way he could have tracked her here. The car was in the lake. No one knew where she was from. He couldn't possibly have found her in this remote place. She was being paranoid.

But the fear grew.

She jerked when Naomi touched her arm. "Sorry," she muttered.

"Talk to us, Elena," Bree said. "You're pale and shaking. Let us help you."

Elena bit her lip and wished she could talk to her friends about it. She didn't even know what to say. Some male figure menaced her dreams, but she didn't know if it was her ex-husband or someone else.

She saw a truck through the trees. Shiny-new and black, it pulled off the side of the road. "There's the deputy."

Bree gave her a last worried glance, then she and Naomi went down the hillside to greet the deputies. Elena called the dogs to her. They both meandered over with their noses pointing down and their tails still between their legs. The dogs plopped down beside her and put their heads in her lap.

Their warm fur strengthened her. Of course this wasn't about her. Her earlier certainty dissipated as fast as Superior's morning fog. She stood as Bree and the deputies arrived on the scene.

Deputy Montgomery was a big man, easily six-five and three hundred pounds, and the white booties he slipped over his boots looked awkward on him. He squatted near the site. "Looks like nicks in some of the bones. I'd say she was stabbed. There's a knife buried here with the bones too."

"Any idea who she is?" Naomi asked.

"Nope." He motioned to the other men. "I'm going to have to call the sheriff in Finland." He dialed his cell phone. "You gals can go. I'll stop by and take your statement when I'm done here." Turning his back on the women, he began to speak into the phone.

"Let's get out of here." Bree snapped her fingers, and Samson came to her. The women and the dogs walked down the slope covered with wildflowers.

Elena drew in a lungful of pure air not tainted by the smell of death. But the scent still clung to her clothes, her hair, and her skin. She longed to get home and shower away the stench. The farther away they moved, the easier it was to tell herself this death had nothing to do with her.

"Hey, wait here a minute." Bree told Samson to stay, then ran back up the hillside. "I want to check the GPS." When Bree returned a few minutes later, her eyes were grim. "It's a match with the cache. The killer intended us to find her. Wasn't there something like that in the news a few months ago?"

Spots danced in Elena's vision, and she swayed. The blackness receded. "It's him," Elena whispered. "I know it's him." A dark, shadowy figure hovered in her memory.

Bree grabbed her hand. "You okay? Sit down." She guided Elena to a nearby rock and pushed her head between her knees. "Take deep breaths."

Elena pushed Bree away. "I'm fine."

"Who do you think it is?" Bree's voice was sharp.

"The man, the one who attacked me." There was a vile taste in Elena's mouth.

"I've got to get Terri and get out of here. It isn't safe. He's found me." Aware she was babbling but unable to stop, Elena leaped up and ran for the Jeep. "Hurry!"

Panic chased her down the hillside to Bree's Jeep. She heard Bree and Naomi shout after her, but nothing could stop the surge of adrenaline that propelled her. Samson caught up with her, then darted in front as if herding her. She stumbled. Her knee dug into the soft earth, then she pitched headfirst into a roll down the hillside.

The scenery rushed past. Her arm slammed into a downed jack pine, and her leg scraped over tiny rocks embedded in the dirt. The scent of moss and dirt invaded her nose. She hurtled down and came to rest at the base of the hill. Dazed, she sat up and began to pick the twigs out of her hair. Every muscle in her body screamed.

Bree reached her. "Are you all right?"

"I think so." Abrasions on her legs and arms began to sting, but she didn't think anything was broken. Her nylon headgear had come off. Samson licked her face, and she pushed him away to take the hand Bree extended. "Thanks." Grass stains and tears marred her favorite jeans.

Bree put her hands on her hips. "Why do you think this has anything to do with you?"

Elena didn't answer. She limped toward the Jeep and got in on the passenger side.

Bree put the dogs in the back and slid behind the wheel. Naomi climbed in behind Elena.

"Lock the doors," Elena said, thumbing down her lock button.

"For heaven's sake, Elena," Bree began.

Elena gave her a fierce look. "Just do it!" The shadows gathered in the forest, hiding him somewhere. She felt vulnerable, exposed. "Drive."

"When are you going to tell us what this is all about?" Bree slipped the transmission into drive and put her foot on the accelerator.

Elena put her head in her hands. "All I know is that there's a man after me." She pressed her fingers over her eyes. Nausea roiled her stomach. "When I saw that grave, all this fear flooded in." She shuddered. "Oh, why can't I remember?" she moaned, pressing fingers over her eyes.

Bree touched Elena's hand. "Are you all right?"

"I feel it *here*." Elena put her hand over her chest. "Call Montgomery and ask him if anything is missing on the woman," she whispered.

"Missing? What do you mean?" Bree asked.

"As in parts of her!" Elena nearly screamed the words. Her hands began to shake, and she clenched them together. She wouldn't panic again. Right now she needed every smart cell in her brain. She didn't know how she knew this, but her certainty was as hard and sure as the seat beneath her.

Bree steered the Jeep to the side of the road and put it in park. She got out her cell phone and dialed. "Doug, is the victim missing any body parts?" She listened a few moments. "I see. Thanks." She clicked off her phone.

"What?" Elena demanded.

"He can't tell yet."

Elena threw open the door and retched, but nothing came up. Perspiration dotted her forehead. "I have to get to Terri! Please, let's go there now."

Bree nodded and put the Jeep back into gear. The vehicle fishtailed around the curves at the speed she drove. "We'll protect you, Elena. Don't panic."

"I don't know who he is though," Elena muttered. "It's hard to protect against a ghost."

"Do you remember anything?" Naomi asked.

"Nothing. But I know it's him."

Bree slowed at the city limits. Rock Harbor had been perfect from Elena's point of view. Her sanctuary. But he'd invaded it. As soon as Bree stopped in front of Anu's house, Elena sprang from the vehicle and ran inside.

Anu never locked the door and had told her not to bother knocking. Elena threw open the door and rushed inside. "Terri!" The scent of baking cookies didn't comfort her.

Anu came from the kitchen. "What is wrong, Elena? You look distraught."

Bree rushed in behind her. "Elena, Montgomery could assign you some protection."

Anu's face creased. "*Kulta,* what is going on?"

Elena looked around for the sight of a bright blonde head. "Where's Terri?"

"She's in the kitchen, decorating cookies."

Elena darted past Anu into the blue-and-yellow kitchen. The sweet scent of sugar cookies permeated the air. Elena went to the children and swept the little girl into her arms.

Terri wiggled. "Down," she commanded. "Cookie." She pointed to a lopsided bunny cookie with more frosting than substance.

"We need to go, Terri." *Far, far away.*

Terri thrust out her lower lip, a trick that usually melted Elena. But today it only upped her frustration. She didn't know where she could go, only that she needed to get away.

Bree and Anu were standing arm in arm and talking in low voices when she turned. "I need to get home," Elena said. "Can you take me now?"

"Of course," Bree said.

"Leave Davy and let him finish decorating his cookies," Anu said.

"You sure?" Bree asked.

"I shall bring him home later," Anu said.

"Okay."

Elena waited by the door until Bree went to tell Davy good-bye. She wanted to scream with the need to hurry. And where could they go? There was no one she could turn to for help. As she carried Terri to the Jeep, the back of her neck prickled. Was he watching her even now from behind the blank stares of some storefront?

And more important — who was he?

Bree held open the back door, and Elena buckled Terri into her car seat in the back. Samson immediately plopped his head on the child's lap. Terri giggled and began to stroke his ears. He gave a blissful groan.

The lighthouse at the end of the road felt like home. Elena felt a pang at the thought of leaving it. She saw it with new eyes, the slate covering its steeply pointed roof and the window mullions that gave it even more character.

Sitting on top of the bluff, she felt safe. Or at least she had until today.

Bree wiggled the mouse, and the computer screen came to life. Elena might not be able to tell her what was going on, but maybe there was some clue they'd overlooked online. She Gooogled "geocache murder." Something touched her shoulder, and she jumped.

She looked up into the smiling blue eyes of her husband. "You scared me to death," she scolded. "Did you lock the door?"

"This is Rock Harbor."

"We found a dead body today." She told him the story. "Elena is terrified, Kade. It was all I could do to talk her into not making any decisions tonight. I thought I'd see what I can find online."

"Snooping?" He pulled a chair up beside her.

"I'm frightened for her." Bree shuddered, and Kade put his arm around her. She snuggled into the comfort of his embrace. The search engine brought up numerous sites.

She clicked on one and leaned forward to read it. "This one was in Bay City just last week," she said. "It says a woman was found stabbed to death in the woods. Geocachers found her. Her hands were amputated." She nearly gagged at the thought. "And her face was missing."

Kade leaned over her shoulder. "Hey, the guy left clues online after the woman was found. 'Authorities were alerted to a post allegedly made by the killer within hours of the body's discovery,' " he read aloud. " 'Oh, ye! Think ye that Incal will accept the blood of innocent animals for your crimes? Whoso sayeth this doth lie! Incal, God, will never take blood of anything, nor symbol of any sort which placeth an innocent in a guilty one's stead!' "

Bree's eyes widened. "That's spooky." She shook her head. I wonder if there's anything at the site where today's cache was listed."

"You should let Montgomery handle it."

"I wish Mason were here." Her sheriff brother-in-law was a rock. He would have known what to do.

"Montgomery isn't a bad sort. How long will Mason and Hilary be in Finland?"

"Another week. They wanted to introduce Zoe to all the Finnish relatives." Hilary was Anu's daughter and part of the family, especially since she'd adopted Kade's niece.

She navigated to the geocaching site. "There are comments posted about today's site." She clicked the comment link and checked the time stamp. "It was just added tonight. 'The heart is deceitful above all things, and desperately wicked.' "

"That's familiar; look it up." He leaned toward the computer.

Bree typed in the beginning of the sentence. "It's from Jeremiah."

"The Bible, New Age mumbo jumbo. Our guy reads from a variety of sources. Seems odd."

She bent over the keyboard again. "Let's see if there are any other geocache murder sites in the past few years." Before she could type in her search, the doorbell rang, and she heard Elena in the hallway.

Bree stood and grabbed Kade's hand to lead him out of the office. "I don't want Elena to see this article. She's already freaked."

They met Elena in the hall, and all three of them went to the living room.

"I'll get the door," Kade said. He stepped to the foyer and returned a few moments later with a young man in tow. Bree recognized him as the man who'd seen her and Elena jogging a couple of weeks ago.

About thirty, the man wore a smile as relaxed as his jeans. His movements suggested a gracefulness she wasn't used to seeing in a man. His gaze shot past Bree and landed on Elena. "I'm so glad I found you."

Elena took a step backward. "Do I know you?"

His smile faltered. "It's me. Will." His gaze darted to Bree. "What have you done to her?"

Elena swayed and grabbed the back of a nearby chair.

"You've been missing for months, girl. I saw a picture in the paper. You were in the background, but I was sure it was you. I showed someone at the coffee shop your picture, and they told me you were staying here. What are you doing going under an assumed name?"

Elena swayed again, then her knees buckled. Kade leaped to catch her, but he wasn't fast enough and she crumpled to the rug.

11

The small building didn't look like a church. Gideon got out of his car and looked around the tiny valley surrounded by a white pine forest. It had been all he could do to squeeze his vehicle through the tree trunks that choked the lane to the compound. He could hear the twang of guitars and the thump of drums.

A young woman got out of a small car and approached the weathered blue building. The fading sunlight struck her, and he realized she was pregnant. Very pregnant. He clicked his tongue. She was much too young to be anything but an unwed mother. Certainly she was no older than Odette. Immorality ran rampant in the world, even in this group he had started. What he saw in front of him proved perfection lay nowhere in this world.

He followed her inside the building. Incense burners intermingled with candles lined the walls. Folding chairs, beanbags, and webbed outdoor seating rather than pews furnished the room. Mostly young people, they wore jeans topped with T-shirts. One girl's shirt read "Job's Children: Accept Life's Pain."

He smiled as he slipped into a sagging patio chair and inhaled the thick scent of patchouli. A few saw him and waved. A hum of excited whispers rose.

Their leader had come home.

The discovery of yet another body after Gideon's alleged death ignited a media firestorm. New theories and speculations about the serial killer, the dead women, and the cop's missing wife — ex-wife, Nick reminded himself — dominated the local news and even made a few national headlines. A flood of sympathetic well-wishers, total strangers, sent their hope and prayers to Nick. Nasty messages from the criminal element poured in too. Taunting e-mails that twisted the knife.

He rubbed his eyes and leaned back in his chair. The past weekend's murder looked to be a mob hit, clean and direct. Gideon tortured his victims, and he clearly preferred women. The man had been identified as Billy DeAngelo, a known drug dealer.

Gideon would make a slip sometime, and when he did, Nick would have him.

Nick flipped open the Gideon file and began to review the remarks the killer posted on the Web. They'd identified the woman found in the pond as Sophie Tallmadge, an exotic dancer known for her graceful — and sensual — moves. So far he hadn't been able to connect her to Eve. And even though they'd kept Sophie's identification out of the media, Gideon had fallen silent about her.

Why no new clues attached to Eve's remains? Did Gideon think the call while Nick was at Eve's house was enough?

His head throbbed from too much caffeine and too little sleep. He should probably eat something other than donuts and coffee.

The door to Nick's office opened, and Fraser stepped in. He came toward the desk with a paper in his hand. "Deputies found bones at a geocaching site in Rock Harbor."

"You think it's another Gideon murder?"

Fraser nodded. "Looks like our guy is taunting us."

"That was fast. It's been less than a week since we stumbled onto the Crandall woman." The woman he'd found on his geocaching jaunt had been identified right away. Yvette Crandall, another blonde dancer. Nick closed the folder. "Did he leave a clue for this one?"

"Yep," Fraser said, holding out the paper.

Nick's muscles clenched at the somber expression on his partner's face. He took the paper and scanned it. " 'The heart is deceitful above all things, and desperately wicked.' " He rubbed his eyes. "A verse, just like the others. This has to be him. Who is it?"

"No identification yet. According to preliminary results, the bones are about five years dead. Coroner thinks maybe the heart was dug out with a knife. There are nicks on the breastbone. No doubt about this one. It's Gideon's MO."

Nick flipped open the Gideon file again. "I showed you this before, and I think it means something." He passed over the passage from Proverbs he'd found.

Fraser took it, and Nick watched his partner read it. "What do you think?" he asked.

Fraser handed it back. "You might be right, Nick. We've got missing eyes, tongue, hands, and maybe heart so far. He finds some woman who he thinks committed one of these abominations and wastes her."

Nick tossed the folder onto the desk. "For

all the good it does us. And what was Eve's sin?"

Fraser didn't answer.

"He seems to be following the order of this passage."

"Maybe. I don't know about the tongue though. Eve had the same verse attached to her as to the Tallmadge woman."

Nick opened his desk drawer and pulled out a Michigan map. "Rock Harbor. Where the heck is that?" He scanned the map and whistled softly through his teeth. "That's in the UP." He looked up at Fraser.

Fraser dropped into a chair. "This could be our break — a murder this old and he's only now revealing it. He's getting bold. Your dad thinks we should get up to Rock Harbor and check it out."

Nick stood and grabbed his sport jacket from the back of his chair. "Let's go now." He stopped in the doorway. "Wait, when was this posted?"

"Saturday night, and the body was found yesterday."

"If we could only figure out his motive. He's a missionary killer, but what triggers him? And why blonde dancers?"

Fraser shrugged. "They all have a similar look — slim and elegant with great bone structure," Fraser said. "Eve fit that profile.

If we knew where he first saw her, we might be able to figure out who he is and why he killed her."

Nick picked up the picture of Eve. "All the victims so far were ballerinas at some point. I think he saw Eve at the ballet."

"In New York? You realize how hard it would be to narrow that field? Thousands of people saw her perform."

Watching her glide across the stage as if she had wings had been the most beautiful thing he'd ever seen. Nick's throat clenched.

He nodded, then grabbed up the files and stuffed them in his briefcase. "Do we have airline tickets?"

"I had Marge check airlines and times. There isn't another one until middle of the afternoon, and the trip is nearly five hours with the layover in Minneapolis. So nine hours away. You might as well drive. You'd get there about the same time, and at least you'd have your car."

"Aren't you coming?"

Fraser shook his head. "I can't go until later this week. My daughter has a dance recital tonight, and Gail's got a short business trip. I'm on Dad Duty. I'll drive up first thing I can."

"If I'd been smart enough to put my family first, they might still be alive," Nick said.

He didn't wait for an answer, since there was none.

He drove home in a fugue of memory. Walking to the front door of his minuscule apartment, he couldn't help his thoughts from wandering to how it used to be. Eve greeting him at the door with a smile. Keri running to meet him. This apartment felt cold and sterile, devoid of memories or life. No plants. Eve loved plants and flowers. Their house had been filled with them.

At least the bedroom looked lived in, since he came home long enough to sleep. He dragged the suitcase off the closet shelf and began to stuff his clothes and toiletries into it. By ten, he was back in his Dodge Durango and heading out of town.

He took I-75 north, barely noticing the names of the towns he passed as the big tires on his SUV ate up the miles: West Branch, Grayling, Wolverine. Only after he crossed the Mackinac Bridge and turned onto Highway 2 at St. Ignace did he manage to tear his thoughts away from the past.

And he remembered he needed help. He pulled out his phone and called Oliver. "Hey, buddy, I've got another one."

"Problems, Nicky?"

"Yeah. Bones found in the UP. I need them identified pronto. You free?"

"Whereabouts in the UP? I have a cabin up near Ontonagon and was planning on going up for some fishing anyway. I was just heading there today, actually."

"Rock Harbor."

He gave his customary *ho-ho* laugh. "Ah, about thirty miles from my fishing hole. Let me get settled, and I'll come over and take a look. Just let me get some fishing in too."

"Thanks, Oliver, I owe you." He ended the call and concentrated on his driving.

There was hardly anything up here. He passed mile after mile of beautiful but desolate scenery and villages barely big enough to slow down for. At Rapid River he turned onto 41 and drove to Marquette, where he stopped to eat. The café waitress recommended something called a pasty — pronounced like *nasty* — and he was surprised to find the meat pie much more delicious than it sounded.

Still wiping his mouth from lunch, he got back in his truck and headed west until he reached 38. Rock Harbor wouldn't be far now. The sun, low on the horizon, glared in his eyes. Eve would have loved this area. She had loved beauty wherever she could find it.

It was after nine by the time he reached the Rock Harbor city limits. Twilight lit the

Victorian buildings with golden light. He drove through a town that could have been the model for a Currier and Ives drawing that hung in their dining room. Totally charming. The street he was on changed to Negaunee, and he saw the twinkle of a lighthouse in the distance.

The glimmer of Lake Superior attracted his gaze. He'd never seen it before today. The Ojibwa called it Kitchigami, which meant "giver of life." He could only wish the magical Great Lake would give him a new lease on his future.

A cold wind blew through his open window, but it wasn't nearly as cold as the look in Eve's eyes the last time he'd seen her.

He parked in front of the sheriff's office. The big stone building seemed out of place among the more elegant storefronts. He stepped inside onto a tile floor and almost ran into a man about forty with brown hair and eyes. "Sorry."

The other man nodded and exited the building. A big blond guy pulled his feet from off a battered desk and turned to face him. His blue eyes looked Nick up and down as if to ask what right he had to come in here.

Nick flipped out his badge. "Captain Nikos Andreakos, Michigan State Police, violent crimes unit."

The man stood, and the challenging expression disappeared. "Deputy Doug Montgomery."

Nick quickly labeled him Deputy Dawg. He looked like the hound in the old cartoon, too, heavy jowls, sleepy eyes. If Nick remembered right, he even had an old comic with the good deputy in it.

Hiding his smile, he tried to pay attention to the deputy. "Is the sheriff in tonight?"

"He's out of the country right now. I'm in charge. You're here about the murder, eh? Have a seat, and I'll get you some coffee. You moved fast after my request for help."

The guy's accent must be the Yooper one he'd heard about. When the deputy returned with a steaming cup of coffee, Nick nodded his thanks. "Can you clue me in?"

"Not much to clue in. Bones found in the forest. Female. That's all we know. A hunter or two missing in the last five or six years, but no one to match her with."

"I've got some help coming up tomorrow. A forensic sculptor."

Montgomery's forehead creased. "Forensic sculptor, eh?"

"He takes casts of remains and adds a layer of clay to simulate flesh and skin so we can put out a picture to the media for identification. We need to nail down the identity ASAP."

"You're thinking the perp will do it again, eh?"

"This is the fourth that I know of."

Montgomery's expression sobered. "Serial killer?"

Nick nodded. "Goes by Gideon. Leaves bodies at geocaching sites. You heard of him?"

"If it doesn't affect us, we don't pay much attention."

Nick grunted. He could only hope the man wouldn't get in his way. "Any evidence at the scene?"

"Clean as the big lake. Not a hair, not a print. We found some mumbo jumbo on the geocaching site, but you probably know all about that." Doug waited until Nick nodded. "You sure it's the same guy?"

"Yeah." Nick put his hands in his pocket and moved to the wall map without answering. "Show me where the body was found."

The deputy joined him and pointed a finger big as a sausage at a point on the map. "Right there."

"Who found the body?"

"Two women out doing the geocaching thing. Bree Matthews and Elena Cox."

"How can I get in touch with them? I'd

like to interview them about what they saw."

"They live at the lighthouse on the outskirts of town. Pretty place."

Nick nodded. "I saw it. I'll head out there now."

Elena's head still swam even though she was lying on the bed. She needed to talk to the man who claimed to know her. Yesterday, when she'd recovered from her faint, she had rushed to her room to be alone. His deep voice had resonated up the stairway and through her door, but she couldn't summon the strength to go talk to him. She fell asleep quickly and then spent most of the next day in her room.

He'd asked why she was using an assumed name. To find she'd been wrong about all she thought she knew made her feel she was swimming over a bottomless pit. What else might she discover when she talked to him?

If only she could pull back the blanket that smothered her memories. Every time she tried to tug away a corner of the blackness, she found nothing but mist. She fingered the small scar on her temple. The cut on her rib had been made by a knife, the doctor had said. Was Terri's father the man in her nightmares? Was Will? She shuddered and dropped her hand.

She had to know. Going on like this any longer wasn't an option.

She decided to face her past and left the room to talk with Bree. The CD player was blaring out Elvis music as she passed Davy's room, and she saw him and Terri dancing with the dog. Samson pranced around the floor with his tail high. The kitten swatted at their feet as they moved past her.

How could she recognize Elvis's voice but not remember her own daughter's birth? It made no sense. She could drive a car, make spaghetti, put on her makeup, remember every ballet movement — a million things that required memory. But she had no idea what she felt for her husband, no clue if she had parents, siblings. No idea of the job she did before Bree found her.

She walked slowly downstairs.

In the living room, Bree glanced up. "You okay?"

Elena sighed. "I'm sorry to bail on you today. Thanks for taking care of Terri."

"Don't worry about it." Bree patted the sofa cushion next to her. Elena sat down.

"Did he tell you who I was?"

Bree shook her head. "I asked, but he said if you were hiding something, he wasn't going to squeal without your permission."

"I'm not hiding anything. I don't remember!"

"I know. That's what I told him, but he was adamant. He left his address. I guess he doesn't have a phone."

Elena took the scrap of paper. A highway and building number were scrawled beneath the words *Job's Children.* "What's Job's Children?" she asked.

Bree frowned. "I'm not exactly sure. It's a community of sorts not far from here. But they're new, and no one I asked seems to know much about them. They keep to themselves."

Elena hadn't come this far to turn back now. If there was some way to discover who she was, she intended to find out tonight. "Can I use the computer a minute?"

"Sure. That's a great idea." Bree came toward her. "I started to look up stuff the other day but got interrupted. We have more information now. Let's see what we can find out about you. Maybe there's something in the news."

Elena's steps lagged. The lost memory felt like a monster swimming below the great waves out on Superior. Just waiting to swallow her up.

"What's wrong?" Bree asked.

"What if it's really bad?"

"You can't fight something you don't know," Bree said, her fingers taking Elena's elbow. "You showed up here, battered and injured. Now we have a dead body. I don't want you to be the next one killed. We have to understand what we're dealing with." She steered Elena to the office and sat her down at the computer.

Elena delayed putting her fingers on the keyboard by reaching over to trim dead leaves from the philodendron on the table.

"Quit fooling with the plant. Let's check it out."

Elena rubbed the dirt from her hands onto her jeans and put her hands on the keyboard, but she wanted to jump and run. She launched the browser and went to Google. She typed in *geocaching serial killer.* Her fingers hovered over the keys. If she was connected with this in some way, maybe it would show up. She added the keywords *missing woman* and hit the enter key.

A flurry of listings appeared. The very first one screamed out at her: MISSING WOMAN FEARED DEAD AT HANDS OF SERIAL KILLER.

Bree gasped beside her and reached over to run the cursor over the link. "How smart to add the search words *missing woman.*" She clicked the link, and the news article appeared. She scrolled down and stopped when a picture of Elena and Terri smiling at each other rolled into view.

"It's you. You and Terri," Bree whispered. Leaning over Elena's shoulder, she touched the screen. "I can't believe it."

"I can't read it," Elena whispered. She covered her face with her hands.

Bree pulled up a chair beside her and sat down. "I'll read it."

Elena had to face this — whatever it was. Terri's life depended on it. She slowly put her hands down and forced herself to read.

Bree was already reading it aloud. "According to this, a serial killer, one who leaves his victims at geocaching sites, was thought to have attacked you and taken your body to dispose of. There's a statewide search going on for you," Bree said, still reading. "Your name is Eve Andreakos, not Elena Cox." She frowned. "And even Terri's name is Keri, not what we thought."

"She doesn't say *K* very well," Elena said. No, not Elena. Eve. She tried on the new name and found it felt oddly familiar. "I was attacked by a serial killer, not . . . not an abusive husband?"

Bree looked up, and their gazes locked. "I'd thought that, too, that maybe you were the victim of domestic violence." She turned her attention back to the screen. "You were married to a Nikos Andreakos, a state cop. You're divorced."

Nikos Andreakos. That name meant nothing. Eve began to read again. "He's been investigating this serial killer, Gideon." The name on her lips felt vile. "Gideon." She jumped to her feet, knocking over her chair in the process. Stumbling back, she clutched her arms around herself.

Bree followed and grabbed her hand. "It's okay, Ele— I mean Eve. We're here for you. We need to let your family know you're alive. The state police will protect you."

"They didn't protect me in the first place."

"They know he's after you now. Do the names trigger anything? Anything at all?" Bree asked.

Eve shook her head. "Nothing." She had to think this through. Figure out what to do, how to protect her daughter.

"Maybe it will come back now."

Eve pulled her hand out of Bree's grasp. "I want to see what else it says." The computer screen called her back. Knowledge was power. Sitting back down in front of the computer, she read through the different articles.

"He's killed at least three people," she said. Then she gasped. "Look! This body they found right after I showed up here — they think it's me! But they haven't got an official identification yet. He puts clues from religious texts on the geocaching site. And mutilates the body in some way." She clutched her stomach. "Before he kills them."

"What a sick puppy," Bree said.

"If only I could remember what he looks like," Eve said, pressing her fingers against her temples. The more she fought against the suffocating blanket around her memories, the more her memories slipped away.

"Don't try to think about it," Bree advised. "You'll just make yourself crazy. Let's go see Doug and have him make a call to Nikos."

"I don't want to see this Nick person." She felt nearly as panicked at the thought of this unknown ex-husband as she did about Gideon. There was something extremely disorienting about thinking of having shared a life — a bed — with a man she didn't know anything about.

"You called him Nick," Bree said. "Not Nikos. Are you remembering?"

Eve put her hand to her throat. "I think everyone calls him Nick." She couldn't explain how she knew this. "I want to see what he looks like." She typed in *Nikos An-*

dreakos Michigan State Police and hit enter.

The first link was to the Michigan State Police site. She went there, but it didn't have a picture, just a press release about Nick being appointed to oversee the special unit in charge of the Gideon investigation. The next few links were news articles. On the third try she hit the jackpot.

The page loaded, and a picture of several men in front of a courthouse popped up. Captain Nikos Andreakos was identified as the man in the middle.

"Hard to see him," Bree observed.

The picture was fuzzy and only showed him from the side. Dark, curly hair was the only clearly distinguishing feature.

Eve felt something break inside. Her eyes burned as she stared at the man in the photo. Clasping her arms around herself, she began to weep, harsh sobs that seemed to erupt from someplace deep inside.

Bree embraced her. "Eve, what is it?"

"I don't know," Eve sobbed. Somehow she knew this man had broken her heart, and she wept from the pain of it even though she didn't understand. How could something she didn't remember hurt so much?

12

It was really too late to come calling, but Nick didn't want to wait until morning. Though it was after ten, it looked like every light in the lighthouse shone out the windows. He parked his SUV in front and went up the steps to the front door. He could smell popcorn through the open window.

A pretty red-haired woman answered his knock. "Did you forget your key?" Her smile faded when she saw Nick. "Oh, I'm sorry, I thought you were my husband." She glanced at her watch.

"I know it's late. My name is Andreakos, and —" Before he could tell her he was with the state police, she put her hand to her mouth and took a step back. "Ma'am, are you okay?"

"Yes, yes, I'm fine." But the color washed out of her cheeks, and she glanced behind her. "Wait here." She shut the door in his face.

Nick stared at the wood three inches from his nose. He rapped again. "Mrs. Matthews?" What had just happened? She'd acted as though she knew his name. Doubling his fist, he pounded harder.

The door opened a crack. "I'm sorry," the woman said. "Listen, could you come back in the morning? It's really too late to deal with this tonight." Her green eyes looked enormous in her pale face.

Deal with what? He hadn't even told her what he wanted. "It's crucial that I talk to you and Ms. Cox. Please, it will only take a moment. I'm with the state police. I don't want to have to throw my weight around, but I can if I have to."

Her gaze went over his shoulder, and he heard the crunch of gravel. "Listen, let me ask my husband what to do."

Nick was ready to throw up his hands. What was the big deal? He turned to see a stocky man about his own age get out of a pickup. Dressed in a park service uniform, he nodded to Nick, then frowned when his wife rushed toward him.

"Bree, what's wrong?" He shot a suspicious gaze toward Nick and gathered his wife close.

Nick couldn't hear their whispered comments, though Bree's agitation was clear.

He stuck out his hand as the other man approached with his wife. "I'm with the Michigan State Police. I'm investigating the serial killer who calls himself Gideon." Nick shook his hand. "Who are you?"

"I'm Kade Matthews. Bree's husband."

"I'd like to interview her and your guest, Elena Cox."

"Not until we talk."

Nick had had enough. "Look, I've told you I'm with the Michigan State Police. We can talk here or we can talk up at the sheriff's office. Those are your options. I'm trying to stop a killer."

Kade studied his face and evidently found something he liked. "Elena is in a fragile state. I'm not sure letting you talk to her is a good idea. You know she was hurt when my wife found her?"

"I'll take it easy with her."

Kade looked away. "Um, Elena was walking along the side of the road just outside town. Bree stopped and picked her up. She had a head wound and a knife cut along her rib. She didn't remember how she got there, who hurt her."

Bree tugged on her husband's arm. "Let's sit down a minute. I don't want her to overhear us."

Nick followed them to the porch swing.

The air smelled faintly of dew and some sweet flower. The light from the old-fashioned street lamp illuminated their corner.

Kade kept staring at him. Nick could almost sense a wave of hostility and suspicion from the other man surging again. "What?"

Bree glanced at his left hand. "You're married."

"I was. She — she was killed by the serial killer I'm tracking." Nick was in no mood to talk about his marital status — or lack thereof. "My daughter is still missing."

Bree put her hand over her mouth. Kade stood and paced the porch. Both of them sent off agitation in waves.

"I think we'd better let you talk to . . . um . . . Elena," Bree finally said.

Car lights swept the front lawn and poked through Eve's bedroom window. A few minutes later, the murmur of voices floated up the stairs from the entry, and the front door opened and closed a few times.

"Elena, where are you?" Kade's voice called from the entry.

Elena? Hadn't Bree told him they'd figured out who she really was? Elena still sounded more familiar than Eve. "I'm up here," she called. "Be right there." She hauled herself up from the rocker by the window and went down to the living room, where she found Kade and Bree standing by the fireplace.

Kade's blue eyes probed Eve's face. "You okay?"

Eve nodded. "As okay as anyone is to discover a serial killer is after her. Did Bree tell you we know my name is Eve Andreakos?"

Kade nodded. "I know. It's just . . ."

"What's wrong?" Eve asked him.

Bree glanced at her husband, then back to Eve. She cleared her throat. "Um, there's someone outside."

Eve wasn't sure how this pertained to her, but it obviously did.

"A Michigan State captain," Bree went on. "Nick Andreakos."

The name sank into her consciousness. She tried to wrap her mind around it. Nick. Here. She rose slowly. "He's . . . in Rock Harbor? You didn't tell him I was here, did you?" She darted a panicked glance toward the entry and moved toward the stairs.

Bree grabbed her arm. "He wants to help you, Eve. Why are you so afraid of him?"

"I don't know. I can't remember." The adrenaline pumping through Eve's veins should have told her something, but she couldn't grasp hold of it.

"Keri has been asking for her daddy," Bree reminded her.

"I know." She sagged against Bree. Even though she didn't remember Nick, Keri did. And she missed him. Eve had no right to deprive her daughter of her daddy.

"I didn't tell him who you were. He thinks you're dead," Kade said.

"Dead?" Eve needed to sit down. She sank into the couch.

Bree nodded. "He thinks Gideon killed you, just like the newspaper said."

"And Keri? Where does he think she is? Dead too?" Just saying the words made Eve shudder.

"He said she's still missing." Bree touched her shoulder. "You okay?"

"No." She wouldn't be okay until this nightmare was over — if it ever was. "Don't you think you'd better warn him?"

"I thought maybe getting his first reaction when he sees you might tell us if he had anything to do with the condition you were in when you got here," Kade said.

Eve nodded. "Okay." She was not ready for this.

"Let me get him." Bree backed out toward the door.

Samson hunkered down and barked, then ran toward the door with his tail wagging hard enough to come off. Eve told herself the dog wouldn't be so welcoming to someone who was a danger. Gracie licked her foot, and she scooped up the kitten for courage while she watched the door for her first glimpse of her husband.

Ex-husband, she reminded herself. He had no power over her.

Voices came her way. First just a murmur, then she could distinguish a deeper voice intermingled with Bree's higher one. The timbre set the hair on the back of her neck to vibrating. She put her hand on her throat and watched for her first glimpse.

Heavy boots clomped along the wooden floor. Eve's pulse rattled against her veins. If she were small enough to squeeze under the sofa, she would have crawled under it.

Two figures loomed in the opening from the hall. Eve's gaze brushed Bree's face, then moved to the figure behind her. The man behind Bree towered over her petite frame. He turned his head and glanced into the room. His eyes widened and his jaw dropped.

The color washed from Nick's olive skin. No words came from his parted lips, just an intake of breath that left a question dangling in the air.

Eve's gaze traced his features. His physical attractiveness made the room seem small. The picture online hadn't captured the magnetism that radiated from his dark eyes. Broad shoulders, dark hair that curled a little at his neck, chiseled lips and bone structure. He could have posed as Adonis.

This man had lived with her in a home somewhere. They once had a life together. He had fathered her child. It was more than she could take in. All this history, and she didn't have a clue how it had played out.

Eve found she was standing. His dark eyes swallowed her whole. The hunger that blazed in them changed to a fierce joy and passion. Before she could move or react, he was in front her. His hands came down on her shoulders. The heat of his fingers burned into her skin where he gripped her.

"Eve," he whispered. "Eve, you're alive." His gaze roamed her face, then lingered on the scar on her temple. His hands moved up to cup her face. Then somehow her face was buried in his shirt that smelled like fabric softener and spicy cologne.

Had she ever felt this way before? Surely she had, but it felt like she'd never been embraced like this before, never inhaled the scent of strength that poured into her nose.

Her bones seemed to melt into wax that left her clinging to his shirt.

She tried to resist the softness that swept over her. How could she feel this way when she didn't remember him? Just when the embrace had gone on longer than she thought she could bear, he released her enough for her to push away from the suffocating folds of fabric.

"I thought you were dead." Nick's words came out in hoarse staccato. "We found bones. We called in a forensic sculptor. The re-creation looked just like you."

His voice was deep, deeper than she'd thought it would be. It made the blood drop from her head to her feet. Any words she might say got stuck somewhere between her intentions and her tongue. All she could do was stare at him.

He stared back with a burning passion in his eyes. Had that been the problem? Maybe he'd been a possessive husband.

"Aren't you going to say hello?" he prodded.

"I . . . I . . ." She swallowed and tried again. "You're . . . Nick?"

He frowned. "What? Of course I'm Nick." His gaze searched her face again. "You're different somehow. What's wrong, Eve?"

The disappointment in his voice wounded

her. "I'm sorry." She looked down at her hands. "I can't remember anything. Until today, I didn't even know my name. I thought it was Elena Cox."

"*You're* Elena? The Elena who found the body?"

She nodded and held up the ballet-slipper necklace that bore the name she'd adopted. "The name Elena is on the back."

"Your old teacher," he said. "She gave you that. You . . . you have amnesia?" He went even paler, if that was possible. "Is that why you let us all go on thinking you were dead for three months?"

She nodded. "I just found out today who I am."

His head jerked around. "Keri? Where's Keri?"

Eve tried to wrap her mind around all she'd discovered. "She's upstairs." She laid her hand on his arm and was surprised by the hard muscles under her fingers. "She's fine."

Nick closed his eyes. "Thank God, thank God," he whispered. He opened his eyes and raked her face with his gaze again. "You look good, Eve."

Eve could have said the same thing back to him if she'd had the nerve. Nick Andreakos had the kind of masculinity that would have made any woman take a second look. She was drawn to him even though she didn't remember him.

Surely she must be some kind of wanton woman to desire a man she didn't know.

She wet her lips, unable to muster a single comment.

"How did you survive Gideon's attack?" He seemed to be drinking her in the way a man in the desert would gulp water.

"I don't remember." She wanted to step away from him, but her legs wouldn't obey.

"I was so afraid." His voice cracked, and he clenched his fists. "There was blood in the living room. All the furniture was messed up. When that skull turned up looking just like you, we were all sure . . ."

"What skull?"

"Animals got to the body, and all we found were scattered bones. I couldn't wait for DNA identification to get back, so I had the re-creation done. It looked just like you. I was sure it *was* you. But all his victims have resembled one another. We still don't have DNA back yet."

She moved slightly away from him. "I'm sorry you had to go through that."

"I wonder if he found another victim when you escaped."

She flinched. "I can't remember anything," she said again.

"Nothing?" The disappointment in his voice sharpened the word.

She curled her hands into fists. "How did you find me if you didn't know I was here?"

"I heard about the body you found yesterday. It fits Gideon's MO. I came to check it out."

She shivered. A headache began to gnaw at her left temple. She backed away from him.

He glanced past her. "I want to see Keri. Let me protect you both."

"Just like you protected us last time?" She should have felt triumph when he flinched, but a hollowness settled in her bones. She was prodding him, and she didn't even know why. She realized Kade and Bree had vanished, probably to give them some privacy.

"That's a low blow." He straightened. "You still haven't forgiven me, have you?"

"I don't remember!" She pressed her fingers to her temples, hoping to stave off the headache. "We're married?"

"Divorced. Just before you disappeared."

She nearly crumpled. "What went wrong between us?"

"It's a long story. Tonight's not the best time to talk about it," he said.

"I need to know," she whispered. "I don't remember anything."

He sighed. "For one thing, you hated my job. You wanted me to quit."

"The work is dangerous?"

"Not so much. I'm mostly stuck doing stuff after the crime. But I work long hours. I'd miss family dinners, have to peel out in the middle of something. You hated that."

Maybe he was right. She wasn't ready to hear all this. Besides, this was his version. Surely he'd done worse than work hard.

"Mommy?" Keri's voice came from the steps.

Nick whirled and stepped to the stairs. "Keri! Come see Daddy."

"Daddy?" Small feet thumped on the steps, and Keri stepped into the foyer. Her blonde hair hung in silken strands on her shoulders. "Daddy!" Her thumb went to her mouth between a smile.

Eve noticed she didn't run to meet him, probably because it had been so long.

He stepped toward her, knelt, and smiled. "Did you miss Daddy?"

She nodded, her eyes never leaving his face. Then she took a step toward him. "Daddy?"

He scooped her up. She nestled into his arms and patted his face with her chubby hands. He buried his face in her hair. "Daddy missed you."

Eve's eyes misted. Their marriage might have ended in divorce, but he'd been a good father. His love for the child radiated brightly.

Moisture ringed his eyes when he lifted his head. His dark gaze swallowed Eve up again. "You don't know how hard it was, how I felt when I thought you were both dead. It changed me, Eve. I can't let you go, either of you. I want us to try again."

Eve heard the words, but she felt nothing other than a need to flee. "I don't know you," she whispered.

Still carrying Keri, he took a step toward her. "You have to remember, Eve. You love me too. I know you do."

She sidled away toward the steps. "I'm sorry, Nick. I don't feel anything."

The light in his eyes faded. "Maybe your memory will come back. What's the doctor say?"

"He says only time will tell." She had to get out of here before this pain in her head crushed her. "Keri, it's time for bed, sweetie."

Keri's lip quivered. "Keri stay Daddy."

Nick passed the reluctant toddler to Eve. "You heard Mommy. It's bedtime for little girls. Besides, I'm not going anywhere."

Eve started toward the steps with her daughter in her arms, then Bree appeared.

"I'll take her," Bree said. She looked over Eve's shoulder to Nick. "You can crash on the couch. Finish your talk."

"I'd rather not," Eve said in a low voice to Bree.

Bree just smiled and took the child up the stairs. Eve turned back to Nick and pressed her back against the wall. Her hands were locked in front of her. "What do you want from me? I can't just go back to where we left off. I want to get away. Right now, before Gideon tries to hurt me or Keri again."

"Don't you want to catch this guy, Evie? Make him pay for what he did to you? You can't keep running forever. What happens if he finds you again? What happens to Keri if he comes and you're not around? If that body you found yesterday means he's tracked you down here, he could do it again."

She shuddered. How would she escape a monster like Gideon? Nick stepped closer, and his hands came down on her shoulders. The heat from his fingers swept down her arms, across her chest, and settled in her belly. She felt the power of his attraction.

"No!" She wrenched away. "Don't touch me, Nick." The safety of her bedroom was just a few steps away.

Through her pain she heard the phone began to ring. She turned to snatch it up before Bree could get it, an excuse to escape this conversation "Hello."

The electronically altered voice sounded like Daffy Duck. "Hello, Eve. You didn't think I'd find you, did you? It was easy, so easy."

"How did you find me?" she whispered.

"A picture in the paper. Hobnobbing with the wrong kind of people."

The picture taken several weeks ago in town. Eve had worried about it at the time and then forgotten. She closed her eyes. "Leave us alone," she said. "I don't know why you want to hurt me. I've done nothing to you."

"You're a sinner of the worst kind. Think, Eve, and you'll remember. I hear you have amnesia, but you and I know that's just a smoke screen."

Her headache ratcheted up a notch. "I don't remember your face or even what you did to me. I'm no threat to you."

"Don't try to fool me, Eve. You're really very clever, very resourceful. But not smart enough. I feel sorry for your daughter."

"Don't hurt Keri."

"I don't want to hurt her. You're the guilty one. You have to pay for your sin."

"I don't know what I did." She straightened and began to walk back and forth across the living room. His smug voice made her want to hit something. If he'd hoped to scare her, he'd accomplished the opposite.

Nick tried to grab the phone. "Let me talk to him."

She hung on and shook her head. He frowned and dropped his hands back to his sides.

"You're still claiming amnesia — to me?" The cartoon laugh sounded eerie. "Oh, this should be fun." The voice hardened. "Don't run away again, Eve. This is between you and me. If you leave town, something might happen to Keri this time. I don't want to do that to an innocent, but I will if you force me."

"Leave her alone! She hasn't done anything."

Gideon chuckled. "Maybe not, but you have. And you're going to pay."

Eve started to cry. "What did I *do*?"

"You know, but you don't want to admit it."

"I don't remember anything," she

screamed into the phone.

"The pain will cleanse you," he said. A click sounded in Eve's ear, returning Gideon to anonymity.

She pulled the phone away from her ear and stared at it.

Nick took the phone out of her hand and put it down on the table. "What did he say?"

She sagged against his chest. "He threatened to hurt Keri if I leave." Something swelled in her soul, a hard core she hadn't known existed. "I'm going to stop him. What do you need me to do?"

13

The spare room of the lighthouse looked out over Lake Superior. With the window open, Eve could hear the foghorn from the automated light buoy offshore that blinked out every few seconds. The rhythmic blare of the horn added a touch of normalcy to the surreal way her life was going right now. On the other side of the bed, Keri slept with her mouth open.

Nick was here, just downstairs on the sofa. She buried her hot face in the pillow as a wave of longing swept through her so intense she thought she'd meld with the sheets. While her mind didn't remember him, her body did.

They were divorced. She needed to remember it. That fact was more important than the way her pulse jumped to life when he looked at her. More relevant than the way Keri's face lit up when she saw him. And he couldn't keep them safe. That was up to Eve. Knowing that something had destroyed their trust in each other, however, didn't eliminate the way she wanted to dump her problems on him and let him handle them.

He exuded strength and reliability, traits she desperately needed right now.

Gideon wasn't going to destroy her life. She wouldn't let him. She rolled over onto her back and stared at the ceiling. Something scratched at her door, and she bolted upright with the sheet clutched in her hands.

"Eve." The hoarse whisper came from the other side of the door. Nick's voice.

She slipped her feet into slippers and tiptoed to the door. Her hand touched the door, then withdrew. He was dangerous to her in ways she couldn't fathom yet. Did she dare go out and talk to him?

The scratch came again. "Eve?"

He'd wake Keri. Grabbing up the robe hanging on the back of the door, she cinched it around her. Her hand went to the door again, and she opened it to see Nick standing in the hallway.

"I need to talk to you."

"It's one in the morning." Even as she protested, her slippered feet moved her through the doorway and closer to the danger Nick represented.

His face was in shadow, but his voice vibrated with longing. "It won't take long. Come downstairs."

"Just for a minute." She brushed past him. He tried to take her hand, but she pulled out of his grip. Padding through the dark house, she felt her way down the creaking steps. She bit back a groan when she barked her shin up against a wooden rocker. This was all his fault.

"You okay?" he asked from the bottom of the steps.

"Fine," she said shortly. Her head shrieked a warning for her to go back to her room, but her feet carried to where Nick stood with his hands in his pockets near the fireplace.

"You had a long drive today and should be in bed," she said.

A smile lifted the corners of his mouth. "Ever the mother. I'm fine."

"Am I the motherly type?"

"The worst kind," he said, a grin lifting his lips. "A mama bear. You mother everyone you meet, not just Keri."

"Lately I'm more like the child," she said. She tightened her robe around her. "What's so important it couldn't wait until morning?"

"I couldn't sleep. I still can't believe you're

here." He took his hands out of his pockets and put them on her shoulders, where they seemed to burn right through the fabric. "These past months have been pure hell on earth. I prayed every prayer I could think of, made every promise to God under the sun, if he'd just let me find you alive."

She spread her hands, palms up. "What do you want me to say, Nick? I can't answer any of this. I don't know you. I don't remember our life together. There is nothing inside that recognizes what you're talking about."

She was a liar. Something inside her heart moved toward him like the tide to the moon.

"Your memory will come back." His hope sounded like desperation.

"It's been three months, Nick. Even the memories I thought I had turned out to be false. I don't even remember the day Keri was born."

He lifted his hands as though to touch her face, then dropped them awkwardly at his sides. "I want you to come home when this is all over," he said. "Give me another chance. Things will be different. Even if your memory never comes back, there is still this attraction between us. You can feel it too — I know you can."

It would help if she could tell him he was

wrong. "Chemistry wasn't enough to save our marriage, and it's nothing to build a future on either. I don't know you. I don't know what you like to eat or drink. What your favorite football team is. Where you went to school, if your parents are living, if you have any siblings. The list goes on and on. I don't know you."

He fell back onto the sofa as though his legs wouldn't hold him. "Nothing? I can't quite believe it."

"It's true. I can't remember what my house looks like. I didn't even know what I looked like until I looked in the mirror. You say you love me. If you do, then give me some space. Take your freedom and make a new life."

"Freedom? A piece of paper changes nothing. I still love you."

She curled her fingers into her palms. "Please don't say that. Let's concentrate on finding this guy."

"I thought you wanted to run away — that you don't think I can protect you."

"Right now you're the best I've got. You've seen Deputy Dawg."

He grinned. "I kept looking around for Ty Coon. Deputy Montgomery is more on the ball than you give him credit for, but I'll ask for more help. Gideon's not going to get to you or Keri."

If only he were right. Deep down, Eve knew Gideon would take her. "Nick, will you make sure Keri is happy?"

He got to his feet again and faced her. His warm fingers touched her chin and tilted her face up. "You'll make sure Keri is happy."

Her chin tingled. She breathed deeply of his masculine scent, so clean and compelling. Eternity by Calvin Klein mixed with the musky aroma of his skin. It was so strange how she could recognize the scent but sense nothing about the man. Nothing other than that her soul longed for him. Surely they'd had good times once for her to feel this security in his strength.

Her lips parted as she stared up into his face. The warmth in her stomach spread. She ached to press her lips against his, to burrow against his chest and hide there forever. But she couldn't betray how she felt. Summoning a reserve of strength she didn't know she had, she put her hands on his chest and pushed him away. She turned on legs that threatened to let her down and walked away.

"This isn't over," he called after her.

It was, but he just didn't know it.

■ ■ ■ ■

Eve had answered so many questions for the past forty-eight hours that her head felt like a watermelon. Not that she'd been able to answer any of them. No matter how hard she tried to batter down the barrier that separated her from her memories, the door remained stubbornly locked.

The media swarmed Rock Harbor, and everywhere she turned, she found a mic thrust in her face. Eve was beginning to see how celebrities lost their tempers and took a swing at the paparazzi.

Nick's presence was constant. Watching every person who approached, he shadowed her movements. Keri hardly let him out of her sight, and it was a joy to see them together. That made up, at least in part, for the way every one of her senses seemed to spring to life when he turned his dark eyes her way.

Eve sat at Keri's bedside on Wednesday night and listened to Nick's deep voice read *The Cat in the Hat* until the little girl's eyes began to droop. The book had been in his SUV, and the way he read it, she could tell it was a story he'd read a zillion times.

He pressed a kiss on Keri's hair, then

tiptoed to the door. Eve kissed the little girl as well and followed him out into the hallway. "I need to talk to you about Keri," he said.

She should have known this was coming. What father would leave a little girl with a mother who didn't even remember her? She would fight with every ounce in her to keep her daughter though. Her mind might not remember the particulars, but her heart burst with love. She marshalled every argument as she led the way to the living room.

Bree and Kade were with Davy, putting him down to bed as well. They would have a few moments of privacy. A cinnamon candle on the fireplace sent its spicy aroma out to greet them as they stepped into the living room. Wasn't aromatherapy supposed to calm the nerves? The fragrance did nothing to soothe her agitation.

"Sit down." Nick's voice was grave.

"You can't have custody of her," she blurted, sinking onto the sofa. She clasped her cold hands together.

He raised his eyebrow. "I wouldn't take her from you, Eve. You should know —" He shook his head and broke off.

She should know better — that's what he had been about to say. But she didn't know. That was the whole problem. Had Keri even had her immunizations? Did she have any medical problems? There were so many things a mother should know that Eve didn't. She was beginning to think she would never recover those lost memories.

"So what about Keri? Is something wrong with her?" Her daughter seemed perfect.

"No, no, she's fine. It's . . ." He sat on the edge of the chair. "It's about your memory, something you don't remember about Keri."

Bree and Kade came into the living room. "I didn't think he was ever going to go to sleep," Bree said of Davy. "He's excited about softball practice." Bree's gaze darted from Kade to Eve. "Are we interrupting something? We can go to the kitchen."

"No, no, it can wait." Relief put a lilt in Nick's voice. "It's not that important."

Eve wanted to hit him. Was he hiding some secret about their baby? "Nick, I'd like the phone numbers of my family," she said. "My parents, any siblings."

He nodded and grabbed his phone. "Get me a paper and pen, and I'll give them to you."

"I'll get it." Bree opened the drawer in an end table and drew out a pad of paper and a pen.

Nick took them and began to write down the numbers. "Your parents live in the same place where you grew up, a small town over near Grand Rapids. Your two brothers live in Grand Rapids. Adam is a bartender, and Seth manages a bowling alley. They're not married. Your sister —" He stopped and looked up. "No one knows where Patti is."

"Oh? Since when?"

"She ran off two years ago."

Nick wasn't meeting her gaze, and Eve frowned. Did he used to date Patti? There was something about her sister he didn't want to tell her.

The sky hung heavy with storm clouds chasing one another in swirls that mirrored the eddies of the harbor. The sky and lake matched Nick's mood. He should have told Eve the truth last night.

It was time for breakfast, but Nick hadn't been able to resist the aroma wafting from the pasty shop. Beef pasties could easily become an addiction. He took another bite and wiped the juice from his chin before entering the Suomi Café. He'd gotten up late, and Kade told him he'd taken the day off to take the kids to the new wildlife exhibition at the ranger station while Eve and Bree were eating breakfast here.

Oliver still hadn't arrived in Rock Harbor, but he'd e-mailed Nick Tuesday saying another project had come up that would delay him a couple of days. Nick hoped the forensic sculptor would make it in today. Oliver could shed some light on the investigation that no one else could.

The aroma of Finnish cardamom bread permeated the Suomi Café. The worn plank floors of the restaurant and the cracked leather booths showed the place was well loved and well used. Nick caught a glimpse of some kind of pancake drizzled with what looked like raspberry syrup. He'd have to eat in here sometime when he hadn't succumbed to the pasty temptation. His gaze scanned the room and came to rest on Eve's bright head. Tension was in every line of her shoulders and downturned head, and he knew she'd seen his entrance.

Even the familiar way she stood — heels together and toes out at the forty-five-degree angle known to all ballet dancers as the first position — caused a wave of love to swell. Eve wrapped herself in a blanket of quiet strength. Her demeanor had always calmed him after a rough day at work, but it could be hard and cold as well.

Her guardedness could cut, and he felt its icy blade when he approached. He zigzagged around the waitress and approached the booth Eve was sliding into. "Mind if I join you?"

"Sit down," Bree said with a quick glance at Eve. Bree scooted over.

Eve still hadn't spoken, and Nick fixed his gaze on her. "Are you okay?"

"I'm fine." Her clipped tone matched her averted eyes.

"Mama is going to come see you," he said.

Her head came up then, and she looked like a felon about to bolt. "Your mother?"

"Yeah. She loves you like a daughter. She took your part over me all through this divorce thing." He studied her face.

Color rushed into her cheeks, but she didn't answer. Nick knew this had to be hard for her, faced with a mother-in-law she couldn't remember. He'd tried to tell his mom not to come right now, but she didn't listen. She often didn't.

When neither of them said anything, Bree cleared her throat. "Have you talked to Montgomery this morning?"

Nick nodded. "Nothing we didn't know though. The preliminary examination showed the woman died of stab wounds. Just like the others."

Eve tore her paper napkin into strips. "We have to find him before he can hurt anyone else, especially Keri."

Nick wanted her to look at him. "I don't

really think Keri is in danger. He's never touched a child before. He's a missionary killer."

"Missionary killer, what does that mean?" Bree asked.

"It's a type of serial killer. He thinks his killing is justified and he's ridding the world of a certain kind of evil. Many kill prostitutes, but we haven't figured out exactly what Gideon's angle is." He decided not to tell her about the verse in Proverbs. It might undo her to know Gideon had targeted her for a supposed sin.

Eve shuddered. "I was never a prostitute, was I?"

Nick wanted to laugh but didn't. "Not hardly." He glanced at Bree. "This is a small town. A stranger is going to stand out here. If he shows up, I think we've got a chance to get him."

"A stranger won't stand out right now," Bree said. "Tourist season just started. We've got strangers in town by the droves."

The bell on the door tinkled behind him, but he didn't pay any attention until a female voice called his name. And Eve's. He turned to look, and a rock seemed to lodge in his throat. As if they didn't have enough problems.

A face he hadn't seen in two years approached. Eve's sister, Patti, walked toward them with purposeful steps. He would have bet money she'd died in a meth house somewhere.

Wishing now he'd had the courage to talk to Eve last night about Keri, he stood and moved to intercept her. "Patti?"

Eve's younger sister had aged some. Tiny lines marred the pale skin around her eyes and mouth. Her blonde hair had darkened to ash, and it hung in dull, lifeless locks that touched her shoulders. The clothes she wore looked like they'd come from a secondhand shop. The garish orange colors of the plaid blouse made her look dull and yellow.

"Nick," Patti said, veering to walk around him. She continued on to join her sister at the booth. "Hello, Eve."

Eve looked from Patti to Nick and back again. "Hello," she said. Her gaze held a plea when she looked back to Nick.

Nick used to think the women looked a lot alike, but drug abuse had transformed Patti into a jaded woman, while Eve still had her fresh skin and clear eyes. He stepped between them again and put his hand on Eve's shoulder.

"Think you have to protect her, Nick?" Patti asked, her voice taunting. "I'm not dangerous. Especially not to my own sister."

Eve's shoulders tensed.

"This is Patti, your sister," Nick said.

"I haven't changed that much," Patti said. Color flooded her cheeks, and she blinked quickly as though forcing back tears. "You've gotten older too." She studied Eve's face. "You don't look it though. The years have been nicer to you."

Nick needed to head off what he sensed was coming. "I'm not sure if you've heard the news, but Eve has been through a lot, Patti. She was attacked, and she doesn't remember anything."

Patti's blue eyes snapped. "What do you mean? I thought the amnesia the paper mentioned meant you didn't remember the attack. You know your own sister."

"No, no. I'm sorry." Eve stood awkwardly. "I wish I did, but I don't remember anyone."

Nick winced. Patti would use that statement if she'd shown up here for the reason he suspected.

"You've got to be kidding me." Patti cheeks reddened even more. "That only happens on soap operas."

"I had a concussion," Eve offered. "How did you find me?"

"You're a media darling," Patti muttered. "It wasn't exactly hard." Her pronounced stare at her sister dragged on.

"Eve will recover in time," Nick said.

"How much time? And what about Keri?"

"What about her?" Nick asked, hoping to head her off. "Would you like to see her? She's with a friend, but you can see her later tonight."

Patti blinked and shrugged. Her smile, when it finally came, looked pinched. "Don't I get a hug?" she asked, looking from Eve to Nick.

Nick wished he could trust her olive branch. He stepped over to hug her and noticed the way her ribs protruded and the reek of tobacco on her clothing and hair. His mind raced through possible ways to talk with her privately before she spilled everything to Eve. He should have told Eve the truth last night. Now she would be blindsided.

Eve slid out of the booth and approached her sister. Patti hugged Eve, but watching her face over Eve's shoulder, Nick suspected Patti would rather hit her.

"Is something wrong?" Eve asked.

"You mean other than the fact you disappeared with my daughter?"

Time slowed. Nick saw Eve recoil, her eyes widen. Bree put her hand over her mouth and froze in place. Stupid, stupid.

He could have prepared Eve for this if he hadn't been such a coward.

Eve's smile came out, an uncertain grimace as if Patti had made a joke she didn't quite know how to take. "Your daughter? Who do you mean?" She glanced toward Nick.

Nick rubbed his eyes. "I wanted to tell you last night." Eve's gaze held his.

Patti crossed her arms over her chest. "I want to see my daughter."

Nick tore his gaze from Eve's and took a step toward Patti. "Let's talk about this later. I need to talk to Eve. Explain things."

"I want to see her. Now," Patti said.

Nick shook his head. "What will that accomplish? She doesn't know anything about you, Patti."

Eve held up her hand. "Wait, wait, you're not talking about Keri, are you?"

Patti glared at her sister. "Of course we're talking about Keri. Don't be a nitwit, Eve."

Eve flinched, and Nick wanted to hurl something through the window. "Don't talk to your sister like that," he growled.

"She's faking," Patti sneered. "She has to be. No one forgets everything about their past." She leaned toward Eve. "Keri is *my* daughter. And I want her back."

Eve began shaking her head. "You're lying." She grabbed Nick's arm. "Tell me she's lying, Nick. Keri is *my* daughter. I would know if she weren't. She's mine."

"I was going to tell you last night," he began.

She held up her hands in a protective motion. "No, this isn't true. Are you saying I'm not Keri's mother? She calls me Mama." She turned back to her sister. "Why are you doing this? You're a liar." Her hands balled into fists at her side, and she took a step closer to her sister, who watched her distress with a supercilious smile.

"Tell her, Nick," Patti jeered. "Surely you don't have amnesia too. Tell her how she couldn't have kids so she had to steal mine."

Nick ignored the younger woman's sneer. He took Eve's hand. "You are her mother — her real mother. We decided not to tell her any different until she was older."

Patti's smile faded. "How dare you? *I'm* her real mother. Do you mean to say she thinks you're her parents? You think you can just steal my daughter away from me?"

Nick faced Patti and squared his shoulders. "Did you want me to tell her that her own mother abandoned her, just walked away without even saying good-bye? That she was too strung up on drugs to care about her baby girl? Is that what you wanted us to do? We love her, Patti. She's happy and content with us. Just go away and leave us alone. Please." Even as he made the plea, Nick knew Patti would never agree.

Nick had heard all the stories. As a child, Patti had guarded all her belongings. And friends. More than once she'd stolen a boyfriend or best friend from Eve. Heck, she'd even tried her wiles on Nick, but he hadn't been interested — not when he had Eve.

Eve's blue eyes turned icy. "I love Keri, and she loves us. You can't have her."

Nick grabbed Patti's arm and tugged her toward the door. "Look, your sister has been through too much to deal with this now. I want you to leave us alone. We'll discuss this when we've caught Gideon."

Patti jerked her arm free. "I'm not leaving town without my daughter," she growled.

"You can't have her."

"We'll see what a judge has to say." Patti turned back toward the door with jerky movements. "The courts generally rule in favor of the biological parents. I'm going to get her back."

"Over my dead body." Nick moved to intercept her. "She's ours, not yours. You gave up all rights the day you left her with us, no diapers, no formula, no money."

For the first time Patti's defiance left her. Her glance held true appeal. "I've changed, Nick. I know I was wrong. Can't you see she belongs with me? What if that killer finds you, Eve?" she said, directing her gaze back to her sister. "Don't you want her to be safe?"

"Of course I do," Eve snapped. "I would do anything for Keri."

"Then let me take her and keep her safe."

"It won't work, Patti," Nick said. "We're not going to let you drag Keri from pillar to post with never a stable home. You've been missing for two years. We thought you were dead."

Patti's pleading smile changed to defiance. "I'm going to get her back, and you can't stop me." She flounced out the door and slammed it behind her so hard that the pictures on the wall shook, and one fell to the floor with a crash. The café customers looked up with curious stares.

Eve almost visibly gathered her coolness around her. Her back straight and her head high, she slid back into the booth and interlaced her fingers together. "Why didn't you tell me, Nick?"

"I started to last night," he said.

"You were only too happy to avoid that conversation. Didn't you think this was something I needed to know?" Her gaze bored into him with a fierce accusation.

He shrugged. "Yeah, you did, and I blew it."

"Tell me how this happened," she demanded.

"You sure you want to hear all this now?"

"I can go," Bree said.

Eve grabbed her hand. "No, stay with me."

Bree nodded and kept hold of Eve's hand.

"Patti was twenty-five when she had Keri. She'd been in and out of drug rehab for three or four years. You were really worried when you found out she was pregnant. You wanted to take her in until the baby was born. I thought she was just mooching off you, but I was gone a lot, and I thought it would get you off my back about work."

He didn't like admitting how unconcerned he'd really been about Keri. The story made him sound like a real jerk. Maybe he was.

"So she was living with us when Keri was born?"

He nodded. "From the first day, she kept leaving you with the baby and running around with her friends. You were working one day, and she left the baby with a friend who had a day care. When she never showed up to pick up Keri, her friend called you and you went to get the baby. We never heard from Patti from that day to this."

"It seems unbelievable," Eve murmured. "Did we just assume she was ours and start teaching her to call us Mommy and Daddy?"

"Not at first. But about two weeks after Patti ran off, I came home from work and you said, 'Keri, Daddy's home.' We looked at each other and knew it was supposed to be that way. Patti wasn't coming back."

"Did you adopt her?" Bree asked.

"Please tell me we did," Eve said.

Nick didn't want to admit how little thought they'd put into the situation. They'd been such idiots.

"Nick?" Eve asked. "We adopted her, didn't we?" Her cool control cracked enough for fear to creep into her voice.

Man, he was slime. If only he didn't have to admit it. "We got guardianship. Adoption was an option, and we started the ball rolling about six months ago, but our marriage started falling apart, and we never finalized it."

Eve took a sip of water, and her hand was steadier. "Why didn't we do something sooner?"

"We thought Patti was dead. There seemed to be no hurry."

"So she could really take Keri?" She put

down the glass and grabbed his hand. "What can we do to stop her? We *have* to stop her, Nick."

He rubbed his thumb over her palm. "We'll need to contact a lawyer, but I guess we've got a battle on our hands." He wanted to point out that their case would be stronger if they remarried, but he didn't want to manipulate her.

Though in another week he might not be above it.

14

Gideon watched the news with avid attention while he slowly ate a bowl of ravioli. He heard steps on the stairs behind him and turned to see his daughter. Odette wore a short denim skirt and a red midriff top. Her sandals covered nothing of her feet. He put down the bowl of ravioli carefully and turned to face her.

"Where do you think you're going dressed like that?" The red on her cheeks and the plum on her eyes made her look like the cartoon of Cinderella. "Is that makeup? You look like a tramp. Go wash and change your clothes."

"Dad, I've got a date." Odette tried to move past him. He grabbed her arm and propelled her down the hallway. "Let go," she protested.

He didn't answer, just pushed her into the bathroom. Once the door was closed and locked, he got out a washcloth and lathered it up. "Sit," he ordered, pointing to the toilet seat.

She knew better than to give him any sass. Her face turned up to his in a gesture of resignation. "Everyone else gets to wear makeup," she muttered with her eyes closed.

He methodically scrubbed every trace of the vileness from her face. It was his job to see his family stayed pure. Her skin was red by the time he finished, but pain would teach this lesson most memorably. With the washcloth rinsed and draped over the towel rod, his gaze swept her attire.

"Change your clothes, Odette," he said in a soft voice.

Her eyes popped open, and an expression of fright pulled her mouth down. "This is a new skirt. I really like it."

Instead of answering, he opened the cabinet and drew out a jar of petroleum jelly. He unscrewed the lid and scooped out a glob of the sticky goo.

"What are you doing, Dad?"

He smeared the jelly over the detestable skirt. "Throw it in the trash. And while you're at it, get rid of that paint you used on your face. There will be no Jezebels in this house."

Odette gave a groan of frustration and got up. Tears rained down her face. "Why do you have to be so mean?" Brushing past him, she fumbled with the lock and finally managed to open the door.

Her sobs echoed down the hall as she ran out. Her feet pounded up the steps, and then her door slammed. It was hard to be a parent, but she'd thank him someday for making sure she stayed righteous.

With that problem taken care of, he began to review his plan. He and the good captain were out for the same thing — justice. Andreakos was still making the mistake of working inside the law. Gideon had discovered the law's shortcomings long ago.

He would have preferred not to make Miranda wait out this cat-and-mouse game, but Eve needed to suffer before he killed her. She would enter the next life better prepared. Pain was purifying. So many of its aspects fascinated him. It was so much more valuable than most people realized.

God had given him the job of wielding the weapon of pain, and he still had much to learn about it.

He listened to his daughter sob a few more minutes, then went to the basement entrance. He unlocked the padlock, opened the door, and turned on the light. Stepping onto the first stair, he locked the door behind him before descending.

At the bottom of the flight, a steel door with two combination locks was to his left. He opened the locks and pulled the door shut behind him, then threw the deadbolt. Turning around, he stepped to the stainless steel worktable in the middle of the room.

The face he had taken wasn't right. No matter what he did to it, it would never be right. The cheekbones weren't high enough — the lips weren't full enough.

He had to have Eve.

Eve cuddled Keri close as the toddler put her thumb in her mouth and closed her eyes. They sat on the back porch in a rocker looking out over the big lake. The sound of the waves and the foghorn should have lulled her as much as it did Keri.

She couldn't lose her baby. The maternal love she felt for the child had welled up the moment Keri called her Mama. Keri belonged with her. If only she could remember everything.

The screen door behind her creaked, and the heavy tread of boots moved across the wood porch. "Mind if I join you?" Nick's deep voice was low and pensive.

"I don't mind." She longed to ask him a million questions.

The other rocker creaked as he settled into

it. Nick cleared his throat. "You okay?"

"Why didn't you tell me, Nick? How could you let me stay in the dark about something so important?"

"I couldn't do it. Keri is your port in the storm, especially right now. It didn't seem pressing anyway. I thought Patti was gone for good."

Eve held Keri closer and pressed her lips against the blonde curls. "What are we going to do?"

"Our first step is to get a lawyer. I expect your sister to go for the throat. We have to be prepared for that."

"I don't know any lawyers. Do we need to get one here or . . . or — ?" She stopped. "I have no idea where we live."

"Bay City."

The name of the town meant nothing to her. "Is that in Michigan?"

"Yes, down on Lake Huron, north of Detroit. I'd guess she'll try to get custody now. For some reason, she seems in a terrific hurry."

"She can't have Keri."

"No," Nick agreed. "The way she abandoned her can't look good to a judge. And she never paid one dime in child support."

"Did you?" The words burst out of Eve.

He ran his hand through his hair. "*Yes,* of

course I pay support. I love Keri. My lawyer drew up a generous support schedule for her."

Eve was past feeling shame. All that mattered was the little girl in her arms. "What did I do before? Did I have a job?"

"You ran a dance studio, ballet. When you were in your twenties, you danced with the New York City Ballet. It was hard for you to give it up when we married."

"Why did I?"

He looked at his hand and twisted the wedding ring on his finger. "It was time."

"There's something you're not telling me. Don't you think the secrets have hurt me enough?"

He shifted and didn't meet her gaze. "It's not important, Eve. Keeping our daughter is important — not rehashing the problems with your career."

So there were problems. Could they have a bearing on this situation? Eve didn't see how, but she needed to know everything in order to understand her past. The blank slate was so frustrating. "What about Keri?"

He seemed to know what she was asking. "You took her to work with you every morning, and she learned to dance almost before she could walk. You've always put her first."

"Then why didn't we put her first when it

came to making sure no one could take her away from us?"

"It was stupid," he admitted, finally lifting his gaze from his ring. "Look, don't freak, okay? We'll get through this. No judge in the world would give Keri to a woman like your sister."

Eve dropped another kiss on her daughter's head and breathed in the scent of her baby shampoo. "Were we happy, Nick? At least for a little while?"

He leaned closer, and she smelled his cologne again. She should pull away, but instead she found herself leaning toward him ever so slightly.

"We can make a new start, Eve. Go on from here."

"What if I never get my memory back?" she whispered.

"Maybe that would be good. You'd have none of the old baggage."

She felt cold and pulled back. "I'd be all ready for a new wound, is that it?"

"That's not what I meant. But sometimes it's hard to believe something can change."

"Did it ever change, Nick?"

He looked off toward the water. "No."

"Surely I made mistakes too," she muttered. "No marriage stands or falls on one person."

He glanced back at her, and something flickered in his eyes. "Let's forget the past, Eve. Both of us. Some things are better left buried."

"What did I do?"

He stood and went toward the house. "It's time for Keri to be in bed."

Someone from her past would tell her the truth. Maybe Will. He still hadn't come to talk to her, but she could go find him.

Nick was gone when Eve got up. Showering and dressing quickly, she found Bree in the kitchen, putting the breakfast dishes in the dishwasher. "I want to talk to Will," Eve said. "Would you take me out to that Job's Children place?"

"Don't you think Nick wants to go with you?"

"He doesn't have the right to make that decision," Eve said, aware her voice was too sharp.

Bree held up her hands. "Don't bite my head off. I'm not too impressed with that Will guy, that's all. He hasn't even checked in on you since his surprise appearance. Don't you think that's a little strange?"

"He probably saw all the hoopla and wanted to stay out of it. But he knows things about my family, about my past. Nick isn't telling me everything, Bree. I have to find out what I can."

"Why do you think Nick is keeping something from you? It's clear he loves you."

"He didn't tell me Patti was Keri's birth mother. I think there's more. Will might be able to tell me."

Bree sighed. "Let me see if Anu will keep the kids."

"You're a good friend," Eve said. While Bree called Anu, Eve went to the office and searched the computer again for anything under Eve Andreakos. She found nothing that might tell her about her past.

She and Bree rode in silence out to the forest. Samson lay on the backseat.

"Don't be mad at me," she told Bree when the car came to a stop in the parking lot.

"I'm not mad, Eve, but this feels like a mistake. I don't like what I've heard about this place. People in town call it a cult. Nick is a good man. Can't you feel that yourself? And you've had your family's phone numbers for two days. Why haven't you called them yet?"

"Because I can't shake the fact that not one of them has tried to contact me yet. What's that all about?"

Bree sighed. "True. That is strange. And I'm sorry. But you don't have to look to some stranger whose motives we don't know."

"Right now, everyone's a stranger. I don't want to depend on Nick. I'm sure we were divorced for a reason, and I want to discover what I need to know without him censoring the facts." Eve threw open her door and got out.

A dingy white building sat surrounded by tall pines. No one seemed to be moving about, but the twang of a guitar came from the piney woods. There were several signs around about "embracing the pain."

Samson bounded out of the backseat when Bree opened his door.

The women followed him into the trees and found a group of young people sitting around a campfire, strumming guitars, sitars, and several other instruments Eve didn't recognize. Her gaze swept the group, and she saw Will in the middle of a circle of teenagers and twentysomethings. He hadn't noticed her yet.

She searched her memory for some trace of his face and came up empty. Any memory of him was as lost as the rest.

Samson bounded into the center of the group, and several women exclaimed over him and stroked his ears.

Will saw Eve, and his smile broke out. He

joined them at the edge of the clearing. "Where's Keri?"

"You know Keri?" Eve asked.

"Of course. She's the cutest toddler you ever saw." He took her elbow and guided her away from the group. "What are you doing here?"

"I wanted to find out how we knew one another."

He glanced at Bree from the corner of his eye, then refocused on Eve. "Maybe you'd rather discuss that in private."

Eve pulled her arm away. "Bree is my best friend. I don't have any secrets from her."

He shrugged. "We were lovers."

Eve put her hand to her throat. Her knees felt wobbly, and she wished she could sit down. Was he joking? If so, it was a poor attempt. She held up her hand. "Start at the beginning and cut the jokes."

"No jokes, Eve. We danced together about five years ago, then lost touch. I never forgot you though and managed to track you down about a year ago. Your marriage was on the rocks, and we just clicked."

"I betrayed my marriage vows?" Eve whispered. It was hard to grasp. She never would have thought she'd do something like that. Maybe that's why Nick didn't want to tell her why their marriage had failed. He was trying to keep this from her. If she knew she loved another man, she would be less apt to try to repair their marriage.

She studied Will's face. His blue eyes returned her gaze. If she loved him, why didn't she feel the same surge of emotion as when she'd seen Nick again for the first time? Or for that matter, every time she still saw Nick?

"We should go," Bree said, tugging at Eve's arm. "We need to get the kids."

"Let me come with you," Will said. "I've missed you."

Eve held up her hands and backed away. "I don't remember you, Will. I think it's best if we don't meet again." She turned and ran back to the Jeep.

Her pulse pounded in her ears. She didn't want to believe it, but it made sense.

Bree caught up with her when they reached the car. "I think he's lying," she said.

"What possible reason would he have to lie?" Eve asked. She hugged herself and shuddered. "I feel so dirty."

Bree took her by the shoulders. "Stop it, Eve! Don't just accept what he says as truth. Talk to Nick about it. Maybe your family too. I don't trust that guy."

Eve wished she could believe Will wasn't

telling the truth. The thought of talking to Nick about this made her feel queasy. But it wasn't going to go away.

A familiar box van sat parked along the street. Nick had been at the sheriff's office, checking on the investigation, when Oliver called. Though barely nine o'clock, the sun was already heating the drops of rain from last night into mist that clung to the ground and sidewalks. It was going to be a hot one.

The back doors stood open on the van, and Nick peered inside to see Oliver bending over a stainless table. "Hey, buddy, thanks for coming." He climbed into the van.

Oliver barely grunted in response, his broad shoulders stooped and intent. The harsh sunlight streaming through the open doors threw the pale bones of the woman Bree and Eve had found into stark relief. Was this all a human being was reduced to in the end, this small pile of calcium and phosphorus?

Oliver touched his arm. "You okay?"

"Yeah. It just got to me a minute." Nick shook off his anger and picked up the skull. "Think you can show us what she looked like? It will take a couple of months to get DNA back, and there's no time for that."

Oliver ran his fingers over the skull. "Let me see what I can do to bring this lovely lady home to her family." His blue eyes held a sheen of moisture.

Nick clapped him on the shoulder. "I know it takes a lot out of you, but some family will be able to have closure because of your work."

Oliver bent back over the remains. A shadow blocked the sunlight, and Nick turned to see a man step into the van. About thirty, he wore an air of authority as real as the police uniform on his body. His thick black hair stood up as though he'd leaped from bed without combing it, but its stiffness told Nick the style was deliberate.

The man's eyes flickered from Oliver to Nick. "You Captain Andreakos?"

"Yep." Nick tried to read the man's demeanor. A tiny smile played at the guy's mouth. Oliver looked up briefly with a distracted expression. "Nick, this is Jason Webster. The Marquette Post sent him to assist."

Nick nodded at the young man. "I didn't think anyone was as nuts as Oliver."

Jason flashed impossibly white teeth. "Interesting stuff, eh?" he said in a thick Yooper twang. "What do we have?"

"Female, young," Oliver said.

Jason took the skull from Oliver and turned it over in his hands. "Why are you so certain she's female, eh?"

"She was wearing a blue silk blouse and jeans, size 4," Nick said.

Jason scrutinized the skull. "You're right, it's female. I'd guess she's African-American and in her twenties."

Oliver raised his bushy white brows and snorted. "She's Caucasian, Scandinavian. Look at those cheekbones and the set of the eyes."

Jason reddened. "I have more experience in our population up here than you do."

Oliver straightened. "Boy, I started sculpting skulls when you were still in diapers. If this is how you plan to behave, then I won't be needing your help."

His Santa Claus personage morphed into something not quite so jolly. Nick didn't blame him. This guy wasn't in Oliver's league.

"I'm in charge of this investigation," Jason shot back. "We'll play it my way."

"I was asked by the task force to get involved, so I would say you're outranked."

Nick decided it was time to step in. "My special task force does have jurisdiction, Jason. I've asked Oliver's help. He's the best in the country. We need a really fast turn-around on identification."

Jason laid the skull back on the table, but his smile grew broader. "I take it you haven't been notified."

"Notified of what?" Nick wished he could wipe the guy's smile off his face.

"You've been suspended. IA will be here sometime today. I'm in charge now."

Internal Affairs. Every officer's worst nightmare. "What are you talking about?"

Jason shrugged. "Someone complained about the violence you used in an arrest."

Probably the Mount Sinai group incident. His dad had warned trouble might be coming because of it. "I'll get this straightened out." He nodded at Oliver. "Our perp has done it before. I need to find out where he seized this woman. The only way to do that is to have her identified as soon as possible."

Jason folded his arms across his chest. "The only ones that have surfaced lately have been dead awhile. What makes you think he'll strike again any faster?"

"He's made threats against my wife."

"I doubt it's coincidence this body turned up," Oliver said, glancing at the bones. "Your man knew Eve was here and was letting her know."

"My thoughts too. He's playing a game with her. She can't remember anything, Oliver. Not even her name. She was going by Elena."

"Elena Cox? Police report says she found the vic," Oliver said, eyebrows winging upward.

"What are you talking about?" Jason demanded. "Why would your wife be here? I thought you lived in Bay City, eh?"

"We're . . . divorced." The word tasted bitter on his lips.

Jason smirked. "Trouble letting go, Captain?"

Nick's fingers curled into his palms. "You have an agenda, or do you just like to work at being a jerk?"

Jason's smile vanished. "Get out of here, Captain. This isn't your baby anymore." He picked up the skull.

Oliver held out his hand. "I'll take that. I want to cast it and get started immediately."

"I can handle it." Jason glanced toward the back door and smiled.

Nick glanced over his shoulder and saw a white van bearing the WBUK-TV 7 logo pull up. A man and a woman erupted from the vehicle and moved toward the forensic van. Nick rolled his eyes. "Did you call them?" he asked Jason.

Jason shrugged, but that annoying smile played at his lips. He moved to the table and began to study the bones.

"He's an idiot," Oliver muttered in an undertone to Nick. "It's going to look nothing like the woman. Can't you stop him?"

"I'll go see what I can do." Nick jumped from the back of the van and jogged down the street to the jail. If Jason slowed down the investigation, they were all in trouble. Especially Eve. He glanced at his watch. Eve would be meeting with the lawyer, and he'd wanted to be there, but first he needed to get this problem here fixed before that numskull ruined their chances of finding Gideon.

He called his dad's phone but the reception was patchy since Cyril was on his way to Rock Harbor. But he got the gist of the conversation. Jason was telling the truth.

He put his phone away and went back to find Oliver. "No go, buddy. This has to play out."

"I might as well go fishing," Oliver said. "I can't watch this butchering." He turned to Jason, who flirted with the tittering brunette journalist. "Get outta my van!"

"What can we do to stop her?" Eve sat in an overstuffed chair in the lawyer's office. The soft green chenille upholstery, the calm décor of the office, was meant to soothe agitated clients, but her distress only mounted. Nick was late.

Ronja Lankinen leaned back in her chair. About fifty, she looked more like a frumpy housewife than the best attorney in town. Her polyester pantsuit strained in all the wrong places, and her mousy brown hair coiled in an untidy knot at the base of her head. She wore no makeup.

"Tell me what you did when your sister disappeared," Ronja said.

"We got guardianship. We meant to adopt Keri, but circumstances . . ." Eve looked down at her hands clasped in her lap. She didn't want to tell the lawyer about her memory problems, though with the hubbub around town, she'd probably heard at least part of it.

"I'm afraid I'm only going on what my ex-husband has told me. I — I'm having some trouble remembering." She touched the tiny scar on her head. "I had a head injury a few months ago, and I can't remember anything from before I arrived in Rock Harbor."

The woman sighed. "You're telling me you can't even remember the details of acquiring your sister's child?"

"Not from personal memory," Eve said. "But Nick has told me how it happened."

"Why isn't he here?"

"He said he'd be here," she said, stealing another glance at her watch. "I'm not sure what happened. Maybe there's a problem at the jail. He wanted to come, but he's in charge of finding the serial killer. You heard about the body that showed up last weekend?" Eve wanted him here, but she wasn't sure she could meet his gaze after hearing what Will had to say.

The lawyer nodded. "Has your sister provided any support in the last two years?"

"No. We thought she might be dead."

"Do you have any proof of her unfitness to raise the little girl?"

"Not really. Isn't the fact she abandoned her enough?"

Ronja twirled a pencil in her fingers. "It could be. It depends on what she's been doing since she left. If she's turned her life around, it might be harder for you. But we'll see. I'll dig around and see if she's been in any trouble, where she's been all this time."

"What should I do? She wants to see Keri. Should I allow it?" More than anything, Eve wanted to grab up her child and protect her. Patti wasn't a fit mother for Keri. A mother needed to put her child first every time. Not just when she felt like it.

Was Eve guilty of the same offense? What

if Patti was able to show that Eve was unfit?

"It would look better to the judge if you're agreeable and reasonable. My gut says to allow her to have supervised visitation. Have her to the house for dinner. Be friendly. See if you can get her to agree to let you adopt Keri. You could allow her to see the little girl occasionally. It's always better for the child if these things can be resolved in an amicable way."

"Okay," Eve said with great reluctance. "I'll arrange it."

Ronja's gaze lingered on Eve's face. "Can you put your differences aside for Keri's sake?"

"It's not that. I just hate to have Keri's life disrupted. I tried to tell her about Patti last night, but she's too young to understand."

"She calls you Mommy and Daddy?" Ronja's eyebrows winged up.

Eve nodded. "It just sort of happened."

It felt odd parroting everything Nick had told her. When would she begin to actually have her own memories?

"She called you Mommy right from the start?"

Eve ducked her head. "Nick says we knew Patti wouldn't be back. She abandoned Keri at the day care and left an empty apartment behind. At least that's what Nick said."

"Do you have any other corroboration, since you don't remember it yourself?"

"Maybe my parents?" Eve needed to call them too. But what did she say to a faceless couple who would want her to love them when she had no idea about them at all?

"Check and see. We might need their testimony. What about the father?"

"Patti never told us who he was, according to Nick. He's never supported her either." Eve tried to stuff her panic back into the dark place from where it had arisen. Everything would be all right. It had to be.

"This is quite a tangle. I really recommend you try to work things out amicably with your sister."

"I'll try, but she seems to be determined to have Keri. I can't let that happen." Eve's voice broke.

Ronja gave her a sharp look. "I do hope you're not thinking of doing something foolish. Like running off with Keri."

Eve bit her lip so hard she tasted blood. "I'm not giving up my daughter."

Ronja sighed. "At least promise me you'll call me before you make any decisions."

Eve didn't answer. She couldn't promise anything. Keri's happiness came first. She stood. "Thanks for your time. Let me know if you find Patti has a record."

"I will. And have faith, Eve."

Eve nodded. Easy enough for the lawyer to say. Her life wasn't hanging in the balance.

She exited the office and walked along Houghton Street. The sidewalks teemed with jostling tourists, and flowers lined the tree lawn. Glancing at her watch, she picked up her pace and headed into the coffee shop. The bell on the door jingled as she pushed it open and inhaled the scent of espresso.

"Good morning," she told the barista before ordering a mocha.

The coffee shop was housed in an old Victorian storefront with high tin ceilings painted blush. Debris was easy to sweep up from the wooden floor, and the bright windows added to the airy feel. She'd quickly fallen in love with the place.

The door opened, and a man with short white hair and a white beard entered. The rosy red cheeks above his beard reminded her of Santa Claus, especially with the smile he leveled at her. "You must be Eve. I've seen your picture on Nick's desk for years." He extended his hand. "Oliver Harding."

Eve took his hand. Hard calluses made it feel like grasping a fistful of sand. Nick had mentioned him. "You're here to re-create our Jane Doe?"

"I was. A young upstart from Marquette hijacked the project, but he was botching it so badly, I couldn't stand to watch. I decided to get a trim to escape the pain. Can you suggest a hair establishment?"

"There's a barber down the street." Eyeing his hair, Eve couldn't see it needed trimming. "How could he take it away from you? Nick says you're the best in the country."

"Bless you, child, for saying that. Nick would have come to my aid, but he's been relieved of duty."

Eve took her mocha from the barista and turned at his words. "What?"

"You haven't heard? Internal Affairs has suspended him pending results of an investigation."

"Nick is one of the most honorable men I know." From the moment he reentered her life, she'd known that.

"I'm sure it will be sorted out soon. Nick won't let any grass grow under his feet." Oliver heaved a large sigh. "In the meantime, I believe our Jane is Caucasian, and the young man from Marquette is sure she's African-American. I don't believe he has much training. If he hadn't been so impudent, I might have taken him under my wing. As it is, I will have to redo the bust.

"But until then, everything is delayed," Eve said slowly.

"It is," Oliver agreed.

And Gideon was drawing ever closer while they were still in the dark.

15

The leaves burst forth with green abandon from the trees that lined Kitchigami Street. Bree sipped the mocha Kade had brought her from the coffee shop. The children walked with them — Davy clinging to her hand and Keri skipping along beside Kade. She found herself looking at every stranger they passed. Was it the man with the hawkish nose or the one who smiled at the children?

They rounded the corner onto Houghton Street and started toward Anu's shop. Samson kept running ahead, then stopping to look back as if to say, "Are you coming?" Four squad cars were parked in front of the sheriff's office and jail. Deputies entered and exited the office with an undercurrent of excitement obvious in their quick movements and intent expressions.

"What's going on?" Kade murmured in her ear.

One of the deputies glanced toward them and frowned. "Should I take the kids and get out of here?" Bree asked.

"I think it's okay," Kade said.

A deputy motioned to them, and they quickened their pace to join him on the steps to the jail. "Deputy Montgomery needs to talk to you," he said. About twenty-five, the rookie wore his cockiness like a suit he wasn't sure quite fit.

Kade cast a quick glance toward Bree. "I'll get my wife settled, then stop back."

The deputy took Kade by the arm. "He wants to see you now."

Kade gave an angry start at the man's insistence, and Samson growled and took a step toward the deputy. Bree put her hand on the dog's head. "It's okay," she said. "We'll just come with you."

Kade's frown didn't leave, but he nodded. A sense of unease settled around Bree's middle as Kade pulled his arm from the deputy's grasp and opened the door for her and the children. She almost thought she saw pity on the deputy's face.

Conversation stopped when they stepped inside. Deputy Montgomery's face creased in a smile that seemed a little too hearty. "Kade, thanks for coming by." His gaze flickered to Bree. "You're free to go visit with Anu or whatever you want, Bree."

"What's going on?" Bree asked. "Are you trying to get rid of me?"

"No, no, nothing like that." Montgomery's eyes darted around the room. "If you'll come back to my office, I'm sure we can get this cleared up."

Kade's eyes narrowed. "Get what cleared up?"

The other deputies shuffled their feet and looked at the floor. Bree took each of the children by the hand and led them toward the heavyset deputy. "Marty, would you mind keeping an eye on the kids?" His daughter went to school with Davy.

"Aw, Bree, I'm not a nursemaid," he muttered.

He hadn't been a deputy long enough to summon the authority another officer might have mustered. Bree almost felt sorry for railroading him. "I'll just be a minute. I have a feeling this isn't for little ears." She knew she was right when he looked away and managed to nod. "Stay. Watch Davy," she told her dog when he started to follow her.

She walked with Kade and Montgomery down the hallway lined with pictures of past sheriffs and deputies. The deputy led them into the last office. "This is Mason's office," she said.

Montgomery's cheeks darkened to red. "I'm filling in for him, so I thought I should be where I could access his files."

Bree wondered if she should warn Mason that Montgomery was gunning for his job. Her brother-in-law probably knew it though. He was pretty savvy about people. She stepped into the office and looked around. Mason usually kept the place as neat as a wind-swept beach, but today it looked like a nor'easter had come calling. Manila folders lay heaped on the desk, and she counted four half-full coffee cups.

Kade stood with his arms folded as Montgomery shuffled around the desk and dropped into the chair. Montgomery moved some papers. "Have a seat."

"I'll stand. We can't leave the kids for long," Kade said.

"What's this all about, Doug?" Bree's flight-or-fight response was surging like a Superior storm.

The man's fingers tightened on his papers before he finally looked up toward Kade. "We found a shovel, Kade. The handle was engraved with your name."

The words were so soft that they didn't register at first with Bree. Kade's shovel? So what?

"Near the body," Doug continued. "There

was a clump of dirt stuck to the metal. A piece of the rotted material from the woman's blouse was in the dirt." He cleared his throat. "I'm going to ask you not to leave town until we get this cleared up."

Bree took a step toward the deputy. "You can't be serious. Anyone could have used that shovel."

Montgomery kept his gaze on Kade. "There are no other prints on the shovel except yours, Kade. Can you explain it?"

Kade spread his hands, palms up. "I use the shovel all the time to move plants or cover waste in the park. I don't know who the woman is or how she got there. I certainly didn't put her there."

Doug finally glanced at Bree. "How did you happen to find the body, Bree? It seems a little suspicious now that we know Kade's shovel may have been used."

"You know the dogs found it," she said. "It was a fluke."

"How did you happen to pick that geocache to go after?"

How had she picked it? She and Kade had been looking through the entries, and he had pointed it out. No way could she tell Doug that bit of information. He would be sure to misunderstand it. "It was close to where we were going to be training the dogs."

"That's it?"

Bree nodded. "It's been a fun hobby until now. We've always picked our sites at random."

Montgomery still didn't look convinced.

Kade took Bree's hand. "I'm not planning on going anywhere. But you're wasting time focusing on me, Doug. The real killer is targeting Eve. She got a threatening phone call. The killer told her not to leave town or he would hurt Keri. We'd like some protection assigned to the house."

Doug frowned. "Did you hear this conversation?" he asked Bree.

"No, Eve told me about it. She was packing up to leave town when he called. She thinks he might really hurt Keri if she leaves. You've got to find him before he hurts Eve or one of the children."

Doug didn't look at Kade, but Bree could almost sense the direction of his focus. "It's not Kade," she said, raising her voice. "Are you going to give us some protection or not?"

"How well do you know Eve?"

"Very well. She's lived with us for three months. You get to know someone pretty well when you live with them. She's not making this up! Ask her ex-husband — he was there when the guy called her. Where is he, anyway? Isn't he in charge of the investigation? He wouldn't let you target Kade."

"Captain Andreakos has been relieved of duty." A smile started on Montgomery's lips but vanished before it could reach its full wattage.

Kade and Bree exchanged glances. Bree could see the warning on Kade's face. They'd have to figure out what was going on without giving the deputy the satisfaction of seeing their shock.

The sun still shone brightly when Eve exited the coffee shop and glanced at her watch. A little after five. She stopped at a pay phone and called Bree's phone. Bree's voice was a little tense, but she assured Eve that Keri was all right.

She ended the call with Bree and started to walk away. She still hadn't heard from Nick. His suspension would have upset him. That was probably what had caused him to miss the attorney appointment. She called his number then listened to the phone ring before being dumped into voice mail. Even listening to the deep tones of his greeting soaked into her soul like rain into soil at the end of a drought.

How could she love another man when Nick made her feel like this? What kind of woman was she that she could sleep with a man she didn't love? She had no doubt she didn't love Will and never had.

A voice called her name, and she turned to look at a black Cadillac that pulled to the curb.

The passenger door flew open, and a short, buxom brunette in her fifties hurried from the car. "Eve!"

Eve found herself enveloped in a hug that felt like coming home. The woman's skin lotion, a concoction of jasmine and other essences, filled her senses. Her arms went around the woman and clung, even though she had no idea whom she held on to.

When the woman finally pulled away, her eyes were misty. "I've missed you, *koukla.*"

Eve didn't trust herself to speak yet. The unconditional love she felt coming off this woman in waves was like balm. "Who — who are you?"

"I'm Rhea. Nick's mother. You poor child." Rhea hugged her again. "You remember nothing?"

Eve shook her head. "Nothing." For a minute, Eve had hoped this was her own mother. Why hadn't she heard from her mom? Studying the other woman's face, she wondered now how she could have missed the resemblance. Nick had Rhea's mouth.

Rhea's pity disappeared. She grasped Eve's shoulders and gave her a shaking. "Where is my granddaughter? Why didn't you seek to find out who you were? I don't understand." She turned to her husband as he exited the car. "Tell her, Cyril."

"Leave her alone, Rhea. Can't you tell she's suffered?" Cyril grabbed her up and hugged her. "But Rhea is right for a change. You could have come to us."

As if she even knew who they were at that point? Cyril was a big man, and Eve could see her ex-husband would look just like him in thirty years. Hadn't Nick said his dad was a cop too?

Eve extricated herself from his arms. "I couldn't," she said. "I didn't know where you lived. I have amnesia. I can't even remember where our house is."

Cyril studied her face. "You really don't remember *anything*?"

She shook her head.

He shook his head and took her hand. "Spotty cell coverage all the way up here. Where is Keri?"

"She's with my friend Bree. I'll take you to her."

They got back into the car, and Eve slid

into the backseat.

Rhea kept up a steady patter of conversation as Eve directed them through town to the lighthouse. Cyril parked the car in the driveway, and Rhea and Cyril spilled out and hurried to the door.

Noting their eagerness to see Keri, Eve wanted to run. The past was here in the present, and she had no idea how to meet the challenges. She went slowly up the steps and entered the house.

Keri was in Rhea's arms as the older woman talked with Bree. Cyril and Kade stood talking in low voices. Having Cyril here made her feel safe. Maybe it was his resemblance to Nick.

She went to stand beside him, and he put his arm around her and pulled her against his bulk. "You need a new sweater," she said, wrinkling her nose at the pilled fabric.

"Hey, it's a relic. Just like me."

It felt natural to return his hug before stepping away. "What's going on with Nick's suspension?"

"Oh, you've heard?" Kade asked.

"Oliver told me. He's Nick's forensic sculptor friend." She told the men about Oliver's fear that the skull's identification was being mishandled. "Can you fix this for Nick, Cyril?"

"I've tried. Someone higher up is ticked and wants to see it go through channels."

"What is Nick accused of?" Kade asked.

"Unnecessary force." Cyril's frown pinched his mouth. "He was investigating a survivalist group, thought Gideon might be part of it. They had a compound outside Indian River. He found a woman hiker they'd kidnapped up near Stoney Creek. There was a scuffle getting her out of there, and the leader, Moses Bechtol, was killed."

"Who's this Bechtol?" Kade wanted to know.

"Nick and Cyril thought he might be Gideon," Rhea said. "But Gideon is still around."

"The shootout turned into a firestorm," Cyril said. "Five of the group's leaders ended up dead or dying. The guy who took over cried foul and filed charges against Nick."

"Won't the kidnapped woman testify?" Eve asked.

"That's where it gets sticky," Cyril said, his mouth pressing to a grim line. "She sides with the group. She's a tree hugger — back to nature and all that. My take is she felt sorry for the kids."

Eve winced. "Kids?"

"A dozen or so saw the whole thing. Some

lost their fathers."

"Are they all okay?"

Cyril's eyebrows arched. "You know how Nick is about kids. You honestly think he'd put them in danger?"

She knew how he was about Keri, but that was all. "So can you get the woman to tell the truth?"

"No dice. She says there were three fatherless kids, and someone had to pay."

"What did she think Nick should have done? Let them cart her off to somewhere else?" Kade put in.

"Exactly what I asked her." Cyril snorted. "She said Nick was just trigger-happy."

"So what is Nick facing?" Eve wanted to know.

"I think he'll be cleared. Eventually. When our boys went through the compound, they took out enough weapons and ammo to keep an army stocked for a year. ATF is having a field day trying to figure out how they got the firepower. And Nick's version of how events went down is borne out by a boatload of expended shells. They were bent on taking him out."

Eve shuddered and clutched herself. The thought of Nick being killed hurt her.

16

Once he'd come to the unwelcome realization that his hands were tied on the investigation, Nick jogged to the lawyer's office but missed Eve. When he tried to call her at the house, he was dumped into Bree's voice mail, so he spent the long day watching Jason cast the skull. It came out a little lopsided, and Nick wondered how this guy had even gotten the job.

If he dared leave Jason alone with the skull, he would have walked around town looking for Eve.

Nick glanced out of the van but saw no one he recognized among the people who had gathered at the sight of the news crew. He would have welcomed a distraction from Jason's ineptitude. Sighing, he cast his gaze back on the bust.

Jason wiped wet plaster from his hands. "Once this is hardened, I can start putting on clay. Maybe tomorrow."

Tomorrow. No wonder the bust looked odd. While Nick sometimes got impatient with Oliver's meticulous attention to detail, it was necessary. Though he was tempted to say something, Nick held his tongue and glanced at the reporters.

The pair looked as if they'd been in a food fight. Bits of plaster clung to their clothing and hair. A streak of white stretched across the woman's left cheek. But her eyes shone, and she still used her hands to punctuate her words. Nick thought she would have kissed Jason if she thought she could get away with it.

"This is so exciting," she gushed. "You'll be famous, Jason." She looked to the photographer. "Did you get enough pictures?"

"I took 100 pictures," the photographer said, his shoulders drooping and fatigue pulling at his lips.

"Perfect. When can I see them?"

He looked at his watch. "It's nearly six. I can email them to you tomorrow."

"Tonight," she said in a hard voice.

He must have been used to her demands, because he just nodded and stumbled out the back door of the van.

Nick wondered how hyped she'd be about this process when it failed to bring an identification. Once Jason made the model, he could get the skull to Oliver. Oliver would redo it the right way.

But how long would it take before Jason let loose of it? Nick sighed and ran his hand around the neck band of his T-shirt. His stomach made a low growl, and he realized he hadn't eaten since the beef pasty around ten. He glanced at Jason, who stood talking with the female reporter. Ogling was more like it. Nick rolled his eyes and hopped out of the van.

Music rolled in bright waves from somewhere, maybe a nearby park. The music was an interesting blend of folk and string band. Must be White Water. He'd heard they were hitting town. He walked to his SUV, jabbed in the key, and gunned it for the lighthouse. He felt faintly miffed that Eve hadn't called him all day. Didn't she realize he was as concerned as she was and would want to know what the attorney said? And he would have thought she'd be at least a little curious about what had caused him to miss the appointment.

The longer he thought about it, the madder he got. The vehicle barely hit the high spots in the road to the lighthouse. When he drew nearer, he realized they had company. He winced when he saw his mom's big Cadillac in front.

He took the steps to the porch two at a time. Bree and Kade had told him to come right in without knocking. He pushed open the door and stepped into the foyer. Samson's nails clicked on the wood floor, and the dog pushed his wet nose into Nick's hand. "Hey, boy, where is everyone?" The dog whined as if he sensed Nick's state of mind.

The kitten ran to him too. She purred and tried to climb his pant leg. He gave the animals a final pat, then went down the hall toward the low murmur of voices.

His parents were in the living room with Bree, Kade, and Eve. "I didn't expect you for hours, maybe not until tomorrow," he told his mother.

"We thought we'd surprise you." His mom hugged him. "We can only stay a couple of days. I wanted to see Eve."

He looked around, eager for a glimpse of his daughter. "Where are Keri and Davy?" he asked.

"In Davy's room. He's trying to teach her to play Candy Land," Bree said. "You look tired."

"I'm bushed. That idiot from Marquette is going to ruin this case."

His dad took on a bulldog stance. "Let me take it over until you get the problems sorted out. You need to get to Detroit and handle the inquiry."

"I'm not going anywhere," Nick said. "Not until we catch that monster."

"You have to go," his mother said. She touched his arm. "You're tense, Son."

"I'm fine, Mama." He managed to smile to show her. "But no one is making me leave when Eve and Keri need me." Why wouldn't Eve look at him? Was the news about Keri that bad? "Eve? What did the lawyer say?"

His mother's head came up to look at Eve. "Lawyer?"

"Patti is back," Nick said shortly. "She wants Keri. Why the heck didn't you call me? What did the lawyer say?"

She finally met his glance. "I tried to call but got your voice mail. She says it would be best to try to settle it amicably. I was going to invite Patti for dinner tonight but got . . . distracted. Why didn't you come? I needed you there. I couldn't answer any of her questions very well."

He winced. "Sorry. I had to babysit the guy from Marquette. He's beyond incompetent."

"Is this how it always was — you putting your work before me and Keri?" Eve whispered, too softly for anyone's ears but his.

He looked at the ceiling and spread his

hands. "This was for you, Eve. I have to find Gideon to protect you." She shrugged and headed out of the room, and he knew she wasn't buying it. Nick's guilt surged. He always made the wrong decision, it seemed.

"I need to talk to you for a minute, Nick," his dad said. The men walked away from the group, and Cyril lowered his voice. "We've got some new developments. I think you're right about that verse in Proverbs. Sophie Tallmadge testified in a trial a week before her death. She claimed the defendant spent the night with her, and the officers investigating were able to prove she perjured herself."

"The lies mentioned in the verse?" Nick asked.

Cyril shrugged. "It fits. So maybe Gideon is watching these women, trying to catch them out in what he calls a sin." He hesitated. "I know you wanted to believe Eve when she said she never slept with that guy, but there has to be a reason Gideon targeted her. We got some information back on the body we thought was Eve. She's been identified as Melissa Howard. The coroner thinks her eyes were gouged out. No indication yet what her sin of pride was — if that verse is connected."

"How'd you figure out who she was?"

"Another clue left by Gideon. Our boy can't stand to have them unclaimed. Or else he likes to taunt us." Cyril's brows gathered into a frown. "Another thing, Nick. It looks like he might have killed Melissa Howard the same night Eve escaped. Maybe as a substitute for Eve. I think you should tell her she's in danger."

Nick was shaking his head before his dad finished the sentence. "He called here already, Dad. She knows he's after her. I don't get it though. If he found a substitute, why is he still after Eve?"

Cyril grimaced. "Would he be satisfied with a substitute now that he's found her again?"

And the pattern. Nick ran through the order of the proverb in his mind: proud look, lying tongue, hands that shed innocent blood, heart that devises wicked plans. "Feet are next," he said.

"What?" his dad asked.

"Later," Nick whispered.

Eve returned to the room. "Nick? Is there news about Gideon?"

He turned and forced a smile. "Nothing new, really. We've identified one of the victims is all. Nothing for you to worry about. Listen, I'll go find Patti. Do you have any idea where she's staying?"

"No. She didn't say." Eve dropped her cool manner a bit and touched his arm. "We'll worry about it tomorrow, Nick. Have you eaten?"

What a dolt he was. The least little crumb of encouragement from her and his pulse leaped and he went dry-mouthed. He and his dad followed Eve back to the group.

"I'll bet you haven't had Greek food since you left, Eve." His mother kicked off her pumps and headed toward the kitchen. "Cyril, I may need you to run to the grocery."

"I'm up for it if you make *kreatopita,*" his dad said from behind Nick.

His mother wouldn't find the ingredients for the meat pie here. Lamb was tough to find in a small town like this. Listening to his parents banter, Nick wondered if Eve missed the family meals with everyone around his mother's dinner table. He did. His mother saw through his excuses, but she'd made her disappointment clear. Maybe he was a coward. The empty spots at the table beside him were too painful to face more than once a month.

When he finally dared to look at Eve, she didn't seem affected. "I'll go see Keri," he said. At least she'd show how glad she was to see him.

■ ■ ■ ■

"Kade and I will go to the store. We know where it is," Bree said.

Eve glanced at Bree. Her friend's smile looked a little strained. Eve followed her and Kade toward the door. "You okay?" she asked.

"Montgomery says they found Kade's shovel near the body," Bree said. "We haven't had a chance to talk about it." She turned her gaze to her husband. "Did you know your shovel was missing?"

He ran his fingers through his thatch of dark hair. "I don't use it every day. I've been trying to think when I saw it last. Maybe last weekend? I moved some hosta."

"Why?" Eve asked. She didn't want to suspect Kade, but she found her gaze drawn to his face. The man was her friend. How could she even entertain a hint of suspicion against him?

"The fire in that area three years ago burned the treetops out. There was too much sunlight for them there, and they were suffering for it." He looked at his wife, his mouth sagging. "You don't doubt me, do you, Bree?"

"Of course not!" Bree cupped his face in

the palms of her hands. "I know you, Kade Matthews. You couldn't hurt anyone. Doug should know better than to suspect you."

"What about you, Eve?" Kade asked, his voice quiet.

Eve tried to infuse confidence in her voice. "Of course not." Kade couldn't be involved. "You don't think he did this deliberately, do you?" she asked Kade.

"Who?"

"Gideon. Maybe he took your spade. Used gloves to bury her without leaving prints."

He stared at her. "If he did, he probably made sure there was DNA on the metal."

"And Montgomery will buy it. I wish the sheriff were here," Bree said.

Eve needed to understand it better. "How did your shovel turn up there, Kade? Any idea?"

"Nope. I'm sure I put it into the back of my truck. Of course, I can't find it now. So it must be mine."

"Why would Gideon want to cast suspicion on you?" Bree asked.

"Maybe he didn't. Maybe I accidentally left it in the forest, and he took the opportunity. I don't think I did, but it's possible."

Bree glanced to Eve. "You're his focus,

Eve. But I don't get it. He left a body here to let you know he'd found you, but he hasn't made any attempt to come after you."

Eve shuddered. "I don't know what he wants," she whispered.

The loons cried out on the lake, and the swans' trumpets sounded in unison all around the island. Such a symphony. The generator hummed beside Gideon, but not enough to distract from the job at hand. The satellite Internet link had been spotty, but it seemed to be working well tonight.

He sat at a makeshift desk and stared at the flickering computer screen. A composite of the woman he'd relocated for Eve to find showed in the window, and he laughed. If this was the best the forensic re-creator could do, they'd never identify the woman. Were they so inept that he had to spoon-feed them every single identity?

Maybe he should wait until the second composite came out. Give them an opportunity to figure it out on their own. The struggle would be beneficial for them, and they would learn from it.

His phone rang with a call from his daughter. He opened the phone. "Odette, is anything wrong?"

"When are you coming home? Betsy and

I had a fight, Dad. I miss you."

"It's good for you to learn to deal with that. The pain will make you stronger."

Odette began to cry. Her childish sobs told him he was doing the right thing. Spare the rod, spoil the child. The rod of this psychological pain would strengthen her spine, make her self-reliant. "That's enough, Odette. I don't want to hear any more whining. Buck up and be an adult."

"Grandma is so awful." Odette hiccupped. "She's got a new boyfriend. He . . . looks at me weird, Dad."

Gideon's fingers clenched around the phone. "Has he touched you?"

"No. But he looks like he'd like to." Disgust coated her words. "He's *old* and has no hair."

"Take a knife to bed with you. If he comes in, stick him with it."

"Daddy! That's gross."

"Do what I say, Odette. Learn to defend yourself."

"Should I tell Grandma?"

"It will do no good. She never believes me. I mean, she won't believe you. Take care of it yourself. It will make you stronger."

"You're my dad!" Her voice rose on a hysterical note. "You're supposed to take care of me. I want to get out of here."

"When the time is right, you will, Odette. You can handle this." He ended the call. *I did.*

The swans trumpeted again, and he smiled. He sat back and glanced around the small structure. He'd paneled it with stainless steel to keep it sanitary for the upcoming operation. All the lights, the operating table, his tools were in order, awaiting their shining moment. Just a few more days to get everything ready.

The scent of caramel corn sweetened the air. Through the open window, Eve could hear the crash of waves on the rocks below the lighthouse. Her attempt at a normal evening of playing Go Fish with the kids fell flat as soon as she'd burned the caramel syrup. Keri hadn't wanted to sit still and insisted on sitting on Nick's lap all evening. Davy had been whiny as well and rarely left his mother's side.

It was as if they sensed change in the wind.

She snipped some dead leaves from the plant on the table and carried the debris to the kitchen to throw it away. She was just trying to put off the inevitable. Sighing, she went back to the living room, caught Bree's gaze, and nodded toward Davy.

Bree nodded. "Time for bed, kids."

"Aw, Mom," Davy said. "I'm beating Dad."

Kade clenched his fist and jerked it in the air. "Yes! And you have to leave before you can say you stomped me."

Davy jumped up and tackled his dad. "I stomped you *bad*!"

Kade tickled him, and the little boy's giggles rang out. Kade stood and hoisted Davy over one shoulder, hanging the boy upside down. "You'll get another chance tomorrow, little man."

Eve watched the Matthews family walk upstairs. If only she could give her daughter that kind of security and stability. She laid her head against the back of the sofa and watched Nick with Keri. The toddler had her head tucked into her daddy's shoulder with her left hand gripping his shirt. The love they shared almost made her feel excluded.

Her gaze locked with Nick's. Keri had to be told tonight. No more waiting for the proper time, no more telling herself that Keri was too young.

Eve wet her lips. "Sweetie, come sit with me for a minute."

Keri tightened her hold on Nick. "Daddy read story."

Forcing her daughter to leave Nick

wouldn't be the best way to move into the necessary conversation. "I need to talk to you about something, baby girl."

The trust in Keri's blue eyes stabbed at Eve's heart. How should she put this? Eve would sooner poke out her own eyes than hurt her little girl. She picked up Keri's hand and kissed her palm. It smelled sweetly of caramel and butter. "I love you very much, Keri."

"Love oo." Keri pulled her hand away and patted Eve's cheek.

This was so hard, with love and grief rising in her chest and choking her. "I'm going to tell you something really wonderful." Eve waited until Keri's eyes grew wide and expectant. "Sometimes little girls and boys are loved so much that they have more than one mommy and daddy who want to share the love."

Nick tried to help. "And you're a very lucky little girl, Keri, because you have two mommies who love you very much."

This was all wrong. Keri was only two. How could she possibly understand this? Eve wanted to roll back the clock to last week, to before she realized Keri hadn't been carried in her womb. "Yes, you're our own little girl forever. But you have another mommy too. She wants to come see you."

Keri's blue eyes mirrored confusion as she stared from Eve to Nick and back again. "Mommy?" Her eyelids drooped, and she put her thumb in her mouth.

Nick's gaze met Eve's in a helpless plea. "She's sleepy," he whispered.

"Maybe we shouldn't try to explain," she whispered. "She's really too young to get it."

"I know your sister. She's going to come in here being melodramatic and telling Keri she's her real mommy."

"Maybe we can ask her not to do that."

"You might not remember her, but you saw how determined she was."

Eve bit her lip. "Should we prevent her from coming here?"

"She'll just go to the court and get it ordered."

"Surely a judge will see the confusion is harmful to Keri." What a mess she was making of this. She knew Keri would never understand. "Time for bed, sweetie," she said, giving up the struggle.

"Dance?" Keri suggested. She scrambled down to the floor and circled her arms over her head, then went demi-pointe.

Eve smiled. "Good form, Keri. Arch your neck a little." She ran her palms over Keri's neck.

"You remember all that?" Nick asked.

Eve arched her brows. "Crazy, isn't it? I can't remember anything important, but I can remember the dance."

"Your ballet has always been important to you."

His tone indicated that maybe her talent had cost him. Eve looked away, knowing there was nothing she could say to that. She didn't remember. Had she put her dance before Nick just as he had put his work first?

She shied away from the thought of bringing up Will.

They watched Keri dance around the room for a few minutes, then Nick insisted she go to bed. Though Keri protested, Nick scooped her up and carried her to Davy's bedroom.

The two children had grown so close that Keri insisted on staying in Davy's room. Eve turned out the lights and followed.

"Bed," Keri said, pointing to the bottom bunk. Davy was a small hump on the top bunk.

Nick slipped her between the covers and planted a kiss on her forehead. " 'Night, baby."

"Night-night, Daddy." Keri's lids fluttered, and her voice was soft.

Eve watched the two of them together.

Guilt crept up behind her and toppled her hopes for ever reclaiming what this small family unit once had. Like Humpty Dumpty, the pieces of their previous lives would never be mended.

17

Sinners gathered at The Fisheries every night to give in to their flesh. Its blinking neon sign attracted them like bugs. Gideon's gaze swept the revelers. It wouldn't be hard to find one deserving of death. He should wait, but something drove him on.

Tonight he was Shiva, the Destroyer.

A group of men and women came reeling from the bar, spilling cigarette smoke and the yeasty odor of beer into the clear air. Their laughter rang into the night. He watched as their little group finally broke apart, each one scurrying to individual cars.

Except for one.

She stood under the watery wash of lamplight looking uncertainly into the darkness. Maybe she felt him hiding there, an avenging puma waiting to rip out her throat. He knew she would come to him though. They always did. Most people tended to ignore that still, small voice inside, dismissed it as superstition.

He knew better.

Dressed in a red dress that barely covered her shapely derriere, and teetering on heels too flimsy to walk in, the woman started toward his hiding place. The silk scarf in his right hand, he waited, his breath catching in his chest.

Fashioning the scarf into a garrote, he was behind her in one movement. Then he had the scarf around her neck, twisting so tightly she couldn't scream. He dragged her back into the welcoming darkness of the trees.

Eve hadn't slept a wink. The thought of losing Keri kept her tossing and turning most of the night. She needed help. Sitting on the edge of her bed beside a napping Keri, she looked from the phone to the number in her hand. What would she say? And why hadn't her parents called her? Nick told her he'd spoken with them, given Bree's number in case they wanted to talk to her.

She called up the number, then waited . . . while she waited for someone to pick up. Did she look like her mother? Her father? Were she and her brothers close? It was already obvious there was no love lost between her and Patti. While it was ringing, she tended to the plants in her room.

"Ya." The voice on the other end had a gruff tone as though the woman smoked three packs of cigarettes a day.

"H-hello, this is Eve." The silence seemed long, but Eve knew it couldn't have been more than a couple of seconds. She longed to hear her mother's concern and love.

"Eve," the gruff voice snapped. "About time, it is! You disappear without a word, to death you worry me and your Fa." The Swedish accent thickened as she talked.

It took Eve a moment to form a response. Nick said he told them she'd lost her memory. "I'm sorry," she said. "I — I don't remember anything."

"Ya, your Nick, he tell us."

The silence between them fell heavy and thick. Too thick to saw through with the sharpest blade. Eve didn't know what questions to ask, how to visualize the woman who raised her.

"I'm afraid," Eve whispered. "I don't know anyone. A man wants to kill me."

"You come home, ya?" The words were said grudgingly.

Eve winced. Her mother obviously didn't really care. "It's okay. I have police protection, but it's frightening not to even know my family. Could you send me some pictures of you and my father? My brothers?"

"We do not take pictures. Is silly," her mother said. "You want to see us, you come home."

"When was I home last?"

"Last Christmas, it was."

Six months ago. There was a world of information in those three words.

"We live not so far you cannot come to see your Fa and Mor more often. Too busy, always too busy."

"Do . . . do you know what happened between me and Nick? Why we divorced? Did I ever talk to you about . . . about another man?"

"You never tell your Mor anything." Her tone changed. "Your Fa, he has doctor bill due. A thousand dollars. I tell Nick, and he says he send it. Make sure, okay? The money, we need."

Was that the guarded tone she'd sensed from Nick whenever she asked about her family? Were they only interested in money? Maybe that was why she never went to visit.

"I don't have any money. Nick and I are divorced. I can't let him give you any money."

"Bad daughter, you. Always you think of yourself." The words were delivered in a harsh growl.

The next thing Eve knew, the dial tone

was ringing in her ear. Her mother had hung up on her? She got to her feet and went out the door. She had to talk to Nick.

She found him on the back porch. The fog had rolled in off the lake, and though she could see the sun would soon burn it off, right now she couldn't make out the buoy offshore, though she could hear its gong and the sound of the foghorn.

Nick glanced up as she settled into the chair beside him. "You okay?"

"I just talked to my mother. Or rather tried to. What's this about her asking you for money?"

He shrugged. "They're always asking for money. I'd hoped she wouldn't ask when she knew what you'd been through."

"But why? Doesn't my dad work?"

"Yeah, in a bar. He and your mom are both alcoholics. Meth smokers too."

She saw him glance at her out of the corner of his eye as if to gauge her reaction. The information didn't surprise her, in light of her mother's aloofness and accusations.

"Were they like this when I was growing up?"

"You lived with the alcohol. And heroin. They found meth just before we were married."

"How did I ever become a dancer?"

"You called it your escape. Elena Cox, the teacher who gave you the necklace, bonded with you when you were in grade school. She gave you free lessons for years."

"My brothers? Are they like . . . her?"

"Great guys, both younger than you and both unmarried. I think they're jaded."

"Have you talked to them — since you found me?"

He shook his head. "I thought your parents would tell them. I guess I should call them."

"And my maiden name?"

"Ostergard." His hand slipped over and took hers.

The warmth of his hand and the interlacing of their fingers brought a level of calm. "Have you always been able to do this?" she whispered.

"What?"

"Make it all better."

His lips turned down. "Not everything. If I could, we'd still be married."

A chill wind blew in from the lake as if summoned by his words. Just about the time she moved closer to him, she was reminded of how little she knew about anything — their pasts, their arguments. Their dreams, their failures. She stood and went to the porch railing.

Her affair.

He joined her. "Can we pretend we have no past?" he whispered. "We have just this minute. We can learn about each other as if we've just met. In a way, we have."

He turned her around to face him, cupped her cheek in his hand, and rubbed her lower lip with his thumb. Eve closed her eyes and inhaled the minty scent of his breath. His lips brushed hers, and she fought the desire to pull him closer.

She turned her head, sliding her lips away. "A new beginning sounds tempting, Nick, but how can we find it until we put the past in its place?"

He stepped back with exasperation in the stiff line of his shoulders. "The past is over, Eve. You don't even remember it."

"What about Will Donaldson?"

He stiffened even more. "You remember him?"

"No, but he's here."

"Son of a —" Nick clamped his mouth shut. His hands curled into fists. "When did you see him?"

Had it just been a few days ago? So much had happened. "He says we were lovers," she said. "Why didn't you tell me it was my fault we divorced?"

He stared at her. "Is it true? You said —"

"I said what?" His gaze wouldn't meet hers, and she braced herself for the news.

"That you never slept with him."

A flame of hope began to burn. "Did you believe me?"

His gaze locked with hers. "Yeah, I did. What's he doing here? You told me you weren't going to see him anymore."

"I don't know." She bit her lip. "Why would he lie?"

"I'm sure he knows you don't remember, and it's a way to hang on. I think he and I should have a talk."

She grabbed his arm. "No!"

"What did you feel when you saw him?" He took her in his arms again, and his lips brushed hers. "I can see you feel something for me, Eve." His fingers pressed against her wrist. "Your pulse is racing."

"I didn't feel anything for him," she admitted. She swallowed the dryness in her throat. "But would he lie to me?"

Nick said nothing. His disappointment and her regret mingled into something as thick as the fog rolling in across the bay.

Jason's bust of the skull found in the grave was shown on TV all over the state by noon Sunday. Nick knew they'd get no hits on it. The guy had rushed through the thing in three days, and it resembled no person he'd ever seen. The lips were too thick for the rest of the bone structure; the nose didn't fit either.

The Marquette officer only wanted the publicity.

Kade talked to Fraser, who arrived in Rock Harbor Sunday afternoon. Nick's partner had arranged to get the skull released and delivered to Oliver. Kade offered the basement of his lighthouse as a workspace.

"I gave Oliver a key so he can come in and out as he likes. He's going to stay at the hotel," Bree said, flipping on an overhead light to show Nick down. "Sorry it's such a mess down here."

"I'm sure Oliver has only made it worse," Nick said. "He didn't want to work in his van in case Jason got wind of it and came in to commandeer the project again." An odor like a damp cave rushed out the open door.

The bare bulb dribbled weak light into the stairwell, but a bright glare from halogen lights illuminated the basement. Over a century of use had packed the dirt floor hard. Stacks of boxes lined the walls, but Oliver's table and supplies took up the center of the room.

Oliver bent over his work. "Hey, Nick, get

me that clay, would you?" He gestured to a tub sitting on boxes about six feet away.

Nick obliged, hefting the heavy tub to his friend. Oliver began to work on the model he'd made of the skull. He had drilled small holes in the cast and inserted vinyl pegs in them to gauge how thick he needed to build up the clay.

"How long is this going to take?" Nick asked. He never tired of watching Oliver at work.

"Another four or five days. Then I'm taking a break and going fishing. Don't call me for a new case for at least a week."

"My dad loves fishing," Bree said.

"I'll take him out one afternoon."

"How'd you get into this line of work?" Bree asked.

Oliver's smile flashed through his neatly trimmed beard. "Indecision," he joked. "First I thought I might be a doctor, but I kept getting distracted. Then I wanted to be a sculptor, but when was the last time you bought a bust?"

"Um, never," Bree said.

"Exactly." He straightened his back, and his grin widened. "Actually, I didn't care about the money. My brother went missing when I was in my twenties. A year later some bones were found. The police couldn't identify them — this was back before DNA typing was around. I had to know if they were my brother's, so I asked the police if I could try to make a cast of the skull."

"You never told me that," Nick said.

"You never asked." Oliver held up a laminated chart. "It helped that I had studied anatomy and art in my academic wanderings. I spent two weeks studying journals until I found a method like this to guide me."

"What's that?" Nick peered closer at the chart but couldn't figure it out.

"It tells me how thick the layers of muscles and skin should be in different areas on the face. This is the most painstaking part of the process. And the most crucial. If you don't get this right, the face won't look like the victim at all." Oliver's voice was muffled as he bent over the skull.

"So was it your brother?" Bree asked in a soft voice.

"It was. But at least I knew and had closure. We buried him and mourned. It helped. There are so many lost souls out there. It's a small thing I do."

"Not so small," Nick said. "You sure you need four or five days?"

"Rushing it at this stage will most assuredly give us the results of our young friend Jason."

Nick knew he had to cool his jets and not push if he wanted to track down this woman — and let them lead her to Gideon. Pulling up a folding wooden chair, he settled down to watch the forensic sculptor.

Layer by layer, Oliver built the cast up, pausing often to gauge the thickness of the clay in different areas.

"How long before we see some results?" Nick asked.

"I'll rush and try to get through in a week or ten days."

"Jason didn't take that long," Bree said.

"Of course not. The young man was inept." He paused. "I think she's blonde too."

"How could you tell? I mean, there was no hair in the grave," Bree said.

Oliver looked up briefly. "There was one strand of blonde inside the skull the first time I looked it over. I didn't tell Jason. I wanted to see which direction he went."

"It was obviously the wrong direction," Nick agreed. "The face he came up with looked out of balance."

"Not surprising," Oliver said, scrutinizing the cheekbones.

Nick watched Oliver smooth the clay

along the cheekbones and reach for more.

"Once I get the clay totally smooth and skinlike, I shall let it dry, then paint it. It will take many layers."

Nick walked over to look at the bust from a different angle. "You know Jason's going to scream foul."

"It won't do him any good. We will have her identified within twenty-four hours of completion." Oliver's gaze stayed on the cast.

"So long as it's before Gideon makes his next move, that will make me very happy."

"I'm going to go meet Eve and your parents at the park," Bree said, heading toward the stairs.

Nick nodded and continued to watch Oliver work. The sculptor's long fingers moved quickly along the face, honing and smoothing. The man really was a master.

Nick's cell phone rang. He had only one bar, so he bounded up the steps to the kitchen. "Andreakos here," he said.

"Captain, this is Grant Campbell with Internal Affairs. I expected you to contact us when you heard of your suspension." The man's voice was heavy with disapproval.

"We've got a situation here," Nick said.

"Well, we've got a situation here," the man snapped. "If you want to be a police officer again, there are some questions that need answering. I expect you in my office tomorrow morning at nine."

"I'm in Rock Harbor, in the UP," Nick said. "It's an eight-hour drive."

"Then I suggest you get started."

"Look, can't you send someone up here? I'm not leaving. A serial killer is after my wife."

"Then I'm sure she has police protection. This can't wait, Captain."

If Eve would go with him, he'd take her, but he knew she'd say no. And he wasn't leaving her here without him. "Then you'll have to send someone to Rock Harbor. I'm not leaving Eve. If it means losing my job, then that's the price I'll pay to protect my wife." From the long silence on the other end, he figured the man had hung up and he'd be getting dismissal papers in a few days. Then he heard Campbell clear his throat.

"I'll be there tomorrow morning. Make yourself available, Andreakos." Without waiting for an answer, he hung up.

Nick rolled his eyes and put his phone away. Just what he didn't need right now. He should probably go over his report of the operation, but it was back at his office. Maybe he could get someone to overnight it. He called headquarters and made the request. His assistant offered to fax them to the sheriff's office, and he jumped on her suggestion.

He went back to the basement and told Oliver what the call was about.

"I'll look after Eve if you need to go," Oliver said, standing and pressing his fist into his back. His eyelids drooped, and his skin was a sallow color.

"Thanks, but I can't leave her." He stretched. "I think I'll go for a walk. Want me to get you a soda or a candy bar?"

"How about a Rolaids?" Oliver said, his white grin breaking out.

"Got plenty of those." Nick started to dig in his pocket, but the older man held up his hand.

"I was only kidding. Those things will kill you, Nick."

"Probably." Nick went toward the steps. "Sure I can't get you something?"

"Just Gideon's head," Oliver said, his gaze going back to the skull.

"I'll do my best." Nick escaped into the sunshine. He decided to walk to the downtown area. The sun shone down from a sky so blue it hurt his eyes. A light breeze wafted off the lake and lifted his hair.

He found himself watching for Eve. Maybe

she and Bree would be walking the children home from the park. Things were strained between them since their discussion about Will Donaldson, but at least she'd admitted she had no feelings for the man now.

Just around the corner from the coffee shop, he saw a familiar black hat and red beard. "Zack? We've got to quit meeting like this!"

His German Baptist friend turned at the sound of his voice and grinned. "Nick! Has the geocaching bug bitten you that much? This is a rather obscure event for you to be attending."

"What planet do you live on, buddy? Haven't you seen the papers? I thought Eve was killed by a serial killer, but I found her up here."

Zack pursed his lips. "I rarely read the paper. It's full of distressing information that pollutes the mind. Is Eve all right?"

"Yes, she's fine." Nick saw the GPS unit in Zack's hand. "You're here looking for a cache?"

Zack nodded. "I live about an hour away. I come here often with my group."

"The folks I met in Bay City?"

"No, the ones from Marquette. Though a big event is going on this weekend, so my friends from Bay City are here as well."

"What were their names again — the guys I met in Bay City?"

"Judd and Hugo. Why?"

Judd. That's who Nick was thinking of. The quiet ones were the ones to watch out for, and this guy just kept cropping up. "Where is Judd?"

"Out scouting the area." Zack frowned. "Is something wrong?"

"How well do you know him?"

"We enjoyed the new adventure for a year before I moved. He's quiet but studious."

Studious. Smart enough to put all those obscure clues online. "I think I need to talk to him," Nick said. "Can we meet for coffee?"

"As you wish." Zack glanced at his watch. "In about two hours?"

"Great. See you then." Nick headed on down the street. He was probably going down a rabbit trail with his suspicion of Judd, but not a single alternative path had opened up to him yet.

When he neared the jail, he saw several cop cars screech to a stop in front. Picking up his pace, he hurried to the building and rushed inside. He might be ordered out since he was technically suspended, but he hoped Montgomery would throw him a bone or two.

"They found her shoe outside the bar this morning," one deputy said as Nick entered the building. "And blood spatter on some leaves in the woods."

"A murder?" Nick asked Montgomery, who stood hiking up his pants by the water-cooler.

"Yeah, some friends reported a young woman missing this morning in Houghton."

"Any resemblance to Eve?" Nick asked.

"Well, she's a blonde," Montgomery said.

"Age?"

"Hannah Pelton, thirty-two. We've got a picture," the deputy said. "I'll call Bree. Maybe she and Samson can track her." He hesitated. "I've got papers to deliver to Eve."

"From Patti?"

Montgomery nodded.

"I'll go with you." If only Nick could shake some sense into his sister-in-law.

Tourists packed the outside seating areas. Eve claimed the last table available outside the coffee shop. Bree was getting their drinks, and both children and the dog had wanted to go inside with her. Through the window, Eve could see the children press their noses to the pastry display case. Nick's parents had returned to their hotel for a rest.

The sun was hot on her head. She glanced around the town street and saw Nick approaching at a brisk pace. Deputy Montgomery lumbered behind him. Patti followed with a triumphant expression brightening her sallow skin.

Nick reached her first. "We knew this was coming," he whispered. "Hang on, we'll get through it."

Eve put her coffee down on the table. Patti's gaze locked with hers. There was no remorse in her sister's face.

Montgomery stopped in front of her. "Eve, I'm sorry, but I have to serve you with these papers. Your sister is suing for custody of Keri." The deputy handed her the bundle.

Eve shook her head. "No."

"Sorry, Eve. You have to take them."

"You can't have her," Nick said, raising his voice. "Just so you know. We'll fight you every step of the way."

Patti tossed her mousy hair back from her face. "She's my daughter."

"The initial hearing is set for Wednesday," Montgomery continued. "One o'clock. The judge will decide temporary custody until the full trial."

Maybe an emotional plea would work. Surely there was some kind of feeling left between her and her sister. Eve's chair scraped as she stood. "Don't do this, Patti. Please. Keri has had enough upheaval in her life." She reached out and took Patti's cold hand.

Patti tugged out of Eve's grip. "I'm her mother. She belongs with me."

"She doesn't know you."

"I never lied to her. You did."

"You abandoned her!" Nick said. "Why are you so set to get her back all of a sudden?"

"Her father wants to meet her."

Eve wet her lips. "Who is it, Patti? Is he a decent man?"

"I think so."

"Why didn't he stand behind you when you were pregnant?" Nick demanded.

"He was married then. His wife couldn't have kids, and he wanted them, so they divorced. If I can get custody of Keri, he'll marry me."

"Oh, he sounds like a real winner." Nick thrust his hands in his pockets.

"Don't do this, Patti," Eve begged. "Please think about it."

Patti's eyes were as hard as ice chips. "He loves kids. And he wants Keri. I'm going to make sure he gets her."

"So it's not that you care about her," Nick said. "You just want to use her as bait to hook some guy who was too much of a good-time Charlie to stick with his wife. He's not getting our baby."

Our baby. Eve was beginning to like the way he wrapped them both in his protection.

Patti's mouth worked, but she said nothing before stomping off. Eve wished she could call her sister back, heal the wounds between them. Instead, she tucked the papers in her purse. "Tell me she won't win, Nick."

"She won't." His gaze held hers.

"Thank you." Little by little he was creeping back into her heart, and she didn't know how to stop him. "Want to join us for coffee?"

His smile emerged. "Sure. I'm supposed to meet someone here later anyway."

She almost warned him not to get his hopes up, but she found that her own kept resurrecting as well. Who was she to tell him not to do something she found impossible to resist?

Eve and Bree left with the children when Montgomery asked for Bree's help, and the rest of the crowd thinned out at the coffee shop. Nick kept the outside table and watched the people walk by. Zack should be along with Judd any minute.

He shouldn't be wasting his time. A better use of these minutes would be combing the woods for the missing woman. He sipped his strong black coffee. The nisu bread was smelling better and better.

He was about to go get a snack when he saw Zack's black hat. The other man spotted his wave and came toward him with Judd in tow. "What can I get for you?" Nick asked when they reached the table.

"Nothing for me," Zack said. "I don't drink caffeine."

"How about you?" Nick asked Judd. It was an excuse to look the guy over better. The casual clothes fit him, but the man looked out of place in the jeans and plaid shirt. He'd be more comfortable in a suit and tie.

Judd nodded. "Thanks, but I limit my coffee to the morning."

"Suit yourself. Have a seat." Nick dropped into the green metal chair again. He waited until the other men were seated. "We've seen each other several times now, Judd, and I've never asked what you do."

"I'm a physician's assistant."

Nick would have guessed he was a lawyer or something. "Did Zack tell you about the serial killer I've been tracking?"

"A bit." Judd looked bored.

"You choose which caches your group goes after, is that right?"

"Yes, of course. They trust my judgment."

"What about the day we went out by the bay? The day we found the woman whose hands were cut off."

"I chose those caches."

"What were your criteria?"

"Just one: I wanted to go out to the bay that day. It was a nice day."

"That was all?"

Judd looked up with an angry flash in his eyes. His cheeks surged with color. "You suspect me, is that it? Typical *pig*," he snarled.

The transformation from confident professional to infuriated man made Nick rear back in his chair. "Whoa, I'm not accusing you of anything."

"No? It sure sounded like you were."

"We know Gideon has some ties to the geocaching sport. I'm just trying to get a feel for how it all works. You've been present at the discovery of two bodies now. Seems strange, don't you think?"

Judd set his chin. "No."

"Do you have much contact with others who play?"

"Of course. It's a small community, so to

speak. I've been to many events."

"Ever been up here?"

"Sure. Many times."

"Is the sport popular up here?"

"It's popular everywhere." Judd stood. "I really need to get going. I'm meeting a friend for dinner." He glanced at Zack. "Coming?"

Zack offered Nick a glance of apology as the two shook hands in parting, but he followed Judd. Nick watched them leave and wondered how he might find out some more information about Judd. That flash of temper just might have been telling.

18

The dogs strained at the leashes. Another twenty people thronged the small sidewalk where the woman's shoe had been found. Bree kept a tight hold on Samson as the handlers listened to the instructions.

Montgomery had them lined up. "You've all got walkie-talkies. Call in your position if you find anything. Don't approach the site. We don't want the evidence contaminated."

"He's sure we're going to find a body and not a survivor," Bree whispered to Naomi.

Naomi took a firmer grip on Charley's leash. "Heel, Charley!" The dog sat back on his haunches.

Deputy Montgomery dismissed the line searchers and went to join the dog teams. "I want you to move fast on this, Bree."

"As long as he didn't put her in a car, we've got a good shot," Bree said. "Are you coming with us?"

He shook his head. "I'll stay at search

headquarters, eh? Call me when you find something."

Bree nodded. "Let's go," she told the other searchers. Naomi followed her. Bree had trained ten other dog teams, but none of them were available today. This victim's chances rested on Bree's and Naomi's shoulders.

She opened the paper sack containing the woman's shoe and let the dogs sniff. "Search, Samson," she said.

His intelligent eyes turned toward the woods, and he strained at the leash anew. Bree unclipped it, and Samson sprang into the underbrush. She ran after him. His tail swished in the air, and she knew he had the scent. The trail led deep into the forest, past stands of white birch and oak trees. Charley barked as he ran in the same direction and caught up with Samson.

Samson leaped over a fallen tree and splashed through a creek. On the opposite side, he stopped. His legs stiffened. His tail came down. While it was exactly what Bree expected, she slowed and hung her head. Dead. Hannah was dead. The dogs had stopped by an old outhouse. The remains of a cabin sat by the stream, a few rotting rafters supported by crumbling walls.

The dogs were milling around outside the

outhouse. "I'd better check it out before I call Montgomery," Bree said. She approached the doorway. The door itself had long since been torn off its hinges.

The body lay just inside the door. Bree stepped away but not so fast she missed seeing the partial peanut butter sandwich on the woman's chest. Or the fact that she had no face. Her feet, severed just above the ankles, were nowhere to be seen.

"She's in there?" Naomi asked.

Bree nodded. She leaned her forehead against a tree and waited for the shakes to pass. No matter how often this happened, she never got used to it.

"Want me to call the deputy?" Naomi asked.

"I'll do it." Bree settled on a fallen tree and dialed the jail. "I found her," she said. She read him the GPS coordinates. When she hung up, she called Kade at the park headquarters. "Can you check the geocaching site? See if there's anything new."

"Sure, hang on."

She listened to his steps move to his computer. "We found her, Kade."

"Oh, baby, I'm sorry. Dead, I assume from your voice?"

"Very. He didn't bury her though." She told him about finding the body's location and listened to the tapping of the computer keys over the phone line.

"Hang on a sec." His keyboard made a few more clicks before silence fell between them for a few seconds. "Nothing here," he said. "Maybe he didn't want it found yet. You might have messed up his plans."

"I'd like to mess up more than his plans," she said. "Thanks, honey."

"You okay?"

"I will be. See you tonight." She ended the call. The brush rustled, and Bree turned to look. They probably shouldn't have come out here without any protection, though most people would hesitate to approach with two dogs guarding them.

Will Donaldson stepped from behind a tree. Two other men with rifles flanked him. One man had a deer over his shoulder — a doe to boot. Will put his hand out to stop their progress when he saw the women.

He looked so different from the other members of Job's Children. Bree had to wonder why he was drawn to the group. His hair was spiked and styled, and his jeans were pressed. He could have stepped out of an *Esquire* magazine, yet here he was in the woods with hunters.

Bree gave a pointed stare at the guns and deer. "Hunting season doesn't start until

November." Will's smile struck her as ingratiating and smug. When he didn't answer, she nodded at the other men. "I'm Bree Matthews. My husband is a park ranger. None of you should be carrying weapons. And that deer is illegal."

"Bree," Naomi murmured. "We're a little outnumbered here."

Will laughed and spread out his hands. "Hey, back off, Mrs. Matthews. We found the deer."

"And I suppose someone else shot it?" She pointed at the gaping hole in the animal's side, an obvious gunshot wound.

"We heard a shot and came running," the man on Will's right said. Bulky and balding, he wore a T-shirt that read "Live Off the Land."

"Then you should have called the park department," Bree said. "I'm afraid I'll have to seize the deer and call this in."

"I don't think so," the man said. "We found it fair and square." The three men turned and plunged back into the thick brush.

Bree started to go after them, but Naomi grabbed her arm.

"Don't be stupid," Naomi said. "They have guns. We can tell Kade about it. It's not like they can get very far. We both identified them anyway."

"I hate poachers," Bree said.

"I hate getting shot more," Naomi pointed out. "I think we've got enough trouble right here without asking for more."

Bree nodded as her phone rang. She pulled it out and saw Kade's number. "Hey, I just found a poacher," she said.

"And the GPS coordinates just popped up," he said. "She's one of Gideon's."

The summer day couldn't be prettier, but Nick was in no mood to enjoy it. Not with the investigation hanging over his head. The last thing he wanted to do today was answer questions from IA.

He popped a Rolaids into his mouth, then got out of his SUV and approached the jail. The village looked quiet and peaceful, too, a chimera that hid the darkness swirling around their heads.

He stepped into the office and saw Montgomery sitting at the desk. "Is IA here yet?" Nick asked him.

"Yeah, Campbell called."

"That's probably him parking." Nick nodded toward the red car that rolled to a stop at the curb. "Where can we meet?"

"The deputy said to use his office. They found the missing woman with the search dogs. Same MO. Missing face too. This time the feet were cut off."

He winced. The door opened, and the man who came through the doorway had to stoop to enter. "What are you, six-ten?" Nick blurted.

The man glowered and ignored the question. "Nick Andreakos?" he asked. "I'm Captain Grant Campbell. Is there somewhere we can talk?"

"Right this way." So no time for niceties. The guy wanted to get right to business, which was fine with Nick. The sooner this thing was laid to rest, the better.

He pointed to the two chairs by the desk, but Campbell went around and sat in the chair behind the desk. A little psychological warfare, but Nick knew where he stood. This guy couldn't intimidate him.

Nick settled into the chair and leaned back, striving for a relaxed pose. Campbell narrowed his eyes, and Nick had to choke back a grin. He'd played this game too many times himself.

"So fire away," Nick said. "I've got a serial killer to catch. The sooner we get this settled, the faster I get him off the streets."

"You seem very flippant about such serious charges." Campbell opened the file he'd laid on the desk. "Excessive force, trespassing, even manslaughter has been mentioned."

Nick's smile faded. "You know that's a boatload of crap. What was I supposed to do? Let Bechtol haul that woman off where we'd never find her?"

"These are serious charges, Captain. I have to investigate them."

"What do the Alpena officers say? You've surely questioned them as well."

Campbell looked down. "Well, yes, I did. They say Mr. Bechtol and his compound fired first, which is exactly what I would have expected them to say. They aren't going to implicate you and themselves willingly. I need proof."

"What more proof do you need? You've got all the ammo recovered from the compound, thousands of bullet casings on the ground, the testimony of the other officers. I don't see what more I can give you."

Nick tried to think of any personal reasons Campbell could have for coming after him but couldn't think of a thing. As far as he knew, they'd never met. Maybe his dad would have an idea.

"The woman you rescued has corroborated these charges. Don't you think she would have been grateful for the rescue if it were done properly?" Campbell asked.

"I'd like to talk to her myself," Nick said. "Have you had a therapist talk to her? I think she was beginning to bond to her captors. It happens. She was with them for several weeks."

"Not to a woman like her. She's a therapist herself and sees no need to speak to anyone."

"I think we should insist on it." Nick wanted to stand and pace, but he couldn't give Campbell the satisfaction of watching his agitation. Acid churned in his belly, and he longed for another antacid.

Campbell flipped the folder shut. "The real issue is that you tend to use force way too often, Captain. I can't believe I'm the only one who has questioned how often you pull your gun."

"I challenge you to come up with a single time I've used force when something else would have worked," Nick said. "I didn't get to my position by letting the bad guy get away. Or by being brutal. I work smart. I'm not bragging — you can read that in my file."

"So you say." Campbell stood. "I'll talk to my supervisor about your answers, but until then you're still on suspension."

"I need to find the man who's after my wife!" Nick jumped to his feet and balled his fists.

"Your ex-wife, Captain." Campbell brushed past Nick and went down the hallway. "You neglected to mention that when we first spoke."

19

Even after two days, Samson was still upset from his discovery of Hannah, so Eve and Bree played hide-and-seek with him and the children along the beach before supper. The spray of cold water from Superior cooled Eve's hot face. It felt good to be *doing something.* Just waiting for Gideon to strike next kept her on edge.

"The initial hearing is tomorrow," Eve told Bree. She sat on a rock and dug her toes into the cool sand. Davy and Keri screamed with excitement as a wave sloshed around their ankles. They ran through the spray, then back to the partially completed sand castle. Samson barked and ran around them. When the cold water hit him, he yelped and ran back to Bree.

Eve laughed and hauled the cold, wet dog onto her lap. He promptly nestled against her and fell asleep.

"It's going to be okay." Bree sat on the sand.

"Ronja thinks so too. She found a rap sheet on Patti. Problem is, I'm not so sure I want to hurt my own sister in court. I left a message at the hotel asking for her to come here to talk to me."

"Has she called?"

"No." Eve would like to believe Patti never got the message, but she knew better.

"Are you remembering anything new at all? Won't that be crucial for your case in court?" Bree voiced Eve's own fears.

"I sometimes get a brief flash of emotion that feels like I'm remembering something. Then it's gone."

Bree didn't seem to be listening. Eve turned to see what had caught her friend's attention and saw Nick's broad-shouldered figure at the top of the cliff. His head turned toward them and he waved, then started down the rock steps that led to the water.

Eve shoved the dog off her lap, tucked her windblown hair behind her ears, and stood. From the grim slant of his mouth, she assumed his appointment with IA hadn't gone well.

Keri ran to him, and he scooped her up, wet sand and all, then put her back down to play and continued on his course to Eve. "I hear you found her," he said to Bree. "You doing okay?"

Bree nodded. "It's never easy."

"How did it go?" Eve asked.

Nick made a face. "Not great. I'm still off the case for now." His phone rang, and he answered it. "Hey, Dad, what do you have?" He listened in silence and moved away. "The next one would have the tongue missing again." His voice was softer as though he didn't want her to hear. "The last one might be the tongue too. Or hands maybe."

Eve studied his back. It sounded like he knew what Gideon was looking for. Why hadn't he told her?

Nick closed his phone and turned back around.

Eve examined his face, the way he wasn't looking at her, the tight line of his lips. "You know something." Funny how she could read him and not even realize she was remembering how to do it.

"I don't *know* anything."

"You *suspect,* then. What's your theory? There seems to be some kind of pattern. He takes a different body part each time. It sounded like you knew what to look for next time."

Bree nodded. "Yeah, give us the scoop. We'll keep it quiet."

Nick's lips pressed together, and he looked away. "I found this passage in Proverbs. It looks like maybe he's following it to rid the world of people who commit things God calls *abominations.*"

The ominous word made Eve shudder. "What passage?"

"Proverbs 6." Nick pulled a notebook out of his shirt pocket, flipped it open, and began to read. " 'These six things the LORD hates, yes, seven are an abomination to Him: a proud look, a lying tongue, hands that shed innocent blood, a heart that devises wicked plans, feet that are swift in running to evil, a false witness who speaks lies, and one who sows discord among brethren.' "

"Which one am I?" Eve hugged her arms around herself, but she still felt cold.

"Look, let's not talk about it. It's just a theory."

"One he's been following so far," she pointed out. "I was the first one he attacked, so does that mean I have the proud look?"

He pocketed his notepad. "The verses he left online when you disappeared indicate he thought of you as the proud look. And the one we think he took in your place also referenced the proud look."

It wasn't what she'd been expecting.

Maybe Gideon's hunt had nothing to do with her relationship with Will Donaldson. "If he took a substitute, why did he follow me here?"

"You seem to be special. You're the only one he's called taunting us about."

"He's called you about me? Why have you never mentioned it before?"

"I didn't want to worry you."

"Good grief, Nick! Don't you think I deserve to know what he has planned? Do you think he plans to kill a few more and then come back for me?"

He ran his hand through his hair. "I'm not inside his head, Eve. I don't know what's inside his warped brain, but I'll protect you. Look, this is getting us nowhere. We're getting more leads every day. We'll find him."

She didn't argue, but she knew if they had a suspect, he would tell her. The police were as much in the dark as she was. A proud look. What had she done to make Gideon choose her to kill for that? If only she could remember.

She decided to let it drop for now. "I need to talk to Patti. Did you happen to see her when you were in town?"

"No, but we could call her at the hotel."

Enduring the way she felt in his presence

right now soured the appeal of having backup when she talked to Patti. Nick took the decision out of her hands by taking Eve's elbow. "We won't be long, Bree, if you don't mind watching Keri."

"We'll be fine. I'll just watch them play until they turn too blue from the water."

Bree's eyes held amusement, and Eve knew her friend guessed her dilemma. "I'll be back in time to help with supper," Eve said, walking quickly ahead to escape Nick's hand on her arm.

His touch evoked a discomfiting warmth. She must be insane to have such a powerful visceral reaction to this man.

"I'll drive." Nick's clipped voice stopped her as she reached the car.

She nodded and slid into the passenger seat. Every time they were alone together, he made her want desperately to remember the reasons they'd split up. On the surface, she could imagine nothing that would have driven her away.

He got in the other side and put the key in the ignition. With his hand on the key, he paused, then turned to look at her. "Whenever we're together, I can feel your tension. I'm sure Keri can too. How do we resolve it?"

"I have no idea what there is to resolve,"

she reminded him. "I'm sorry if being around me makes you uncomfortable, but we're just going to have to put up with each other."

"I didn't say that! I want to be around you. You're the one who keeps pulling away."

"You expect something from me that I can't give," she whispered. "You want me to have some kind of response to you, to our past, but I don't remember any of it. There's a world of incidents that shaped our lives together, and I don't have any recollection of them."

He sighed and gripped the wheel with both hands. "I'm not making demands on you."

"Not verbally. But in your attitude, your manner. There's this whole undercurrent of expectation that I just can't handle."

He nodded. "Fair enough. I don't know how to change it, since I do remember."

He leaned over, and she smelled the spicy scent of his cologne. He touched her chin. "I remember the walks along Lake Huron when we were dating, the way you like to eat ice cream so slowly it melts before it's gone, the way you look when you get out of the shower with your hair still damp at the temples. I can still smell the baby wash you use and the night cream you put on your face before bed. Your peach pajamas that make you look like you're fifteen are still at the house. What am I supposed to do with all those memories, Eve? You tell me."

She looked down at her hands, but the motion just pressed the flesh of her chin deeper into his fingers. "I don't have any answers. Only questions. You said you wanted to start over, but it feels like you're trying to pick up where we left off. I've forgotten the directions to that location."

His hand dropped away, and she wanted to call back the warmth of his fingers. Fickle, fickle. No wonder Nick didn't know which way was up. She didn't know what she wanted herself.

"So we act like we're strangers?"

She faced him then, chin up, anger chilling her words. "We *are* strangers, Nick. We only met a few days ago."

The muscles in his jaw clenched. He faced the dash without another word and twisted the key in the steering column. The engine sprang to life, and he gunned the SUV away from the curb.

Eve leaned her cheek against the cool glass. Right now, she had to admit her attraction to the man. If she remembered all the history between them, maybe all she'd feel would be dislike. She'd never quite understood how love could turn to hate.

Had she felt hatred, loathing the man who had shared her bed and her life? If so, maybe she didn't want to remember.

Nick parked the SUV outside the small hotel. The small neon sign read "Rock Harbor Inn." Bree had told Eve that the building was a French trading post in the town's glory days in the 1800s. Her gaze swept the vehicles parked in the lot, but she didn't know what Patti was driving.

"Let's see if she's here," Nick said, opening his door.

Eve's legs felt heavy. Confrontation seemed unpleasant, though she knew it was necessary. She was willing to do anything to avoid baring their many problems in front of a strange judge.

Nick's fingers touched hers, then he drew away and an impassive expression replaced the concern that had flickered in his eyes. No doubt he was trying to honor her request to forget their past. She tried to feel gratitude for his effort, but a chill swept through her, and she had to resist grabbing his hand and hanging on.

She could tackle this. Lifting her head, she walked briskly toward the entrance. Nick reached for the door, but she jerked it open herself and stepped inside. The air smelled fragrant with some kind of spicy candle. The warm colors of the interior added to the welcoming aura.

The clerk at the desk put down her magazine and smiled. Before she could ask how she could help them, Eve stepped to the desk. "Is Patti, uh . . ." She glanced at Nick.

"Patti Ostergard." He supplied the name with a quick glance.

The clerk wiggled the computer mouse, looked at the screen, then reached for the phone. "Who should I say is here to see her?"

"Her sister," Eve said.

The clerk paused with upraised brows. She looked as though she wanted to ask why Eve didn't know her own sister's name, but she dialed the phone anyway. "Ms. Ostergard? Your sister is in the lobby." She listened. "I'll tell her." She hung up the phone. "She'll be right down."

Thank you, God. Eve had been afraid Patti would refuse to see her. "Thanks."

"Sit down over here." Nick walked toward a seating area with a sofa, two chairs, and a coffee table. "I'll run across the street and get you a peppermint latte."

Eve took the terra-cotta-colored sofa while Nick darted out the door. Through the big windows, she watched him jog across the street. A large vase of flowers on the coffee table hid her from the lobby. Her sight of the elevator was unobstructed.

Her fingers tapped on the chenille fabric until she realized what she was doing and stilled her restlessness. Classical music played softly from hidden speakers, and she found herself humming along. What was the song? Bach's Mass in B Minor.

A smile lifted her lips. She remembered the title! Maybe she should listen to more classical music. Her fingers tapped out the melody. Could she play the piano? She'd have to ask Nick.

Sitting here was driving her crazy. Was Patti deliberately keeping her waiting? She stood and stretched and walked through the lobby toward the restroom. Stepping into the bathroom, she ran a comb through her hair and slicked on some lipstick. She went into a stall for paper to blot it. She heard the door open.

Steps moved across the tile. They were heavy for a woman, and Eve turned her head from her downward position and caught a glimpse of movement. A hard hand shoved her, and she nearly toppled into the toilet. Her stall door slammed shut, and she caught a glimpse of a man's shoes under the door. A finger poked through the broken lock hole and held the door closed.

"Don't think you've escaped me, Eve," a harsh whisper said. "Our fun is about to begin. Only your sacrifice will accomplish its purpose."

Eve shrank away from the door. Her tongue worked, but only clicking sounds emerged from her dry throat. Her gaze stayed on the man's finger. She glanced at the toilet. She could climb on top of it and look down on him, see his face. Or she could slide under the sidewall to another stall and run out.

But her limbs refused to connect with either idea. Then the finger disappeared, and she heard his steps run across the floor. The door whooshed open, and she felt the emptiness of the room.

She threw open the stall door and ran to the exit. The hallway was empty.

Still shaking, she walked on wobbly legs back to the sitting area where Nick stood holding two lattes, looking around for her.

He saw her and started toward her. "What's wrong?"

"Gideon was here." She collapsed onto the sofa.

"What?"

"In the bathroom. He trapped me in the stall." She told him what Gideon had said.

"Did you see him?"

"Just his shoes. And his finger." Hysterical laughter bubbled in her throat.

Nick sat beside her and shoved the coffee into her hand. "Take a sip. You're shaking. I'll go look for him."

"No!" She grabbed his hand. "Don't leave me."

"He'll get away, Eve."

"He already has." She sipped her latte. "He wanted to scare me, not hurt me. Not yet."

"I want him." Nick walked to the window and looked out. "Just tourists out there. Any one of them could be Gideon." He took out his phone and made the call. "Fraser, come to the Rock Harbor Inn. Gideon was here and threatened Eve." He put away his phone and joined her on the sofa. "You're safe now."

She leaned against his strong shoulder. "How do we catch him, Nick? He never seems to make a mistake."

"He will." Nick pressed a kiss against her temple. "Where's Patti?" He hesitated. "I wonder if she has some connection with him. She's taking a long time. Maybe to allow him time to threaten you."

"She's my sister, Nick."

"She's not a good person. I think you've

figured that out by now. I wouldn't put anything past her."

Eve shuddered. "I don't believe she'd do something like that."

"You don't remember all the things she's done. She stole money and used it for drugs once. She's capable of anything, especially when she's high. I'm going to have Fraser check her out."

Eve nodded. "This was a mistake to come here. She probably won't listen anyway."

The light on the elevator flickered from floor 4 to 3 to 2. Without realizing she'd moved, Eve was standing with her hands clenched together. Fear gripped her throat, suffocating terror like she'd felt in the car before Bree had found her.

Nothing here should evoke this kind of terror. She forced her gaze to sweep the lobby, but the elevator drew her back. The danger would come from there. Flashes of memory assaulted her: the dark hallway of a familiar building, the scent of peanut butter, a weightlessness of white feathers.

She stumbled back against the sofa, then put down her latte before she could drop it.

Nick sprang to his feet. "Eve, what is it?"

"I don't know," she whispered. "The elevator . . ."

He turned to look at the elevator as the

doors dinged and began to open. Eve saw a flash of red, the color of blood. Her vision wavered, and she whirled.

Nick grabbed her arm and hauled her to his chest. "It's okay," he murmured in her hair.

Though the safety of his arms calmed her, Eve pulled away and turned her head to the elevator door. Her sister stepped out, wearing a red sweater. Eve peered past Patti, but the elevator doors closed on an empty space. Why was her heart rate still ratcheted up to Mach speeds?

"Eve?" Patti cast an uneasy glance around the room. "You look like you're about to faint."

"I . . . I'm fine." Eve sank onto the sofa, the flashes of insight gone. She felt stupid. There was nothing here.

Patti advanced into the sitting area. "What do you want?"

Eve tried to collect her scattered thoughts. "I'm your sister, Patti. I'd like to be your friend too."

"Yeah, right. You don't even remember me."

Eve chose to believe the hurt in Patti's blue eyes was genuine, and she reached for her sister's hand. "Sit down a minute."

Patti sat on the sofa's edge beside Eve.

"Spit it out and let's get it over with."

"Give her a break, Patti," Nick said. "You don't have to prove you're a hard case."

Eve waited for the explosion, but instead Patti laughed. "I've always liked you, Nick. You don't pull any punches."

Eve rushed in to take advantage of the broken ice. "Patti, we both only want what's best for Keri. I'd like to see us work together to resolve this."

"Like we'd ever agree to what's best for Keri."

"Would you like to see her? Come to dinner tonight?"

Patti stared at her. "You're serious?"

"My mom's veal stew has been cooking all afternoon," Nick said.

Patti's face relaxed. She twisted a lock of lank hair between her fingers. "You know to get me where it hurts, Nicky."

"It's her favorite," Nick told Eve with a smile.

A flare of resentment made Eve grit her teeth. Her ex-husband knew her own sister better than she did. And how had he even remembered that sweet little detail? Patti had been gone for two years.

"How about we head over there now?" Nick stood and put his hands in his pockets.

Patti rose and looked down at Eve. "Okay.

But no pressure."

Eve's gaze locked with Nick's. She knew he planned to try to see if Patti had anything to do with Gideon.

20

The swans' voices lifted in a melody that raised Gideon's spirit to God. He closed his eyes and drank in the magic of their song. The perfect summer day ministered to his soul where he sat on a grassy knoll in the sunshine.

Miranda sat in a wheelchair beside him. He'd moved her to the Rock Harbor nursing home, and she seemed to love the sunshine. She was strapped in and her head was in a headrest. Her blue eyes blinked slowly.

He averted his eyes from her scars. "Isn't it lovely, Miranda? I was thinking about the geocaching tournament coming up. I was trying to think about what I want to hide. I think I'll do a treasure hunt and lay about five clues that lead to the big cache." His face tingled at the thought.

A nurse approached from across the lawn. "I need to take Miranda back inside," she said. "The doctor would like to speak with you."

Gideon drew back. "I don't have time today."

"He's rather insistent," the nurse said gently. "It won't take long." She nodded back toward the building. "In fact, here he comes now."

Gideon stood and mentally armed himself as the nurse wheeled his wife away. The doctor's grim expression lightened with a forced smile. "Hello, Doctor," Gideon said.

"I thought I might find you out here." The doctor waited until the wheelchair was out of sight. "I'm afraid your wife has been declining since you brought her here."

Gideon stared at the doctor until the man looked away. "She's fine," he said. "It's temporary. She's had these episodes before, and she'll rally."

"I'm afraid not this time." The doctor hesitated. "I ran some routine tests. She's got leukemia too."

Gideon closed his eyes and sank back onto the lawn chair. "No," he said. His weak voice disgusted him. Miranda deserved a strong defender.

"She only has another month or so."

"No!" Gideon jumped up with his fists balled. "What about treatment?"

"She's too weak to withstand any chemo or bone marrow transplant. The treatment would likely shorten her life even more. I'm sorry." The doctor laid his hand on Gideon's arm.

Gideon shook it off. His wife would not die. They would all see the miracle that would happen. He would take Eve, and Miranda would rally.

Patti was silent in the backseat. Nick cleared his throat. "Hey, Patti, where've you been all this time, anyway?"

"Around."

"Where? You seem to be off the drugs now. How'd you do that?"

"Some friends helped me. Which was more than you ever did."

"We tried," he said. "You have to want to get well before it happens. I just wondered how you got to that point."

"No, you're trying to figure out who Keri's father is. Well, I'm not saying. So drop it."

Nick waggled his eyebrows at Eve. Patti wouldn't tell them anything. He parked the SUV outside the lighthouse. When they got out, he could hear the children squealing and shouting in the backyard.

"Go on in, and I'll get Keri," he told the women.

Eve nodded and ushered Patti to the front door. He stepped around back.

"Watch me, Keri!" Davy shouted. He ran along the sand and hurtled himself into a cartwheel, but his feet didn't go very far up.

"Good try," Nick shouted.

The little boy gave a delighted grin. "She can't do it yet. She's too little. But I'm big."

"You're quite the little man," Nick said. He rubbed the boy's head as he passed. "With you showing her, Keri will learn it in no time."

"I'll teach her." Davy turned to try another one.

"You practice. I need to take her to see her mommy a little while." He scooped up Keri, sand and all. "Hey, baby girl, let's go inside."

"No!" She wiggled to get down.

"Your mommy wants you." Holding her over his head until she squealed and laughed, he crossed his eyes at her, then cradled her against his chest. "And Grammy made you cookies."

"Tookies?" She quit fighting.

Nick carried her onto the back porch, then brushed the sand off both of them before stepping inside.

His mother was still working at the stove when he walked through. "I can't believe you're letting that woman see her," she said, shooting him a glare that usually made him quail.

He snagged a cookie for Keri and himself. "It's for the best, Mom." He didn't want to argue with her. Stepping through the doorway into the living room, he listened, but there was no fighting. In fact, there was no talking.

Patti sat on the sofa, and Eve sat opposite her on the armchair. Patti was staring at her hands, and Eve looked out the window. Both looked up with relief lighting their eyes when he arrived.

"Here she is," he said in a voice he recognized as too hearty. "Keri, this is Aunt Patti. She's kind of your mommy too." He set her on the floor.

"Kind of?" Patti's eyes narrowed, and venom spread over her face. She opened her mouth, then shut it again when he shook his head. The smile she turned on Keri didn't reach her eyes. "Hi, sweetie. Come see me."

Keri hung back, her eyes wide and questioning. She backed up until she bumped against Nick's legs. "Where Mommy?" Spotting Eve, she ran to her and climbed into her lap. "Mommy," she said, her gaze still on Patti.

"Let's go see your Aunt Patti," Eve said. Carrying Keri, she moved to the sofa beside her sister.

"Would you like some candy?" Patti asked, rummaging in her purse. She pulled out a Jolly Rancher.

"She's not old enough for hard candy," Eve said, intercepting the candy when Keri reached for it. Keri began to cry, and Eve jiggled her legs. "Eat your cookie."

"I can say whether she's old enough or not," Patti snapped.

"You don't have any experience," Nick told her. "Eve knows what's appropriate."

"I'm her mother. I should be able to say if she can have candy or not." Patti took another piece out of her purse and dangled it in front of the little girl.

Eve stood with Keri in her arms. Keri started to cry. "This isn't going to work. Patti, you have to always think about what's best for Keri, not about who's got the most power."

Nick could see the meeting going south in a hurry. "Sit down," he whispered to Eve. He pointed to the chair.

Carrying the squalling child, she went back to the armchair. "Hush, Keri," she said. "You've got a cookie."

Keri threw the cookie onto the coffee table. "Want tandy!"

Nick picked up the cookie. "That's enough, Keri," he said, his voice stern.

She sniffled with her gaze on him. Her wailing stopped, and she took the cookie he held out. Her eyes wide, she watched him go back to his chair.

He decided the firm, direct approach would work best. "Patti, we asked you here for two reasons. We want you to get to know Keri, and we'd like to find a way to settle this out of court. How about if we agree to liberal visitation? How often would you like to see her?"

"How often would *you* like to see her?" Patti countered. "I'd let you have liberal rights to her too. Maybe every other weekend?"

"We're not giving her up," Eve said. "You don't even know how to take care of her."

"You don't know any more than I do. I bet you don't remember her favorite snack or which toy she likes best. When the judge hears you can't remember anything, I'll be awarded custody."

"You don't know those things either," Eve pointed out.

"I remember," Nick put in. "How will you

get around that?"

"You're not married," Patti pointed out. "That's not going to help you."

"I'm her father. The only one she's ever known. Keri's never even met this great guy who's so ready to throw his wife over for you. Who is he?"

Patti snapped the latch on her purse open and shut several times. Nick could almost see the wheels turning.

"None of your business," she said finally. "You'll meet him at the right time."

"He's a real stand-up guy if he lets you do all the dirty work." Nick had disdain in his voice. "A real man would help you."

Patti unwrapped the Jolly Rancher she held without looking at him. "He's a great guy. You don't know him." She popped the candy into her mouth.

"But we'd like to." Eve's voice was gentle. "Could we meet him?"

"No! He wants to stay out of the picture until it's all over."

Nick didn't like the sound of this guy. What a weasel.

"Would you like to hold Keri?" Eve stood again and approached the sofa.

Patti put her purse on the floor and held out her arms, but her hands shook. "Come see your mama, Keri."

Keri's small brow wrinkled, and she looked up at Eve. Nick wanted to slap someone. Patti was determined to push her own way. He and Eve locked gazes, and he saw the same awareness in her eyes. They should have kept Patti as far away from Keri as possible.

Eve settled the little girl on Patti's lap and sat beside them. Patti jiggled the child awkwardly on her knees. "Can you say *Daddy,* Keri?"

Keri's head swiveled toward Nick. "Daddy," she said. She reached her arms for him.

Patti exhaled. "He's not your daddy, not your real daddy."

"Daddy. My daddy," Keri said, pooching out her lower lip.

Nick had had enough. He stood and scooped his daughter out of Patti's arms. "This was a mistake," he said. "You don't even know the proper way to behave around children, Patti. I thought maybe you'd grown up the last few years, but I was wrong. We'll have to deal with this in court."

Patti blinked, then bit her lip. She reached down and grabbed her purse. "The judge will give her back to me. You'll see." Casting an angry glance at her sister, she rushed to the door, slamming it behind her.

■ ■ ■ ■

"Have another piece of *tiropita,*" Rhea urged Eve. "You too, Nicky."

The darkness outside the kitchen windows made the bright kitchen seem even more welcoming, and Eve's full tummy contributed to her sense of well-being in spite of how badly it went with Patti. She refused to stay for dinner, so Nick had run her back to the hotel. Oliver had emerged from the basement, following the aromas of Rhea's meal.

"I'm stuffed, Mom," Nick said.

Eve wondered how many family dinners like this she couldn't remember. From the familiarity Nick's parents showed, she would guess there were a lot.

"I'll get the kids ready for bed," Bree said. She lifted Keri from the booster seat and took Davy's hand. "I'll be right back."

"Thanks," Eve called after her.

"How's our Jane Doe coming?" Cyril asked Oliver.

Oliver was on his third helping of stew. "Almost ready to paint. After dinner I will show you. She's quite lovely."

Oliver looked totally drained — as well he should when he finished the thing in record time. Eve wondered if he'd had more then two or three hours of sleep a night.

"Let's go see her." Nick half rose, but Oliver waved him back down.

"Not until I have some dessert. Your mother has cooked in the kitchen all day, and the least we can do is appreciate her labor. The meals I get at the bed-and-breakfast are not nearly so excellent."

The doorbell sounded, and Bree called from upstairs. "I'll get it." She passed the kitchen and returned with Deputy Montgomery in tow.

"Sorry to interrupt your supper," Montgomery said.

"Have an almond biscuit." Bree grabbed the plate and offered them to the officer, who grinned and took one.

"I was hoping to find all of you here," Montgomery mumbled around his mouthful of biscuit. "Town is crawling with cops. I've been sent to ask you something, eh? I don't agree with it myself, but I'm just the messenger, so don't shoot me." He glanced at Cyril. "You tell them yet?"

Cyril shook his head.

"A lead on Gideon's threat today?" Nick asked.

Cyril looked down at his plate. "I was just getting to it," he said. When he looked up, his face was set and strained. "Son, you aren't going to like this, but it's the only way we can go with this. We want to use Eve as a decoy to flush out Gideon."

Eve came forward in her chair, moved first by shock, then by surprise that someone hadn't come up with a plan like this before now. She gripped her water glass. The idea wasn't terribly far-fetched.

"No!" Nick slammed his fist on the table, and the dinnerware rattled. "That's not going to happen. No way. I can't believe you'd even ask."

Cyril spread his hands. "What else have we got, Son? Gideon's a phantom. He'll just keep killing."

"I'll find him. I'm not risking Eve."

"I'll do it," Eve said, projecting as much confidence into her voice as possible.

"You will not! I won't allow it."

"You have no say in it." Eve tried to say the words with gentleness, but Nick flinched. "I'm sorry, but I can't let this guy keep on going just because I'm afraid." The water glass shook in her hand, and she put it back on the table.

"You don't get it," Nick said. "He's following a plan, a script. I think when he gets through it, he'll start over at the beginning again. With you."

"What are you talking about?"

"The passage from Proverbs. A few more deaths, and he'll make his move on you to be the first in a new round."

Eve's hands shook, but she clasped them together. "If that's the case, I've got some time. I'm not going to just sit and wait for him to show up when he's good and ready. Maybe I could even save someone's life."

Nick's eyes flashed, and he glanced to his dad. "What did you have in mind?" he asked.

"The geocaching event is this weekend."

Bree nodded. "I need to get my team assembled. Eve could be part of my team, and she'd be visible."

"Me? I'm not very good at geocaching."

"Absolutely not," Nick said. "She's got a killer after her. The last thing she needs to do is be in the middle of his territory, where he can pick her off whenever he wants to."

"I'm tired of looking over my shoulder," Eve shot back. "And like I said, it's not your call."

Kade held up his hand. "Truce, you guys. Look, Nick, she wouldn't be alone. There will be a whole team, with hundreds of people combing the woods. If Gideon makes a move, we'll grab him."

Nick lifted his eyebrows. "How would you

feel if he were after Bree?" Kade looked down. "See, you'd feel the same way."

"It's hard not to worry when you love someone," Kade agreed. "You can come along too, Nick. Keep an eye on her."

"I don't want her anywhere near the forest."

"Stop talking about me like I'm not here," Eve snapped. "I don't know what a normal, fun day is. I won't live my life afraid of my own shadow." She leaned back in her chair, her shoulders sagging. "This has to end, Nick. I'll do whatever it takes."

"I'm working on it, Eve."

She looked up at Montgomery. "You can go back and tell the police I'll cooperate. Tell me what to do."

"She'll have all of us to protect her," Oliver said. "I'll offer my eyes and ears too."

Montgomery nodded. "I'll be back once we have it figured out, eh?" He grabbed another biscuit. "Good cookie," he said before he walked off.

"I'm sorry if I'm out of line," Kade said. "But Bree and I have had some experience. Can we help?"

"I don't see how," Nick said.

"He's left these bodies at geocaches, right?" Bree asked. "Kade and I know a lot about the sport. We might see something you've missed in the evidence."

Nick stared at them. "Why not? I've got nothing new to go on by myself. What do you think, Dad?"

Cyril cleared his throat. "I've got copies of the file in the trunk. Let me go get them."

"While he's getting the files, you want to see our Jane Doe?" Oliver asked. "She's coming along."

Nick's chair scraped on the floor as he stood. "You bet."

Eve didn't want to see the woman, but she followed the rest down the narrow steps to the basement. In the brightly lit room, the halogen beams spotlighted the victim's head.

Eve heard Nick gasp before she really focused on the face. The walls of the basement wavered as she stared into her own face. "It's me," she whispered.

"Nicky, you should know better," Rhea scolded. "Bringing your wife down here. Let's go have some tea, Eve." She grasped Eve's arm.

Eve pulled gently out of her grip. Fascination pulled her closer to the worktable.

Oliver had finished the sculpting, and the bust stared sightlessly toward a dark corner of the basement. It had to be painted yet, but there was no mistaking the woman's resemblance to Eve.

"It's not you, not really," Oliver said. "Her nose isn't as finely sculpted as yours. And she's older. I'd say by ten years or so. Her hair is darker too."

"How do you know?" Rhea asked. She put a comforting arm around Eve.

"I found a strand inside the skull. Of course, there's no telling where it came from on her head. If it was on the underside, it could be darker than the hair that got sunlight. But I used my best judgment."

Eve walked around the stainless steel table, looking at her own face, feeling disembodied. If they didn't find Gideon, she might someday be on a table just like this one. The morbid thought made her stomach heave.

She bolted for the stairs.

21

Eve rooted through several folders, scattering their contents across the table. The photographs of the murders made her wince and avert her eyes, but she scanned the reports. If she was going to put her life on the line, she was going to see it all and know what she was dealing with.

"This was his first listing on the geocaching site." Cyril pulled a photo and report from the stack.

"How long has he been killing?" Kade asked.

Cyril handed Eve the report. "We thought it was about four months. But we know he was only *telling* us about his kills for that long. Now we know he's killed before. The body you found, Bree, is at least five years old."

Bree read through the report over Eve's shoulder. "The first woman was found floating in a pond in Bay City."

Nick nodded. "Gideon identified himself pretty quickly on the geocaching site. His user name was Gideon right from the start."

"Did you try tracking him by computer tracing?" Oliver asked. He sat opposite Kade, nursing his fatigue with a cup of hot tea.

"Yep." Cyril frowned and leaned back in his chair. "He's got some fancy scrambler on his system. It looks like it's coming from overseas, but we know he's right here in Michigan."

Bree frowned. "Do you have someone watch the geocaching site daily for any new posts related to these murders?"

"Not daily but occasionally," Nick said. "I check them myself weekly. I haven't looked in a few days though."

"Does he mutilate every victim?" Kade asked.

"He takes the face and some other body part." Cyril wrinkled his nose. "The coroner believes he does the amputations while the victims are still alive."

"Ick." Bree put her hand on her midsection. "This guy is so sick. It's always women too."

"Blonde women," Eve said. "Ones who look like me."

"What do we know about this first

woman?" Kade took the report from Eve and looked it over.

"Sophie Tallmadge," Nick said. "The clue was from the Koran. It read, 'Then Musa cast down his staff and lo! it swallowed up the lies they told.' "

"Lying?" Oliver asked. "Do we know what she lied about?"

Cyril shrugged. "We heard she testified in a trial about the defendant spending the night in question with her. Seems she perjured herself."

"All the women have some connection to dancing." Nick slid a picture of Sophie to Eve. You recognize her, Eve?"

Eve studied the woman's face, then shook her head. "Sorry." Some help she was going to be. This might be a mistake. She moved to the next report. "How about victim number two?"

"We found her a couple of months later, but animals had gotten to the body and all we had were bones."

"Has she been identified?" Eve asked.

Cyril nodded. "We thought it was you for a while. I put Oliver's bust out on the news as soon as I knew it wasn't you, and her mother identified her as Melissa Howard."

"What was the clue for that one?" Kade asked.

Nick read from the file. "The clue reads, 'For pride is the beginning of sin, and he that hath it shall pour out abomination: and therefore the Lord brought upon them strange calamities, and overthrew them utterly.' " He looked up. "The same as the one he left for you."

"What was missing?" Bree asked.

"All we had were bones, so we aren't sure. We suspect the eyes were taken maybe. And of course the face," Cyril said.

"How do you know for sure it was Gideon who attacked Eve?" Kade asked.

Nick's mouth tightened. "He left his calling card."

"Which is?"

Cyril frowned. "I'd rather not say. It's something we're holding back for identification."

"It's a peanut butter sandwich," Eve blurted out. She closed her eyes, and she could smell peanut butter.

They all stared at her. "How do you know that?" Nick asked.

Eve rubbed her forehead. "I don't know, but that's right, isn't it?"

"Yes," Nick said, shooting a swift glance toward his father. "But that goes no further than this room. It's the one clue we're holding back."

"Are you remembering anything else?" Cyril asked.

Eve wanted to bolt, but she stayed in her chair and shook her head. She could get through this. "Who's next?"

"Yvette Crandall. Her hands were cut off. And the face, of course." The women covered their mouths. "Sorry," Cyril added.

"Holy cow," Kade said softly.

Eve wasn't sure she'd be able to sleep tonight. "What's her story?"

"I found her when I went out geocaching with my friend Zack." Nick glanced at Eve. "He used to be our neighbor — German Baptist, wears black. Does that ring a bell at all?"

She shook her head. "I can't even remember what our neighborhood looks like."

"Clue?" Bree asked.

Cyril grimaced. " 'Oh, ye! Think ye that Incal will accept the blood of innocent animals for your crimes? Whose sayeth this doth lie! Incal, God, will never take blood of anything, nor symbol of any sort which placeth an innocent in a guilty one's stead!' "

"What the heck?" Kade asked. "Where's that from?"

"*Dweller on Two Planets* by Phylos the Tibetan."

"What religion?" Bree asked.

"New Age," Cyril said. "Our guy gets around."

"What was her sin?" Eve asked. She wasn't sure she wanted to know.

"She had her cat put down when she moved to take a new job. At least that's what we make of the reference to innocent animals. Again, she took ballet as a kid and continued with it as a hobby."

Bree crossed her arms. "That's just wrong. She should have taken the cat to a shelter."

"Evidently Gideon thought so too."

Eve rested her hand on her chin as she thought about it. "So he's punishing women for what he calls a sin and using different religious texts for justification."

"Yeah, that seems to be the tie-in," Nick said.

"How about the next victim?" Kade asked.

"The bones Bree and Eve found. No identity yet, though now we know this one might actually be the first victim."

"Clues?" Bree asked. "I can't remember."

" 'The heart is deceitful above all things, and desperately wicked.' " Cyril leaned back in the chair.

"So he probably took her heart," Bree said.

Cyril agreed. "Knife nicks around the rib

cage would suggest that."

Kade rubbed his forehead. "And the one he just killed. Hannah Pelton?"

" 'Her feet go down to death, her steps lay hold of hell.' Proverbs 5:5," Cyril said. "Pretty obvious with her. Her friends said she had sex with some guy she just met in the parking lot before she disappeared.' "

"Could Gideon be someone who teaches world religions?" Oliver asked. "He knows a lot of different religious books."

"Maybe," Cyril said. "He's what we call a missionary killer. He's on a mission to rid the world of sinners, ones that he picks out for some reason."

"He could catch every one of us in something if he looked long enough," Bree said. "Since the women he chooses are all blondes, is he picking the victims, then watching to see what he can convict them of?"

Nick was flipping to the next page, but he stopped. "There's an idea. I assumed he identified the sin first, but you might be right, Bree."

Eve swallowed the bile in her throat. "What about our Jane Doe? Why is Gideon only now showing her to us?"

"Maybe she doesn't fit the mold in some way?" Bree suggested.

"She looks the same as the others," Cyril pointed out. "And she suffered like the others."

Eve couldn't think about it anymore. She rose. "I'm going to bed."

Built in the late 1800s, the grand old courthouse was constructed of dressed fieldstone. Eve's pumps echoed on the polished marble floor of the hallway. Anu had kept the children so Bree could come along. Her sneakers squeaked in time with Eve's heels. Nick walked on Eve's other side, and his parents followed him. Eve tried not to notice the way his hand brushed hers as though he wanted to hold it.

At least they hadn't been forced to bring Keri. Eve had been afraid the judge would want to talk with the little girl. Fortunately, Keri was too young.

Ronja met them at the door to the courtroom. "Smile," she whispered. "Act confident and in control."

Eve felt anything but confident, but she managed to put on a weak smile. Her lawyer held the door open for her. The smell of old wood and leather felt comforting somehow. Eve stopped at the last row of seats and looked around. The imposing judge's bench loomed over the room, but at least it was empty. Patti wasn't here yet either.

Ronja led Nick and Eve to a table and chairs while Bree and Nick's parents took seats behind the bar. Eve rubbed her cold hands together, even though the action might betray how scared she was. She pulled out her chair and sat down, then sprang to her feet as Patti entered with her attorney. The sharp, put-together African-American woman had penetrating eyes capable of skewering a person. The attorney's competence made Eve clench her hands together. She guessed Patti had brought her in from Detroit or Milwaukee.

Nick leaned over and whispered, "Where'd she get the money for a big gun like that? She has to be costing a fortune."

"Maybe her man is loaded," Eve whispered back. She smiled at her sister, but Patti looked away with her chin hiked in the air.

Patti and her attorney were barely seated before the bailiff entered. "All rise," he said. "The Honorable Judge Haskins presiding."

Eve bolted to her feet and forced her hands to relax at her sides. A tall, thin man entered the courtroom. His black robe flapped around him like wings on a giant bat. His scowl made her shiver. Talking to a judge when he had a wild hair about something might not be a good idea.

"Be seated," the bailiff called.

The judge riffled through the papers in front of him. The echo of a cough and a foot shuffling made Eve even more tense. How long would it take for him to decide to listen to them? Ronja's smile reassured her, but Eve caught herself tapping her foot.

The judge finally put down his glasses and pressed his fingers together in a steeple. "You're Patti Ostergard?"

Patti nodded jerkily. "Yes, Your Honor."

"Can you explain to this court why you have not had any contact with your daughter for the past two years?"

Patti tucked a lank lock of hair behind her ear. "I have no good excuse, Your Honor. I was young and immature. While I was away, I grew up and realized my daughter needed me. I want to make it up to her."

The judge nodded, and his gaze went to Eve. "You're the adoptive parents?"

"We are, Your Honor." Eve stood. Nick bolted up beside her. "We'd like to follow through with the adoption we started."

"You're divorced now, according to my file. Is that true?"

Nick answered. "Unfortunately, yes, Your Honor. But we're working on ironing out our difficulties."

The judge harrumphed. He shuffled his papers again. "You didn't finish the adoption proceedings, and you had good reason to do so. Why not?"

"We'd intended to, Your Honor," Eve said, choosing her words with care. "We started the procedure six months ago. Then our marriage began to struggle, and we never followed through. That was a mistake. Keri is our baby. We love her very much."

She took hope in the way the judge smiled and nodded. He had to see they'd been the responsible party. They'd taken care of Keri when no one else would.

"Eve can't even remember my daughter, Your Honor!" Patti bolted out of her chair and pointed her finger at Eve. "She has amnesia. She's wording things so you can't tell, but ask her. Ask if she even remembers the day Keri was born."

Ronja bolted to her feet. "Objection, Your Honor. Hearsay, and besides, it has no bearing on this case."

"I think I'd like to hear this," the judge said. "I've heard rumors to that effect. Could one of you illuminate this court?"

Eve closed her eyes and prayed for strength. She'd known Patti would likely bring this up, but it seemed so cruel that she'd held on to a tiny glimmer of hope that her sister wouldn't put her through this.

"Judge, if I may answer?" Nick said. When the judge nodded, he rushed on. "A serial killer targeted my wife. She barely escaped with her life and somehow managed to protect our daughter during the attack. Her injuries caused a temporary amnesia, but if you would see her with Keri, you would know her mother's love is still intact. She is a wonderful mother, even in the face of danger and trauma."

"You talking about this Gideon I've heard so much about?" the judge asked.

"Yes, Your Honor."

"You close to finding him?"

"Closer than ever, sir," Cyril called out.

The judge banged his gavel. "There will be no outbursts, or I'll order the courtroom cleared."

Rhea tugged on her husband's arm, and he sat back down.

"What about danger to the child?" The judge closed his folder.

"We have police protection."

Judge Haskins directed his gaze to Patti. "I'm not convinced you're a better choice. The file says you abandoned your daughter at a day care when she was two weeks old. Just never went back to get her."

Patti hung her head. "That's right, Your

Honor. It's a poor choice that haunts me."

"How do I know you won't do it again?"

Patti lifted her head, and her eyes held a shimmer of tears. "You don't. But I know. I'd do anything for my daughter."

Good performance. Eve's cynicism grew. Patti was no more ready to put Keri first than she'd ever been. She hoped the judge would see through her claims.

"I'm not going to make a decision today. I'm going to order an in-home study of both of you and wait for that report." He banged the gavel on the desk. "Adjourned."

Eve glanced up into Nick's eyes. "Thanks for sticking up for me today," she whispered. Tenderness stirred in her heart, catching her by surprise. Was it possible to learn to love this man? She'd like to believe that.

"You would have done the same for me." He squeezed her hand.

His parents and Bree joined them at the table.

"That went well, I think," Rhea said. She hugged Eve. "It will be okay."

Ronja gathered her papers. "She's right. I think you made a good impression on the judge."

"I hope so," Eve said.

Patti stopped at their table. "I knew he would believe me," she said. "Why fight it,

Eve? You're just going to get hurt. The court always rules in favor of the real mother."

"Then Eve will retain custody," Rhea snapped. "She's Keri's real mother. And what century are you living in? The court strips rights away from parents all the time. Don't think the judge bought your tearful act. He's seen better actresses than you come through his courtroom."

Patti flushed and ignored the older woman. She shook her finger in Eve's face. "You can't keep her away from me."

"Neither of us is going to look like a prize, Patti. Have you thought of that?" Eve asked. "I'm living with friends, and you're living at a hotel with no visible means of support. Where are you getting your money for this, anyway? The social service worker is going to ask those kinds of hard questions. You'd better be ready for them."

Patti's confident smile twitched. "You'd better be ready to turn my daughter over to me. I won't be denied my rights."

"Do you think she'd try to take Keri and run if this goes badly for her?" Eve asked, watching her sister's stiff shoulders.

"Over my dead body," Rhea said fiercely. She hugged Nick and Eve. "We've got to get going, kids. Cyril will turn around and come right back as soon as he takes me home. I hate to go, but the nursing home called about Mother. They've been adjusting her Alzheimer's medication."

Patti turned and flounced away. Rhea and Cyril followed as if they were making sure she wasn't coming back.

22

The cool breeze hit Eve's face, but nothing stopped the burning in her cheeks. They were in danger of losing Keri because of her sin. How could she have torn her family apart for another man? What kind of person was she? Maybe she didn't want to get her memory back — not if it meant facing all kinds of sordidness.

Holding on to the handrail, she raced down the stone steps to the water. She kicked off her shoes when she reached the shoreline and let her toes sink into the cold sand.

"Eve?" Nick's voice came from behind her.

She turned and saw him coming across the beach. "Just leave me alone," she told him.

He slogged through the sand to her side, stopping about four feet away with his hands in his pockets. "Eve?"

"We're really nothing alike, are we?" Eve was just beginning to realize how different they were. "You're the savior, the rescuer in the darkest hour. You thrive on responsibility. I love music, art, dance. Spontaneity is what I crave, and you long for regimented hours, isn't that right?"

"I thought you couldn't remember."

"I don't. But I'm not blind." She turned her back and stared out over the water. "How can you even want to try again when I might remember my love for another man at any minute?"

"I don't believe you're in love with Will," Nick said. He turned her around to face him. "You only used him to find the courage to tell me you'd had enough." His fingers tipped her chin up.

She didn't resist. When she tasted his minty lips, she knew her heart had never forgotten him. Her soul remembered his strength, his commitment. Her arms went around his neck, and she pressed into his embrace. Her fingers touched the rough stubble on his cheeks, then moved around to the back of his head to become entangled in his thick hair. She closed her eyes and gave herself to the kiss.

His strong arms were a safe haven, her

port in the storm. Nick loved her unconditionally.

He broke the kiss, then trailed his lips across her cheeks, her eyes. "Come to the hotel with me tonight. Let's start over."

The tender yearning in his gaze scorched her, and she was tempted to go with him, to ignore what she'd learned about herself. But she would hate herself tomorrow if more terrible revelations were to come. She couldn't love Nick until she knew she could trust herself. And the only way to know that was to regain her memory.

She pulled away from his embrace and ran for the safety of the house.

Eve tossed and turned on the bed until the clock read 12:05. She was never going to get any rest like this. Maybe some chamomile tea would help her relax. Gracie objected with a loud meow when she moved the kitten off her chest and got up.

Samson's nails clicked on the wood floor as he moved to meet her outside her door. Eve rubbed his ears, then went past him down the stairs and through the silent house to the kitchen. Nick was staying at the hotel with his parents tonight. She thought her rejection had cut especially deep.

She filled the kettle and put it on the

stove. Nights were the worst, when those gossamer memories teased her, flitting so briefly through her thoughts.

At the sound of the whistle, she poured the steaming water into the waiting cup. Setting the kettle onto a cool burner, she picked up her cup and started toward the living room.

The hair raised on the back of her neck. Did she hear something, a slight scratch? She should go get Kade, but she hated to wake him if a squirrel or raccoon had taken up residence on the back porch. Maybe she should call Samson from upstairs. She approached the kitchen's rear door and listened. The only sound was the wind.

She looked at the doorknob, then backed away. What was she thinking? No way was she going to open the door and look. She turned to leave the kitchen, but something about the door bothered her, and she looked back at it. The deadbolt lever was in the wrong position. It hadn't been locked.

She set her cup on the counter and moved to the door to lock it. She heard a whisper of movement behind her, and her danger registered. Before she could turn, an arm came around her waist and pulled her against a man's chest. His other hand clasped her mouth and forced her head back into his neck.

"Hello, Eve. We meet again," the man whispered. "I hope you've been anticipating this as much as I have."

She couldn't see him, but she could feel some cloth over his face where it rested against her cheek. Fear drained the strength from her limbs, moving through her legs and arms with an icy grip. She tried to scream, but nothing made it past his hand over her lips.

The arm tightened around her waist, and his thumb moved to caress her cheek. "So lovely. Your skin is the finest I've ever seen. So much better than the others."

She began to struggle then. Her hands came up to tear at his arm, but she couldn't begin to match his strength.

The arm around her waist moved higher until his hand came around her throat. "A lovely neck. Long and slim. Though we know you're not pure, don't we, Eve? You have to pay for your sin."

She kicked out, kept kicking. Keri was upstairs. Her baby needed her. She would not allow this man to rip her from her daughter. She tore at his arm with renewed vigor, using her nails like talons.

He flinched and swore under his breath. "Enough. We have to go."

Her heels dug into the flooring, but she couldn't get any purchase, and he pulled her as though she weighed nothing. The door rattled, and the cool breeze rushed into the kitchen. Then she was on the threshold and moving out onto the porch. Even grabbing the doorjamb barely slowed her attacker's progress.

A low growl came from the living room, then Samson ran toward them. The man swore again, and his arm relaxed a fraction as he moved to pull the door shut against the dog.

Eve secured her hold on the doorjamb and tried to lurch back into the kitchen, using her strong legs for leverage, but he ripped her fingers free. She heard him kick at the door, trying to close it as the dog's snarls grew closer. But he was too late.

Samson barreled through the door before it latched, then leaped into the air toward them. He came at her attacker with silent intent. The force of the big dog's leap drove Eve and Gideon against the railing. The man's leg lashed out past her, connecting with Samson's flank, but the dog kept on coming. His teeth bared, he sprang toward Gideon.

Gideon released her mouth and threw his arm up to protect his throat as the dog leaped onto him. Eve managed to wrench out of his other arm's grip. She dove to the deck, letting her weight assist her.

A dark blur, dog and man, grappled beside her. Samson snarled again, and Gideon shouted hoarsely. Eve's chest hurt, and she struggled to draw enough air into her lungs.

The dog yelped, and the sound galvanized her into action. "Samson?" She grabbed the rough railing and hauled herself up as she heard someone run across the planks. A dim shadow leaped from the porch into the yard, and she saw a man's stooped form rush away.

"Samson?" she said again. Something squeezed in her chest. The dog had to be all right.

She heard the dog's nails on the boards, then his fur brushed against her. Samson licked her face and whined, but Gideon had vanished. Eve peered into the dark, but the moonlight couldn't penetrate it. He could be anywhere, behind the bushes, skulking in the well house. Samson was still barking and growling, but he pressed close to her legs as though to protect her.

"Good boy." Her voice sounded shaky. "Let's get inside." Her fingers in his collar, she pulled him into the kitchen with her.

She locked the door and threw the deadbolt.

She heard Bree call her name from upstairs, then the floor over her head squeaked as someone moved on it. Sinking to her knees, Eve saw a white feather on the floor and picked it up. Gideon must have dropped it. Samson came to her, and she put her arms around the dog. She thanked God he was okay.

Her eyes widened as memories of another attack assaulted her. She reeled as the onslaught of memories rushed in. Her heart strained against her ribs as terror surged through her veins.

She remembered the night he'd entered her house.

The scent of chili hung in the air. Eve stirred it with hands still shaking from her scare and glanced at the clock. Late again. Just a half hour ago, she gave the signed divorce papers to her lawyer to give to the judge on Monday. Nick had begged for another chance in spite of everything, and she'd thrown caution to the wind and invited him for dinner.

He should have been here an hour ago. The phone rang and she grabbed it when she saw it was Nick. "Where are you?" she demanded.

"I'm not going to make it," he said. "I got a lead on the sniper case, and I have to follow up."

A familiar weariness swept over her. "I see."

"Look, don't be mad, okay? This is important."

She needed to tell him about the man who had followed her onto the elevator at her loft studio, who had touched her arm, then backed her into a corner for several seconds, but Nick didn't care. Maybe she'd call Will and invite him over. He might care.

She ended the call without answering him. She should have been angry, but instead she was numb. Numb and broken. He'd taken all she had to give, and there was nothing left.

She bent her head and pressed her fingers against her closed lids. When she straightened and opened her eyes, the lights flickered, then went out. The room plunged into darkness. Eve's fingers brushed the hot pot of chili. She dropped the spoon and put her burning finger to her mouth.

Nick had promised to get the house rewired, but of course he'd never gotten it done. She probably had too many things going in the kitchen. She moved through the dark house, feeling her way to the utility room. Something tripped her, a doll or a stuffed animal, and she stumbled over it and nearly fell.

A sound caught her ear. Stealthy and furtive. It made her breath catch in her tight throat.

Someone was in the house. The man who tried to grab her in the elevator? She tried to tell herself he couldn't know where she lived. Clear out here in the country, not even a streetlight shining through the window pierced the deep darkness inside the house.

She opened her mouth to call out, then closed it. It would be stupid to give away her location. If she could get to Keri, she would run to the car in the garage and escape.

The blackness watched, waited.

Without warning, he struck. Something went over her head. The struggle went on in silence. His hands, smelling of peanut butter, pressed her against the wall, and duct tape came around her wrists.

With her hands bound with tape, he dragged her onto her back.

"Such a pretty face," he crooned in a distorted voice. "I'll take your eyes first, Eve, and then your face."

Fingers traced her cheekbones, her eye sockets.

She was fighting with a psychopath.

His touch left her, and she sensed him looming over her in the dark. Lying on her back, she coiled her legs to her chest, then kicked out, connecting with his chest. She heard the sound of a table crashing over and the contents toppling to the floor. She scrabbled away on her back. He came at her again. Something pierced her chest, and she cried out. Then a heavy weight crashed against her head. Stars sparkled in her vision, and she felt herself fading.

"Mommy?" Keri's voice.

Her cry had awakened her daughter. Eve fought harder, knowing Keri's life hung in the balance, as well as her own. She flipped to her stomach and tried to crawl away, but he grabbed her right ankle and began to haul her back. With a hard kick of her right leg, she thrust him back and flung out her bound arms. Her hands touched a heavy brass candlestick. It wasn't much of a weapon, but it was all she had.

Grasping it just above its base, she rolled onto her back. She felt rather than saw him approach. Praying for strength, she brought the candlestick down on his shoulder. He fell onto her, and she brought it down again, aiming for where she thought his head was.

The blow landed square and solid, and he went limp. His weight nearly crushed her lungs. She rolled him off her and sat up.

He moved, so she hit him again. And again. Then he lay still. Dead, she hoped.

Something warm and sticky soaked her blouse. She couldn't think, couldn't focus. *Get away. Take the little girl and get away.* Using her teeth, she tore the duct tape away from her wrists. She scooped up the child and ran for the garage door.

Rocking back and forth on the kitchen floor with her arms around the dog, Eve remembered it all. A hand came down on her shoulder, and she screamed.

Red marks stood out in sharp relief against the white flesh of Eve's neck. Nick held out a cup of hot tea. "Drink it," he ordered. He hadn't been here. Again.

Eve started to take the tea, but there was something in her hand. "He dropped this." She held it out.

Nick took it and glanced to Kade. "Any idea what kind of feather this is?"

Kade cinched his bathrobe tighter and took the feather from Nick's fingers. "Too big for a gull. Maybe a swan. I'll find out."

"Now drink your tea," Nick said.

She took it and cupped both hands around it. "Thanks." She took a sip, and a bit of color came back to her cheeks.

"I still think we should call the doctor," Bree said. She carried a blanket with her into the room. Shaking it out, she tucked it around Eve.

"I'm not hurt," Eve said. "Thanks to Samson." The dog's ears flickered at the sound of his name. He padded to the sofa and pressed his nose against Eve's leg. She rubbed his head.

"I'm going to get him the biggest steak in the grocery store," Nick told her. She didn't look up. In fact, she'd barely looked at him since he arrived after the frantic phone call.

It had been all he could do to find a place to park with all the sheriff and police cars lining the road along the lighthouse. Dozens of cops roamed the yard, but all he cared about was getting to Eve. Fraser stopped him outside to tell him he was personally going to guard Eve. Nick managed to thank him even though all he wanted to do was get to his wife.

He sat beside her on the sofa, and she leaned slightly away. His gaze met Bree's, and he saw sympathy there. He had no idea what the undercurrent meant, but he had a feeling he was about to find out.

"I remember, Nick," Eve said, her gaze finally meeting his. "I remember everything." Her voice was remote and as cool as Lake Superior.

"Everything? You mean you have your memory back?"

"Yes. After Samson saved me. You weren't there again, Nick. Not when Gideon first came for me and not tonight." She rose and pulled the blanket around her more closely. "You're never there!"

He flinched at her words. "Eve, I had no way of knowing he would come here tonight."

"It's your job to protect us!" She screamed the words at him. "Instead, Samson had to do it." The dog whined and pressed harder against her leg.

Nick felt the blows hit home. Protecting people was his job, and he'd failed his own family. "I'm sorry, Eve."

"Sorry? Do you know how many times I've heard that, Nick? Sorry doesn't change how he cut me. How he almost killed me. Sorry wouldn't have helped if he'd hurt Keri. I don't want your apologies." She sank back onto the sofa.

"Let it alone for now," Bree said, sitting down beside Eve and taking her hand. "This isn't the time to discuss it."

"The time is never right, is it?" Eve asked, a weary edge to her voice.

"Exactly what happened?" Nick asked.

Eve stared at him again. "When emotions get involved, your cop persona kicks in."

"Eve, I'm trying to catch him," Nick said between gritted teeth. "Do you want me to let him go on killing women? Others haven't been as lucky as you."

Her fingers tightened on the blanket. She leaned back against the sofa. "I'm sorry. Go." She shooed him away with her hand. "Go see what you can find out."

"I want to hear it from you. What happened here tonight?"

She stared at him, and he didn't know if he could stand to hear how Gideon had tormented her.

He glanced at Bree when Eve didn't answer. "Bree? What happened here?"

"Good grief, put the man out of his misery," Kade said from his seat by the fireplace. "Eve came down for some tea. Gideon got in while she was fixing it. I don't know how — I'm positive I threw the deadbolt. He grabbed her from behind and started to drag her outside. Samson heard them struggling and came to help. He drove off Gideon."

"Samson was pacing in the bedroom," Bree said. "He kept whining, and I told him to shut up. He went out into the hall then. We had the fan on, so I didn't hear anything from downstairs. If only I'd checked things out. I just thought he was restless."

Nick stared at Kade. Could he be the killer? Someone had unlocked the door. He liked Kade and didn't want to suspect him, but maybe he should.

"Did you see him, Eve?" Bree asked.

"No, he grabbed me from behind. And in Bay City, he shut off the lights." Eve plucked at some threads on the blanket and didn't look up.

Nick preferred the Eve who responded to him without all the baggage. He'd hoped to find a new start. Maybe it wasn't possible.

The memories haunted even her sleep. The next morning, Eve felt hollow eyed and exhausted. Even a shower didn't clear away her cobwebs. Keri seemed to pick up on Eve's distraction. She whined and cried until Eve finally put her down for nap. Though Keri hadn't awakened last night, she surely sensed the tension in the household.

Samson shadowed her all morning, and

his company reassured her. If not for the dog, she would be dead right now.

Gideon wasn't going to do this to her again. She would have to save herself.

She went down the hall to the office and sat in front of the computer. Nick had surely checked out the Web site by now, but she was done waiting for him to protect her. The geocaching site came up, and she scanned down the list of caches in the area.

"Anything new?" Bree asked, coming to the doorway.

"Nope. It's all the same as the last time we looked." She didn't know what she was expecting — some grand revelation maybe.

"Nick will find him. You're being too hard on him, Eve."

"You don't waste any time, do you? Get right to the point." Eve could feel the sermon coming.

"Maybe all the memories coming at one time made it hard to sort through," Bree suggested. "You have to give Nick credit for trying."

"Our marriage went through some pretty rough times the past two years. I don't see it changing."

Bree didn't say anything for a long minute. Eve peeked up at her. "I can see your wheels turning. Just say what you're thinking."

"No marriage rises or falls on the actions of one person. How does Will fit in?"

Heat rushed to Eve's face. That was one memory she hadn't wanted to examine — the nights she met Will at the studio and danced until ten while Keri slept on a blanket at the edge of the dance floor. The way she lit up when he told her she was beautiful. Only by the grace of God had she not fallen into bed with him. At least there was that much. But realizing how close she'd come made her squirm. She'd actually gone to meet him at a hotel once. They talked for about an hour, but when it came down to breaking her bent wedding vows, she pulled back and rushed out.

She didn't love Will. There was relief in that realization at least.

Had Gideon followed her that night?

Eve realized Bree was still waiting for an answer. "I didn't have an affair."

"What was it, then?"

"A flirtation, I guess you'd call it. Nick was gone more than he was home, and I was lonely. I was used to adulation in the ballet, and suddenly I was just a wife whose husband barely noticed her. That went on for five years." She looked down at her hands. "I'm not proud of it. Will and I shared a passion for dance, and he came from humble beginnings just like me. At the time, it seemed we had more in common than Nick and I did."

"You had Keri."

The sound of her daughter's name brought the first smile to Eve's face. "We both love her so much."

"You still love Nick."

"It doesn't matter. He'll never change," Eve said.

"Was he a cop when you married him?"

"Yes, but I thought . . ." She stopped, realizing what she'd been about to say.

"But you thought he'd change," Bree finished for her. "What do you want from a husband?"

"A man who loves me unconditionally. Who puts me above his job and everything else. I went to church alone almost every Sunday because he got called into the office."

"There's no doubt Nick loves you."

"He doesn't show it. No wonder I couldn't get pregnant. I hardly saw him." Eve realized how bitter her words sounded. Was any of this her fault?

"How were things when you were first married?"

"Our honeymoon was the only time I had him to myself. Work always intruded on everything we tried to do."

"Aren't you proud of what he does though, Eve? He saves people every day. There's a sacrifice in that. Just like a soldier who leaves his family and goes off to war. The family pays a price for our safety. You knew he was created to be a cop when you married him. Did you think that would just fade away because he loved you?"

Eve thought about what Bree said. "Maybe I did," she admitted. "I don't think I realized what it would be like to be a law-enforcement wife."

"Let me ask you something — would you feel the same way about Nick if he were a store owner? What if he worked in an office? Left in the morning at nine and came home at five. Wore a suit to work every day. Talked about numbers on a spreadsheet instead of criminals he'd tracked down. How would that affect your feelings?"

Eve wanted to flippantly say she'd love it, but would she really? The thought felt vaguely distasteful.

Bree was watching her face. "The same thing that drives Nick to love you so completely is also what makes him good at his job. Focus and determination. Passion. He's rather heroic. What if he were just a normal man who hid behind a counter when a bank robber broke in?"

Eve didn't want to admit it, but Bree was right. "I wouldn't have nearly as much respect for him."

"One thing I've seen is how wives want to change who they're married to. You fell in love with Nick's passion and commitment. He hasn't changed. He can't. But you can change how you react to him. You can partner with him instead of fight him."

"You make it sound so easy. I don't know if I'm strong enough."

"You're stronger than you think. You haven't been able to strangle the love you have for Nick either. It's still there if you look for it." Bree smiled. "Sermon over. I hope you forgive me for interfering."

"I love you. You can say anything to me. I might get mad, but I know you care." Eve stood and hugged her. "I'll think about what you said."

She'd be lucky to ever forget it.

23

The small white building didn't look much like a church to Bree. Kade parked their Jeep beside it. They'd left Eve and Nick waiting for the home study guy to show up. In spite of Eve's trauma the night before, they wanted to move forward to settle Keri's custody issues.

Bree glanced at the group's headquarters. It squatted in the thick overhead trees like a pale mushroom with its rounded roof and dingy white paint. The windows were fly streaked and dusty, and the yard around it was overgrown with weeds.

"I'm not sure about this," Kade said. "I don't see how they could have anything to do with planting my shovel at the scene."

"Just humor me, okay?" Bree opened her door and got out. She met Kade at the front of the vehicle. He took her hand, and they went toward the front of the building. This place gave her an uneasy feeling. The idea of a Thursday afternoon meeting was kind of weird too.

Will met them at the front door. His slacks were pressed and spotless, and he wore a jacket with no tie. His easy smile told her he intended to forget that she'd challenged him over the hunting episode, and the arrogance raised her hackles. As if he was forgiving her, though he was the one who broke the law.

She didn't return his smile, and his dimmed a trifle, then came back full wattage. Bree could feel Kade bristle, and she squeezed his fingers. "Let's find a seat."

"Sit here," Will said, leading to a row of ladder-back wooden chairs near the middle of the room.

Bree and Kade stepped into the row and sat. Will took the chair on the aisle. Bree glanced around the room. A banner hung above the battered podium at the front of the room: SUPERIOR — NOT JUST A STATE BUT A WAY OF LIFE. Deer heads and black bearskin rugs hung on the walls.

She leaned over and whispered to Kade, "Are they pushing for secession from Michigan?"

"Looks like it."

There was always some talk going on above the bridge about breaking away from the trolls and forming their own state. Bree didn't see it ever happening. The UP depended too much on Michigan's infrastructure.

A man stepped to the podium and held up his hands. "Welcome to our visitors. I think we're about to get started. My son will come and play for the singing."

A young man who looked like a younger version of the leader stood and went to the front, where he picked up a guitar and began to strum it. Bree joined in on the verses of "As the Deer." At least she'd heard the song before. The people in the room — about forty — were mostly young adults in their twenties and thirties. There were quite a few teenagers too. Everyone clapped in time to the music and swayed in their seats.

"Now for our announcements," the older man said. "Our supplies for the winter are growing, but we need more meat laid up." Will began to frown and shook his head, catching the man's eye. The man smiled weakly. "Um, let's move on to other business."

Bree felt Kade's arm tighten under her fingers. He moved her hand off his arm and stood. "If you were about to say what I think you were, let me say right now that I'm a ranger. There is no legal taking of animals right now. If you're going to lay up meat, it needs to be store-bought."

Mutterings rippled around them. Bree saw several resentful glances sent their way. She tugged on Kade's arm, and he sat back down.

"Thanks for that reminder," the leader said. "On to other business. I heard from the Superior Coalition. They're going to send a speaker for our meeting next weekend to report on the status of the movement. Secession would be best for Job's Children as well as for the whole area. For one thing, Yoopers understand living off the land and being self-sufficient." His gaze touched Kade. "At least most do."

Bree was tempted to get up and walk out, but she wanted to know exactly how this group figured into what had been going on.

A young man with curly blond hair strode up the aisle. His blond beard looked more like peach fuzz. Dressed in ragged jeans and a long-sleeved T-shirt, he stepped to the podium. "Today I'd like to talk about the role of pain in shaping our lives. We should really pray that God cares enough about us to give us pain. Only pain shakes us out of our stupor and wakens us to God's working in our lives. In fact, when I pray, I usually cut myself with a razor." He pulled up his left sleeve to reveal red slashes on his arm. "It really puts me in tune with God."

Bree choked back a gasp. These poor kids. Yes, pain shaped their lives, but God didn't expect them to cut themselves. He'd send the necessary circumstances to mold them. She moved restlessly in her seat, then glanced to the back of the room.

The door opened, and Patti peeked in.

Bree grabbed Kade's arm, but before she could explain, Patti ducked back out.

What was Patti doing here? Bree didn't get it. She tried to focus on the meeting. She wouldn't have called it a church service by any stretch of the imagination. There was no glorifying God's work, only a pitiful effort to meet him with self-inflicted pain.

Once the meeting adjourned with a prayer for pain that would show the way, she and Kade bolted to their feet. "Let's go," she whispered.

Bree somehow managed to hold her tongue long enough to shake Will's hand and smile. Kade took her hand, and they made their escape into the sunshine. The rest of the group stayed inside talking in small groups.

"They've got it partly right," she told Kade. "Pain shapes us and molds us. But that cutting thing was too weird for words.

And there was no mention of just embracing the pain God brings to our lives and looking for the good that he brings out of it."

"I agree. They seem misguided, but not criminal."

Bree told him about Patti's appearance. "She and Will are both connected to Eve. I can't believe we're too far off base to think something's going on here."

"Let's look around," Kade said.

Discarded candy wrappers and soda cans littered the grounds. "For a back-to-nature group, they sure don't take care of the environment," Bree said.

They ducked through thick white pines and headed back toward a rock face. "Someone in town said they live in the old mine shaft," Bree said. "It should be close by."

"There's the opening." Kade pointed out the gaping hole in the mountain.

"Do we dare go in?"

Kade shrugged. "What can they do except throw us out?"

"True." Bree clutched Kade's hand, and they approached the opening framed in rough, weathered wood. "It doesn't look very safe. It's hard to imagine an acclaimed dancer living here, but I think his acclaim is long gone. Eve said he came from humble beginnings just like she did. It was something they had in common."

The opening was about twelve feet wide and eight feet high. The top beam sagged, and the interior was dark. A dozen or so lanterns were clustered on the ground near the opening. Several lighters lay beside them.

"You game to go in?" Kade asked. He picked up a lantern.

"If you're with me. I wish we'd brought Samson." She stooped and grabbed one of the lighters and lit the lantern in Kade's hand.

"I'm surprised they don't use flashlights or battery-powered lamps," Kade said. He trimmed the wick. "Let's go before they start wandering this way."

Bree followed him into the mine. The hewn rock walls seemed to press in on them. Several tunnels branched off in various directions.

"Let's try this one," Kade said, tugging her to the right.

They had to duck to enter the room just off the tunnel. Kade lifted the lantern to illuminate the space. Two sleeping bags, a pail upended to serve as a makeshift table, piles of discarded clothing, and several pairs of shoes were in the room.

Bree stepped closer to examine the pictures on top of the pail. "Look, Kade. Patti and Will. And a picture of Eve with Keri." The whole setup creeped her out, but she picked up the picture of Patti and Will, who was dressed in his leotards. They had their arms entwined, and she was looking up at him with an adoring expression.

It looked recent.

Bree put the picture back. "I bet this is Will's space. What if he's Keri's father?"

"Then why is he so interested in Eve?"

Bree shuddered. "Maybe he's using her to get to Keri. He asked her where Keri was the other day when we came out here."

"I think we'd better find out," Kade said, his voice grim.

Eve glanced out the living room curtains. The social worker would be there any minute.

"Quit pacing. It will be okay," Nick said. "You've got your memory back, so you'll be able to answer all her questions."

"But the situation is still far from ideal," Eve said. She walked back into the living room, where Keri sat on the floor fitting wooden puzzle pieces into their frame. The quiet house had her listening for a sound at the door or the creak of a foot on floorboards. She told herself Fraser was watching the house and had it all under control. The Matthewses would be back soon.

And Nick was here. No one would try to hurt her with him hulking around. Her fingers touched the tender spots on her neck.

"It will be okay. We'll deal with it," Nick said.

Easy for him to say. He had a good job and knew where he fit in. By now all her dance students would have found other teachers. "Did you sell my studio?"

"No. I've been making the payments."

"Why would you do that if you thought I was dead?"

"You loved that studio and put so much work into making it look nice. I couldn't stand to let it go yet." Nick's steady gaze stayed on her, and he started to extend his hand to her, then dropped it. "I heard a car door." He went into the hall.

Eve followed him. Her chest felt as though someone were sitting on it.

The man wore an easy smile and carried a briefcase. With thin dark hair and muddy hazel eyes, he was dressed in jeans and a polo shirt. "I'm Mark Haskell with Child Protective Services."

"Come in." Nick held the door open and

stepped out of the way.

"This way," Eve said, leading him into the living room. "This is our daughter, Keri." Intent on her puzzle, Keri ignored her mother's introduction.

Mark smiled. "Let's sit down and talk a bit, shall we?" He went to the armchair and sat down. Balancing his briefcase on his knees, he flipped it open and withdrew a file and something to write with. He closed the lid and placed the file on top of the case for support. He clicked the end of the spring-loaded pen.

Eve and Nick sat on the sofa. They answered Mark's questions about how they came to have Keri and what they knew of Patti's background.

"Have you talked to Patti yet?" Nick asked.

"Not yet. We have an appointment this afternoon." He clicked his pen.

Mark's pen-clicking habit was beginning to annoy Eve. But he seemed to be a nice guy and was clearly listening to them.

Mark wrote down a few more notes. "Now to your circumstances presently. This is your home?"

"Um, no," Eve said. "I'm staying with a friend while I'm here in Rock Harbor. I actually live in Bay City."

"I see. How long have you been here? And why is this case being settled here and not in Bay City? You intend to move here?"

As soon as he asked the question, Eve knew the answer. Rock Harbor had entwined itself around her heart and soul. This was where she wanted to raise Keri. But how would that affect Nick? After her talk with Bree, Eve was beginning to see her own role in the failure of her marriage. A tiny seed of hope had begun to sprout, but there was no way it would come to full flower if she didn't go back home — Nick needed law enforcement.

"I'm going to see about finding my own place here," Eve said before she could change her mind. She felt Nick's startled glance. "I'm going to sell my house in Bay City."

"I see. How long have you been here?"

"Three months."

Mark paused writing. "Seems a long time for a visit. What's the history of this decision?"

She was going to have to tell him. Patti would anyway if Eve didn't. She sighed and plunged into the story. He jotted down notes while she spoke. His expression gave nothing away, and she had no idea if she'd just shot herself in the foot.

"You say you've regained your memory now. If I may say so, that seems convenient. Do you have proof of this? What does the doctor say? Is it possible the amnesia will return?"

"I haven't been to the doctor yet." Stupid. She should have made sure she had the doctor's diagnosis. There hadn't been time, and she hadn't wanted to leave the house after Gideon's attack. Her fingers touched the bruises on her neck without thinking.

Mark's gaze followed her hand. "You're bruised. Those look like finger marks." He looked at Nick with accusation.

Nick held up his hands. "She was attacked last night."

"Attacked? By the same man you fled from?"

"Yes," Eve admitted. "He broke in."

"And where was your daughter during this time?"

"Sleeping upstairs with everyone else. He didn't bother anyone but me."

"But she was still in danger," Mark said.

"Isn't everyone?" Nick stood and paced. "Look, we live in a scary world. Terrorists and murderers seem everywhere. But it only seems that way. You can't stick your head in the sand and pretend they aren't out there. But you can't hide out from life either." He stopped and scooped Keri into his arms.

She reached up and patted his face. "Daddy," she said.

His face dissolved in tenderness. "The fact is we love her. She's our world. Patti will never be able to say that. Her own interests are always more important than her daughter's."

"According to the court report, she says she's changed."

"You'll have to decide that for yourself," Eve said. "But we've raised Keri for two years. Patti left her at a day care and never went back to get her. From that day until she showed up here last week, we hadn't heard a word from her. If she really loved Keri, wouldn't she at least call and inquire about her?"

"I would think so," Mark admitted. He closed his file. "What is the status of your relationship? Who would have custody?"

"I would. But Nick will see her often."

"And I'll pay child support. But frankly, I want my family back again. I haven't given up on our marriage."

"I see." Mark glanced to Eve. "And you, Ms. Andreakos?"

Eve and Nick locked eyes. "I'd like that as well," she said, unable to tear her gaze away.

Joy lit Nick's face. He took a step toward

her, then stopped. But the warmth in his eyes only grew more brilliant.

"I'd like to observe Keri with you for a few minutes, if I may," Mark said.

Eve stood and held out her hands for the little girl. "Let's do your puzzle, baby girl."

Keri lurched out of Nick's arms toward her. Eve and Nick sat cross-legged on the floor with Keri between them. Memories of other times like this flooded Eve's mind, and she forgot about Mark sitting behind them taking notes. Her hand grazed Nick's, and their eyes met again.

She looked away. They had work to do on their relationship before she was willing to risk her heart again. Trust had to be rebuilt on both sides. She hoped it was possible.

Keri played happily with them, and Eve hoped Mark could see how secure the little girl felt with them around her.

About fifteen minutes later, Mark cleared his throat. "I think that's enough for now." He clicked his pen again and slipped it into his briefcase. His folder followed, and he snapped shut the latches on the case, then stood. "I'll file my report with the judge next week. I know you all need closure."

Eve wished she could read his opinion in his face, but he'd undoubtedly had a lot of experience hiding his emotions. "Thank you," she said. She walked him to the door and closed it behind him.

When she returned to the living room, Nick had picked up Keri and was rocking her. Her eyes were beginning to close, and she nestled against Nick's chest.

They belonged together. Eve could see that so clearly now. But there seemed to be no easy resolution to their conflicts.

24

Nick laid his sleeping daughter on the sofa and covered her with her favorite silky pink blanket. He pulled it up around her neck and went in search of Eve.

She was nowhere in the downstairs, and he hadn't heard her go upstairs, so he glanced out the yellow ruffled curtains into the backyard. She stood out on the farthest promontory that overlooked Superior.

He made sure Keri was still asleep, locked the front door, then stepped out the back door and joined her.

She jumped when he put his hand on her shoulder. "You shouldn't be out here alone," he said.

"I'm tired of being afraid," she said softly. "I'm not going to let him terrorize me. I thought about that when you told Mark that we can't be afraid to live our lives. I've been afraid to stick my head out of my hidey-hole. I was just starting to emerge, and he came at me again. I found myself retreating, and I'm not going to do it."

The waves beat at the rocks offshore. The clouds hung low over the gray water, and the wind blew Eve's hair into his face, but Nick didn't mind. He slipped his arm around her waist and watched nature's show. They didn't need to talk, not yet. In fact, he wasn't sure he was ready.

In one breath she said she hadn't given up on their marriage, and in the other she said she was going to move here permanently. The two didn't mesh. At least not in his mind. He didn't see how they could in hers either.

"Life has beat us up some, Nick," Eve said, her gaze on the horizon. "Like those rocks, we're worn down and battered. Do you think we can withstand the waves?"

"Our foundations are deep in bedrock. Our faith, our love for each other and for Keri — they're as solid as they come."

"We divorced," she reminded him. "I think the waves moved us along the sand a bit."

They stood spoon fashion, and he rested his chin on her head. "We started looking at the waves instead of into each other's eyes."

She didn't answer right away. A sigh eased out, and she relaxed against his chest a minute before turning around in his arms and looking up into his face. "I don't want to leave here, Nick. I can't go back to Bay City. Maybe we'd better talk about that before we go overboard with discussing how solid we are."

He cupped her cheek in his hand and brushed his thumb across her soft lips. Words wouldn't do nearly as much as showing her how he felt. He bent his head and brushed his lips across hers. When the kiss deepened, he wasn't sure who had initiated it.

She wound her arms around his neck, and the passion between them spiked quickly to the power of the waves. He crushed her to him and forgot all the problems they faced. There was only the softness of her body pressing against him, and the heady feel of her lips on his. It had been so long since they'd loved.

The wind swept around them as if to drive them more tightly together. Nick wanted only to prolong this moment. It had been so long in coming.

"Daddy."

Only gradually did he become aware that Keri had been tugging at his pant leg. He and Eve broke apart. His brain felt fuzzy, and he couldn't tear his gaze away from

Eve's blue eyes for a moment.

Keri tugged again. "Up, Daddy. Keri up."

He scooped her into his arms, almost thankful for the defense. "You didn't sleep very long."

"Phone," she said.

"You answered the phone?" Eve asked.

Keri nodded.

"Who was it?" Nick carried her back toward the house with Eve keeping step.

"Duck."

Nick's smile faltered. Eve's eyes registered fear.

"What did he say, Keri?" Nick asked, careful to keep his voice interested and nonthreatening.

"Come visit," she said. "Duck visit."

Eve's legs trembled as she ran into the house. She couldn't quite clear her head enough to understand what Gideon's purpose had been in calling.

The phone lay on the floor. She picked it up. "Hello?" There was only silence. She clicked it on and off and heard the dial tone. It was useless to check the caller ID, but she punched the button anyway. *Unknown* was all that came up. Nick had put a recording device on the phone. She went into the living room to check it. The red light was on, indicating something had been taped.

She started to punch the button, then dropped her hand. Nick would be in here shortly, and she'd wait to hear it with him. His footsteps approached on the wooden floors. "In here, Nick," she called.

He joined her by the desk.

"There's a message," she said.

"Down," Keri said.

Nick set her on the floor, and she ran to her puzzle. "Did you listen to it yet?"

Eve shook her head. "I wanted to wait on you." She shuddered. He pushed the button to play the message.

A voice like Daffy Duck's blared out of the recorder. "You're Keri, aren't you? How are you, Keri?"

"Fine," Keri's voice was clear and loud.

"Where is your mommy?"

"Out."

"You're there all alone? Oh dear, I shall have to come visit and help you, Keri. You shouldn't be alone. Something might happen to you."

"Puzzle?" Keri asked. "Duck play puzzle."

"I like puzzles. I think your mommy does too. But she's not very good at them. I think she'll never figure this puzzle out. Can I talk to your mommy, Keri? Go get her."

" 'Tay." There was a clatter as Keri evidently dropped the phone on the floor. "Mommy!" she called. The back door clattered.

The machine continued to play. "You're recording this, I'm sure, Eve. The other night didn't go well. I've taken it as a sign. I won't break into the house again." The line clicked, and there was nothing more.

"You think he's telling the truth?" Eve asked. She was afraid to believe that he'd decided to leave her alone.

"I wish we could believe it, but I wouldn't count on it. He might not break in here, but he hasn't given up his plans." He dug out his phone and made the call. "Dad? We got a call here from Gideon. The machine taped it." He listened a minute. "Okay, see you later." He ended the call. "He wants me to digitize it and send a copy to forensics in Bay City."

"Should you call Deputy Montgomery?"

"Yeah." He called Montgomery and told him what had happened.

Eve wondered if the nightmare could possibly be over, though it didn't make sense Gideon would just give up. Not after all he'd done to find her. Her calmness surprised her, but facing him twice and living to tell about it had given her courage.

Nick closed his phone. He went to the

sofa and patted the spot next to him. “Come here, I want to talk to you.”

“Talk?” She lifted an eyebrow. “Are you sure that’s all?”

“I’d rather kiss you,” he said, grinning. “But we need to talk.”

She tried to keep from smiling, but it came out anyway. She’d rather kiss him too. Joining him on the sofa, she settled into the arm he put around her. The scent of his cologne made her want to turn and throw herself against him. To kiss him until he couldn’t speak, to drag him upstairs to her bedroom.

In fact, her feelings quite shocked her.

She wet her lips and fought her instincts. “Okay.”

“I can’t live here, Eve.”

She’d known he would say that. “You could get transferred to the Marquette Post.”

“That’s an hour and a half from here. Three hours’ driving time a day. How about if we look into getting a weekend cabin here?”

“What weekends? You’re always working.”

“What about your dance studio? You love it. Do you really think you could round up enough students up here to continue your work? You love dancing.”

She hadn't thought about that part of it. She loved her studio with the sunlit wood floors and the high ceilings. It looked out over the bay. "I feel so safe here."

"Why? There are none of the shops you like. Your friends, our church, our home, they're all back in Bay City."

"I do feel safe here, Nick. But more than that, I feel like I can be me with no masks. Bree and Kade, they accepted me from day one, when I didn't even know my name. These people are different. I want to be like them. My life in Bay City was all about putting on a happy face, never showing anyone the real me."

"What am I supposed to do here, Eve? Arrest poachers?" Though his words were soft, the passion behind them came through. His warm fingers touched her chin to turn her face toward him. "I love law enforcement. You've always known that. Are you trying to make me choose between you and my job?"

"No, it's not that, Nick." She grabbed his wrist and moved his hand so his fingers rested against her lips. She kissed them. "This is about me and Keri, not you."

"I don't think so. I feel manipulated. And you're very good at that, honey. I often don't recognize it, but this time I see it. If I could live this way, I'd do it in a heartbeat, because I love you. But I'd shrivel up and die here. If you don't see that, you don't know me very well."

Her eyes burned, and pressure built behind them. "I do know that. And I'm not saying forever. Just for now, I need this place."

"And what about what I need? What Keri needs? She needs me in her life."

"You can be in her life."

"Eve, it's an eight-hour drive one way to get here. When am I going to see her with my schedule? You're not looking at it clearly."

"Maybe I'm not." She turned her head so his fingers dropped away. "I can breathe here. If you stay awhile, you'll love it too."

"It would be easy to give in, to just find a little Podunk deputy job. But we both know what would happen. I'd start to blame you eventually for the way I was stagnating. I don't want that to happen."

"I know," she whispered past the knot in her throat.

"How about if we find a place in a little smaller town? Maybe Oakhurst or Bay Park."

If she loved him, she'd go with him. The truth whispered in her heart. Leaving Rock

Harbor would be like losing a piece of herself, but maybe that was better than losing Nick. And he was right — Keri needed him.

"I'll think about it," was all she could promise.

25

The life-support machines that surrounded Miranda beeped in the background. Gideon barely noticed them or the stink of antiseptic that burned his nose. He sat in a hard-backed chair and held his wife's hand.

"Is she going to die?" Odette asked, her voice trembling. She turned to her father for reassurance.

He'd hoped seeing Odette would rouse Miranda, so he'd gone after her. "She's not going to die."

"How do you know? The doctor said we should stay here because it wouldn't be long." Odette took her mother's other hand. "She's been like this forever. I kind of forget what she was like, Dad. I remember her baking cookies and reading *The Swan Princess* to me. But I almost can't hear her voice in my head anymore."

"Don't be ridiculous. You have to remember her, Odette. She will be devastated when she awakens if you've forgotten her."

"I was only eleven when it happened." Odette looked down at her mother. "Six years is a long time."

"Not so long. She's going to be fine." He dipped a sponge into water and ran it along Miranda's lips.

A shadow fell over the bed. He looked up to see the doctor standing at the foot. Clipboard in hand, he wasn't smiling.

Gideon's gut tightened. "Doctor."

"We need to talk," the doctor said.

"Not in front of her. Perhaps a room somewhere?"

"There's a conference room down the hall."

"Stay with your mother, Odette," Gideon said.

"No! I'm old enough to hear this, Dad. I want to come."

"Doctor?" Gideon asked.

"Fine with me."

The doctor led them down the tiled hallway to a sparse office: brown utilitarian furniture, an end table that held only a couple of magazines. Gideon wouldn't need the box of tissues on the coffee table.

He perched on the edge of the hard sofa. Odette looked young and frightened when she sat beside him. Probably he should take her hand to appear as a loving father, but he cared only about Miranda.

"Proceed, Doctor," he said.

"I'm sorry it has come to this, but the latest tests on your wife show no brain activity."

Odette gasped, and tears pooled in her eyes. "Daddy?" she asked in a small voice. "Does that mean . . ."

"It means nothing. My wife is going to wake up, Doctor." He turned an icy stare onto the physician, who squirmed but didn't look away.

"I'm sorry, but the machines are the only thing keeping her alive. It's time for you and your daughter to make a decision about turning them off."

"My decision is no." Gideon stood. "This conversation is over."

"Dad," Odette said. Her hands twisted together in her lap. "We can't keep living like this. The doctor says Mom is gone."

"You'd like that, wouldn't you? Not to have to come see her any longer and do your duty. No one is going to kill my wife. She's going to wake up."

The doctor rose. "I realize you may not be ready for this step, but it's really the best one."

"For whom, Doctor? The nursing home?

You need the room for someone else?"

The doctor flushed. "Not at all. But when hope is gone, it helps no one to deny the truth."

"Hope is not gone. Not my hope anyway." He jerked Odette to her feet and hustled her toward the door. "Go home if you want, but I'm going to go sit with your mother."

"Daddy!" Odette resisted his pushing. "You have to face it."

"Murderess," he hissed. "You don't love your mother." He opened the door and shoved her out it. "Go home. I don't want to see your face." Leaving her sobbing in the hall, he strode back to Miranda's room.

Nothing had changed since he'd left. The machines still beeped. She lay sleeping peacefully. Healing. But she needed the final offering.

"Hold on, my love," he murmured, tucking the sheet around her. "Tomorrow you'll be reborn."

Bree knew she needed to tell Nick and Eve about the pictures she'd seen in the mine. She should have told them last night, but they were so tense and upset that she hadn't wanted to add to their worry.

Bree went downstairs. Today she'd start registering visitors for the weekend geocaching event. Participants had been showing up throughout the week. The aroma of bacon drew her through the living room to find everyone at the table eating breakfast. Eve looked a little bleary-eyed, but she was smiling. Bree caught Kade's eye and nodded for him to start the conversation.

His answering nod was almost imperceptible. He pulled out the chair beside him so Bree could sit down. "Eve, how much do you know about Will?" Kade asked.

Eve's smile faded. "What's this all about?"

"It affects Keri."

Every head in the room turned to look at Kade. "Keri? What are you talking about?" Eve asked.

"We saw some pictures yesterday," Bree said.

"What pictures?"

"One of Will and Patti standing arm and arm. And another of you holding Keri in the backyard," Kade said.

Bree watched Eve closely. There was no missing the way she blanched, the sudden inhalation. "What do you know about him?" Bree asked gently.

"He — he was married once, but they're divorced. He's a great dancer."

Kade frowned. "Is he older than he looks?"

"He's twenty-eight."

"He looks about twenty-two," Bree said.

"Eve, I think Will might be Keri's father. And I think he's using you to get access to Keri. I'm worried he may try to take her."

"I'll talk to Patti, see what I can find out." Eve's smile had disappeared. "Why would he want Keri now, after all this time? That makes no sense."

"The service was kind of strange," Bree said. "One guy talked about using self-inflicted pain to meet God. Maybe having no kids was a source of pain for him. Though after listening to the service, I would think he would consider pain a good thing."

"Maybe he wants to make sure Keri is brought up 'right,' " Kade said.

"This might help our case," Nick said. "What judge would award a child to parents who live in a mine shaft? That's hardly safe."

Bree kept back her other fear. If the judge ruled against Patti, would Will try to take her anyway?

Nick didn't know what to think of the Patti-and-Will thing. He needed to find out though. The rest of them finished their breakfast in somber silence.

"Deputy Montgomery needs to see me,"

Nick said. "I'll meet you at the ranger station in a little while, Kade." He glanced at Eve. "Fraser will be outside again today, watching over you."

She nodded. She'd barely spoken to him this morning, and he wondered if she'd gotten as little sleep last night as he did.

He drove to town and parked in front of the sheriff's station. He welcomed the opportunity to think about something other than Eve's desire to stay here. It was enough to drive a man bonkers.

Inside, he dropped into the chair across from Montgomery. "What've we got?"

Montgomery shoved a file toward him. "See for yourself, eh?"

Nick flipped open the manila folder and began to read. "She's from Marquette. That's a surprise. Since he moved her, I thought she might have been a troll."

"I expected someone from under the bridge too," Montgomery agreed. "Maybe he hid her until now to help hide his identity. Maybe he's from around here after all."

"Could be." Nick continued to read. "Whoa, she's been missing six years. That means Gideon has been operating longer than we imagined."

"I noticed that. What do you make of it, eh?"

"Did he just get careless and we finally noticed him, or did he decide to be more deliberate and flaunt what he was doing?"

"You're the expert. What do these types do?"

"It varies. The BTK killer in Kansas sent letters to the police, taunting them for their failure to find him. Ted Bundy operated in anonymity." Nick closed the file. "We've checked out every geocaching group in Michigan. At least the ones we know about, though there are probably more. And some people work the caches alone, not in a group."

"You have anything on him dating before the Tallmadge woman?"

"No. But if he's been active six years, maybe we need to check the groups again. It would make sense that he was emboldened when he found a vehicle like geocaching that protected his anonymity."

"Why haven't we been able to track him down through the computer pathways, eh?"

"We've had a couple of problems doing that. One, he spoofs his address and bounces it through at least ten other computers, many of them overseas. Two, he changes the log every time he gets onto the geocaching site. He's smart."

"How many geocachers are there in Michigan?"

"Hard to say, since it's all so informal. Some teams appoint just one person to retrieve the data for the caches. The real number might be much higher than the number of registered users at the Michigan site even. Many of the users don't bother with state levels and only register with the national organizations. It's all so fuzzy."

"How many do you think will show this weekend? Bree is registering the entrants, isn't she?"

"Yes. I'm going to look over her list tonight and tomorrow night, and we'll see how many show. You can bet Gideon will be among them. How do you plan to use Eve to draw him out?" His gut still clenched at the thought of the danger she would be in, but it seemed to be the only way to catch the monster.

"Kade hid the big cache for us out near Reed Lake. There's a small ice fishing lean-to at the site that Bree is going to set up as the final check-in. Eve will man it. There will seem to be no one around, but there's a tree stand close by. I thought you'd want that station to guard her, eh?"

"I like it. Will anyone else be around?"

"Some state boys are going to be across

the way with high-powered binoculars. She'll be safe, and we'll get him."

"I'll make sure of it. Fraser is watching out for her too. With that many eyes peeled, we'll protect her." Nick opened the door. "Listen, I've got to go. Kade and I are going to take a walk through the planned caches, see if there's anything new." He went out the door and down the hall.

The sunshine began to warm up the morning as he drove out to the forest. He rolled his window down and inhaled the scent of vegetation and mossy woods. The appeal of the area hadn't escaped him like Eve thought. But what did a man like him do up here? He wasn't a hunter. He hated fishing. The thought of camping felt juvenile. He'd been created to be in law enforcement. Denying it would be turning away from the best he had, to throw the gifts he'd been given back into God's face.

By the time he reached the ranger station, he didn't want to think about it anymore. The receptionist directed him through the doors to a wildlife rehabilitation center, where he found Kade feeding a baby bird.

"I didn't know you could raise birds that small," he said. "It doesn't even have feathers. What are you feeding it?"

"Dry cat food softened with water." Kade

poked a bit of mash down the bird's gaping gullet. "I can't always save them, but I manage to pull quite a few through. This little one is a robin."

"Do they all like cat food?"

"At the beginning. They eventually graduate to suet mixed with peanut butter and seeds."

"Peanut butter?"

"Yeah, it's full of protein, and most birds love it. Some of my swans are addicted to peanut butter sandwiches."

The men looked at one another. "Peanut butter sandwiches," Nick said slowly. "Could Gideon be connected to the swans? Eve found a white feather on the floor after he attacked her. I don't have the report back yet on what kind of feather it was, but you said you thought it might be a swan. Eve's greatest performance was *Swan Lake.*" He stopped and inhaled. "I wonder . . ."

"What?" Kade asked.

"Eve last danced professionally when she was twenty-five — about six years ago. I found a picture of that night. It was in the possession of the man I thought was Gideon. Anyway, something else happened that night. Another dancer fell when Eve — well, she didn't use the best judgment. The girl fell off the stage into camera lights, and her costume caught fire. The fire scarred her. She became catatonic. I don't know what ever happened to her. But I wonder if the attacks on Eve could be related to the accident."

"What did Eve do?"

"She doesn't like to talk about it. It changed her. I'd rather she told you." Eve hadn't even told him everything. Every time the subject came up, she cried and said she was so ashamed.

"What was the girl's name? I could get Montgomery on it," Kade said.

"Ah, Miranda. I can't remember the last name."

"We'll check it out," Kade said. The bird quit opening its beak, and he put it back into the aviary. "I'm finished here."

"What kinds of animals do you have here?"

"Just about any orphaned babies, from deer to bear to birds. I've got a prey aviary on the other side of the center. Bald eagles, osprey, cranes. You name it, I've got it."

Nick saw no white birds. "Must be rewarding," he said, following Kade to his truck.

"I like to feel I'm making a difference." Kade opened his truck door and glanced at Nick. "Kind of the way you feel, I'm sure. You save people. I save the environment and our wildlife."

Nick got in the truck and slammed the door behind him with more force than necessary. "Yeah, well, tell that to my wife."

Kade switched on the engine. "Eve is just afraid, Nick. Afraid that one of these days you're not going to come home. She protects herself the only way she knows how."

"Fear? You think so? I thought she was jealous of my job."

"It's more likely fear. You still love her?"

"Sometimes I wish I didn't. I wonder if we'll ever be strong again." In a quiet moment, Nick thought he might examine what Kade said. That Eve might be afraid had never occurred to him. She'd never said that was the problem.

He watched out the window as Kade drove through the narrow, tree-lined lane. The truck bottomed out several times in potholes. The forest was so thick through here that the sunlight barely dappled the ground, and the gloom felt like twilight. Thick patches of black flies hovered in the air as they passed.

What did Eve like so much about this place anyway? Give him city lights, people jostling shoulder to shoulder, and fast-food places on every corner.

Kade braked hard. "What the heck?"

Nick peered through the window in the direction in which Kade's gaze had locked. A flutter of white moved through the trees. "What is it?"

"The swans are back."

"What swans?"

"I moved a flock of mute swans from this lake. It's a nesting spot for trumpeter swans, and the mutes were taking the place over." Kade groaned and smacked his hand on the steering wheel.

"So move them again."

"My boss was sure they'd just come back. He said if they did, I'd have to shoot them." Kade's voice was thick. "Dang, I don't want to kill them. They're beautiful creatures."

"Can you move them farther away? I'll help you. What do we have to do?"

"I don't have the equipment I need with me." A muddy SUV approached on the lane. Kade groaned. "He's seen them."

The SUV, a forest-service vehicle, stopped next to them, and the window ran down. Another park ranger, about sixty with heavy jowls and white hair, looked out toward them. "You saw, Kade?"

"Yeah. I'd like to try moving them farther away, maybe down to Porcupine."

The head ranger nodded, then ran his window up and drove on.

"I'd better check out how many there are."

"I'll go with you." When Nick stepped outside, the black flies swarmed him. "You got any bug spray? I may not survive the trip otherwise."

"Yeah." Kade came around the front of the truck and reached into the glove box. He tossed Nick a can of spray.

Nick coated his skin with the stuff and tossed it back inside. The flies still hovered, but at least they weren't landing. "Let's go."

The men stepped off the lane and into the thick brush. Nick could hear the swans squawking and fighting as they neared the lake. Kade broke through the trees just ahead of him, and Nick followed. He stopped and stared at the sight. At least thirty swans glided on the lake's placid surface. Near the shore, two orange-billed swans pecked at a large black-beaked one.

Kade grabbed up a branch and leaped forward, driving the aggressive swans away.

"Are the orange-billed ones the mutes?"

"Yes. The one they were picking on is a trumpeter."

Small flecks of blood showed against the bedraggled trumpeter's white feathers. It listed, then righted itself and swam away. Kade moved closer to the water, and four mutes swam toward him. Before he could react, two of them came ashore, beating their wings and hissing. He moved away, but they followed, stabbing at him with their beaks and beating their wings.

"Run!" he told Nick.

The two men ran, and the swans came after them only as far as the trees before they stopped and moved in triumph back to the water.

"How do you capture them and move them?" Nick asked, panting.

"We tranquilize them. Swans are territorial and can be dangerous. They can break an arm with their wings or poke out an eye. There have been a few instances where they've killed a human. You don't mess around with them when they're mad, though most of the time they're fine."

The men stopped in a small clearing. The truck was only another thirty feet away, just through the trees on the other side of the clearing.

Nick saw a red marker. "What's this?" He squatted to take a look. "The ground's dug up here. Looks like someone buried something."

"Maybe one of the caches for tomorrow?" Kade glanced around. "The caches aren't usually buried."

"It's big. Almost the size of —" Nick

stopped, not sure he wanted to voice it.

"A grave," Kade finished. "Let me get my new shovel."

26

Bree needed to get out and smell the fresh air. She'd head into town to start taking registrations in about an hour.

Her phone rang, and she nearly groaned when she saw it was the nursing home. "Bree Matthews," she said.

"Mrs. Matthews, your father hit the aide again." The nursing home director's voice announced the news with all the seriousness of a doctor delivering a death sentence.

Bree's anticipation of the day shattered. Samson came to lean against her leg when she sank onto the bench and said, "Oh no!"

"I'm going to ask the doctor to sedate him."

"Look, we've talked about this before. I don't want my father spending his remaining days in some kind of half twilight."

The director sighed. Bree always had a hard time thinking of him other than in large letters. THE DIRECTOR. Not Nathan Johnson, a mild-mannered milquetoast of a man, but the one person who had the power to help or hurt her father. The fact that he'd called Bree himself instead of letting one of his minions do it told her he was dead serious about fixing this "problem."

"I'm afraid I must insist, Mrs. Matthews. He not only hit Ruby; he tried to choke her too."

"Choke?" Bree faltered. "I don't believe it. He's a gentle man."

"Bernard is not the man he once was. I'm afraid you haven't accepted that fact, Mrs. Matthews. When can I expect you to come take care of this? The doctor will require your agreement."

How could she let them drug her father so that he was merely a breathing shell lying on the bed? He was once a great man, extremely smart and talented. A scientist who commanded respect. What were her options? They'd narrowed week by week, month by month.

"I'll come now."

"If you fight me on this, Mrs. Matthews, I'm afraid I'll have to expel your father from our facility. I have a responsibility to keep my staff safe too." He rang off without saying good-bye.

Bree closed her phone. Samson pressed his nose against her hand and whined. She rubbed his ears. "I'm okay, boy." But she wasn't. Agreeing to this would be the hardest thing she'd ever done.

"Trouble?" Eve asked.

"My dad. He tried to choke a nurse." The worst part about all this was that Bree had only come to know him in the past few years. Their time had been all too short, and it was about to be over. "The director wants to dope him."

"Have they tried some anticonvulsant meds?" Eve asked. "Valproic acid is especially helpful. It won't knock him out either."

"I don't think so." Bree allowed herself to feel hope. "How do you know this?"

"Nick's grandmother has Alzheimer's, and I've read up on everything I can find." A shadow darkened Eve's eyes. "I'd forgotten her until now. I should ask Nick how she is."

"Would you come with me to the nursing home? I don't know much about the medication side of this."

"Sure."

The bright promise of the day tarnished, Bree took Davy and Keri to Anu's shop, then pointed the Jeep to town and drove to the nursing home. The only facility of its kind, Rock Harbor Nursing Home had a good reputation as a caring place. Bree had worked hard to maintain a good relationship with the staff. Most of the time she thought her gifts of candy and cookies as merely a goodwill gesture. Today that favor she'd earned might be all that prevented her father from being shipped out to somewhere farther away like Houghton or Marquette.

Ruby waved to her from the nurses' center. Bree walked over to see how badly Bernard had hurt her. As Bree neared the counter, she could see the ugly red marks on the woman's neck. A cocker spaniel sort of woman, even down to the medium brown color of her hair, Ruby had been nothing but kind to Bree and her father. Seeing Ruby injured made Bree squirm inside.

Ruby touched her throat when Bree's gaze lingered there. "Don't fret so. It's not as bad as it looks. He just caught me off guard."

"What happened?"

"I'd just helped him get his shower. He'd been a little agitated all morning, kept saying he had to go see the swans."

"The swans? I've never heard him talk about swans."

"There are some in the pond in the backyard. They arrived about a month ago. He loves to watch them. Anyway, when I told him we'd go later, he tried to push me out of the way and go to the door. I grabbed his arm and tried to lead him back to the bed, but he turned and grabbed me by the throat. I had no idea he was that strong. One of the orderlies saw the struggle and rushed to help."

"I'm so sorry," Bree said. "Did you see the doctor?"

"No, I'm fine. It will bruise, but I'm okay. Let me tell Mr. Johnson you're here." Ruby picked up the phone and dialed. She told the director that Bree had arrived, then hung up and motioned to her. "He said to come on back." She opened the door, and the women stepped inside the office. "The doctor's here already too," she whispered.

At least she'd been warned. The battle was just past the smooth wooden door. She knocked and waited until she heard the director's voice tell her to come in. Pushing open the door, she stepped aside to let Eve enter, then followed and shut the door behind them.

"You brought reinforcements?" Mr. Johnson smiled, but the lift of his lips looked pained. His eyes stayed sharp and determined.

"This is my friend Eve Andreakos."

"Let me get another chair. You know Dr. Ferguson, I'm sure."

"Yes, hello, Doctor," Bree said. She tried to hide her distaste. The doctor always reminded her of Snidely Whiplash come to life. Davy was addicted to the old *Dudley Do-Right* cartoons, and she'd seen more than her fair share. With his handlebar mustache and penchant for black suits, the doctor could have walked right out of the TV.

The fact that she was always in defense mode with him didn't help.

She seated herself in the armchair that Mr. Johnson pulled up. Eve sat beside her in the chair that was already in front of the massive cherry desk. The director's office furniture left no doubt that he was important.

Her defense hovered on her tongue, but she choked it back. Let them state their case first. It would turn the tables on them. They would be expecting her to react to Mr. Johnson's call. She sat quietly and stared at him until he cleared his throat and shot a quick glance toward Dr. Ferguson.

"Ah, as we discussed on the phone, something must be done about your father. He's becoming a danger to others." He sat back and folded his hands, waiting for her response.

Bree considered her words. She didn't want to appear as a hysterical daughter. Facts were the only thing these men would respect. "How many times has this occurred?" she asked.

"This is the third time. Each incident has escalated."

"I think he needs to be on Haldol," Dr. Ferguson said.

"Oh, I disagree," Eve said before Bree could ask what side effects the drug might have. "Major studies indicate that such strong sedation is not only unnecessary but dangerous. What has he been on up to now?"

Dr. Ferguson scowled, and Bree could almost see him mentally twirling his mustache. She tensed, certain he was going to give them a major argument over the proper course of treatment.

He flipped open his folder. "Aricept and Razadyne."

"No antidepressants or anticonvulsants?" Eve asked.

"No. I'm not convinced they're helpful in this case."

"How about trying Cipramil daily with a possible dose of Xanax if he becomes agitated? I think you'll see a major improvement."

"I disagree," Dr. Ferguson said. "And what is your background in making these suggestions?"

"I have a family member with the disease. We've consulted with the best doctors in the country."

"These types of people are much easier to handle if they're sedated," the doctor said.

"The purpose isn't to make them easy to handle," Bree said, clenching her hands. "And he's not just a nameless person. He's Bernard Hecko, my father. He has dignity and value. I want to visit with him while he's himself as many times as I possibly can. He's not here just putting in his time until he dies. This is his home, where he should be able to interact with friends and family. It's supposed to be a safe haven where he can't hurt himself and no one else can hurt him either. You're not going to drug him. I want him prescribed what Eve suggests. If you won't do it, we'll change doctors." Bree knew she could find a doctor who would listen.

Dr. Ferguson's black eyes went even darker. "Very well," he said. "But one more incident, and you'll have to move him to another facility."

Bree rose and motioned to Eve. "Thank you for your time," she said in a voice that left no doubt the interview was over and she expected her instructions to be followed. "I'm going to go see my father now. I'll check in over the next few days and see how he's getting along on the new meds."

She didn't wait for the men to try to talk her out of her decision. Eve followed her, and Bree rushed through the door. She left it open behind her and hurried past Ruby. The air-conditioning cooled her hot face.

"You handled that well," Eve said.

"Thanks to you. I was clueless in there. They could have drugged him and I wouldn't have known about any alternatives."

"I was glad to help. Let's go see your dad."

Bree nodded and led her friend down the hall to the last room on the left. "Hey, Dad," she said, pushing open the door.

He sat in an armchair staring out the window. Tall and distinguished still, Bernard had the kind of face that aged well. His disease shrouded the intelligence in his eyes, but Bree still saw glimmers of the man he used to be.

"Did you see the swans, Cassie?" he asked.

"It's Bree, Dad." She touched his shoulder, and he looked up at her.

"Of course it is," he said. "You were only a baby when I saw you last."

Bree choked back a sigh. How long had it been? Two days? Yes, just two. She touched his cheek. "I heard you got some swans. What kind?" She squinted out the window and saw the white birds gliding along the pond's surface. "Black bills. They're trumpeters. You're lucky. The mutes are more common."

"Lucky," he agreed. His chin touched his chest, and his eyes closed.

Bree sighed. "I guess we'd better go get the kids."

They left Bernard sleeping and went back out into the sunshine. The traffic was bumper to bumper all the way to the downtown area. "The geocachers are going to have to camp out," Eve said. "There aren't enough rooms to house them."

"A bunch of them are staying at the forest campground," Bree said. "Looks like we've got a great turnout. But I'm still uneasy about you being bait."

"It may end up being a bust. When he called, he said he wouldn't break into the house again."

"And you believe that?"

"No. I think he was talking in riddles. I'm just trying to *make* myself believe it. It's the only way I can function."

"I'm afraid for you."

Eve shrugged. "Nick got me a little gun that I'm going to start carrying."

"If you're not familiar with handling it, that's not going to do you a lot of good."

"It fit in my hand like it was made for me." Eve's brief smile came. "I'd almost like a chance to shoot him. Almost. I just want it to be over. I might as well be a target while everyone is watching and can help."

"I don't like it."

"It will be over soon." Eve got out of the Jeep and followed Bree to the store.

Several customers were at the checkout. Bree smiled and chatted with the customers a minute, then the women went back to the break room for some cardamom bread and tea. Bree watched Anu put the kettle on to boil, then get down the Arabia cups and saucers.

"I'll get the tea." Bree opened the tin and peeked inside. "You've got Nordqvist."

"Yes, a fresh shipment came in two days ago. I knew you'd love it."

Bree lifted out four tea bags and inhaled the aroma of China Rose tea. "I would have come over sooner if I'd known you had this."

With the tea and bread on the table, Anu pulled out her chair and sat down. "Now tell me," she said.

Bree and Eve settled at the table with her, and Bree explained what had happened at the nursing home. "He's such a gentle man," she said. "I never expected him to be violent, not ever. It seems so unfair for a sweet and godly man to have to go through this."

Anu stirred sugar into her tea and didn't answer at first. Her gaze was soft and faraway. "I, too, was surprised at first, *kulta,*" she said finally. "This morning, a woman brought back a lace tablecloth she bought two weeks ago."

Bree frowned, unsure why Anu changed the subject. But the older woman usually had a purpose in her rabbit trails, so Bree said nothing.

"I knew at once she had used it. She said it was stained when she bought it, but several times I had opened that cloth and admired the pattern before folding it back up. I knew she did not tell the truth." Her gaze locked with Bree's, and she smiled. "And you think, *This crazy woman, where is she going with this story?*"

Bree chuckled. "Go on, I'm listening."

"I was angry, very angry. I wanted to call the woman a liar, to throw her out of my store. All the ugliness of my inner person wanted to rise up and scream at her. This is what surprised me. But I didn't, *kulta.* The control I have learned as a Christian helped me, and I held my tongue. Your father's disease has stripped away that control. If there was ever proof that man is evil at his core, just as the Bible says, it's when we see a man afflicted like your father. With his control gone, the natural man that is at the heart of all of us is revealed in all his deformity and vileness."

Bree thought about the times she raged inside and subdued it, the way she bit back unkind words, the way she often didn't feel like helping her neighbor but did anyway. "I see what you mean."

"There, but for God's grace, are we," Anu said, lifting her cup of tea to her lips.

27

Perspiration dripped down Nick's back as he heaved another shovel load of dirt onto the growing pile. They'd gone down two feet and found nothing. Maybe whatever was buried here had already been moved.

Then his shovel clanged on a metallic surface. "Found it," he said to Kade. Nick wiped perspiration out of his eyes and redoubled his efforts.

His shovel kept clanging on whatever was down there. Shovelful by shovelful, the men uncovered their find. Kade swiped the last of the dirt from the top to reveal a long metal box.

"Looks like ammunition or guns," Kade said, brushing dirt off the green metal.

"I suppose we should call Montgomery," Nick said. "I'd guess they belong to Job's Children."

Kade tried to pry up the lid, but it resisted. "Yeah, good call." He pulled up Montgomery's number.

While Kade spoke to the deputy, Nick meandered around the clearing looking for more disturbed dirt. Leaves from last autumn lay in drifts around the edge of the clearing and crunched underfoot as he kicked through them. The place was peaceful, and he was beginning to think his intuition was off when he stepped into soft dirt under the leaves.

Brushing them aside, he found another burial spot. "Here's another one," he called.

Kade joined him. "Montgomery is on his way. I wonder how many other sites they have out here? And what's the point?"

"So they wouldn't be found with the weapons. And they like to sprinkle their stuff in different locations in case they have to bug out. They can find these caches quickly."

"Let's try that box again," Kade said, heading back to the one they'd already dug up.

"What will Montgomery say?"

"He probably thinks we already opened it." Kade put the shovel blade under the lid and pried. It popped open this time, and he used the blade as a wedge.

Nick began to pry the other end. Adrenaline pumped through his body at the find.

He hated these kinds of groups. If it were up to him, he'd pass a law forbidding them. He jabbed with his shovel again, and the lid popped loose. He and Kade lifted it off and stared down.

Cans of food. Green beans, corn, sweet potatoes. Tomato sauce, soups, ravioli. No weapons, no ammo.

He kicked at his shovel. "Crap. I thought there would be guns."

Kade leaned on his shovel. "Me too. Bree and I went to listen to that group. There were bearskins on the walls, and Bree found them poaching."

"I know they're involved with Gideon somehow. He had a hand in the last group I broke up, and he's here now. I can smell him."

"Maybe. Don't forget to have your dad check on that woman who was injured in the ballet. There might be a connection there," Kade reminded him.

Nick nodded and called his dad. He doubted an accident so obscure could be connected to a serial killer, but it wouldn't hurt to check. His gaze went back to the metal chests.

He just might have to scout around the headquarters of Job's Children this weekend. The forest would be thronged by people out for the geocaching event. No one would notice him wandering close to the compound. If there was a connection, he would find it.

Eve jumped at Nick's offer to take Keri for a "date." A little time to herself before Bree got home was just what she needed. Kade was there, and Nick's partner Fraser was parked in an unmarked car across the street, adding more security.

She fertilized the plants and grabbed the new Denise Hunter book. Just having time to lose herself in a good book was heaven.

Kade came into the living room. "Hey, Bree's got a flat tire. Would you mind going with me? I don't want to leave you here alone."

"Oh, go ahead. Fraser's still out there. I'll be fine. I think I'll go down to the beach and read."

"I shouldn't be gone more than fifteen minutes."

With Kade gone, Eve went outside and told Fraser she would be on the beach reading. He nodded and told her he'd keep watch.

Carrying her book, Eve went down the steps to the sand. A stone bench perched just past the sand at the base of the hillside where the lighthouse looked out over the water. She got situated, then dug her bare toes into the cool sand. The sun was an orange ball dropping into the endless blue of the water. She sat there watching the sun go down.

She heard a footstep behind her but didn't turn. It was probably Kade back already. "You're back early," she called. Her smile faltered when she realized it wasn't Kade.

"Mind if I join you?" Oliver stood with a half smile just behind her.

"I suppose Nick called you to come check on me." She smiled and moved over on the bench. "It's sweet of you to worry, but I'm really okay, Oliver. There's a policeman out front."

"I saw. But the guy is sleeping. There was little protection he could offer." He paused. "Listen, I've got something I need to show you. I think it might be important for the investigation. Can you come to my van?"

"Now? Don't you want to wait until Nick gets back so you can show him?"

"He's seen it already and doesn't know what to make of it. I think you might be able to shed some light on it." Oliver rose and held out his hand.

She took it and rose. "Okay." The book tumbled to the sand, but she left it there, knowing it would be a good excuse to leave Oliver and come back to the beach.

The stone steps to the water had crumbled over time, and Eve was careful as she went ahead of Oliver up the cliff. The lighthouse beam blinked, and she walked toward the car in the dusk. She heard Samson barking inside the house. She'd have to let him out when she got back.

Oliver was right. Fraser's head lolled back, and his mouth was open. Some help he was. But then, he'd been on duty all day. Oliver's van was parked across the street under a tree. He went to the back and opened the doors. Climbing inside, he turned to offer his hand to her. She reached up and grasped his fingers, then stepped into the vehicle.

Eve glanced around at the various containers and busts. "How many victims have you brought home to their families?"

"Oh, upwards of two hundred, I think." Oliver's back was to her, and when he turned around, he held a set of handcuffs. One end was clasped around a hand rest on the back of the front seat.

"Where did you find those?" She stepped closer to look at them, but they seemed much too ordinary to be the reason he'd brought her here.

His hand snaked out and caught hers,

then slapped the other end of the handcuff around her wrist. “I bought them for this moment.” His fingers bit into her arm.

“What are you doing?” She figured it was some kind of stunt he wanted to show her. Until he brought a red cloth toward her face. She jerked on the handcuff, but it held fast. His calloused fingers grabbed the back of her head while his other hand forced the cloth into her mouth.

She tried to spit it out, but it was wedged in too tightly.

“I see by your eyes you’re finally afraid,” he said. “Good.” He bent down and flipped on a recorder.

The Daffy Duck voice that came out made her shudder. Gideon? Oliver was Gideon? His work had been praised all over the country. Nick trusted him. She couldn’t wrap her mind around it.

He slammed the van door closed, then brushed past her to clamber into the front seat. The van engine sprang to life.

The lurch of the vehicle threw Eve to her knees. She crouched there and looked for some tool to unlock the handcuff, but none lay within reach. Only tubs of clay. She thumped on the side of the van with her hand, hoping someone would hear her.

Oliver turned around, and the malice in

his eyes made the last of the spit in her mouth dry up. "You don't want me to come back there," was all he said, but it was enough.

Eve dropped her hand and huddled on the floor. She would never see Keri or Nick again. The thought made her eyes sting. All the petty reasons she'd given Nick for not going home with him blew away.

She gritted her teeth and pulled on her cuffs. If she kept her wits, there would be an opportunity to escape. She'd outwitted him twice already, and Gideon was no longer a faceless, unknown attacker.

He was driving too fast for the rough road. The van lurched and kicked like a failing ski boat. Night had fallen with the suddenness common in the North Woods. Darkness shrouded the landscape, but the glow from the dash illuminated Oliver's profile enough for her to see his narrowed eyes and set mouth.

Tree limbs brushed the side of the van, so she guessed the road was a private lane. It seemed to go on forever. At one point a larger branch screeched across the frame and made her jump.

Oliver slammed on the brakes, and she slid into the back side of the passenger seat. He said nothing as he switched off the engine and got out.

Eve scrambled to her feet and tried to peer around the seat and out the window, but it was too dark to see with the forest blocking out the moonlight. The metal door clanked as Oliver wrenched it open. He stepped inside, but she was too blind even to make out his features.

Eve worried the gag with her tongue, but it still refused to budge. Something metallic jingled, and she felt Oliver's cold hands on her arm, then the handcuff came free from the seat. She tried to spring away from him, but his hand forced her back to her knees. He brought her hands in front of her, slapped the other side of the handcuff onto her free wrist, and dragged her to her feet.

Battling with her in silence, he tossed her out the van door. She fell hard, her chin slamming into the dirt, her palms scraping across some rocks. She didn't understand, couldn't figure out how this could have happened.

She should at least have a fighting chance.

Her right knee screamed when he dragged her to her feet again. Brush tore at her exposed skin as he propelled her forward. The lashes from the vegetation seemed to come out of nowhere in the utter blackness.

Then her foot banged against something,

a ledge maybe.

"Step up," he growled.

The cloth in her mouth was soaked now, and choking her. She desperately wanted it gone. Her foot sought and found the step up, and Oliver pushed her about three steps, then stopped.

She heard something creak. A door? He pushed her across the threshold and into a building that smelled of damp and mouse. A light flared, and she saw his face thrown into sharp relief by the match flame. He bent over a lantern. Adjusting its wick, he got the light going and held it aloft.

Eve got her first good look at the place. A one-room cabin with a dirt floor, it had only a cot, a chair, and a wooden table. No indoor plumbing or kitchen.

Oliver pushed her onto the end of the cot with one hand and ripped out her gag with the other. It felt like half her tongue went with the cloth, but the relief was exquisite.

He pulled up the chair and straddled it with its back toward Eve in a casual gesture that confirmed his command of the situation.

She wet her lips. "I don't understand, Oliver. I liked you. I thought you were my friend."

"Don't bother using any psychobabble on

me. I'm too intelligent for it to work." His smile held no humor.

"What did I do?"

"It angers me a great deal that you've dismissed your sin so completely. I've given you space to repent of it, to make amends, but you've ignored it."

"Ignored what? I really don't know."

He pulled a picture from his pocket and handed it to her. She took it with her wrists chained together. In the dim light she could make out her own face smiling back at her. Dressed in a white tutu and feathered tiara, she looked so happy and carefree. Everything had changed that night.

"Ah. I see by your expression, you're finally understanding."

She handed the photo back. "No, no. I really don't. Were you in the audience?"

"I was there. Watching my wife dance."

"Your wife danced that night? Which part? What was her name?"

"Miranda."

The single word was enough. Eve shrank back in her chair. "You — you're Miranda's husband?" She didn't remember his last name. Nick always just called him Oliver.

His gaze never left her face. She shuddered. "I . . . I lost track of Miranda. How is she?"

"You never paid for your sin that night. Never even said you were sorry."

Eve wet her lips. "I did, but she was . . . was unresponsive by then."

He frowned then. "You went to the hospital?"

"Yes."

"I don't believe it. I would have known." He shook his head. "No, you're trying to make light of what you did, and there was no excuse."

"You're right, there wasn't. I still think of it with shame."

Eve could sense he was barely hanging on to his composure. Maybe silence would be the best option here. Her hands were small, and she wondered if maybe she could wiggle them free from the handcuffs.

He clenched and released his fists, maybe because he wanted to wrap them around her neck. She wrenched her wrists, but the cuffs refused to budge. Her feet were free though. If he would just leave her alone for a few minutes, maybe she could escape. It was so dark, he'd never find her once she lost herself in the woods.

"What are you going to do?" Her voice trembled.

"Pain will purify you. The sin of envy is grievous, Eve. It caused you to commit every one of the abominations. Pride, lies, all of them. Have you ever read Dante's *Divine Comedy*?"

She'd read it in college, but right now, while her pulse thundered in her ears, she couldn't remember what it was about. Something about descending into purgatory — perhaps where she was now.

When Eve didn't answer, he smiled. "With your eyes sewn shut, envy will not be possible, Eve, and you should thank me that you shall enter purgatory partially cleansed."

He meant to sew her eyes shut!

She remembered the scene now. The sinners' eyes had been sewn shut with wire.

"Ah, I see you remember," Oliver said. "Your flesh shrinks from pain, but your spirit will revel in it."

"How will my suffering help Miranda?"

"Miranda is catatonic because she lost her beauty. *You* took it from her, and you'll give it back."

Her mind threw the crime scene photos of faceless women down before her eyes. They released fearful tears. "How will I do that if you sew my eyes shut? My face will be mutilated too."

"I'll be careful not to harm your skin."

She jumped to her feet, straining against her bonds. "Let me go!"

He smiled then, amused. "You think I'm mad. No matter. You'll soon see. But not tonight. Tomorrow, everything will be in place." He stood and went outside.

Eve heard a lock click, followed by the sound of a wooden bar falling into place. She ran to the door and tried to open it, but it wouldn't budge. He'd taken the lantern with him, and darkness shrouded the cabin. She couldn't see anything.

She recalled a reflection of the lantern about three feet from the door. A window? Maybe she could get out that way. Eve felt along the wall until her hand touched cool glass. She peered out the window and made out the outline of the van. Where had he gone?

Did she dare break the glass and try to crawl out? Surely he'd hear her. Biting her lip, she considered her options. If she stayed here, she had no chance. Even if he heard her attempt to escape, he was saving her for some diabolical scheme and would be unlikely to take revenge right then. She had to try it.

Groping across the floor, she tried to find some kind of weapon. A rock, anything. Her hand touched cool, bare earth, then the leg of his chair. Maybe the chair. She picked it up, hands still cuffed, and had raised it to shoulder height when she heard his tread on the porch.

She barely made it back to the cot before the door opened and he stepped back inside.

28

While Kade changed the tire, Bree sat on the curb and watched the pedestrians amble around town. More than two hundred geocachers had registered this afternoon, and she was spent. But she went on alert when she saw Patti disappear into the coffee shop. "I want to talk to her, Kade," she said.

Kade tightened a lug nut. "You sure you want to do this tonight? Eve is home alone."

"You're not quite done. I'll be back before you're finished." She hopped up and hurried into the shop. Inhaling the rich scent of coffee, she glanced around for Patti. She expected to find her at the register, but instead Patti sat at a back corner table.

Will was with her.

Bree marched to the table. Patti saw Bree when she was three feet away. The soft expression she wore vanished, and she snatched her hand away from Will's. He whipped around in his chair and stared up at Bree.

Bree pulled a chair out and sat down. They might as well keep it quiet and civilized. "I have some questions," she said.

"This isn't what it looks like," Patti began. She looked a little pale, and beads of perspiration dotted her upper lip and forehead.

Will had his fingers pressed to the side of his head as though it ached. "Don't bother making excuses, Patti. Someone saw her and her nosy husband coming out of the mine. I'm betting she knows."

"I saw the pictures," Bree said. "You and Patti together. Eve and Keri. You're Keri's father, isn't that right?"

"Bingo. What are you going to do about it?"

Bree glanced at Patti. "Did he tell you he was romancing your sister?"

Patti's eyes widened. "What are you talking about?"

"He's using you to get Keri, because his plan to get her through Eve failed."

Patti's gaze swiveled to Will. "Is this true? Do you know Eve?"

His laugh was hollow. "Don't you see what she's trying to do?"

Bree thrust her chair back and left them

arguing. She had never wanted to hit someone so badly in her life. When she got back outside, Kade was letting the Jeep down off the jack.

He took one look at her face and said, "We were right?"

Bree grabbed his arm as he started toward the café. "Don't bother, honey. He isn't worth it. Let's get home and check on Eve."

The lighthouse was dark when Nick parked and shut off the engine. He glanced in the backseat, and just as he'd expected, Keri was sleeping in her car seat. They'd gone to the petting zoo at the ranger station, then to Houghton for her to play in the McDonald's play area.

He eyed the dark house again. Where had Eve gone? She'd said she was going to stay home and relax. And where were the Matthewses?

After unbuckling Keri and lifting her into his arms, he carried her around back to see if Eve was sitting out watching the stars, but the backyard and porch were deserted. He moved to the edge of the cliff and looked down onto the beach. No Eve.

A vague sense of unease gripped him. Samson was barking from inside. He glanced across the street. The dark shape of the police car was still there. If she had left, why hadn't Fraser followed her?

The lighthouse was at the end of the road and had no close neighbors. The Blue Bonnet B and B was the closest, but no one from there could see into the backyard here.

He tried to tell himself not to worry, but his unease mounted when he found the back door unlocked. Pushing inside, he flipped on the light. "Anyone home?"

Samson woofed, and his nails clicked on the floor as he rushed to greet Nick. He whined and kept going to the door.

"You have to go out?" Nick opened the door, and the dog rushed through. Instead of going to the yard to do his business as Nick expected, Samson turned and gave him an "Are you coming?" look.

The dog was clearly agitated. Nick laid Keri on the sofa, then dug out his cell phone and called Bree. "Hey, do you know where Eve is?"

"Isn't she at the house?" Bree asked.

"No, and the house is dark. The back door is unlocked, and no lights are on. And Samson is upset."

"I had a flat, and Kade came to help me. He hasn't been gone long. We're almost home. I'll call Montgomery. Eve wouldn't leave the house unlocked. She was going to stay in with the doors locked."

"I know." Nick's gut turned over. He closed his phone and went to search the house. Nothing. Maybe she was down on the beach. She liked to walk along there. But not at night. He could only pray she'd sprained her ankle or something and was sitting there waiting for him. But wouldn't she have shouted for help? His mind ran through all the possible scenarios, but he didn't think any of them held up to scrutiny.

Leaving Keri sleeping on the sofa, he grabbed the flashlight by the back door and stepped outside. He rushed to the steps leading to the beach. The dark night made it hard to watch his step on the stone flight, and he nearly fell twice.

Once his sneakers sank into the soft sand, he cupped his hands to his mouth and shouted for Eve. He listened but heard nothing more than the waves crashing on the rocks. The wind kicked up, and lightning flickered overhead.

"Eve!" he shouted again. When there was no answer, he walked along the shore, shining the flashlight along the sand. Nothing. He turned to go back to the lighthouse and caught sight of a paperback book lying on the ground. He picked it up.

It was the book she'd been reading the

last few days. His throat closed, and fear numbed his limbs. She wouldn't have just left it here. Something had happened to her.

Using the handrail to steady himself, he took the steps two at a time. There was no note, no indication of where she'd gone. He called her name in the house, but there was no answer. Keri was still sleeping.

Nick's concern exploded into full-blown worry. Fraser should know what had happened. He jogged out the front door and over to the officer's car. "Fraser, Eve's missing."

Fraser didn't answer. Nick shined his light into the car, but the glass reflected too much glare to see clearly. He jerked open the car door. Fraser's head was back, and a wet stain covered his chest. A knife protruded from it.

Nick pressed his fingers to the man's throat. "Fraser?" His partner's flesh was cold. Dead. Nick tried to wrap his mind around the fact as panic and grief closed his vocal cords.

Nick swallowed, and his panic released its grip. He wheeled as Kade's pickup and Bree's Jeep parked in front of the lighthouse. "Bree, Kade! Fraser is dead. Gideon's got Eve."

Bree didn't waste time asking questions.

She darted for the house. "I'll get Samson." The men followed her inside. Samson hunkered down on the floor and barked when they entered the house, then bounded to the door. Bree stood and went to grab her search-and-rescue backpack out of the closet. Samson began running around and barking when she got out his search vest. She slipped it on him.

"Come with me, Samson." She ran upstairs with the dog on her heels.

"Where's she going?" Nick asked Kade.

"She's having Samson smell Eve's things and get a fix on her scent." Kade grabbed the phone. "I'll call Anu and ask if we can drop Keri off at her place. She's already got Davy. We'll need everyone we can get."

"Samson is on her trail," Bree said. She held the leash, and Samson pulled her along the yard.

His nose in the air, he bounded toward the side of the house. Nick and Kade ran after Bree and Samson. The dog reached the front yard and tugged Bree toward the road. He stopped at the end of the driveway. His tail, which had been wagging excitedly, drooped.

Bree unclipped the leash. "Search, Samson."

The dog ran back and forth across the

yard and street. He went down the street a few yards, then turned back. His ears lay back and his eyes looked mournful.

"She left in a vehicle," Bree said. "He's lost her scent."

The peanut butter sandwich was dry and tasteless, but Eve acknowledged her fear might have made the food flavorless. It was all she could do to summon enough saliva to swallow the first bite.

Her eyes on Oliver, she managed another bite, though she longed to throw it to the ground. She'd already done that once, but he'd picked it up and handed it back to her. After hesitating, she took it and decided it was best to keep him calm until she figured out how to get out of this.

He seemed so sane and rational. Even now, as he sat quietly eating his own sandwich and swigging a Pepsi.

Maybe she deserved this. She didn't like to think about Miranda, didn't like to remember the night she'd sunk lower than she ever dreamed she could. Her eyes burned from the effort to keep the tears at bay.

She wet her lips. "I've always loved swans. I thought I heard some outside. Do you have swans here?"

He threw back the last of his Pepsi and set the can on the floor. "On the pond. A glorious family. Come, I'll show you." He stood and helped her to her feet, then held the door open for her.

Such a contradiction. So courteous and yet so evil. Eve couldn't wrap her mind around it. He kept a tight grip on her arm as they went around to the back of the cabin. Thunder rumbled overhead, and fingers of lightning illuminated the mostly overgrown path. In the next flash, Eve saw the white birds gliding along the pond's surface.

"Trumpeters," she said.

"That one is Odette," he said, pointing to the nearest swan.

The swan glided nearer and fluttered out of the water and onto the ground. She ran at them, and Oliver backed up. "Careful, she's quite territorial. She has a penchant for taking the skin from my hand. I'm sure she'll find yours just as tasty."

If only he'd loosen his grip on her arm. Out here in the open, freedom felt as close as the smattering of mist on her face. At the next lightning flicker, Eve darted a glance into the thick brush and tried to see where she could hide if she managed to get away.

"Odette, just like in *Swan Lake.* You must

know the story."

"I watched a recording of it every day when I was growing up," he said in a monotone, his rapt gaze on the swans. "It was a copy of the Bolshoi Ballet. Maya Plisetskaya was the greatest ballerina ever to dance in it."

"She was lovely," Eve agreed.

"The swans were my escape. When my foster father would come to my room at night, I could see the swans from my window. Until he was done with me, I would shut my eyes and imagine I was swimming with them, watching their feet move through the water, seeing them dive for fish."

"I'm sorry," she said.

He glanced at her. "No need to pity me. The pain shaped me. It set me on my journey to be one with the universe. I'm aware that you think I'm quite mad. Nothing could be further from the truth." He smiled. "Pain and sacrifice are good for the soul."

"And what have you sacrificed?"

His mouth twisted. "Enough talk." He turned her around and propelled her back toward the cabin.

Eve dragged her feet and waited to see if his grasp would lessen even a fraction. But his fingers dug into her flesh with a relentless grip. When they reached the entry, he stumbled slightly over the step up, and she took her chance.

She tore out of his hand and darted toward the woods. He shouted after her, and she ran faster over the uneven ground. Wet leaves and branches lashed at her face, and she fought them blindly. Thunder rumbled again, and the rain let loose from the clouds. She was soaked to the skin and shivering in seconds.

The ground grew slick. The patter of rain on leaves drowned out any noise of pursuit. She spared a glance backward just as Gideon tackled her and drove her into the mud. Her face smashed into the cold muck, which filled her mouth and nose. She couldn't breathe, and she fought the suffocating bulk of Oliver on top of her. Stars exploded in her vision as she failed to inhale a last gulp of oxygen.

The blackness deepened around her, and with it a final regret. She wished she could have seen Nick and Keri one last time. The darkness took her down.

Every dog unit in the area responded to Bree's call for help, though she wasn't optimistic about their chances. Since Gideon had taken Eve in a vehicle, it would be a miracle if they managed to get her scent. He could have taken her anywhere, back to his lair in some other county even. They had no idea where to begin looking.

She sent two teams to each of the roads out of town while the men combed homes and businesses to see if a resident had noticed anything out of the ordinary. Since the forest was also a possibility, she and Naomi took their dogs and drove out to the Ottawa forest. Samson's soulful eyes watched her from the backseat, and Bree could feel her dog's distress.

Parking along the road, she and Naomi got out and opened the doors for the dogs. Charley and Samson leaped out. Bree let them smell one of Eve's socks, which she'd double bagged and brought with her. The dogs sniffed, then strained at their leashes.

Bree released the clip on Samson's leash. "Search, Samson!"

The dog disappeared across the road. Bree trained her high-powered flashlight on him and watched as he bounded through high weeds with his nose in the air. Charley followed, and both dogs crisscrossed the dark meadow where it joined the inky forest. They ran back out onto the pavement and took off down the road about a hundred feet, then circled back.

"They don't have a scent," Bree said, watching the aimless way they wandered from the ditch to the other side of the path. Lightning flickered overhead, and thunder chased it.

"Let's go on down the road." Naomi called Charley to her.

Bree snapped her fingers, and Samson ran to sniff at her leg. "Let's go, boy." They walked along the side of the road deeper into the forest. She could only hope Gideon had driven along here and the dogs would catch a whiff of Eve when she exited the vehicle.

The trees grew thick through here, and the heavy foliage of the oak trees on one side joined with the tangled branches of maple on the other side to form a canopy over their heads. Bree heard a smatter of rain, but no moisture reached her head.

It was so dark she wouldn't have been able to see the pavement if not for the flashlight. She swept the beam of light back and forth across the road to guide them. The dogs needed no help. They ran ahead, and she could hear their soft woofs. The moisture would make scents strong and easier to follow.

If they picked up a trail.

"This feels pretty fruitless," Naomi said,

kneeling to tie her right sneaker.

Bree didn't answer. She felt the futility, but they had to keep going. Eve depended on them.

If she was still alive.

They spent the next three hours walking down the road, then circling back to the Jeep and driving farther. The sprinkles of rain changed to a full-blown downpour, and the women and dogs were drenched.

Bree shivered under the rain slicker she'd pulled from her ready pack. She had no idea whether they were searching in the right place. "Let's go back where our phones work," she told Naomi. "Maybe someone has heard something."

They jogged back to the Jeep and drove out to where the tree canopy broke. Two bars on her cell phone, good enough. There were four missed calls. Trying not to let her hope get out of hand, Bree called up the missed-call log and started to scroll through it.

They were all from the nursing home. Her pulse hammered in her throat. Something had happened to her dad.

Bree's cell phone rang before she could call the nursing home back. She answered it, but the call dropped. Driving back into the open air where rain rattled the roof of the car, she scrolled through her menus again to see who had called.

The nursing home showed again. Before she could return the call, the phone rang again. "Hello, this is Bree," she said.

Ruby's voice spoke. "Bree, I'm so sorry, but your father has gone missing again."

Bree tensed. "Are you sure?"

"We've checked everywhere. He's gone."

"It's nearly one in the morning, and it's been raining for hours. When did he go missing?"

"About two hours ago. I called the sheriff already. He sent a deputy over, but he said everyone else is out searching for a missing woman."

"I'm searching for her too," Bree said. "But I'll be right there." She disconnected and told Naomi what had happened. "I have to trust that everyone's doing their best to help Eve. But I've got to help Dad. He's in danger too."

"Of course you do," Naomi said. "We'll find him fast and get back here. We're not doing much good for Eve at the moment. Maybe someone else is having better luck."

"Call Montgomery and check in," Bree said. She accelerated down the wet road to the highway and listened with half an ear while Naomi talked to the deputy. From this side of the conversation, it was clear that no one had found Eve.

She tried not to think what that might mean.

All the lights were on in the nursing home when she parked and got out. She let the dogs out and snatched the end of Samson's leash while Naomi corralled Charley. They jogged through the rain to the entrance.

Deputy Montgomery met them at the front door. Rain dripped from his wide-brimmed hat, and his yellow slicker deposited more moisture on the floor. The corners of his eyes drooped with exhaustion, and mud streaked his pale face.

"Sorry about this, Bree," he said. "I couldn't pick up a trail on him at all. The dogs will locate him fast, eh?"

"You bet," she assured him. Without wasting any time, she led Samson down the hall to her father's room. What a sense of déjà vu. She'd just done this. The dogs sniffed around the room, then took off down the hall when given the order to search. She quickly called Kade's phone and left a message when he didn't answer.

Bree expected them to go out the back door to the yard again, but they went straight for the front door. How could he have slipped out past the nurses' station again? Her gaze touched Ruby's face, and the woman looked down with red creeping into her cheeks.

Montgomery held the door open for them. The dogs ran across the road and disappeared into the trees. Their frantic barking grew fainter, then louder again as they circled back to let the women catch up. Then they were off again.

She'd hoped to find him quickly, but when she stopped to catch her breath and call Samson to her, her watch showed over an hour had passed. She shivered in the cool, wet air. Exhaustion slowed her movements, and she found it hard to think, to reason through where he might have gone.

Was he wandering aimlessly, or did he have a destination in mind? There was nothing out this way that she'd ever seen but a deserted cabin deep in the forest. He'd never make it that far. It was another ten or fifteen miles into the forest at least.

Bree stood. "Let's keep going." They were wandering in a dark maze with no end in sight, but giving up wasn't an option.

29

Nick hung with Kade as he helped organize searchers to go door-to-door throughout Rock Harbor. Not that he thought Gideon would have kept Eve somewhere here in town. But someone might have seen something.

The men had been walking for hours. Nick's feet throbbed, and his back ached. It was nearly two in the morning. "Has anyone checked Job's Children?" he asked Kade.

"We probably should," Kade said.

"I thought about it earlier, but I made an assumption about Gideon once and didn't want to make the same mistake again." Nick turned and walked back down the sidewalk in the direction of the lighthouse. The beacon flashed and illuminated his SUV where he'd left it along the side of the road.

"I'll go with you. We're getting nowhere here," Kade said.

The men climbed into the vehicle and

drove out of town. Rain sluiced over the windshield so fast the wipers could barely keep up. He eased up on the accelerator when the tires slid on the wet pavement.

Kade glanced at Nick. "There's something you should know. Will is Keri's father."

Nick slammed on the brakes, and the SUV fishtailed. He brought the vehicle under control, then turned his head to stare at Kade. "And you're just now telling me this?"

"Sorry. I was focused on finding Eve, and it slipped my mind. We just found out tonight for sure."

"There has to be a connection." Nick tried to pick up his speed a little, but it was impossible with the road conditions. He eased off on the accelerator again and concentrated on peering through the windshield.

"Maybe Gideon didn't take her. Maybe Will is going to hold her and demand I hand over our daughter."

"But why kidnap Eve before the judge even makes a custody ruling? And Fraser is dead too. The trouble coming down on his head would be huge." Kade took a napkin from the dash and wiped the moisture from the inside of the windshield. "Of course, maybe he's arrogant enough to think no one can pin anything on him."

Nick reached the turnoff into the compound. The place was as dark as an underwater cave and about as wet. The tires sank into muddy holes, and he had to fight the wheel to stay on the lane. "Any idea where to go?" He peered through the window and could barely make out a building.

"That's the church. They all live back in the copper mine." Kade reached into the backseat and grabbed a battery-powered lantern and a flashlight. He handed the Maglite to Nick. "I'll show you."

Nick flipped on the flashlight and got out into the driving rain. The beam barely pushed back the shadows enough to see where to put his feet. Cold rain from his wet hair trickled into his yellow slicker. Kade struck off through the driving rain like he knew where he was going, and Nick followed.

Kade stopped in front of the mine's mouth and lifted the lantern he carried so it shone into the darkness. "Follow me." He disappeared into the dark opening.

Nick focused his flashlight beam after him and stepped into the dark, dry space. The cessation of rain was a relief. He followed Kade, who was moving through an opening to the right.

Moans filtered to their ears.

"Something's wrong," Nick said. The stink of sickness burned his nose.

"This way." Kade led the way down a corridor to the right. The lantern illuminated a sleeping bag and the face of the man who thrashed on it.

Will Donaldson. And Patti beside him.

"Help me, man," Will whispered. His voice sounded hoarse and weak, and his words were slurred. His eyelids drooped, and it was clear he was having trouble focusing.

"What's happening here?" Nick knelt by the couple. He could hear other people crying out farther back in the mine.

"Bad food," Will whispered.

"Water, need water." Patti licked her lips.

Nick found a bottle of water and started to give her a sip, but Kade stopped him.

"We don't know what's caused this," Kade said. "The water could be contaminated." He scratched his head. "Bree saw them earlier. She said Will acted like he had a headache, and Patti was sweating and looked pale." He knelt by Will. "How long have you been sick?"

"Since nightfall," he slurred.

"I'll call an ambulance," Nick told Kade. He ran down the corridor back into the rain and placed a call to 911 before going back inside.

"Is Eve here?" he asked Will as soon as he got inside the mine again.

Will mumbled and tossed but didn't answer.

"He's out of it," Kade said. "I looked around while you were outside. Everyone in here is sick."

"Any idea what it is? Or if it's contagious?"

"Will said bad food. It could be botulism. Paralysis is one of the main symptoms. They're slurring their words and their eyes are drooping."

Nick knelt by Patti. "Patti, where is Eve?"

She blinked and tried to rise, then fell back onto the sleeping bag. Her eyes weren't focusing on Nick.

"Where's your sister, Patti?"

She shook her head. "Not here," she managed to get out.

Nick stood. "Is there anything we can do?"

"Pray they hang on until help arrives."

"Eve too," Nick whispered. If his wife wasn't here, where was she?

A thick substance glued her lips together. Eve swam up out of unconsciousness that only reluctantly released her. She rubbed something stiff and dry from her face and pried her eyes open. The dim light of early morning showed the small cabin she thought she'd escaped.

She choked back a sob and struggled into a sitting position. Every muscle ached. Her mouth tasted like mud.

She was alone.

Handcuffs still chained her wrists together, but at least Gideon wasn't here. Dried mud coated her arms and clothing. Running her hand over her face, she realized mud caked every bit of her skin.

She staggered to her feet and tottered to the window. The van was gone. Maybe she could get out again. Rushing to the door, she twisted the handle, but it wouldn't open. He'd probably dropped a bar into place on the outside. She glanced around to see if there was anything she could use as a battering ram.

Her gaze lit on the chair. Battered and old, the wood was strong, but it was no match for the massive door. The cot was too heavy for her to lift. There was nothing. She went back to the window. It was barred. How had she not noticed that last night?

There was a second window on the opposite wall that she hadn't seen last night. It was barred too. Through the glass, she could see the swans on the pond. There was a shack on an island of dirt in the middle of the water. She leaned her forehead against the cold glass and let the tears moisten the dry mud on her cheeks. It was hopeless. This prison was as tight as any the government had erected.

A sound came to her ears. Some kind of scratching or pecking. She turned around to see a face peering back at her through the front window. She yelped in surprise. The old man looked familiar, and she realized it was Bree's father, Bernard.

Eve sprinted to the window and looked past the old man to an empty yard.

He was alone.

"Did you wander off again?" she asked. "Where's Bree?"

"I caught the biggest fish in the record of the state here," he said. "My father was so proud of me."

"Bernard, where is Bree? Do you remember me? I'm Eve, Bree's friend."

"I still have that fish mounted over my fireplace."

"Bernard, can you unlock the door?" Eve pointed. "See the bar on the door? Can you lift it?"

The old man shuffled to the door and fumbled with the wooden bar. Eve heard it scrape across the wood as he lifted it. "Can you unlock the door?" she called.

The knob twisted, but the door didn't open. It probably took a key. Maybe Oliver left it somewhere out there. "See if there's a mat," she called. "There might be a key under it."

She heard more movement, but the door stayed closed. When she went back to the window, she heard the sound of an engine, and Oliver's van came down the narrow lane.

She put her hands on the window. "Bernard, run! Go hide!"

The old man shuffled back to the window. "I caught the biggest fish right out back of this cabin. We should go fishing."

The van stopped, and Oliver got out. He smiled when he saw Bernard. "Good to see you, my friend. Would you like to fish today? Come inside, sir." He tugged the old man toward the door.

Eve heard the key slide into the lock, then the door opened and Oliver shoved Bernard into the cabin.

"Sit," Oliver ordered, pointing to the chair.

Bernard sat on the chair with his hands on his knees and looked up with an expectant smile. When Oliver said nothing more, the old man glanced around and picked up one of Eve's flip-flops, which she'd kicked off.

"Don't move." Oliver left the cabin. The bar on the door clanged into place.

Eve turned to see what he was doing. Jogging to the van, he opened the side door. A handicap access ramp came out, and he stepped in only to emerge a few moments later with a woman lying on a gurney.

Eve couldn't make out much detail, only straggly blonde hair at the top of the sheet. Oliver wheeled the bed to the cabin, then placed a piece of plywood over the steps in front of the door. After the scrape of the bar being lifted again, the door opened, and he pushed her up the jerry-rigged ramp inside.

When he rolled the gurney past Bernard, the old man walked out the door while Oliver's back was turned.

Eve turned her face away, hoping Oliver wouldn't notice. Now all she could do was pray Bernard remembered where they were and lead someone back to help.

"He's just disappeared." Bree leaned her head against the rough bark of an oak tree. At least the rain had stopped, but slogging through the mud had left her muscles sore and wobbly.

Naomi looked as bedraggled as Bree felt.

Her hair had dried, plastered to her head, and twigs sprouted from her scalp. She was breathing hard as she selected a spot on the downed tree near where Bree sat.

"We need to rest," Bree said, though her nerves strummed with the urgency to keep going.

"Maybe we could just climb in the Jeep and sleep an hour," Naomi said.

"The Jeep is miles behind us," Bree said, shading her eyes to help focus on the truck that rattled up the fire lane. "It's Kade." He must have tracked her GPS unit. Though she was tired, she stood and went to meet him.

He strode to meet her, and she went into his arms, the safe haven she'd craved.

"No luck?" he whispered into her hair.

"No." Lifting her head, she searched his face. "He's been gone all night, Kade. Eve too."

"It wasn't that cold last night. He's probably fine."

"Samson still seems to have a trail. We just can't go fast enough. Everyone is tired, including the dogs."

"I brought them some food." Kade kept his arm around her, and they walked back to his truck, where he lifted a bag of dog food from the back.

Bree caught a glimpse of Nick in the truck. He was on his phone. "Hard night for you guys too."

"Yeah. Nick is sick with worry. Just like you."

"Nothing on Eve at all? Any leads?"

"Nope. We even checked out the Job's Children compound." He hesitated.

"What is it?"

"They were all sick. We think it's botulism. Patti was with them. Since the food was in them so long before help arrived, they may all die."

"Oh no," she whispered. "You know, they both looked a little pale when we saw them."

"Yeah, they were in a bad way when we got out there. Patti is already on a respirator. Will too. They seem the sickest."

Eve would hate to hear this. In spite of the trouble Patti had caused, she was still Eve's sister. "What about Eve? Have the dogs gotten a scent?"

Kade shook his head. "She's vanished. None of the other dog teams have gotten a whiff of her scent either. He must have hauled her out of town with the windows shut." Kade carried the bag to where Naomi lay on the fallen tree with her eyes closed.

The dogs got up and stretched when he dumped some food for them. The truck door slammed, and Bree turned to see Nick walking toward them with slow steps.

"You didn't find your dad?" he asked.

"No."

Nick handed her a bag. "Here's some food for you two."

Bree pulled out a beef pasty. Even though it was lukewarm when she bit into it, it was the most delicious thing she'd ever eaten. The beef juice exploded on her tongue with flavor, and her fatigue began to fall away.

"I needed that," she said. "I was even out of pistachios."

"I brought you more of those too." Kade smiled and handed over another bag.

"A man after my heart," she said, tucking them into her ready pack.

"That's the idea."

Naomi was still sleeping, but Bree knew her friend needed food. She poked Naomi's leg with the toe of her shoe. "Hey, sleepy-head, grub's here."

Naomi opened one bleary eye. "Food? Do I smell food?"

"You do indeed." Bree shoved the bag into Naomi's hand. "Kade and Nick are here."

"They found Eve?" Naomi asked, sitting up with a hopeful glint in her eyes.

"No."

The light in Naomi's face faded. She

opened the bag and took out her food. "Bliss," she said when she took her first bite. "What time is it?"

"Nine," Nick said.

"The geocachers should be out in force by now," Bree said. Maybe they'd stumble across evidence of Eve's or Bernard's whereabouts. Bree was beginning to worry that her dad was lying dead under a bush somewhere. She didn't want to even think about what was happening to Eve.

"I think I'm going to go talk to Oliver," Nick said. "He knows a lot about the criminal mind. Just maybe he'll have an idea of where Gideon would think to take Eve."

Bree nodded. "How are the kids?" she asked Kade.

"I called Anu on the way out here. They're doing fine."

"They don't know what's going on, do they?"

Kade shook his head. "She's kept the TV off."

That was a relief. Bree had been afraid Davy and Keri would see Eve's face on the morning news. Kade kissed her. "I'll stay with Nick. We're praying for you. Call me when you find him."

"I will." Bree watched the men jog back to the truck. Kade turned the vehicle around, and the truck rolled away.

Birds chirped overhead, and the sun began to burn off the fog left by the rain. Bree's hope lifted with the sunshine. "You ready to get going again?" she asked Naomi.

Her friend nodded and held up her hand for Bree to haul her to her feet. "I can't understand how he could have gotten this far. He's an old man."

"Have you ever seen his stride when he's on a mission? He's got long legs and loves to walk. He's probably covered twice our distance." Not for the first time, Bree regretted the slowness of searching. Whenever the dogs lost a scent, it took time to find it again.

Bree called Samson to her and rubbed his head. His dark eyes stared up soulfully. The dogs were even more exhausted than she and Naomi were. They might even be following the wrong scent by now.

"Maybe we should freshen their scent." She dug in her backpack and rooted until she found the bag with her father's T-shirt. She held it open for the dogs to sniff, then closed it and put it away. "Search, Samson. Find Grandpa."

Samson's tail wagged, and he set off the way they had just come. She locked gazes with Naomi.

"If we've been going the wrong direction all this time, I'll shoot myself," Naomi muttered.

Bree could have kicked herself. Samson was an awesome search dog, but any dog could get distracted by other scents. They may have wandered far off course. The dogs didn't seem to have a scent now. They crisscrossed the area with their noses in the air. Samson turned and looked back at Bree as if to ask what had happened.

Bree sighed. "I think we'd better head back a ways and see if we can figure out where we went wrong." The minutes ticked by, and Bree swatted at black flies that came buzzing out of wet vegetation.

This was her fault. She should have refreshed the scent every hour or so. Stupid, stupid. The sort of thing an amateur would do.

After walking about an hour, Samson's ears went on alert. Just to make sure she wasn't misreading her dog, Bree had him and Charley smell the T-shirt again. Both dogs began to wag their tails and bound off toward the east.

"They've got it!" Naomi ran after the dogs.

Bree jogged after them. Samson laid his ears back and raced down a lane that barely cut through the vegetation. From the dog's body language, she thought her dad must be very close. She almost called Kade, then decided to wait until she actually found her dad.

Samson, followed by Charley, leaped over a fallen tree and disappeared over a hillside. Moments later, Bree heard happy barking.

"They've found him!" She kicked up her speed a notch and ran to the top of the hill. Looking down, she saw both dogs licking her father, who sat on a tree stump. "Dad!"

Her father looked up. His eyes were alert, though he looked tired. He stood, and she neared and hugged him. "You had us worried sick."

"I just went for a walk," he said. "Me and Eve."

Bree ended the hug and stared at her father. "Eve? Did you see Eve?" He was probably confused. A trek that long with no food or water would disorient anyone.

"She lost her shoe," Bernard said, holding up a flip-flop.

It was hot pink. Bree had seen Eve wear these sandals. "Where is Eve, Dad?" she asked. "Can you take us to her?"

"I thought I'd go fishing," her father said. His blue eyes clouded.

"Eve, Dad. Where's Eve?"

Her father stared off into the trees. "I caught the biggest fish out of that pond," he muttered.

Bree's eyes stung. He knew where Eve was, but how could she get through to him? She got out her phone and called her husband. "I found Dad, and he's got Eve's shoe. Can you meet us at the nursing home? I'm taking Dad there now, then we'll come back here."

30

Nick paced the sidewalk outside the nursing home. Kade waited in the Durango. Bree still wasn't back yet, but he knew it would take awhile. They'd have to hike to the Jeep before returning to town. He should have gotten her coordinates and started looking for Eve, but without the dogs it wouldn't do much good. He'd have no idea which direction Bernard had wandered.

Popping a Rolaids into his mouth, he paced some more until he finally saw her red Jeep round the corner. He jogged to the vehicle as Bree got out with her dad and Samson. "Where is Eve?" he asked.

Bree shook her head. "He's confused again."

"How do you know he even saw her?"

Bree held up a hot pink flip-flop. "Recognize this?"

"Yeah." He took the sandal in his hand.

"So we know she's in the woods somewhere. How do we find her?"

"We'll go back out as soon as I take care of Dad. I marked the coordinates where we were. I left Naomi there. She was going to have Charley follow the trail until we get back."

At least they had a jump start. "I should have gone straight out there with her," Nick said.

"I'll be right back, and we'll go. Did Oliver have any ideas?"

"I can't reach him. He might be out fishing though. I'll try his phone again while you get your dad settled."

Bree nodded and guided her dad toward the building. "Stay, Samson," she said. The dog lay down at Nick's feet and closed his eyes. "He's exhausted," she said. She and Bernard disappeared inside.

Nick got out his phone and dialed Oliver again. The voice mail came on almost immediately. Where could he be? Nick hoped everything was okay.

He started to put his cell phone back when it rang. "Andreakos here."

"Nick, I got the information you wanted," his dad said. "Uh, it's a little strange."

"What is?"

"Well, this Miranda you wanted me to

find? Her name is Miranda Harding."

"That's right, I remember now. Harding is a common name. Were you able to trace her?"

"This is where it gets weird. She's been catatonic for seven years. Her husband recently moved her to Rock Harbor. Nick, her husband is Oliver."

"Oliver? Our Oliver?" Nick stammered.

"Yeah. And get this. She's missing."

Nick's mind raced. He hadn't spoken to Oliver since before Eve disappeared. Miranda's husband could want revenge. It would be understandable. "He's got her, Dad."

"That's what I'm thinking. I'm on my way to the bed-and-breakfast where he's been staying now. I'll call you if there's any clue to where he's gone."

"Get a scent sample."

"Will do. Oh, and, Nick? I just heard from IA. You've been cleared of the charges. This is your investigation. Not that you ever really lost it."

Still in shock, Nick disconnected. He couldn't believe his friend would betray him this way. The news about his job paled in comparison.

The door opened, and Bree stepped out.

"Let's go," she said. "Any luck raising Oliver?"

Kade exited the Durango and joined them.

"He's got Eve," Nick said.

"What?" Kade stared at him. "Who has Eve?"

"Oliver. Miranda's last name is Harding. She's Oliver's wife."

Bree held up her hand. "Wait, who's Miranda?"

"A woman Eve hurt a long time ago. She's been in a hospital ever since. This is all about revenge."

"*Oliver* is Gideon?"

"Yes!" Nick grabbed her arm. "We have to find them."

"Can we get a sample of Oliver's scent?" Kade suggested. "Maybe the dogs could pick it up."

"I already told Dad to get a sock."

Bree shook her head. "The dogs led us in the wrong direction for a while. My fault though, not theirs. I won't make that mistake again." Bree prodded Samson with the toe of her boot. "Come on, boy." The dog stood and stretched, then hopped into the backseat when she opened the door. She shut it and got behind the wheel while Nick climbed in. Kade offered to go get Oliver's sock from Cyril, and Nick tossed Kade his keys to the SUV.

"The easiest thing to do would be to drive out the fire road until we get where we found my dad. Or wherever Naomi is. Your dad can send out Oliver's sock, and we'll try that scent once we get it too."

"I'll call Naomi. What's her number?" Nick punched in the numbers Bree rattled off. Naomi's voice mail came on. "Dead spot, I guess," he said, closing his phone. "I got her voice mail."

"I've got the coordinates where she started." Bree gunned the Jeep through a narrow opening in thick brush. "We'll be there in about fifteen minutes."

"Why don't you pull over and I'll drive? You're beat."

"I'm okay. Got my second wind."

Nick leaned forward in his seat and scanned the forest as it passed. What were the chances Eve was even still alive? He didn't want to consider the possibility she was gone, but he couldn't ignore the facts. Still, he'd thought she was dead once before. Until he saw her lifeless body with his own eyes, he would keep the faith.

"Here we are." Bree pulled the Jeep off into the waist-high weeds. "We have to hike about a quarter of a mile into the brush."

She let Samson out.

Nick scrambled out and struck off through the thick brush. Brambles tore at his pants and shirt. He battered down the vegetation as best he could to make the going a little easier for Bree, but nearly half an hour passed before Bree held up her hand.

"We're here." She knelt on the ground and rummaged in her pack. Samson crowded her, poking his nose into the contents. "I already fed you all the food I had," she said. "Want some water?" She dug out a small plastic bowl and a water bottle. Samson lapped the bowl dry, then she shoved everything back inside and opened a bag for him to sniff. "Ready, boy? Search, Samson. Find out where Grandpa was."

The dog sniffed the air, then started back the way they'd come. "The other way, Samson," Bree told him. "Backtrack."

The dog stopped and looked at her, his dark eyes hesitant. "This is something new for him," she told Nick.

Great. Eve's life was dependent on the dog learning something new. Nick was tempted to strike off on his own. "Which direction was he walking from?"

"We don't know. He was sitting when we found him." Bree took the dog's head in her hands. "You can do it, Samson. Back.

Where did he walk from? Go the other way."

Samson nosed around the fallen log, then took off east and north of his original heading. "I think he's on to something," Nick said.

"Yes, I think so."

They ran after the dog, but he quickly paused to nose some wildflowers. "He still doesn't understand," Bree said. "He wants to follow the freshest scent because that's the way he's been trained."

They tromped all afternoon. Kade brought them sandwiches and Oliver's scent, then returned to the sheriff's office to check on the progress of the other searchers. Nick almost went back with him. This felt like a total waste of time. Eve probably wasn't even in the woods. It was hard to say where Oliver had taken her. They could be back in Cheboygan for all he knew.

He rubbed his burning eyes. His fight against despair grew more and more feeble. Eve had been gone now nearly twenty-four hours. What were the chances she was still alive? Oliver had shown no mercy to any other woman. He would be unlikely to show any to the woman he hated most in the world.

Even in the daytime hours, the deep woods never got brighter than twilight. Dark clouds had begun to cover the sun, and the shadows lengthened. Every tree seemed to hide a figure watching them, though Nick knew it was his imagination.

He and Bree rested in a meadow. Lying back with his hand over his eyes, he wished he could sleep, then wake up to find out it had all been a nightmare. The odor of mud, crushed grass, and wildflowers lulled him, and his eyes closed, then he jerked awake. He couldn't sleep, no matter how tired he was. Eve was depending on him.

He lurched to his feet and wished he didn't have to awaken Bree, but he didn't know how to work with Samson. Kneeling, he shook her shoulder gently, and she came instantly awake.

"Let's go," she said.

They took off again. Even though they walked for hours, evening surprised him when it fell. They stopped to let Samson rest, and Nick heard a vehicle moving slowly down the lane. They stayed on the ground where they rested and watched its approach. It was Kade's truck. He pulled it to the side of the road and got out.

"I brought some food," Kade said.

Nick realized he was ravenous. "Thanks," he said.

The night sounds echoed around him.

Crickets chirped, and an owl hooted overhead. The wind in the treetops brought the scent of pine to his nose.

Bree got up and hugged her husband. "You're a lifesaver." The dog yawned and stretched, then stood. "Any news?" Bree asked.

"No." Kade put his arm around her. "Naomi came back to town. She and Charley are exhausted and never did get a trail."

"How are the kids?" Nick asked.

"Fine. Still with Anu."

Bree glanced down at her dog. "He's rested some. Maybe he'll get it." She dug in her bag and pulled out three bags. "We'll let him sniff all of them. Maybe he'll get a whiff of Eve or Dad."

Samson sniffed each bag. His head came up.

"Search, Samson," Bree said without much hope in her voice.

The dog moved around the clearing. He stopped and sampled the air again. His tail began to wag, and his ears came up. He leaped across a patch of wildflowers and headed south, away from the place they had found Bernard.

"He's got a scent!" Bree shouted.

Fresh strength flowed through Nick's muscles, and he sprang after the dog.

■ ■ ■ ■

Eve couldn't figure out what Oliver was waiting for. The day had been strange in the extreme. He'd wheeled his wife into the cabin, then left them to do something outside.

She gazed down into Miranda's face. The room was so dark she could barely make out the woman's face, but everything about her was etched in Eve's memory by now.

There was little resemblance of the lovely young woman she'd once been. Her hair was thin and dry now, lying almost without color on the pillow. Her sallow skin didn't have a hint of the pink it used to. She was so gaunt that she barely raised the sheet from the gurney.

Worst of all, her face was pitted with deep scars. Her mouth twisted in a hideous grimace.

And it was all Eve's fault.

"I'm sorry, Miranda," she whispered. "You don't know how sorry I am. There was no excuse, but I was young and blind."

She approached the gurney, wishing she could make amends. Miranda hadn't stirred since Oliver brought her in. Eve touched her hand, then snatched it away. It was cold, so cold. Could Miranda be dead?

Eve shuddered and told herself it wasn't possible.

Eve tried not to imagine — in graphic detail — what Oliver intended to do to her. Reading Dante's *Divine Comedy* had left her nightmare-ridden for a week when she was nineteen. He'd be sure to make it as painful as possible.

She heard him coming and turned to face the door. Metal to metal, the key grated in the door, then it creaked open and allowed the light from the lantern he held aloft to spill into the room.

He was smiling.

The expression made her feel worse. Blood pulsed in her throat, and she vowed she wouldn't make it easy for him. Whatever he planned was outside, and she intended to take any opportunity to escape. Better to die trying than to just let him have his little game.

Oliver approached the gurney that held his wife. "How are you, my dear?" He didn't wait for an answer but opened the door and wheeled her out.

Eve sprang to her feet. She intended to try to squeeze through the doorway, but he slammed and locked the door before she could.

"Are you so eager to begin? How self-sacrificing." The door muted the words.

The rattle of the gurney as it passed around the side of the cabin was muffled by the cabin walls, but Eve was able to track their progress. When the noise reached the back, she stepped to the window and looked out to see him lift his wife from the gurney and lay her in a boat. Miranda seemed strangely stiff. He stepped into the craft, and the sound of the motor started.

Miranda had died. Eve was sure of it. She tried to remember what she'd heard about rigor mortis. Didn't it start about three hours after death? Miranda wasn't fully stiff yet, so maybe she'd been dead about that long.

Eve watched him guide the boat out across the water toward the tiny island in the middle.

The swans trumpeted and flapped their wings to signal their protest as the boat passed, but they didn't fly away. Instead, they swam toward Oliver, and he threw them bits of a sandwich.

Eve guessed it was a peanut butter sandwich.

She lost sight of him, and it seemed like forever before she heard the sound of the boat returning. When the boat docked, he looked up and saw her staring out the window and gave a jaunty wave. Still smiling, he approached the cabin and disappeared around the side.

Waiting for his key to scrape in the lock again, she felt nearly faint. When the wait had gone on longer than expected, she darted to the window and saw him exiting the van with a soft suitcase.

She grabbed up the chair and hefted it over her head. The key rattled in the lock, and he entered the cabin. Using all her strength, she swung the chair at his head.

He leaped out of the way and knocked it out of her hand with the smile still in place. He tossed her the small satchel. "Put that on."

Shaking her head, she backed away.

"You would rather I kill you now?" With a casual gesture, he showed her the knife in his hand.

She shrank back with her eyes on the blade. She had no doubt he knew how to use it. "I can't change with you in here."

"Five minutes." He went to the door and locked it behind him.

Her only chance was to get outside this cabin. Eve knelt and unzipped the satchel. What a strange-looking getup. She touched the brown garment and realized it was a gown made of some incredibly rough, greasy cloth that scratched her fingers when she touched it.

A haircloth, just like Dante's sinners wore.

Dropping the gown, she shuddered and rubbed her palms on her jeans. The thing was nasty. What was she going to do? She couldn't put it on.

But he'd make her.

Either she could do it willingly and with courage, or he'd kill her here and now. While there was life, there was hope. Shucking off her jeans and shirt, she picked up the oily cloth and dropped it over her head. The material itched and irritated.

She missed hearing Oliver's entrance until he was right behind her.

"Shall we go?" He wrapped a rope around her wrists and began to tie her up.

She flexed her wrists as much as she could as he secured her hands behind her, then he took her arm in a tight grip and marched her outside.

Eve stumbled over the rough ground as he pushed her. The night air had never tasted so fresh. He forced her into the boat and cuffed her to a mooring cleat. Without another word, he stepped in and pushed the boat into the lake. He started the motor, then guided it toward the island, overgrown and wild. Eve watched its approach. Her bare arms pebbled with goose bumps. Working the ropes, she felt them give a little.

The swans swam to meet them. Digging into a bag on the bottom of the boat, Gideon began to throw bits of peanut butter sandwiches all around in the water. They flocked to the food.

Eve couldn't see the water because of the birds. There had to be hundreds of them.

He switched off the motor and threw an anchor overboard before stepping into the water and dragging the boat ashore.

"What are you going to do?" Eve's voice trembled. "Why am I dressed like this if you're going to blind me and take my face?"

He unlocked the cuffs and tossed them into the pond. His face was set but serene, and he didn't seem to be listening.

"I know *sorry* isn't good enough, Oliver, but I really am sorry. I was young and stupid. If only I could do it all over again." She remembered that night like it was yesterday.

She heard the music, saw herself imitating the intricate steps she'd seen Miranda perform in practice, a routine Miranda had choreographed herself. It had been so natural to steal the steps she admired. Eve almost didn't realize she'd done it until the crowd was on its feet, cheering.

Eve would never forget the look on Miranda's face when she started her own performance.

Moments later, Miranda lost her balance and fell headfirst from the stage into the lights. Then her clothes had burst into flames. Eve shuddered at the memory.

"You stole Miranda's dance steps. She could only compensate for it by trying something daring and different. Something dangerous." He stood on the bank, pointing his finger at her. "You brought this on yourself."

"I know," she whispered. "But why now, after all these years?"

"The first years we spent going from doctor to doctor. With every one who told me there was nothing he could do, my hatred of you grew. For solace, I turned to learning, to seeking the truth. The truth is that pain shapes us. Even Miranda. She'll be stronger for all this. But she's suffered long enough. Now it's your turn to be educated. And her turn to have a new face."

He grabbed her arm, hauled her out of the boat, then propelled her to the cabin that squatted in the center of the tiny circle of land that wasn't much bigger than the building.

She fought him, trying to bite him, to kick him, but her struggles were futile with her hands tied behind her. He thrust open the door and dragged her inside. Music blared from speakers, and bright lights shocked her unadjusted eyes. She shuddered at the music — "Black Swan Pas de Deux."

Blinking in the bright wash of light, she stood swaying in the middle of the room while he shut and locked the door. In the Swan Queen's white costume, Miranda lay on what looked like an operating table under the lights. Other medical equipment flanked the room.

Her gaze went to the table holding a big sewing needle and wire. Her stomach cramped, and she nearly doubled over. He was ready to inflict plenty of pain.

Oliver went to the metal table and picked up the needle and wire. His smile seemed easy and relaxed.

The needle's evil glint drew Eve's attention. "You don't know how to transplant a face," she whispered. "You'll kill Miranda as well as me." Her gaze went to the other woman. There was now no doubt in her mind that Miranda had died already. Should she tell Oliver, or would it inflame him more?

"I went to medical school, you know," he

said. "And I've extensively studied the procedure. She'll die anyway if I don't try. She has leukemia."

She might as well go for it. Eve nodded to the gurney. "She's dead already, Oliver. Look at her. You killed her by taking her from care."

His eyes flashed. "Your lies won't work. Miranda will live and love me again."

Eve backed away as he came toward her. Twisting her wrists in the ropes, she felt them give more. If she could keep him talking until she got her hands free, she had a chance. "Why did you take the other women if you wanted me?"

"Ballerinas should be above reproach. Gifted with so much beauty and grace, you should guard your morals. When I found one who fell, I removed her."

She knew she had to tread carefully. Goad him enough to keep him talking and explaining himself without pushing him over the edge.

"But they're all blonde like me. And Miranda. I think you like killing. You justify your urges by telling yourself you were ordained to preserve the ballet's status, but it's not true."

His smile faltered. "That's not true. I have a mission."

"What happens when I'm dead? Will you keep watching for more blonde ballerinas to kill? I think you will. I don't think it's about Miranda at all. It's about you."

He was shaking his head, coming nearer with the wicked needle and wire.

She wrenched her wrists so hard that pain radiated up to her shoulder. One hand slid out of the rope, then the other. She was free! Still backing away, she calculated her opportunity. He'd locked the door, so she needed time to get it unlocked and open.

Oliver began to thread the curved needle with wire. Eve took the chance. She ran at him, using her strong legs to drive her headfirst into his pudgy stomach. He reeled, knocking over a stainless steel cart and sending the scalpels and other instruments falling to the floor. His head slammed into the cart, and he slumped at its base.

Eve darted past his feet and fumbled with the deadbolt. The thing was new and stiff and resisted her efforts until she realized she was twisting it the wrong way. She got it open and ran outside.

Gideon shouted behind her, but she was already shoving the boat into the water. She got in and managed to get the motor started. It puttered much slower than she would have liked. Turning, she saw Gideon wading in after her. Oliver, teeth bared, threw himself at the boat and managed to grab the edge. She turned to dive out, then reconsidered.

The swans were coming to meet them. Hundreds of swans.

31

Perspiration dripped down Nick's forehead. The terrain had been mostly uphill, and they had to sidestep heavy vegetation often. At least the moon was out, though the thick trees blocked much of its glow.

He broke through the underbrush to find Bree and Kade sitting on a tree stump. Bree's mouth drooped, and Samson lay at her feet.

"What's wrong?" Nick asked.

"Samson's exhausted, and he's lost the trail again," Kade said softly. "I'm letting Bree sleep awhile. She's about to drop where she stands."

"I'm awake." Bree sighed and got up. "Now that I've got a little strength back, I'm going to climb a tree and try to get a signal so I can talk to my dad."

"It's nearly eleven," Kade pointed out.

"Maybe he'll be lucid. I just need some kind of clue to where we're going. You know these woods, Kade. If he could just tell us something, we might know where to head."

"I'll climb," Nick said.

"He wouldn't talk to you. Kade offered, too, but I'm the one he'd be most apt to talk to." She got up and went to an oak tree. "One of you want to give me a hand up? Sorry to be a weenie, but I'm so tired."

"I'll do it." Kade went to his wife. Lacing his fingers together, he made a ledge of his hands for her to put her foot on. He hoisted her higher when she stepped onto his laced fingers.

She grabbed the tree limb and swung up into the branches. "Be right back." She disappeared into the foliage.

Nick swept the beam of his flashlight around while he waited. The light didn't penetrate much, and every tree looked like another. It would be easy to get lost out here. He could hear Bree's voice, muffled by the leaves. Settling on the ground, he leaned his head back and closed his eyes.

The first time he'd seen Eve had been magic. She was dancing in *The Nutcracker*. He'd never seen anyone so graceful. Floating around the dance floor, she embodied the music. He hadn't anticipated his reaction, because he wasn't a ballet sort of guy. His mother had wanted them all to go for her birthday, and she'd dragged him kicking and screaming.

But he'd fallen for Eve in that moment. He hung around backstage until she'd changed and was leaving for the night. Her face scrubbed clean of makeup, she was even more beautiful up close.

He smiled, remembering how hard it had been to talk her into going out for coffee.

Bree gave a wild yell from the tree, and her feet slid into view. "He gave me something!"

Kade reached up and helped her down, holding her a minute before he let go. "What'd he say?"

"He kept talking about fishing. And he said something about the swans on the pond. Isn't there an old fishing cabin clear at the end of the fire trail? I seem to remember something about it."

"Yeah. I haven't been back that way in ages though. You think he could have gotten that far?" Kade asked.

"It's worth a shot. Let's go look."

"How far are we?" Nick asked.

Bree consulted her GPS and showed it to Kade. "What do you think — maybe a half mile?"

"I'd guess about that," Kade said. "I think the trail is about a quarter mile west of here.

If we get on it first, we can make better time."

"Lead the way," Nick said. "Maybe we're not too late."

A swan rose off the water and beat at her face with its wings. Eve fell back in the boat, landing on the wooden bottom. The hair-shirt tore at her flesh, and she thought she felt a trickle of blood. The swan advanced with its neck outstretched. Trumpeting its outrage, the swan jabbed at her leg with its beak, breaking the skin and drawing blood.

She kicked out, and the swan toppled into the water.

Oliver climbed into the boat, rocking it wildly as she tried to right herself. He cut the motor. "They want more food." Oliver stooped to lift the bag of sandwiches.

Not stopping to think or plan, Eve sprang to her feet, braced her legs, and rocked the boat powerfully to the right. If she went into the water with the swans, at least she'd go down fighting.

When the boat dipped, Oliver flung out his hands to try to balance himself. It looked as though he might succeed as the boat settled.

Eve balanced herself and lifted her leg in a quick *grande battement.* Her toe struck him on the shoulder, and he flailed, but it wasn't enough to keep him from toppling headfirst into the water. He went under, then his head popped up in the midst of the swans.

The birds began to jab at him with their beaks. He screamed, an almost womanly sound, and struck back at them. His cries seemed to agitate them further.

A flurry of feathers churned the waters. Trumpeting calls drowned out his screams. Covering her ears, Eve screamed with him. It was horrible, horrible. Then there was silence.

She dropped onto the seat and put her face in her hands. She didn't want to give in to tears, not yet. She still had to get out of here. When she lifted her head, she found herself nose to beak with a huge swan. A drop of blood dripped from the swan's beak. She shuddered and scrabbled back. The swan came closer, craning its neck toward her. Then it dipped its head and bit her on the leg.

She screamed again, but her back was already against the motor. The other swans drifted closer, and terror closed her throat. Bree had told her swans could be dangerous, but until tonight, she hadn't believed her.

The big swan in the boat trumpeted, and another swan landed on the edge of the boat, rocking it in the water.

"Shoo, go on, get out of here." Eve made a shooing motion with her hand. She picked up an old towel lying in the bottom of the boat and flapped it around.

A third swan landed in the boat. The same fear and disorientation she'd felt the first time she watched *The Birds* multiplied.

Another swan lifted in the air. Its wing struck her face, and the force knocked her to the bottom of the boat. She struggled to her feet and saw a patch of clear water past the swans. If she could dive past them and swim for shore, she might make it.

She stood, but the swan knocked her down again. Another hissed and bit at her ankle. Dimly, she heard a splash. Her head still reeling, she tried to sit up. It sounded like someone was swimming, but surely Oliver was dead.

A man's hand slapped the top of the boat.

When Nick saw the swans attacking his wife, he didn't think; he reacted. A broken paddle lay on the ground. He grabbed it, kicked off his shoes, and dove into the water. Eve's screams tore his heart out. His arms churned the water, and his feet propelled him in her direction.

Gulping in oxygen, Nick's head surfaced. He was only two feet away. He reached the boat and tossed the paddle in, then climbed in himself. Snatching up the paddle, he began to whack the swans with it.

"Get out of here!" *Thwack, thwack.* He struck the swans on the tail feathers with the flat end of the paddle. After several indignant squawks and trumpets, the swans flew back to the water and glided away.

Nick dropped the paddle and knelt beside Eve. Her eyes looked dazed. A smear of blood marred the pale skin of her cheek. "Eve, honey, are you okay?" He still couldn't quite believe she wasn't already dead.

"I . . . I'm okay," she whispered. She touched the stubble on his chin. "You need a shave."

He barked a laugh. "I need more than a shave. I stink to high heaven. I haven't seen the inside of a building since you disappeared." He hugged her to his chest. "I thought I'd lost you."

She was wet and shivering. "He's dead," she said. "The swans killed him."

"Swans? Holy cow." He released her and stood, waving to Kade and Bree, who stood on the shore. Samson was barking. "She's okay!"

Eve held up her hand for Nick to help her stand. "It's Miranda, Oliver's wife. He thought a new face — my face — would heal her." She turned and pointed to the island. "She's in that cabin."

"I figured out it was Oliver. I still can't believe it."

"I'm so tired." She leaned her head against his chest again.

The full explanation of what had happened could wait. He needed to get her home and in bed. Thankfulness welled in his soul. It could have turned out much differently. "Sit down. I'll get us to shore."

Nick started the engine and guided the boat through the ripples of water to shore.

Kade waded out and grabbed the bow, and Nick cut the motor. Kade pulled the boat onto the bank.

Bree rushed to Eve. "Oh, Eve, I prayed and prayed. Thank God you're all right."

Samson leaped into the boat and began to lick Eve's face. She put her arms around him. "Good boy, Samson. I bet you're the one who found me, aren't you?"

"It was tough going, but he brought us in the right direction. And my dad helped."

"Oh, thank God Bernard made it back. I was so worried about him."

"He's fine."

"What happened?" Eve asked.

"It's a long story," Bree said. "Let's go home."

Eve's shivers finally stopped. She sat in Bree's living room in front of a roaring fire with a mug of hot tea. With her palms cupped around it, she inhaled the aroma and the moist heat. Though it was summer, her ordeal had left her cold, inside and out.

Bree stepped into the room. "The kids are sleeping. We should be too. It's after one, but I want to know everything."

Eve's mind had been running around and around it anyway. "I don't really understand it all myself. I'm hoping Nick and Kade will have more information when they hear what Cyril finds out at Oliver's house in Cheboygan. All I really know is he thought he could bring his wife out of her state and back to life with my face." She shuddered.

Bree glanced at her with guarded eyes. "Um, Eve, I've got something to tell you. It's going to be hard."

"What's wrong?" Eve's insides clenched.

"It's about Patti."

Eve closed her eyes. "She got custody?" she whispered.

"No, no, nothing like that. There was an . . . incident . . . at the camp. Some tainted food got into the food supply. Ten people are already dead." Bree took her hand. "I'm sorry, but Patti and Will are two of them. They were the worst off when Nick and Kade found them and called the ambulance."

Eve inhaled softly. "They're dead?" Bree's hand was her anchor. Memories flooded her mind. "Patti wasn't always this way. I remember when she was a little girl and I'd read stories to her. We'd bake cookies together, play games when my parents were out drinking." She swallowed the pain. "I'd always hoped things between us would change."

"I know."

The tears she'd been holding at bay flooded her eyes. "I should be happy," she sobbed. "They can't take Keri from me. But I feel like I cheated. I got everything I want, and she only got pain in her life."

"She made her own choices, Eve. We all do. We all have pain. It's up to us to decide how to let God use that pain for our good."

"Some of us don't pay the price for our sins." Eve locked gazes with Bree. "I deserved what Oliver had planned for me."

"A single mistake isn't the same as a lifetime of destructive choices." Bree squeezed her fingers.

"Maybe not." Eve swiped the last of the tears off her face. "But I know I don't deserve the good things God has given me."

"None of us does." Bree's smile came out. "I don't deserve the blessing I get to tell Kade about when he gets home."

"You don't mean —"

Bree nodded, and tears glistened in her green eyes. "Davy is going to get that baby brother or sister."

Eve hugged her. "Oh, I'm so happy for you!" And she was relieved to find she meant it. God had given her Keri. That was enough.

Bree glanced behind her when the front door opened. "The guys are home."

Both men looked ready to drop. Nick's dark curls were plastered to his head, and his jeans still looked damp. Kade's blue eyes drooped. Nick grabbed a wooden chair and turned it around to lean against the back when he sat. Kade rested his hand on Bree's shoulder.

"Did you talk to your dad?" Eve asked.

Nick nodded. "He talked to Oliver's daughter. She let them take a peek at his office in Cheboygan. He had a video library of women in their homes, taken through the windows. He had everything documented in a spreadsheet. Oliver was a detail-oriented sort of guy. According to his daughter, he had always been strict, but when her mother was injured, he went off the deep end. Started studying every religion known to man, every natural medicine remedy, every obscure culture. There were a ton of obscure religious texts in his office. The one open on the desk was occult."

"The guy had an intellect the size of China. And an ego to match," Kade said.

"How old is his daughter?" Eve asked.

"About seventeen. She stayed with her grandmother a lot, and the old lady's a real nutcase. Cyril —" Nick stopped. "What?"

"Odette. He named his daughter Odette?" Eve could see his obsession with *Swan Lake* had been long.

"I'd forgotten — that's the Swan Queen's name, isn't it?" Nick asked.

Eve nodded. "Did Odette know about his passion for the ballet?"

"Oh yeah. He made her take lessons, and she hated it. Skipped out every chance she got. He watched the tape of *Swan Lake* nearly every night for as long as she could remember."

"He told me the swans were his escape when his foster dad came to his room at night."

Nick shook his head. "Anyway, Cyril has

Odette out of Grandma's house and with a social services counselor. They're going to try to find a foster home for her until she turns eighteen." Eve yawned, and he stood and held out his hand. "Let's get you to bed. This can all wait until morning."

Eve put her hand in his palm. The warmth of his hand warmed her like the tea hadn't. He pulled her up from the sofa and kept possession of her hand.

"I'll see you in the morning."

"I'll walk you to your room." He glanced to Bree. "Your sofa still mine?"

"Of course. I'll get the bedding."

"I'll get it, honey. You go on to bed," Kade said. He patted her on the behind as she passed.

Eve realized all she'd wanted here in Rock Harbor was wrapped up in the relationship she saw between Kade and Bree. It wasn't the town at all, though she loved the slow pace. She'd thought the kinder, gentler life would give Nick time to love her the way Kade loved Bree.

But he already did.

Love wasn't a one-size-fits-all sort of thing. Everyone showed love in a different way. She'd been wanting Nick to fit into her pre-conceived idea of how a man in love acted. Her main agenda had been to try to get him to fit her ideal.

She was becoming like his sister, Layna. The thought gave her pause.

Nick was already the perfect man for her. The same passion that drove him to find her when he was exhausted was the same passion that made him such an excellent public protector. If she'd ever succeeded in her quest to change him, she would have found he wasn't the man she fell in love with.

Her thoughts tumbled in a morass of longing and realization of how wrong she'd been. He walked her to her door. She turned and stepped into his arms. His chin rested on her hair, and his arms held her tight. His shirt smelled of mud, perspiration, and Nick. A heady combination, when she realized all he'd gone through to rescue her.

His lips moved against her hair. "I realized when I thought I'd lost you that where we live doesn't matter. I can be a deputy here in Rock Harbor and still be in law enforcement."

She lifted her head. "No, Nick. Saving people is what you do best. We'll find us a place on Lake Huron, out away from the hustle and bustle. When you're late for dinner, I'll remember all the meals you missed to rescue me."

His arms tightened around her. "I can come home?"

She lost herself in his gaze. "Yes. Come home, Nick."

A corner of his mouth turned up. "I wasn't quite sure how to tell you, but the divorce was never finalized. When your lawyer learned you were missing, she didn't file it. She left a message on the answering machine last week after you showed up."

"We're still married?" She couldn't still the leap of joy.

He nodded.

She pushed open the door. "I guess that means this bed had better be big enough for two."

His eyes widened, and she smiled as she led him inside and shut the world out.

ACKNOWLEDGMENTS

Oh, the joy of going back to Rock Harbor! You'd think these people were real. Well, they are to me. I hope you, dear reader, enjoyed this foray back into the lives of the Rock Harbor folks as much as I did. I've received many requests from you over the past few years to write more stories set there. I and the Nelson folks listened.

My unending love and gratitude to my Thomas Nelson family: publisher Allen Arnold, who jumped on the whole geocaching/serial-killer idea with both feet; editor Ami McConnell, my friend and cheerleader, who had many great suggestions on taking this book to the next level of suspense and romance; editor extraordinaire Natalie Hanemann, who puts up with my numerous requests for help with a smile and a hug; marketing manager Jennifer Deshler, who brings both friendship and fabulous marketing ideas to the table; superorganized publicist Carrie Wagner, who helps me plan the right strategies and is always willing to listen; fabulous cover guru Mark Ross (you *so* rock!), who works hard to create the perfect cover — and does it; fellow Hoosier Lisa Young, who lends a shoulder to cry on when needed; and my sweet Amanda Bostic, who is still my friend even though she doesn't work on my books anymore. I love you all more than I can say.

My agent, Karen Solem, was the first one to love this idea. She's my biggest cheerleader, and that includes kicking an idea to the curb when necessary. I wouldn't be anywhere without her. Thanks, Karen — you're the best!

Erin Healy is the best freelance editor in the business — bar none. Her magic touch on my book has to be seen to be believed. Thanks, Erin! I couldn't do it without you.

Writing can be a lonely business, but God has blessed me with great writing friends and critique partners. Kristin Billerbeck, Diann Hunt, and Denise Hunter make up the Girls Write Out squad (www.GirlsWriteOut.blogspot.com). I couldn't make it through a day without my peeps! And another one of those is Robin Miller, president of ACFW (www.acfw.com), who spots inconsistencies in a suspense plot with an eagle eye. Thanks to all of you for the work you do on my behalf and for your friendship.

I have a super-supportive family that puts up with my crazy work schedule. My husband, Dave, carts me around from city to city, washes towels, and runs after dinner without complaint. Thanks, honey! I couldn't do anything without you. My kids, Dave and Kara (and now Donna) Coble, and my new grandsons, James and Jorden Packer, love and support me in every way possible. Love you guys! And thanks to my parents, George and Peggy Rhoads; my brothers, Rick and Dave Rhoads, and their wives, Mary and Teresa; and my "other parents," Carroll and Lena Coble. One of them is often the first to hear a new idea, and they never laugh at me. Love you all!

Most important, I give my thanks to God, who has opened such amazing doors for me and makes the journey a golden one.

I love to hear from readers! Drop me an e-mail at colleen@colleencoble.com and check out my author site at www.colleencoble.com. There's a forum to chat about books, and I try to stop in since books are my favorite things in the world. If you have a book club, I'd be happy to call and chat when you're discussing one of my books.

Thank you all for spending your most precious commodity — *time* — with me and my stories.

DISCUSSION QUESTIONS

1. Gideon's life spiraled downward because of his obsession over a wrong, and he really had been harmed. Have you ever obsessed over something? If so, what did you do to put it behind you?

2. Eve and Nick had a second chance to correct a relationship gone wrong. But sometimes it's hard to forget the past. List three things you could do right now to turn around a relationship that's gone bad for you.

3. Nick and Eve's marriage suffered because of Nick's skewed priorities toward his job. What is the most important thing in your life right now? What should it be? If your priorities are in the wrong order, what can you do today to turn it around?

4. Is there some talent or part of your

personality that you believe you would never be able to forget, just as Eve innately remembered her ballet? How does that happen?

5. Bree was showing God's love to a stranger when she took in "Elena." In today's world, many times we're afraid to reach out to strangers. How can we overcome that tendency and become the salt we're meant to be?

6. Law enforcement personnel today face such horrific things. Nick wanted to make a difference, be a hero. Do you think he was the exception or the rule among law enforcers?

7. How can you be a hero in your circle of influence?

8. Have you ever seen *Swan Lake*? If so, what was your favorite part and why?

9. Have you ever been geocaching? Why do you think it's become so popular?

10. What did you feel when Gideon told his daughter she had to learn to deal with the

situation at her grandmother's?

11. What theme came through to you in *Haven of Swans*?

12. When you've read Proverbs 6, have you ever worried that you're guilty of something God considers an abomination?

ABOUT THE AUTHOR

Colleen Coble is a *USA Today* bestselling author and RITA finalist best known for her romantic suspense novels, including *Tidewater Inn, Rosemary Cottage,* and the Mercy Falls, Lonestar, and Rock Harbor series.

Visit her website at www.colleencoble.com
Twitter: @colleencoble
Facebook: colleencoblebooks

The employees of Thorndike Press hope you have enjoyed this Large Print book. All our Thorndike, Wheeler, and Kennebec Large Print titles are designed for easy reading, and all our books are made to last. Other Thorndike Press Large Print books are available at your library, through selected bookstores, or directly from us.

For information about titles, please call:
(800) 223-1244

or visit our website at:
gale.com/thorndike

To share your comments, please write:
Publisher
Thorndike Press
10 Water St., Suite 310
Waterville, ME 04901